JOSEPH CONRAD

UNDER WESTERN EYES

In the first decade of this century, Conrad wrote three political novels that have had constant influence on the way we look at contemporary history. The third of these, UNDER WESTERN EYES, is the eternally pertinent story of Russian radicals exiled in Geneva, those who spy on them, and the iron links that chain them to each other and to their motherland.

EVERYMAN,
I WILL GO WITH THEE,
AND BE THY GUIDE,
IN THY MOST NEED
TO GO BY THY SIDE

JOSEPH CONRAD

Under Western Eyes

with an Introduction by
Cedric Watts

EVERYMAN'S LIBRARY

Alfred A. Knopf New York Toronto

43

THIS IS A BORZOI BOOK

PUBLISHED BY ALFRED A. KNOPF, INC.

First published 1911
First included in Everyman's Library, 1991
Introduction, Bibliography, and Chronology Copyright © 1991 by
David Campbell Publishers Ltd.
Typography by Peter B. Willberg
Second printing

ISBN 0-679-40554-2
LC 91-52993

Library of Congress Cataloging-in-Publication Data
Conrad, Joseph, 1857–1924.
Under western eyes / Joseph Conrad.
p.   cm.—(Everyman's library)
ISBN 0-679-40554-2
1. Soviet Union—History—1904–1914—Fiction.   I. Title.
PR6005.O4U5   1991   91-52993
823'.912—dc20   CIP

Book Design by Barbara de Wilde and Carol Devine Carson

Printed and bound in Germany
by Graphischer Grossbetrieb Pössneck GmbH
A member of the Mohndruck printing group

CONTENTS

———

INTRODUCTION

Under Western Eyes is one of Joseph Conrad's best novels: a vivid, eloquent and subtle study of political conflict, personal betrayal, guilt and atonement.

Like other novels by Conrad, it was originally planned as a short story; but, as the project grew, the writing extended with painful difficulty from December 1907 to January 1910; and, after delivering the manuscript to his literary agent, Conrad suffered a physical and mental collapse. In a letter given stressful immediacy by its ungrammatical phrasing ('let even I', 'It lays'), his wife Jessie reported:

> The novel is finished, but the penalaty [*sic*] has to be paid. Months of nervous strain have resulted in a complete nervous breakdown ... There is the M.S. complete but uncorrected and his fierce refusal to let even I touch it. It lays on a table at the foot of his bed and he lives mixed up in the scenes and holds converse with the characters.[1]

There were several reasons for this breakdown. One was Conrad's recent quarrel with his literary agent (J. B. Pinker), who had become exasperated by the slow progress of the novel and by Conrad's repeated demands for loans: at this time the author was heavily indebted to him. Another was that Conrad had angrily severed his relationship with Ford Madox Hueffer, a former literary collaborator. But the main reason, almost certainly, was the imaginative and emotional strain entailed by the writing of a novel which related so directly to the stresses and griefs of Conrad's childhood in Poland.

In December 1857, Conrad – then Józef Teodor Konrad Korzeniowski – was born into a country which had vanished from the map of Europe. By means of a series of partitions in 1772, 1792 and 1795, Poland had been annexed by Russia from the east and by Prussia and Austria from the west and south-west. The Poles were, and remained, a proudly patriotic nation, their sense of national identity being all the more intense for their lack of autonomy; and, when a nation is annexed by hostile powers, its preoccupation with the inter-linked problems of loyalty and treachery is intensified.

Conrad's father, Apollo Korzeniowski, poet and translator, was fervently patriotic; with his wife, Ewa, he conspired against the Russian authorities; and both were arrested, tried and sentenced to exile. Their four-year-old son accompanied them on the bleak journey to remote Vologda. Partly as a result of the privations of exile, Ewa died of tuberculosis in 1865; and four years later her grieving widower joined her in death. By the age of eleven, Conrad was an orphan, heading the vast procession of mourners that followed his father's coffin through the streets of Kraków in a funeral which was simulta-neously a huge patriotic demonstration of Poles against Rus-sians. Already, stamped on the boy's imagination, was an image of the lethal cost exacted from domestic, familial life by political concerns; a recognition that a man may be seen both as a subversive criminal and as a loyal martyr; and already he knew personally the isolation which was to be rendered with such intensity in so many of the novels and tales of his mature years.

In 1903 Conrad called himself 'homo duplex': the double man.[2] There are many senses in which that epithet is apt. He was Polish by birth and allegiance, yet he settled in England and became a British citizen who wrote in English. He was a seaman who, after nearly twenty years of voyages in which he had reached the rank of captain, abandoned that vocation to embark on a second career, that of a novelist. Partly because of his years as an orphan and as a voyager (when he was the only Pole in the crew), and partly because of his melancholy temperament, he had a keen sense of human isolation; yet he also expressed a strong allegiance to the principles of loyalty, solidarity and tradition, whether evoked by the cause of Polish nationalism, the ethics of the British merchant navy, or the liberal values for which Britain was celebrated. He felt in-tensely loyal both to Poland and to his adopted country, and when he took British nationality in 1886 he was formally discarding Russian citizenship; yet leading Polish novelists complained that by settling in England as a writer he had betrayed his homeland.[3] Not surprisingly, betrayal was to be a recurrent theme in almost all his major works: the Razumov of *Under Western Eyes* has notable precursors in Lord Jim and Nostromo. While writing *Under Western Eyes*, Conrad found time to produce a superb short story, 'The Secret Sharer', in which another protagonist is surprised by the arrival of a killer who is a fugitive from justice; but, in this tale, which may be seen as a counterpoint to the story of Razumov, the hero loyally harbours the fugitive, helps him to escape, and thereby gains new authority.

There were other and related tensions in Conrad's outlook. A tendency to sceptical introspection, coupled with a distrust of the corrosively sceptical intelligence; Quixotic impulses and Hamlet-like brooding; a romantic responsiveness to heroic individualism, yet a very modern readiness to see the folly, absurdity and futility of many apparently heroic actions; a keen political indignation on behalf of the humble, the downtrodden and exploited, yet also a strong awareness that, historically, revolutionary aspirations to redeem the downtrodden have so often culminated in new dictatorships and new forms of exploitation. The son of a conspirator, he could sympathize with rebels and outsiders of various kinds, while distrusting the rhetoric and jargon of political rebels. As a writer, he displayed intense dedication to his craft, while yet expressing scepticism about the adequacy of language: he was capable of eloquent warnings about eloquence. Could it be that 'words ... are the great foes of reality' and that 'speech has been given to us for the purpose of concealing our thoughts'? If so, are such claims, necessarily made in words and speech, false?

All these tensions and paradoxes help to account for the verve and power of *Under Western Eyes*. Conrad's intense interest in the figure of the isolated and alienated individual (previously displayed in the treatment of Jim in *Lord Jim* and Decoud in *Nostromo*, for example) is evident in the central characterization of Razumov, illegitimate and largely disowned, struggling to find solace in work, yet having his life disrupted by the startling arrival of a bomb-throwing young revolutionary who seeks sanctuary. This single incident, leading to the betrayal of the revolutionary, Haldin, and to

Razumov's bitter task as a spy for the Tsarist regime, imposes on Razumov a burden of duplicity and guilt which eventually leads to his confession and maiming. Conrad's profound hostility, as a Pole, to Tsarist Russia inevitably sought keen expression; nevertheless, as his 'Author's Note' declared:

My greatest anxiety was in being able to strike and sustain the note of scrupulous impartiality. The obligation of absolute fairness was imposed on me historically and hereditarily, by the peculiar experience of race and family, in addition to my primary conviction that truth alone is the justification of any fiction which makes the least claim to the quality of art ... I had never been called before to a greater effort of detachment: detachment from all passions, prejudices, and even from personal memories.

A cynic might, of course, remark that in matters of morality (and therefore of politics) nobody is impartial; nobody can be fully detached; and Conrad had long taken a bleakly pessimistic view of most political activities by 'men, shortsighted in good and evil'.[4] Nevertheless, the *endeavour* to be impartial in observing and rendering such matters is laudable and salutary; and his declared aim accounts for numerous features of *Under Western Eyes*. Repeatedly Conrad strives to balance and discriminate. On the Tsarist side, he distinguishes between the relatively decent and the relatively contemptible upholders of the oppressive system. The range includes Prince K— , the aloofly conservative nobleman who is unable to repress fully his paternal feelings towards Razumov; General T— , ruthless guardian of despotism; and Councillor Mikulin, the deviously sophisticated manipulator. The revolutionaries and 'nihilists' opposed to the régime are more fully diversified. Victor Haldin is briefly but memorably depicted as the idealist intoxicated by a vision of freedom: an idealist whose bomb kills not only a notorious Minister of State but also a fellow-revolutionary and several innocent spectators. His sister Natalia (or Nathalie) is a relatively stereotypical characterization: the vulnerably ardent young believer in an eventual era of concord, freedom and harmony. Then there is the vivid characterization of the monstrously egoistic arch-conspirator, Peter Ivanovitch, companion of his grotesque patroness,

Madame de S——. Sophia Antonovna is treated with some sympathy as the dedicated, experienced and selfless worker for a tainted cause. At the meeting-point of oppressive extremes, there is Nikita (alias Necator: Killer), the sadistic double agent in whose characterization this sophisticated political and psychological novel merges with the modes of satire, melodrama and the popular thriller. The text's predominant realism frequently modulates, as its ironies intensify, towards satiric mordancy and even black comedy. As in his other works, Conrad punishes his villains by caricaturing them.

The English teacher seems to echo Conrad's views when he says:

'A violent revolution falls into the hands of narrow-minded fanatics and of tyrannical hypocrites at first. Afterwards comes the turn of all the pretentious intellectual failures of the time. Such are the chiefs and the leaders. You will notice that I have left out the mere rogues. The scrupulous and the just, the noble, humane, and devoted natures; the unselfish and the intelligent may begin a movement – but it passes away from them. They are not the leaders of a revolution. They are its victims: the victims of disgust, of disenchantment – often of remorse. Hopes grotesquely betrayed, ideals caricatured – that is the definition of revolutionary success.'

In formulating such views, Conrad was recalling the decline of the French Revolution from the initial fervour for 'Liberty, Equality, Fraternity' to the carnage of the Terror and the eventual emergence of Napoleon as dictator–emperor: this would form part of the subject-matter of his later novels, *The Rover* and the unfinished *Suspense*. The author of *Under Western Eyes*, however pessimistic his outlook, might well feel vindicated by history. In 1917, six years after the novel's publication, the Russian Revolution occurred; and, in his subsequent 'Author's Note' (1920), Conrad claimed that the 'ferocity and imbecility' of autocratic rule had been superseded by 'the no less imbecile and atrocious answer' of the revolutionaries: 'the tiger cannot change his stripes nor the leopard his spots'. Between 1941 and 1945, that tiger fortunately devoured Hitler's eastern armies; but many victims of Stalinist dictatorship in the 1930s, and of Russian imperialism later in the century, might well have agreed with Conrad's assessment.

(Not surprisingly, that 'Author's Note' was for many years banned in the USSR and eastern Europe.) Conrad's quest for impartiality is nevertheless evident in the epigraph chosen for *Under Western Eyes*: he quotes his own fictional character, Natalia Haldin: 'I would take liberty from any hand as a hungry man would snatch a piece of bread.'[5] Inevitably, for such is the discipline of good fiction, the political views presented explicitly and implicitly in *Under Western Eyes* constitute a more volatile, rich and exploratory mixture than can be found in any of Conrad's non-fictional writings.

The art of Conrad, who was Polish and British, seaman and novelist, victim of Russian imperialism and extoller of the British navy, naturally aspires to paradox. The preoccupation with paradox and the endeavour for impartiality are implicit in the oblique narrative technique of *Under Western Eyes*. The ostensible narrator is not an omniscient authority but the English teacher of languages who so candidly confesses his limitations; he is, he explains, an unimaginative translator of Razumov's memoirs. As a literary device, the use of the language teacher as narrator is not wholly successful. His intrusions are sometimes irritating disruptions: his presence as an eavesdropper at crucial scenes is sometimes implausible; and frequently he is the reporter of matters which he cannot have known. The reader may share the annoyance of the Razumov who asks: 'How did this old man come here?' Often his presence as intermediary is forgotten not only by the reader but also, it seems, by the author; and the writing then gains imaginative freedom and richness. To the extent that the narrative is effective, it is inevitably inconsistent with the narrator's avowedly unimaginative character. In *Heart of Darkness*, Conrad had deployed Marlow as story-teller: an imaginative, astute, reflective and abundantly creative figure; and there the oblique narration had been boldly exploratory, incisively questioning common assumptions about rationality, communication, perception and civilized order. In *Under Western Eyes*, such questioning is relatively muted: Conrad is clearly evolving from that early phase of turbulent experimentalism towards the more conventional and 'affirmative' works of his last years.

On the other hand, the narrative device does generate some radical ironies. Typically, in the very passage of Chapter 1 in which he condemns the Russian readiness to become intoxicated by words, their 'ardour of speech' which is 'too disconnected to be classed as eloquence', the teacher concludes with: 'But I must apologize for this digression.' He, too, can become verbally intoxicated; he, too, can digress. This narrator purports to be observing, with a mixture of incomprehension and distaste, the irrationalities, passions and corruptions of the Russian character; yet his repeated attempts to impose a national stereotype on Russian matters (e.g., 'the spirit of Russia is the spirit of cynicism') are defeated by the complexities which he is obliged to record and report. Furthermore, his own stance of civilized restraint is clearly subject to some ironic criticism. A literary descendant of the inhibited Mr Lockwood in *Wuthering Heights*, he observes with irritably repressed jealousy Natalia's increasing emotional involvement with Razumov. The Russian passions he observes may be variously histrionic, immature, dangerous and corrupt: but at least these are intensities of feeling, compared with which his rational restraint can resemble the dullness of a subjugated personality. 'In life, you see,' says Sophia Antonovna, 'there is not much choice. You have either to rot or to burn.' If some of the Russians choose to 'burn', and are led by passionate conviction to destruction or despair, the teacher of languages perhaps represents those who, opting for cool detachment, may seem to 'rot' in spectatorial impotence. Complicating Conrad's critical stance towards both the revolutionaries and the upholders of corrupt autocracy is his sense of conflict between the rational and the vital; against the attractions of sceptical intelligence and democratic liberalism are ranged the attractions of a mode of life which, if erring and dangerous, is at least intense and vivid.

The same paradox, the same contrast, is implicit in the very descriptions of landscape. Critics have generally praised Conrad's rendering of the Russian landscape, and particularly of the snowbound city of St Petersburg amid the icy northern vastness. Innumerable plausible details lend graphic immediacy to the opening sequences depicting Razumov's impoverished life-style, his startling encounter with Haldin, the assassination in the street, Razumov's anxious errand to Ziemianitch's slum, and the further journeys into the labyrinths of power following his decision to betray the revolutionary. Close confinement, yet open wide streets; mean garret and opulent palace; agonized introspection, brutal physical action; penetrating cold, and firelit state chambers; the 'greasy rancid steam' of the sordid eating-house, and the 'clear black sky of the northern winter, decorated with the sumptuous fires of the stars': it is a richly credible Russian world that Conrad evokes. In contrast is the peaceful orderly domesticity of democratic Geneva, with its tidy parks and hotels, its Boulevard des Philosophes (which, with predictable irony, is described as 'a singularly arid and dusty thoroughfare'), and 'its orderly roof-slopes ... comely without grace, and hospitable without sympathy'. The Genevan setting is repeatedly disparaged and belittled: excessively so, given that both Razumov and (implausibly) the language teacher take identically jaundiced views of its 'banality' and 'mediocrity'. The two guests vie with each other in insulting the land whose hospitality they accept. Largely by means of such landscape descriptions, Conrad suggests that while autocracy may be cruelly repressive and revolution bloodily dangerous, established democracy may entail a taming of the spirit. Natalia says to the Englishman: 'You belong to a people which has made a bargain with fate and wouldn't like to be rude to it. But we have made no bargain. It has never been offered to us – so much liberty for so much hard cash.' And later even that teacher, in metaphors which adroitly link the political and the personal, concedes: 'It is not for us, the staid lovers calmed by the possession of a conquered liberty, to condemn without appeal the fierceness of thwarted desire.' The idea anticipates W. B. Yeats' epigram in 'The Second Coming' (1920):

> The best lack all conviction, while the worst
> Are full of passionate intensity.

There is even some anticipation of that diabolical paradox expressed by T. S. Eliot in his essay on Baudelaire:

INTRODUCTION

[T]he possibility of damnation is so immense a relief in a world of electoral reform, plebiscites, sex reform and dress reform, that damnation itself is an immediate form of salvation – of salvation from the ennui of modern life, because it at last gives some significance to living.[6]

In the great film by Graham Greene and Carol Reed, *The Third Man*, Orson Welles remarks that while the violent era of the Borgias in Italy produced some of the world's finest works of art, centuries of democracy in Switzerland have produced merely 'the cuckoo-clock'.

The interest of *Under Western Eyes* lies largely, therefore, in its sustained political ironies; but repeatedly the novel exploits the ironic disparity between illusion and reality, word and deed, seeming and being. Razumov's egoistic reserve is misinterpreted by Haldin as an inner nobility; his lack of family connections encourages Haldin to confide in him; so his very alienation leads to his unwilling and bitter entanglement in the world of conspiracy and espionage. If Razumov is later tempted by sexual desire, it is desire for the trustful sister of the very man he has betrayed. The suicide of Ziemianitch averts any suspicion that Razumov was the betrayer, yet the trust of Natalia Haldin leads Razumov to confess his guilt: an act which severs him not only from her but from his remote father who has promised to foster his career. Cleansed in conscience yet maimed in body, he regains his integrity only to become a reclusive invalid. At least Razumov is delivered from the purgatory of moral isolation by the attentions of 'Tekla the Samaritan' and by sociable visits from various revolutionaries who (with strangely imprudent lenity) call on the stone-deaf invalid for enlightening conversation as they pass by. Meanwhile, Natalia Haldin devotes herself not to grandiose dreams of the ideal future but to charitable social work among the needy; a career not so different from that of the 'Lady Almoner' heroines of the past. Thus one political recommendation of *Under Western Eyes* is the traditional conservative recommendation popularized in nineteenth-century novels by Charles Dickens, George Eliot and Elizabeth Gaskell: within a generally irremediable large-scale situation, the best that can be hoped for is local amelioration by means of personal charitable, kindly and loving deeds. If Conrad was often modernistic in his radical scepticism, he could also be remarkably traditional in his moral affirmations.

Another source of this novel's irony is the sustained theme of the haunting of the living by the dead. Even before his betrayal of Haldin, Razumov has a hallucination of him lying in the snowy street; the next day, the 'familiar phantom' appears in his room; and repeatedly thereafter, Razumov's guilt expresses itself in thoughts of Haldin as a vivid 'phantom'. The victim had prophesied that his soul would walk the earth, and the prophecy is amply fulfilled.[7] Victor Haldin even seems to live on within his sister, who, though so femininely attractive, has some oddly masculine traits: a 'deep' and 'masculine' voice, a glance 'trustful as that of a young man', and a handshake of 'exquisite virility'. It is the name 'Victor Haldin', not her own, that Natalia utters when introducing herself to Razumov (who reels with a shock which is misconstrued as evidence that his relationship to Victor was a 'brotherhood of souls'). Ingeniously, this Gothic theme of the power of the dead is linked by Conrad to the political machinations of Madame de S— , who bizarrely hopes to employ 'evoked ghosts' to aid her demented revolutionary schemes (in which 'rivers would part like Jordan, and ramparts fall down like the walls of Jericho'). The linkage is made explicit by Razumov when he remarks of Haldin: 'I am not sure that he is beyond the influence of one woman at least; the one over there – Madame de S— , you know. Formerly the dead were allowed to rest, but now it seems that they are at the beck and call of a crazy old harridan.' The ironies are multiple: not only is Madame de S— , who hopes to evoke the spirits of the dead, herself so grotesquely decrepit as to resemble 'a galvanized corpse out of some Hoffmann's tale', but also her superstitious belief, though nonsense if taken literally, has metaphorical force which Razumov knows all too well: for, in his guilty mind, the dead Haldin is a remorselessly pursuing phantom.

In the 'Author's Note' to *The Shadow-Line*, Conrad explicitly repudiated a supernatural interpretation of that novel, explaining that his concern was with the secular world. Nevertheless, several of his tales and novels, among them *The*

INTRODUCTION

Nigger of the 'Narcissus', 'The Secret Sharer', *The Shadow-Line*
itself and *Under Western Eyes*, do have a theme of 'haunting and
exorcism' which is so resonant, consistent and sustained as not
to be fully reducible to secular terms. It is typical of our
'double man', Joseph Conrad, that though he poured scorn on
Christianity in letters to his sceptical friends Edward Garnett
and Cunninghame Graham, he later told his son John (a
nominal Anglican) that he, like 'all true seamen', was a
believer.[8]

A lonely Russian student who commits a lethal act; who is
tormented by guilt, and eventually cleanses himself by confession and atonement: for many readers of *Under Western Eyes*,
these features will inevitably recall Fyodor Dostoyevsky's
Crime and Punishment. That Russian novel was indeed one of the
main influences on Conrad's, and it provides a fine instance of
what may be called 'dialectical influence', which occurs when
a text offers provocation and challenge to a subsequent writer.
   Of the Russian novelists, Conrad greatly admired Turgenev
but harboured an almost pathological hostility to Dostoyevsky, whom he termed 'the grimacing haunted creature'
evoking 'fierce mouthings from prehistoric ages'.[9] This makes
even more remarkable the extent to which *Under Western Eyes*
seems indebted to *Crime and Punishment*. Conrad has not only
repeated the theme of the guilt-tormented young man who
eventually confesses; he has also derived a variety of related
material from Dostoyevsky's novel. Near the end of *Crime and
Punishment*, Raskolnikov, the former student who lives in
St Petersburg, is impelled towards the confession by the
idealistic and loving Sonya, whose appearance reminds him of
Lizaveta, whom he had killed. Near the end of *Under Western
Eyes*, Razumov, the former student who had lived in St
Petersburg, is impelled towards confession by the idealistic
and loving Natalia, whose appearance reminds him of Victor,
for whose death he is responsible. Both protagonists are lonely,
introspective, intelligent, neurotic, bad-tempered and sardonically contemptuous of others. Both have repeated inter-
views with an astute representative of the police; in each case
the interviewer sees more deeply into the truth of the matter

than the exasperated interviewee expects. As Raskolnikov contrives a philosophical rationale for murder, so Razumov contrives a political rationale for lethal treachery. Raskolnikov seems to be fortuitously freed from suspicion when the workman Nikolay confesses to the crime; and Razumov seems to be fortuitously freed from suspicion when the carter Ziemianitch hangs himself and is deemed the betrayer of Haldin. While deciding to proclaim the truth, Raskolnikov becomes drenched with rain; and Razumov, with consciously symbolic phrasing, declares himself 'washed clean' during a thunderstorm. Raskolnikov, living as a convict in Siberia, is lovingly tended by the devoted Sonya; while Razumov, living as a cripple in a remote region of Russia, is lovingly tended by the devoted Tekla, and Natalia serves as a compassionate visitor to 'overcrowded jails'. There even appear to be verbal echoes. Razumov's question, 'Do you conceive the desolation of the thought – no one – to – go – to?', recalls Marmeladov's 'Do you realize ... what it means when you have nowhere to go to?'; and Razumov's 'It was myself, after all, whom I have betrayed' may have been suggested by Raskolnikov's 'I killed myself, and not the old hag.' Even the name Razumov, which, appropriately for a reflective student, means 'Son of Reason' (*razum* being Russian for reason or mind), may have been suggested by the name of Raskolnikov's friend Razumikhin: a surname which, another character remarks, 'deriving as it does from the word "reason", ... leads me to believe that he must be a student of theology'.[10]

Nevertheless, the relationship between Conrad's novel and Dostoyevsky's is more often critical than derivative. Conrad offers a relatively concise narrative; the confessional garrulity of many of Dostoyevsky's characters is implicitly criticized not only by the more economical dialogue of Conrad's but also by the language teacher's strictures on the Russians' 'extraordinary love of words'. In contrast to Dostoyevsky's concluding Christian emphasis on confession as the key to redemption and joyful regeneration, Conrad concludes with a sombre and relatively secular emphasis on disillusionment and withdrawal from struggle: Razumov becomes a reclusive invalid, Natalia turns from revolutionary conspiracy to charitable visiting, and the arch-conspirator Peter Ivanovitch opts for quiet married life with 'a peasant girl'. Above all, Conrad vindicates the title *Under Western Eyes* by lucidly depicting what Dostoyevsky (who revered Tsarism) could not: the relationship between violent revolt and the oppressive autocratic system. Instead of the turbulently voluble emotional bounty with which Dostoyevsky renders the interaction of lives which are so often tormented, desperate and anguished, Conrad strives for a more austere, lucid and ironic overview of lives distorted and riven by political ideologies. Yet there remains common ground: Raskolnikov, in temperament, in his bitter alienation and in his eventual confessional accession to the claims of truthful humanity, resembles a twin brother of the lonely Razumov.

In addition to *Crime and Punishment*, Conrad drew on a diversity of historical and literary sources when writing *Under Western Eyes*. In July 1904, V. K. de Plehve, the Russian Minister of the Interior, was blown to pieces in his carriage by a man called Sazonov, an incident which (Conrad told John Galsworthy) suggested the basis of Haldin's crime against 'Mr de P— '.[11] The fictional circumstances, however, also recall the assassination of Tsar Alexander II in 1881, when two bombs were used: the first damaged the Tsar's sleigh; he alighted to inquire about the injured; and a second bomb then killed him and people in the crowd. The assassins were subsequently betrayed by a member of their group.

The novel's Father Zosim was based on the historic Father Gapon (with a glance at Dostoyevsky's Father Zossima); General T— was suggested by the notorious General Trepov, who was shot by Vera Zasulich. Mikulin's warning to Peter Ivanovitch that Nikita is a double agent adapts a warning given to a revolutionary leader by A. A. Lopuhin (head of the Police Department) that Evno Azev was a double agent working among revolutionaries on behalf of the authorities. As in the fictional narrative, the police chief and the revolutionary met by chance during a journey by rail; and Lopuhin, like Mikulin, was exiled for his indiscretion. This unmasking of Azev may have led Conrad to change his plan for the novel so as to make Razumov himself a double agent. In Conrad's original plan, outlined in a letter to Galsworthy, there is no mention of this development. After betraying Haldin, Razumov was to travel abroad, meet and marry Haldin's sister, and eventually confess to her: a confession provoked 'mainly by the resemblance of their child to the late Haldin'. A vestige of the original scheme survives incongruously at a crucial moment in the finished novel: Razumov admits to Natalia that he had contemplated 'the unpardonable sin of stealing a soul' – which appears to be a melodramatic way of saying that he had intended to exploit her trust by marrying her.[12]

Peter Ivanovitch, the hypocritical feminist who dictates his praises of womanhood to a browbeaten secretary, was based on several figures. Michael Bakunin, a leading anarchist, was certainly one of these: like Ivanovitch, Bakunin was imprisoned in a fortress, was exiled to Siberia, and escaped by making a long trek across Russia to the Pacific coast; his exploits 'made him a legendary figure in western Europe'; and subsequently Switzerland (which, like England, was patiently hospitable to political extremists) provided a base for his revolutionary activities. Bakunin has been described as 'a man who idealized womankind and lived largely on the contributions of his infatuated followers (which included a villa on a Swiss lake); an inflated, almost comic figure in mind and body'.[13] The manuscript of *Under Western Eyes* shows that Conrad also had Tolstoy in mind: there Peter Ivanovitch is said to be the author of *Resurrection of Yegor*, *The Pride of Darkness* and *The Pfennig Cantata*, echoing Tolstoy's *Resurrection*, *The Power of Darkness* and *The Kreutzer Sonata*. Commentators have suggested other possibilities: Alexander Herzen, the revolutionary propagandist, and Prince Kropotkin, the celebrated anarchist, may have been recalled by Conrad. The privations of Ivanovitch as starving fugitive were associated in the author's mind with the sufferings of his great-uncle Nicholas, who, during the retreat from Moscow, had been driven by starvation to eat a dog.[14] Furthermore, as the text repeatedly reminds us, Ivanovitch's patroness, Madame de S— , is a grotesquely parodic counterpart of Madame de Staël, admirer of Rousseau and patroness of a salon of literary and political radicals. Ivanovitch is even satirically likened to King Numa, the legendary second king of Rome, whose lover and adviser was supposedly the nymph Egeria. From all these diverse source-materials, Conrad has constructed a strikingly vivid character: a compound of charismatic power and ludicrous hypocrisy; a pretentious but plausible giant whose escape from captivity provides one of the most memorable sequences of Conradian ironic description. Here aesthetic relish, sympathy and mild mockery are focused, typically, by the sense that a paradoxical 'homo duplex' has emerged:

His clothing dropped off him gradually. His naked, tawny figure glimpsed vaguely through the bushes with a cloud of mosquitoes and flies hovering about the shaggy head, spread tales of terror through whole districts. His temper grew savage as the days went by, and he was glad to discover that there was so much of a brute in him. He had nothing else to put his trust in. For it was as though there had been two human beings indissolubly joined in that enterprise. The civilized man, the enthusiast of advanced humanitarian ideals thirsting for the triumph of spiritual love and political liberty; and the stealthy, primeval savage, pitilessly cunning in the preservation of his freedom from day to day, like a tracked wild beast.

The wild beast was making its way instinctively eastward to the Pacific coast, and the civilised humanitarian in fearful anxious dependence watched the proceedings with awe.

A minor character, Julius Laspara, seems to have been based on Sergei Stepniak, who had assassinated the Russian chief of police, General Mesentsev, in 1878.[15] The assassin escaped, lived for a while in Switzerland, and eventually settled in London, where he became well known to Conrad's friends, Edward and Constance Garnett. Laspara and Stepniak are similar in physical appearance (short but powerfully built, with a high forehead, almond-shaped eyes and thick beard); and Conrad may have drawn on Stepniak's partly autobiographical novel, *The Career of a Nihilist*. Its revolutionary hero, Andrey, resides for a while at Geneva among conspirators and exiles from Russia: and his character, like Razumov's, is thrown into relief by scornful reference to the orderly, artificial Genevan setting and the lakeside gardens frequented by tourists. Like Razumov, Andrey has the habit of gazing down, as if hypnotized, into the rushing waters of the Rhône. In Andrey, this attraction is intended to illustrate his romantic and aspiring nature; whereas, in Razumov, it becomes the subject of incisive critical comment by the narrator.[16] Both heroes reach a crucial decision after wandering, preoccupied, by the lake, away from it, and back again, their introspections punctuated by reference to the sound of the waters and the wind; and in both cases the authors make explicit reference to Rousseau. During his walk, Razumov has considered the execution of a plan (writing a journal) of which he has been reminded by his meeting with Laspara. Stepniak was killed when, apparently deaf, he failed to hear a train which then struck him down as he walked across the track; and this may be the source of the incident in which the deafened Razumov is struck down and crippled by the tramcar. Of Stepniak's writings, both *The Career of a Nihilist* and *Underground Russia* celebrate womanhood, platonic friendships and self-sacrificing idealism; and the feminism of Peter Ivanovitch may derive in part from Stepniak's belief in the superiority of the female revolutionists. *Underground Russia* declares:

> Women, it must be confessed, are much more richly endowed with this divine flame [i.e. ruthless zeal] than men. This is why the almost religious fervour of the Russian Revolutionary movement must in great part be attributed to them; and while they take part in it, it will be invincible.[17]

When Razumov begins to confide to his journal his own 'confessions', he is seated by the lakeside statue of Jean-Jacques Rousseau, the philosopher whose *Confessions* express those romantically republican ideals which will be mocked in Razumov's narrative. On an islet (an ironic location, as the narrator notes), 'the exiled effigy of the author of the *Social Contract* sat enthroned above the bowed head of Razumov in the sombre immobility of bronze'. Chapter 1 of *The Social Contract* had opened with the declaration that 'Man is born free; and everywhere he is in chains':[18] and the chains, as Peter Ivanovitch demonstrates, are still being worn by Russians. Switzerland may be placid, Conrad suggests, but its past hospitality to Voltaire and Rousseau nurtured the radical ideas which, by helping to precipitate the French Revolution, proved a very mixed blessing. As that revolution gave way to the 'Napoleonic despotism, the booted heir', perhaps Russian agitators based in Geneva might be preparing the ground for new tyranny. Conrad prophesied in his essay 'Autocracy and War' (1905) that the Russian people were so inured to dictatorial government that even after a revolution there, 'tyranny, assuming a thousand protean shapes, will remain clinging to her struggles for a long time before her blind multitudes succeed at last in trampling her out of existence . . .'[19] Razumov's address in Geneva is the Rue de Carouge; and this was also the address of Lenin, whose *coup d'état* in 1917 would deflect the Russian Revolution away from democracy and towards dictatorship.[20]

A seductively influential outlook (which may sometimes have politically conservative implications) is tragic humanism, according to which the oppressive circumstances at least enable the suffering individual to be regarded as a noble martyr. Razumov tells Mikulin: 'I know I am but a reed. But I beg you to allow me the superiority of the thinking reed over the unthinking forces that are about to crush him out of existence.' There he is citing Blaise Pascal's *Pensées*:

> Man is only a reed, the weakest in nature, but he is a thinking reed. There is no need for the whole universe to take up arms to crush him: a vapour, a drop of water is enough to kill him. But even if the universe were to crush him, man would still be nobler than his slayer, because he knows that he is dying and the advantage the universe has over him. The universe knows none of this.[21]

Conrad was probably recalling this passage when, in the essay 'Henry James', he claimed that, as human life becomes extinct on a dying planet, 'it will be the imaginative man who would be moved to speak on the eve of that day without to-morrow'.[22] At the end of *Under Western Eyes*, Razumov, though crushed in body, remains a source of intelligent ideas for those who, like Sophia Antonovna, choose to visit him; and, by means of his journal which is transmitted by the teacher, he achieves a limited but significant degree of nobility as a man who indicts the forces of violence and reaction which oppressed him, and who, by confession, exalts tardy integrity above survival and success.

We have noted that *Under Western Eyes* is flawed in various ways. The oblique narrative procedure leads to inconsistencies and awkwardness. Democracy is demeaningly caricatured, while the international conspiracy of Ivanovitch and his associates eventually dwindles into insignificance; and some sequences (particularly in Part Fourth) are marred by melodramatic dialogue and incidents. As so often in Conrad, the depiction of the oppressively isolated self and of harsh or absurd ironies seems generally more effective than the voicing of hopes and affirmations. Nevertheless, the novel powerfully voices the plight of the individual who, seeking only to live in peace with others, must undergo an inner purgatory imposed by oppressive ideologies. *Under Western Eyes* has protean adaptability: the distinguished Kenyan writer, Ngugi wa Thiong'o, adapted the story to an African setting in his narrative of betrayal and guilt, *A Grain of Wheat* (1967); and it underwent another vivid transformation in Howard Brenton's televized play about British terrorism, *The Saliva Milkshake* (1977). These works boldly extend the implications that Conrad's 'teacher of languages' had sought to limit. Victor Haldin has fulfilled his own prophecy by continuing to haunt the earth: sometimes in Africa, like Ngugi's Kihika, or in England, like Brenton's Joan; while Razumov, who renounced marriage, has nevertheless fathered the later betrayers, Mugo and Martin.

E. M. Forster once wrote: 'If I had to choose between betraying my country and betraying my friend, I hope I should have the guts to betray my country.'[23] For Conrad, Pole and Englishman, seaman and novelist, Roman Catholic and sceptic, son of political conspirators and chronicler of the myopia of politicians, the choices were never so simple. As he wrote in *A Personal Record:*

The part of the inexplicable should be allowed for in appraising the conduct of men in a world where no explanation is final. No charge of faithlessness ought to be lightly uttered. The appearances of this perishable life are deceptive like everything else that falls under the judgment of our imperfect senses ...

INTRODUCTION

It would take too long to explain the intimate alliance of contradictions in human nature which makes love itself wear at times the desperate shape of betrayal.[24]

One of the necessary burdens of civilized life is the burden of repeated compromises between imperious demands, personal, social, moral, political; and there are few such compromises which cannot, in conscience, seem to be tainted by treachery. For many years to come, therefore, and in many parts of the world, Conrad's *Under Western Eyes* is likely to remain a sombrely cogent text.

Cedric Watts

CEDRIC WATTS is Professor of English at Sussex University, and author of *Joseph Conrad: A Literary Life*.

NOTES

1. William Blackburn, ed., *Joseph Conrad: Letters to William Blackwood and David S. Meldrum*, Duke University Press, 1958, p. 192.

2. Z. Najder, ed., *Conrad's Polish Background*, Oxford University Press, 1966, p. 240.

3. The novelists were Eliza Orzeszkowa and Stefan Zeromski. See Z. Najder, *Joseph Conrad: A Chronicle*, Cambridge University Press, 1983, pp. 255–7; and W. T. Zyla and W. M. Aycock, eds., *Joseph Conrad: Theory and World Fiction*, Texas Tech Press, 1974, p. 58.

4. Joseph Conrad, *Nostromo*, Harper, 1904, pp. 352–3.

5. The epigraph, which gives 'snatch' instead of 'snatch at', slightly misquotes her speech.

6. T. S. Eliot, *Selected Essays*, Faber & Faber, 1951, p. 427.

7. The terrorist Stepniak once remarked that 'the Terrorist is immortal'. (Sergei Stepniak: *Underground Russia*, Smith, Elder, 1883, p. 44.)

8. John Conrad, *Times Remembered*, Cambridge University Press, 1981, p. 152.

9. Jocelyn Baines, *Joseph Conrad: A Critical Biography*, Weidenfeld & Nicolson, 1960, p. 360. Dostoyevsky was a Russophile who detested Poles, which partly explains Conrad's antipathy; nevertheless, Dostoyevsky's *The Devils* anticipates *Under Western Eyes* in its satiric treatment of revolutionary conspirators.

10. *Crime and Punishment*, tr. D. Magarshack, Penguin, 1951, p. 63; *Crime and Punishment*, p. 433; *Crime and Punishment*, p. 487.

11. G. Jean-Aubry, *Joseph Conrad: Life & Letters*, Heinemann, 1927, vol. II, pp. 64–5.

12. *Joseph Conrad: Life & Letters*, p. 65.

13. George Woodcock, *Anarchism*, Penguin, 1963, p. 151; Avrom Fleishman, *Conrad's Politics*, Johns Hopkins Press, 1967, pp. 218–19.

14. This linkage was noted by Keith Carabine at a Conrad Conference in Copenhagen in 1990.

15. On Stepniak and Conrad, see: Cedric Watts, 'Stepniak and *Under Western Eyes*': *Notes and Queries*, CCXI, 1966, pp. 410–11; Thomas C. Moser, 'An English Context for Conrad's Russian Characters', *Journal of Modern Literature*, XI, 1984, pp. 3–44.

16. Sergei Stepniak, *The Career of a Nihilist*, Scott, 1889, p. 16.

17. Stepniak, *Underground Russia*, p. 139.

18. Jean-Jacques Rousseau, *The Social Contract and Discourses*, Dent, 1913, p. 3. (Some translations read 'Man was born free . . .')

19. Joseph Conrad, *Notes on Life and Letters*, Dent, 1949, pp. 102–3.

20. Paul Kirschner, 'Conrad under French Eyes', *The Conradian*, vol. 15, June 1990, pp. 80–81.

21. Blaise Pascal, *Pensées*, tr. A. J. Krailsheimer, Penguin, 1966, p. 95.
22. *Notes on Life and Letters*, p. 14.
23. E. M. Forster, *Two Cheers for Democracy*, Arnold, 1951, p. 78.
24. Joseph Conrad, *A Personal Record*, Dent, 1946, pp. 35-6.

SELECT BIBLIOGRAPHY

CONRAD'S LETTERS

FREDERICK R. KARL and LAURENCE DAVIES, eds., *The Collected Letters of Joseph Conrad*, Cambridge University Press, 1983 onwards.

AUTOBIOGRAPHICAL WORKS

The Mirror of the Sea and *A Personal Record* (two works in one volume), Dent, 1946. The writing of *A Personal Record* overlapped that of *Under Western Eyes*: while Razumov was writing his confessions, so was Conrad; and parts of *A Personal Record* illuminate the political background of the novel.
Notes on Life and Letters, Dent, 1949. The essays entitled 'Autocracy and War' and 'The Crime of Partition' are particularly relevant to *Under Western Eyes*.

BIOGRAPHICAL WORKS

JOCELYN BAINES, *Joseph Conrad: A Critical Biography*, Weidenfeld and Nicolson, 1960; subsequently reprinted by Penguin Books. This remains an admirably concise, lucid and informative work.
NORMAN SHERRY, *Conrad and His World*, Thames & Hudson, 1972. An excellent introductory biography, generously illustrated.
FREDERICK R. KARL, *Joseph Conrad: The Three Lives*, Farrar, Straus & Giroux, 1979. A massive interpretative account.
ZDZISLAW NAJDER, *Joseph Conrad: A Chronicle*, Cambridge University Press, 1983. More factual and less speculative than Karl's book.
CEDRIC WATTS, *Joseph Conrad: A Literary Life*, Macmillan, 1989. This emphasizes the practicalities of Conrad's career, particularly his dealings with publishers.

CRITICAL STUDIES

F. R. LEAVIS, *The Great Tradition*, Chatto & Windus, 1948; Penguin, 1962. Chapter 4 of this very influential work is devoted to Conrad.
DOUGLAS HEWITT, *Conrad: A Reassessment*, Bowes & Bowes, 1952. Hewitt distinguishes sharply between the 'defensive irony' of *Under Western Eyes* and the 'offensive irony' of *The Secret Agent*.
ALBERT GUERARD, *Conrad the Novelist*, Harvard University Press, 1958. Excellent discussions of Conrad's tensions and techniques.
ELOISE KNAPP HAY, *The Political Novels of Joseph Conrad*, Chicago University Press, 1963. A widely ranging political discussion.

AVROM FLEISHMAN, *Conrad's Politics*, Johns Hopkins, 1967. Chapter VIII offers a lucid analysis of *Under Western Eyes*.

PAUL KIRSCHNER, *Conrad: The Psychologist as Artist*, Oliver & Boyd, 1968. Sees a Conrad who, in *Under Western Eyes*, has 'come to terms with his own deepest conflict'.

TERRY EAGLETON, *Exiles and Emigrés*, Chatto & Windus, 1970. Chapter 1 shrewdly postulates various political limitations of Conrad's novel.

NORMAN SHERRY, ed., *Conrad: The Critical Heritage*, Routledge & Kegan Paul, 1973. This reprints early reviews of *Under Western Eyes*.

C. B. COX, *Joseph Conrad: The Modern Imagination*, Dent, 1974. Chapter 6 suggests that the deafened Razumov may be seen as a symbol of the ageing Conrad, who became 'increasingly deaf to the problems of modernism'.

CEDRIC WATTS, *A Preface to Conrad*, Longman, 1982. A general introduction to the range of Conrad's works.

TED BILLY, ed., *Critical Essays on Joseph Conrad*, Hall, 1987. Includes an essay by P. R. Szittya which argues that *Under Western Eyes* is 'fiction about fiction'.

JAKOB LOTHE, *Conrad's Narrative Method*, Oxford University Press, 1989. Chapter 12 gives sensitive attention to the narrative techniques of *Under Western Eyes*.

MARK A. WOLLAEGER, *Joseph Conrad and the Fictions of Skepticism*, Stanford University Press, 1990. Claims that *Under Western Eyes* is 'the last of Conrad's great fictions of skepticism'.

PERIODICALS DEVOTED TO CONRAD

The magazines *Conradiana* (Texas Tech University) and *The Conradian* (Joseph Conrad Society) frequently include critical and scholarly essays on *Under Western Eyes*.

LITERARY WORKS INDEBTED TO *UNDER WESTERN EYES*

NGUGI WA THIONG'O, *A Grain of Wheat*, Heinemann, 1967.

HOWARD BRENTON, *The Saliva Milkshake*, 1977, in *Plays for the Poor Theatre*, Methuen, 1980.

CHRONOLOGY

DATE	AUTHOR'S LIFE	LITERARY CONTEXT
1853		Charlotte Brontë: *Villette*.
1856	Marriage of Apollo Korzeniowski to Ewelina Bobrowska in Oratów.	Bernard Shaw born.
1857	December 3: birth of their son, Józef Teodor Konrad Korzeniowski (later to be known as Joseph Conrad).	Flaubert: *Madame Bovary*. Baudelaire: *Fleurs du mal*.
1859	Family moves to Żytomierz.	Dickens: *A Tale of Two Cities*.
1861	Apollo Korzeniowski arrested in Warsaw for patriotic conspiracy.	Dickens: *Great Expectations*.
1862	Conrad's parents exiled to Vologda, Russia: he accompanies them.	Turgenev: *Fathers and Sons*. Ruskin: *Unto This Last*.
1863	Family moved to Chernikhov.	Thackeray dies.
1865	Death of Conrad's mother.	Birth of Kipling and Yeats.
1866	Stays with uncle at Nowochwastów.	Dostoyevsky: *Crime and Punishment*.
1869	Death of Apollo Korzeniowski; Conrad becomes ward of relatives.	Tolstoy: *War and Peace*.
1870	Taught by Adam Pulman in Kraków.	Charles Dickens dies.
1871	Also taught by Isydor Kopernicki.	Dostoyevsky: *The Devils*.
1872	Resolves to go to sea.	George Eliot: *Middlemarch*.
1874	Leaves Poland for Marseille to join French merchant navy.	Hardy: *Far from the Madding Crowd*.
1875	Sails Atlantic on *Mont-Blanc*.	Thomas Mann born.
1876	Serves as steward on *Saint-Antoine*.	Death of George Sand.
1877	Possibly involved in smuggling arms to Spanish royalists.	Tolstoy: *Anna Karenina*.
1878	Shoots himself in chest, recovers, and joins British ship *Mavis*.	Hardy: *The Return of the Native*.
1879	Serves on clipper *Duke of Sutherland*.	Ibsen: *A Doll's House*.
1880	Sails to Australia on *Loch Etive*.	Dostoyevsky: *The Brothers Karamazov*.

HISTORICAL EVENTS

Crimean War begins.
Crimean War ends. Freud born.

Indian Mutiny.

Darwin's *Origin of Species*.
Emancipation of Russian serfs.
American Civil War begins.
Bismarck gains power in Prussia.

American slaves freed. Polish uprising.
American Civil War ends.

Gandhi born. Suez Canal opens.

Franco-Prussian War. Lenin born.

Paris Commune.

Mazzini dies. Bertrand Russell born.
Winston Churchill born.

Bakunin dies.

Russia declares war on Turkey.

Afghan War. Congress of Berlin.

Zulu War. Einstein and Stalin born.

DATE	AUTHOR'S LIFE	LITERARY CONTEXT
1881	Second mate of *Palestine*.	Death of Dostoyevsky and Carlyle.
1882	Storm-damaged *Palestine* repaired.	Birth of Virginia Woolf and James Joyce.
1883	Shipwrecked when *Palestine* sinks.	Nietzsche: *Thus Spake Zarathustra*.
1885	Sails to Calcutta on *Tilkhurst*.	Birth of D. H. Lawrence.
1886	Takes British nationality; qualifies as captain.	Stevenson: *Dr Jekyll and Mr Hyde*.
1887	Sails to Java on *Highland Forest*.	Birth of Marianne Moore.
1888	Master of the ship *Otago*.	Birth of T. S. Eliot.
1889	Resigns from *Otago* and settles in London, writing *Almayer's Folly*.	Death of Robert Browning.
1890	Works in Belgian Congo.	Ibsen: *Hedda Gabler*.
1891	Officer of *Torrens* until 1893.	Hardy: *Tess of the D'Urbervilles*.
1894	*Almayer's Folly* accepted by Unwin. Meets Edward Garnett and Jessie George.	R. L. Stevenson dies; Aldous Huxley born. Kipling: *The Jungle Book*.
1895	*Almayer's Folly* published.	Crane: *The Red Badge of Courage*. Hardy: *Jude the Obscure*.
1896	*An Outcast of the Islands*. Marries Jessie George. Meets H. G. Wells.	William Morris dies; Scott Fitzgerald born.
1897	Corresponds with Cunninghame Graham. *The Nigger of the 'Narcissus'*.	Kipling: *Captains Courageous*.
1898	*Tales of Unrest*. Enters collaboration with Ford Madox Hueffer (later known as Ford Madox Ford). First son, Borys, born.	Wilde: 'Ballad of Reading Gaol'. Wells: *War of the Worlds*. Rilke: *Advent*.
1899	'Heart of Darkness' serialized. Serialization of *Lord Jim* begins.	Birth of Hemingway.
1900	*Lord Jim* (book). J. B. Pinker becomes Conrad's agent.	Death of Ruskin, Nietzsche, Oscar Wilde and Stephen Crane.
1901	*The Inheritors* (co-author Hueffer).	Kipling: *Kim*.
1902	*Youth* volume.	Gorky: *The Lower Depths*.
1903	*Typhoon* volume. *Romance* (co-author Hueffer).	James: *The Ambassadors*. Birth of George Orwell.
1904	*Nostromo*.	Chekhov: *The Cherry Orchard*.
1905	*One Day More* (play) fails.	Wells: *Kipps*.

CHRONOLOGY

DATE	AUTHOR'S LIFE	LITERARY CONTEXT
1906	*The Mirror of the Sea* (with Hueffer). Second son, John, born.	Samuel Beckett born. Ibsen dies.
1907	*The Secret Agent.*	Birth of W. H. Auden.
1908	*A Set of Six* (tales).	Bennett: *Old Wives' Tale.*
1909	Quarrels with Hueffer.	Death of Swinburne.
1910	Moves to Capel House, near Ashford.	Yeats: *The Green Helmet.*
1911	*Under Western Eyes.*	William Golding born.
1912	*A Personal Record.* '*Twixt Land and Sea* (tales). *Chance* serialized in *New York Herald.*	Patrick White born. Pound: *Ripostes.*
1913	Meets Bertrand Russell.	Lawrence: *Sons and Lovers.*
1914	Book of *Chance* has large sales. Conrad becomes prosperous at last.	Joyce: *Dubliners.* Birth of Dylan Thomas.
1915	*Within the Tides* (tales); *Victory.*	Lawrence: *The Rainbow.*
1916	*The Shadow-Line* serialized.	Henry James dies.
1917	*The Shadow-Line* (book).	Anthony Burgess born.
1918	Borys Conrad wounded in war.	Death of Wilfred Owen.
1919	*The Arrow of Gold.*	Woolf: *Night and Day.*
1920	*The Rescue.*	Lawrence: *Women in Love.* Katherine Mansfield: *Bliss.*
1921	*Notes on Life and Letters.*	Huxley: *Crome Yellow.*
1922	*The Secret Agent* (play) fails.	Eliot: *The Waste Land.* Joyce: *Ulysses.*
1923	Visits USA to acclamation. *The Rover.*	Yeats wins Nobel Prize. Huxley: *Antic Hay.*
1924	Declines knighthood. Dies of heart attack; buried at Canterbury.	Forster: *A Passage to India* Shaw: *Saint Joan.*
1925	Publication of *Tales of Hearsay* and the unfinished *Suspense.*	Eliot: *Poems 1909–25.* Shaw wins Nobel Prize.
1926	*Last Essays.*	Kafka: *The Castle.*
1927	*Joseph Conrad: Life & Letters*, written and edited by G. Jean-Aubry.	Woolf: *To the Lighthouse.*

CHRONOLOGY

AUTHOR'S NOTE

It must be admitted that by the mere force of circumstances *Under Western Eyes* has become already a sort of historical novel dealing with the past.

This reflection bears entirely upon the events of the tale; but being as a whole an attempt to render not so much the political state as the psychology of Russia itself, I venture to hope that it has not lost all its interest. I am encouraged in this flattering belief by noticing that in many articles on Russian affairs of the present day reference is made to certain sayings and opinions uttered in the pages that follow, in a manner testifying to the clearness of my vision and the correctness of my judgment. I need not say that in writing this novel I had no other object in view than to express imaginatively the general truth which underlies its action, together with my honest convictions as to the moral complexion of certain facts more or less known to the whole world.

As to the actual creation I may say that when I began to write I had a distinct conception of the first part only, with the three figures of Haldin, Razumov, and Councillor Mikulin, defined exactly in my mind. It was only after I had finished writing the first part that the whole story revealed itself to me in its tragic character and in the march of its events as unavoidable and sufficiently ample in its outline to give free play to my creative instinct and to the dramatic possibilities of the subject.

The course of action need not be explained. It has suggested itself more as a matter of feeling than a matter of thinking. It is the result not of a special experience but of general knowledge, fortified by earnest meditation. My greatest anxiety was in being able to strike and sustain the note of scrupulous impartiality. The obligation of absolute fairness was imposed on me historically and hereditarily, by the peculiar experience of race and family, in addition to my primary conviction that truth alone is the justification of any fiction which makes the least claim to the quality of art or may hope to take its place in the culture of men and women of its time. I had never been called before to a greater effort of detachment: detachment from all passions, prejudices, and even from personal memories. *Under Western Eyes* on its first appearance in England was a failure with the public, perhaps because of that very detachment. I obtained my reward some six years later when I first heard that the book had found universal recognition in Russia and had been republished there in many editions.

The various figures playing their part in the story also owe their existence to no special experience but to the general knowledge of the condition of Russia and of the moral and emotional reactions of the Russian temperament to the pressure of tyrannical lawlessness, which, in general human terms, could be reduced to the formula of senseless desperation provoked by senseless tyranny. What I was concerned with mainly was the aspect, the character, and the fate of the individuals as they appeared to the Western Eyes of the old teacher of languages. He himself has been much criticized; but I will not at this late hour undertake to justify his existence. He was useful to me and therefore I think that he must be useful to the reader both in the way of comment and by the part he plays in the development of the story. In my desire to produce the effect of actuality it seemed to me indispensable to have an eye-witness of the transactions in Geneva. I needed also a sympathetic friend for Miss Haldin, who otherwise would have been too much alone and unsupported to be perfectly credible. She would have had no one to whom she could give a glimpse of her idealistic faith, of her great heart, and of her simple emotions.

Razumov is treated sympathetically. Why should he not be? He is an ordinary young man, with a healthy capacity for work and sane ambitions. He has an average conscience. If he is slightly abnormal it is only in his sensitiveness to his position. Being nobody's child he feels rather more keenly than another would that he is a Russian – or he is nothing. He is perfectly right in looking on all Russia as his heritage. The sanguinary futility of the crimes and the sacrifices seething in that amorphous mass envelops and crushes him. But I don't think that in his distraction he is ever monstrous. Nobody is exhibited as a monster here – neither the simple-minded Tekla nor the wrong-headed Sophia Antonovna. Peter Ivanovitch and Madame de S. are fair game. They are the apes of a sinister jungle and are treated as their grimaces deserve. As to Nikita – nicknamed Necator – he is the perfect flower of the terroristic wilderness. What troubled me most in dealing with him was not his monstrosity but his banality. He has been exhibited to the public eye for years in so-called 'disclosures' in newspaper articles, in secret histories, in sensation novels.

The most terrifying reflection (I am speaking now for myself) is that all these people are not the product of the exceptional but of the general – of the normality of their place, and time, and race. The ferocity and imbecility of an auto-cratic rule rejecting all legality and in fact basing itself upon complete moral anarchism provokes the no less imbecile and atrocious answer of a purely Utopian revolutionism encom-passing destruction by the first means to hand, in the strange conviction that a fundamental change of hearts must follow the downfall of any given human institutions. These people are unable to see that all they can effect is merely a change of names. The oppressors and the oppressed are all Russians together; and the world is brought once more face to face with the truth of the saying that the tiger cannot change his stripes nor the leopard his spots.

1920.   J. C.

To Agnes Tobin
Who brought to our door
her genius for friendship
from the uttermost shore
of the west

UNDER WESTERN EYES

'I would take liberty from any hand as a hungry man would snatch a piece of bread.'—MISS HALDIN

UNDER WESTERN EYES

PART FIRST

TO begin with, I wish to disclaim the possession of those high gifts of imagination and expression which would have enabled my pen to create for the reader the personality of the man who called himself, after the Russian custom, Cyril son of Isidor—Kirylo Sidorovitch—Razumov.

If I have ever had these gifts in any sort of living form they have been smothered out of existence a long time ago under a wilderness of words. Words, as is well known, are the great foes of reality. I have been for many years a teacher of languages. It is an occupation which at length becomes fatal to whatever share of imagination, observation, and insight an ordinary person may be heir to. To a teacher of languages there comes a time when the world is but a place of many words, and man appears a mere talking animal not much more wonderful than a parrot.

This being so, I could not have observed Mr. Razumov or guessed at his reality by the force of insight, much less have imagined him as he was.

Even to invent the mere bald facts of his life would have been utterly beyond my powers. But I think that without this declaration the readers of these pages will be able to detect in the story the marks of documentary evidence. And that is perfectly correct. It is based on a document; all I have brought to it is my knowledge of the Russian language, which is sufficient for what is attempted here. The document, of course, is something in the nature of a journal, a diary, yet not exactly that in its actual form. For instance, most of it was not written up from day to day, though all the entries are dated. Some of these entries cover months of time and extend over dozens of pages. All the earlier part is a retrospect, in a narrative form, relating to an event which took place about a year before.

I must mention that I have lived for a long time in Geneva. A whole quarter of that town, on account of many Russians residing there, is called La Petite Russie—Little Russia. I had a rather extensive connection in Little Russia at that time. Yet I confess that I have no comprehension of the Russian character. The illogicality of their attitude, the arbitrariness of their conclusions, the frequency of the exceptional, should present no difficulty to a student of many grammars; but there must be something else in the way, some special human trait—one of those subtle differences that are beyond the ken of mere professors. What must remain striking to a teacher of languages is the Russians' extraordinary love of words. They gather them up ; they cherish them, but they don't hoard them in their breasts ; on the contrary, they are always ready to pour them out by the hour or by the night with an enthusiasm, a sweeping abundance, with such an aptness of application sometimes that, as in the case of very accomplished parrots, one can't defend oneself from the suspicion that they really understand what they say. There is a generosity in their ardour of speech which removes it as far as possible from common loquacity ; and it is ever too disconnected to be classed as eloquence. . . . But I must apologise for this digression.

It would be idle to inquire why Mr. Razumov has left this record behind him. It is inconceivable that he should have wished any human eye to see it. A mysterious impulse of human nature comes into play here. Putting aside Samuel Pepys, who has forced in this way the door of immortality, innumerable people, criminals, saints, philosophers, young girls, statesmen, and simple imbeciles, have kept self-revealing records from vanity no doubt, but also from other more inscrutable motives. There must be a wonderful soothing power in mere words since so many men have used them for self-communion. Being myself a quiet individual, I take it that what all men are really after is some form, or perhaps only some formula, of peace.

Certainly they are crying loud enough for it at the present day. What sort of peace Kirylo Sidorovitch Razumov expected to find in the writing up of his record it passeth my understanding to guess.

The fact remains that he has written it.

Mr. Razumov was a tall, well-proportioned young man, quite unusually dark for a Russian from the Central Provinces. His good looks would have been unquestionable if it had not been for a peculiar lack of fineness in the features. It was as if a face modelled vigorously in wax (with some approach even to a classical correctness of type) had been held close to a fire till all sharpness of line had been lost in the softening of the material. But even thus he was sufficiently good-looking. His manner, too, was good. In discussion he was easily swayed by argument and authority. With his younger compatriots he took the attitude of an inscrutable listener, a listener of the kind that hears you out intelligently and then—just changes the subject.

This sort of trick, which may arise either from intellectual insufficiency or from an imperfect trust in one's own convictions, procured for Mr. Razumov a reputation of profundity. Amongst a lot of exuberant talkers, in the habit of exhausting themselves daily by ardent discussion, a comparatively taciturn personality is naturally credited with reserve power. By his comrades at the St. Petersburg University, Kirylo Sidorovitch Razumov, third

year's student in philosophy, was looked upon as
a strong nature—an altogether trustworthy man.
This, in a country where an opinion may be a legal
crime visited by death or sometimes by a fate worse
than mere death, meant that he was worthy of
being trusted with forbidden opinions. He was
liked also for his amiability and for his quiet readiness to oblige his comrades even at the cost of
personal inconvenience.

Mr. Razumov was supposed to be the son of an
archpriest and to be protected by a distinguished
nobleman—perhaps of his own distant province.
But his outward appearance accorded badly with
such humble origin. Such a descent was not credible. It was, indeed, suggested that Mr. Razumov
was the son of an archpriest's pretty daughter—
which, of course, would put a different complexion
on the matter. This theory also rendered intelligible the protection of the distinguished nobleman.
All this, however, had never been investigated,
maliciously or otherwise. No one knew or cared
who the nobleman in question was. Razumov
received a modest but very sufficient allowance
from the hands of an obscure attorney, who seemed
to act as his guardian in some measure. Now and
then he appeared at some professor's informal
reception. Apart from that, Razumov was not
known to have any social relations in the town. He
attended the obligatory lectures regularly, and was
considered by the authorities as a very promising

student. He worked at home in the manner of a man who means to get on, but did not shut himself up severely for that purpose. He was always accessible, and there was nothing secret or reserved in his life.

I

The origin of Mr. Razumov's record is connected with an event characteristic of modern Russia in the actual fact: the assassination of a prominent statesman — and still more characteristic of the moral corruption of an oppressed society where the noblest aspirations of humanity, the desire of freedom, an ardent patriotism, the love of justice, the sense of pity, and even the fidelity of simple minds are prostituted to the lusts of hate and fear, the inseparable companions of an uneasy despotism.

The fact alluded to above is the successful attempt on the life of Mr. de P——, the President of the notorious Repressive Commission of some years ago, the Minister of State invested with extraordinary powers. The newspapers made noise enough about that fanatical, narrow-chested figure in gold-laced uniform, with a face of crumpled parchment, insipid, bespectacled eyes, and the cross of the Order of St. Procopius hung under the skinny throat. For a time, it may be remembered, not a month passed without his portrait appearing in some one of the illustrated papers of Europe. He served the monarchy by imprisoning, exiling, or sending to the gallows men and women, young and old, with an equable, unwearied industry. In his mystic acceptance of the principle of autocracy he was bent on extirpating from the land every vestige of anything that resembled freedom in public institutions ; and in his ruthless persecution of the rising generation he seemed to aim at the destruction of the very hope of liberty itself.

It is said that this execrated personality had not enough imagination to be aware of the hate he inspired. It is hardly credible ; but it is a fact that he took very few precautions for his safety. In the preamble of a certain famous State paper he had declared once that " the thought of liberty has never existed in the Act of the Creator. From the multitude of men's counsel nothing could come but revolt and disorder ; and revolt and disorder in a world created for obedience and stability is sin. It was not Reason but Authority which expressed the Divine Intention. God was the Autocrat of the Universe. . . ." It may be that the man who made this declaration believed that heaven itself was bound to protect him in his remorseless defence of autocracy on this earth.

No doubt the vigilance of the police saved him many times ; but, as a matter of fact, when his appointed fate overtook him, the competent authorities could not have given him any warning. They had no knowledge of any conspiracy against the

Minister's life, had no hint of any plot through their usual channels of information, had seen no signs, were aware of no suspicious movements or dangerous persons.

Mr. de P—— was being driven towards the railway station in a two-horse uncovered sleigh with footman and coachman on the box. Snow had been falling all night, making the roadway, uncleared as yet at this early hour, very heavy for the horses. It was still falling thickly. But the sleigh must have been observed and marked down. As it drew over to the left before taking a turn, the footman noticed a peasant walking slowly on the edge of the pavement with his hands in the pockets of his sheepskin coat and his shoulders hunched up to his ears under the falling snow. On being overtaken this peasant suddenly faced about and swung his arm. In an instant there was a terrible shock, a detonation muffled in the multitude of snowflakes; both horses lay dead and mangled on the ground, and the coachman, with a shrill cry, had fallen off the box mortally wounded. The footman (who survived) had no time to see the face of the man in the sheepskin coat. After throwing the bomb this last got away, but it is supposed that, seeing a lot of people surging up on all sides of him in the falling snow, and all running towards the scene of the explosion, he thought it safer to turn back with them.

In an incredibly short time an excited crowd

assembled round the sledge. The Minister-President, getting out unhurt into the deep snow, stood near the groaning coachman and addressed the people repeatedly in his weak, colourless voice : " I beg of you to keep off. For the love of God, I beg of you good people to keep off."

It was then that a tall young man who had remained standing perfectly still within a carriage gateway, two houses lower down, stepped out into the street and walking up rapidly flung another bomb over the heads of the crowd. It actually struck the Minister-President on the shoulder as he stooped over his dying servant, then falling between his feet exploded with a terrific concentrated violence, striking him dead to the ground, finishing the wounded man and practically annihilating the empty sledge in the twinkling of an eye. With a yell of horror the crowd broke up and fled in all directions, except for those who fell dead or dying where they stood nearest to the Minister-President, and one or two others who did not fall till they had run a little way.

The first explosion had brought together a crowd as if by enchantment, the second made as swiftly a solitude in the street for hundreds of yards in each direction. Through the falling snow people looked from afar at the small heap of dead bodies lying upon each other near the carcasses of the two horses. Nobody dared to approach till some Cossacks of a street-patrol galloped up and, dismounting, began to turn over the dead. Amongst the innocent victims of the second explosion laid out on the pavement there was a body dressed in a peasant's sheepskin coat ; but the face was unrecognisable, there was absolutely nothing found in the pockets of its poor clothing, and it was the only one whose identity was never established.

That day Mr. Razumov got up at his usual hour and spent the morning within the university buildings listening to the lectures and working for some time in the library. He heard the first vague rumour of something in the way of bomb-throwing at the table of the students' ordinary, where he was accustomed to eat his two o'clock dinner. But this rumour was made up of mere whispers, and this was Russia, where it was not always safe, for a student especially, to appear too much interested in certain kinds of whispers. Razumov was one of those men who, living in a period of mental and political unrest, keep an instinctive hold on normal, practical, everyday life. He was aware of the emotional tension of his time ; he even responded to it in an indefinite way. But his main concern was with his work, his studies, and with his own future.

Officially and in fact without a family (for the daughter of the archpriest had long been dead), no home influences had shaped his opinions or his feelings. He was as lonely in the world as a man swimming in the deep sea. The word Razumov was the mere label of a solitary individuality. There were no Razumovs belonging to him anywhere. His closest parentage was defined in the statement that he was a Russian. Whatever good he expected from life would be given to or withheld from his hopes by that connection alone. This immense parentage suffered from the throes of internal dissensions, and he shrank mentally from the fray as a good-natured man may shrink from taking definite sides in a violent family quarrel.

Razumov, going home, reflected that having prepared all the matters of the forthcoming examination, he could now devote his time to the subject of the prize essay. He hankered after the silver medal. The prize was offered by the Ministry of Education ; the names of the competitors would be submitted to the Minister himself. The mere fact of trying would be considered meritorious in the higher quarters ; and the possessor of the prize would have a claim to an administrative appointment of the better sort after he had taken his degree. The student Razumov in an access of elation forgot the dangers menacing the stability of the institutions which give rewards and appointments. But, remembering the medallist of the year before, Razumov, the young man of no parentage, was sobered. He and some others happened to be assembled in their comrade's rooms at the very time when that last received the official advice of his success. He was a quiet, unassuming young man : " Forgive me," he had said, with a faint apologetic smile and taking up his cap, " I am going out to order up some wine. But I must first send a telegram to my folk at home. I say! Won't the old people make it a festive time for the neighbours for twenty miles around our place?"

Razumov thought there was nothing of that sort for him in the world. His success would matter to no one. But he felt no bitterness against the nobleman his protector, who was not a provincial magnate as was generally supposed. He was in fact nobody less than Prince K——, once a great and splendid figure in the world, and now, his day being over, a senator and a gouty invalid, living in a still splendid but more domestic manner. He had some young children, and a wife as aristocratic and proud as himself.

In all his life Razumov was allowed only once to come into personal contact with the prince.

It had the air of a chance meeting in the little attorney's office. One day Razumov, coming in by appointment, found a stranger standing there—a tall, aristocratic-looking personage with silky grey side-whiskers. The bald-headed, sly little lawyer-fellow called out, " Come in—come in, Mr. Razumov," with a sort of ironic heartiness. Then turning deferentially to the stranger with the grand air, " A ward of mine, your Excellency. One of the most promising students of his faculty in the St. Petersburg University."

To his intense surprise Razumov saw a white

shapely hand extended to him. He took it in great
confusion (it was soft and passive) and heard at the
same time a condescending murmur in which he
caught only the words " Satisfactory " and " Persevere." But the most amazing thing of all was
to feel suddenly a distinct pressure of the white
shapely hand just before it was withdrawn : a
light pressure like a secret sign. The emotion
of it was terrible. Razumov's heart seemed to
leap into his throat. When he raised his eyes the
aristocratic personage, motioning the little lawyer
aside, had opened the door and was going out.

The attorney rummaged amongst the papers
on his desk for a time. " Do you know who that
was ? " he asked suddenly.

Razumov, whose heart was thumping hard yet,
shook his head in silence.

" That was Prince K——. You wonder what
he could be doing in the hole of a poor legal rat
like myself—eh ? These awfully great people have
their sentimental curiosities like common sinners.
But if I were you, Kirylo Sidorovitch," he continued, leering and laying a peculiar emphasis on
the patronymic, " I wouldn't boast at large of the
introduction. It would not be prudent, Kirylo
Sidorovitch. Oh dear, no ! It would be, in fact,
dangerous for your future."

The young man's ears burned like fire ; his
sight was dim. " That man ! " Razumov was
saying to himself. " He ! "

Henceforth it was by this monosyllable that Mr. Razumov got into the habit of referring mentally to the stranger with grey silky side-whiskers. From that time too, when walking in the more fashionable quarters, he noted with interest the magnificent horses and carriages with Prince K——'s liveries on the box. Once he saw the princess get out— she was shopping—followed by two girls, of which one was nearly a head taller than the other. Their fair hair hung loose down their backs in the English style ; they had merry eyes ; their coats, muffs, and little fur caps were exactly alike ; and their cheeks and noses were tinged a cheerful pink by the frost. They crossed the pavement in front of him, and Razumov went on his way smiling shyly to himself. " His " daughters. They resembled " Him." The young man felt a glow of warm friendliness towards these girls who would never know of his existence. Presently they would marry generals or Kammer-herrs and have girls and boys of their own, who perhaps would be aware of him as a celebrated old professor, decorated, possibly a Privy Councillor, one of the glories of Russia—nothing more !

But a celebrated professor was a somebody. Distinction would convert the label Razumov into an honoured name. There was nothing strange in the student Razumov's wish for distinction. A man's real life is that accorded to him in the thoughts of other men by reason of respect or natural love. Returning home on the day of the attempt on Mr.

de P——'s life, Razumov resolved to have a good
try for the silver medal.

Climbing slowly the four flights of the dark,
dirty staircase in the house where he had his lodgings,
he felt confident of success. The winner's name
would be published in the papers on New Year's
Day. And at the thought that " He " would most
probably read it there, Razumov stopped short on
the stairs for an instant, then went on smiling
faintly at his own emotion. " This is but a shadow,"
he said to himself, " but the medal is a solid beginning."

With those ideas of industry in his head the
warmth of his room was agreeable and encouraging.
" I shall put in four hours of good work," he thought.
But no sooner had he closed the door than he was
horribly startled. All black against the usual tall
stove of white tiles gleaming in the dusk, stood
a strange figure, wearing a skirted, close-fitting,
brown cloth coat strapped round the waist, in long
boots, and with a little Astrakhan cap on its head.
It loomed lithe and martial. Razumov was utterly
confounded. It was only when the figure, advancing
two paces, asked in an untroubled, grave voice if
the outer door was closed, that he regained his
power of speech.

" Haldin ! . . . Victor Victorovitch ! . . . Is
that you ? . . . Yes. The outer door is shut all
right. But this is indeed unexpected."

Victor Haldin, a student older than most of his

contemporaries at the university, was not one of the industrious set. He was hardly ever seen at lectures ; the authorities had marked him as " restless " and " unsound "—very bad notes. But he had a great personal prestige with his comrades and influenced their thoughts. Razumov had never been intimate with him. They had met from time to time at gatherings in other students' houses. They had even had a discussion together—one of those discussions on first principles dear to the sanguine minds of youth.

Razumov wished the man had chosen some other time to come for a chat. He felt in good trim to tackle the prize essay. But as Haldin could not be slightingly dismissed, Razumov adopted the tone of hospitality, asking him to sit down and smoke.

" Kirylo Sidorovitch," said the other, flinging off his cap, " we are not perhaps in exactly the same camp. Your judgment is more philosophical. You are a man of few words, but I haven't met anybody who dared to doubt the generosity of your sentiments. There is a solidity about your character which cannot exist without courage."

Razumov felt flattered and began to murmur shyly something about being very glad of his good opinion, when Haldin raised his hand.

" That is what I was saying to myself," he continued, " as I dodged in the wood-yard down by the riverside. ' He has a strong character, this young

man,' I said to myself. ' He does not throw his
soul to the winds.' Your reserve has always fascinated me, Kirylo Sidorovitch. So I tried to remember your address. But look here—it was a
piece of luck. Your dvornik was away from the
gate talking to a sleigh-driver on the other side of
the street. I met no one on the stairs, not a soul.
As I came up to your floor I caught sight of your
landlady coming out of your rooms. But she did
not see me. She crossed the landing to her own
side, and then I slipped in. I have been here two
hours expecting you to come in every moment."

Razumov had listened in astonishment ; but
before he could open his mouth Haldin added,
speaking deliberately, " It was I who removed
de P—— this morning."

Razumov kept down a cry of dismay. The
sentiment of his life being utterly ruined by this
contact with such a crime, expressed itself quaintly
by a sort of half-derisive mental exclamation,
" There goes my silver medal ! "

Haldin continued after waiting a while :

" You say nothing, Kirylo Sidorovitch ! I understand your silence. To be sure, I cannot expect
you with your frigid English manner to embrace
me. But never mind your manners. You have
enough heart to have heard the sound of weeping
and gnashing of teeth this man raised in the land.
That would be enough to get over any philosophical
hopes. He was uprooting the tender plant. He

2

had to be stopped. He was a dangerous man—a convinced man. Three more years of his work would have put us back fifty years into bondage—and look at all the lives wasted, at all the souls lost in that time."

His curt, self-confident voice suddenly lost its ring and it was in a dull tone that he added, " Yes, brother, I have killed him. It's weary work."

Razumov had sunk into a chair. Every moment he expected a crowd of policemen to rush in. There must have been thousands of them out looking for that man walking up and down in his room. Haldin was talking again in a restrained, steady voice. Now and then he flourished an arm, slowly, without excitement.

He told Razumov how he had brooded for a year ; how he had not slept properly for weeks. He and " Another " had a warning of the Minister's movements from " a certain person " late the evening before. He and that " Another " prepared their " engines " and resolved to have no sleep till " the deed " was done. They walked the streets under the falling snow with the " engines " on them, exchanging not a word the livelong night. When they happened to meet a police patrol they took each other by the arm and pretended to be a couple of peasants on the spree. They reeled and talked in drunken hoarse voices. Except for these strange outbreaks they kept silence, moving on ceaselessly. Their plans had been previously arranged. At daybreak they made their way to the spot which they knew the sledge must pass. When it appeared in sight they exchanged a muttered good-bye and separated. The " other " remained at the corner, Haldin took up a position a little farther up the street. . . .

After throwing his " engine " he ran off and in a moment was overtaken by the panic-struck people flying away from the spot after the second explosion. They were wild with terror. He was jostled once or twice. He slowed down for the rush to pass him and then turned to the left into a narrow street. There he was alone.

He marvelled at this immediate escape. The work was done. He could hardly believe it. He fought with an almost irresistible longing to lie down on the pavement and sleep. But this sort of faint-ness—a drowsy faintness—passed off quickly. He walked faster, making his way to one of the poorer parts of the town in order to look up Ziemianitch.

This Ziemianitch, Razumov understood, was a sort of town-peasant who had got on ; owner of a small number of sledges and horses for hire. Haldin paused in his narrative to exclaim :

" A bright spirit ! A hardy soul ! The best driver in St. Petersburg. He has a team of three horses there. . . . Ah ! He's a fellow ! "

This man had declared himself willing to take out safely, at any time, one or two persons to the second or third railway station on one of the southern lines. But there had been no time to warn him the night before. His usual haunt seemed to be a low-class eating-house on the outskirts of the town. When Haldin got there the man was not to be found. He was not expected to turn up again till the evening. Haldin wandered away restlessly.

He saw the gate of a wood-yard open and went in to get out of the wind which swept the bleak, broad thoroughfare. The great rectangular piles of cut wood loaded with snow resembled the huts of a village. At first the watchman who discovered him crouching amongst them talked in a friendly manner. He was a dried-up old man wearing two ragged army coats one over the other ; his wizened little face, tied up under the jaw and over the ears in a dirty red handkerchief, looked comical. Presently he grew sulky, and then all at once without rhyme or reason began to shout furiously :

" Aren't you ever going to clear out of this, you loafer ? We know all about factory hands of your sort. A big, strong, young chap ! You aren't even drunk. What do you want here ? You don't frighten us. Take yourself and your ugly eyes away."

Haldin stopped before the sitting Razumov. His supple figure, with the white forehead above which the fair hair stood straight up, had an aspect of lofty daring.

" He did not like my eyes," he said. " And so . . . here I am."

Razumov made an effort to speak calmly.

"But pardon me, Victor Victorovitch. We know each other so little. . . . I don't see why you . . ."

"Confidence," said Haldin.

This word sealed Razumov's lips as if a hand had been clapped on his mouth. His brain seethed with arguments.

"And so—here you are," he muttered through his teeth.

The other did not detect the tone of anger. Never suspected it.

"Yes. And nobody knows I am here. You are the last person that could be suspected—should I get caught. That's an advantage, you see. And then—speaking to a superior mind like yours I can well say all the truth. It occurred to me that you—you have no one belonging to you—no ties, no one to suffer for it if this came out by some means. There have been enough ruined Russian homes as it is. But I don't see how my passage through your rooms can be ever known. If I should be got hold of, I'll know how to keep silent—no matter what they may be pleased to do to me," he added grimly.

He began to walk again while Razumov sat still appalled.

"You thought that——" he faltered out, almost sick with indignation.

"Yes, Razumov. Yes, brother. Some day you shall help to build. You suppose that I am a terrorist, now—a destructor of what is. But consider that the true destroyers are they who destroy the spirit of progress and truth, not the avengers who merely kill the bodies of the persecutors of human dignity. Men like me are necessary to make room for self-contained, thinking men like you. Well, we have made the sacrifice of our lives, but all the same I want to escape if it can be done. It is not my life I want to save, but my power to do. I won't live idle. Oh no! Don't make any mistake, Razumov. Men like me are rare. And, besides, an example like this is more awful to oppressors when the perpetrator vanishes without a trace. They sit in their offices and palaces and quake. All I want you to do is to help me to vanish. No great matter that. Only to go by-and-by and see Ziemianitch for me at that place where I went this morning. Just tell him, ' He whom you know wants a well-horsed sledge to pull up half an hour after midnight at the seventh lamp-post on the left counting from the upper end of Karabelnaya. If nobody gets in, the sledge is to run round a block or two, so as to come back past the same spot in ten minutes' time.' "

Razumov wondered why he had not cut short that talk and told this man to go away long before. Was it weakness or what ?

He concluded that it was a sound instinct. Haldin must have been seen. It was impossible that some people should not have noticed the face and appearance of the man who threw the second bomb. Haldin was a noticeable person. The police in their thousands must have had his description within the hour. With every moment the danger grew. Sent out to wander in the streets he could not escape being caught in the end.

The police would very soon find out all about him. They would set about discovering a conspiracy. Everybody Haldin had ever known would be in the greatest danger. Unguarded expressions, little facts in themselves innocent would be counted for crimes. Razumov remembered certain words he said, the speeches he had listened to, the harmless gatherings he had attended—it was almost impossible for a student to keep out of that sort of thing, without becoming suspect to his comrades.

Razumov saw himself shut up in a fortress, worried, badgered, perhaps ill-used. He saw himself deported by an administrative order, his life broken, ruined, and robbed of all hope. He saw himself—at best—leading a miserable existence under police supervision, in some small far-away provincial town, without friend to assist his necessities or even take any steps to alleviate his lot—as others had. Others had fathers, mothers, brothers, relations, connections, to move heaven and earth on their behalf—he had no one. The very officials that sentenced him some morning would forget his existence before sunset.

He saw his youth pass away from him in misery and half-starvation—his strength give way, his mind become an abject thing. He saw himself creeping, broken down and shabby, about the streets—dying unattended in some filthy hole of a room, or on the sordid bed of a Government hospital.

He shuddered. Then the peace of bitter calmness came over him. It was best to keep this man out of the streets till he could be got rid of with some chance of escaping. That was the best that could be done. Razumov, of course, felt the safety of his lonely existence to be permanently endangered. This evening's doings could turn up against him at any time as long as this man lived and the present institutions endured. They appeared to him rational and indestructible at that moment. They had a force of harmony—in contrast with the horrible discord of this man's presence. He hated the man. He said quietly :

" Yes, of course, I will go. You must give me precise directions, and for the rest—depend on me."

" Ah ! You are a fellow ! Collected—cool as a cucumber. A regular Englishman. Where did you get your soul from ? There aren't many like you. Look here, brother ! Men like me leave no posterity, but their souls are not lost. No man's soul is ever lost. It works for itself—or else where would be the sense of self-sacrifice, of martyrdom, of conviction, of faith—the labours of the soul ?

What will become of my soul when I die in the way I must die—soon—very soon perhaps? It shall not perish. Don't make a mistake, Razumov. This is not murder—it is war, war. My spirit shall go on warring in some Russian body till all falsehood is swept out of the world. The modern civilisation is false, but a new revelation shall come out of Russia. Ha! you say nothing. You are a sceptic. I respect your philosophical scepticism, Razumov, but don't touch the soul—the Russian soul that lives in all of us. It has a future. It has a mission, I tell you, or else why should I have been moved to do this—reckless—like a butcher —in the middle of all these innocent people— scattering death? I! I! . . . I wouldn't hurt a fly!"

" Not so loud," warned Razumov harshly.

Haldin sat down abruptly, and leaning his head on his folded arms burst into tears. He wept for a long time. The dusk had deepened in the room. Razumov, motionless in sombre wonder, listened to the sobs.

The other raised his head, got up and with an effort mastered his voice.

"Yes. Men like me leave no posterity," he repeated in a subdued tone. "I have a sister though. She's with my old mother—I persuaded them to go abroad this year—thank God. Not a bad little girl my sister. She has the most trustful eyes of any human being that ever walked this

earth. She will marry well, I hope. She may
have children—sons perhaps. Look at me. My
father was a Government official in the provinces.
He had a little land too. A simple servant of God
—a true Russian in his way. His was the soul of
obedience. But I am not like him. They say I
resemble my mother's eldest brother, an officer.
They shot him in '28. Under Nicholas, you know.
Haven't I told you that this is war, war? . . . But,
God of Justice! this is weary work."

Razumov, in his chair, leaning his head on his
hand, spoke as if from the bottom of an abyss.

" You believe in God, Haldin ? "

" There you go catching at words that are wrung
from one. What does it matter ? What was it the
Englishman said : ' There is a divine soul in
things . . .'? Devil take him—I don't remember
now. But he spoke the truth. When the day of
you thinkers comes don't you forget what's divine
in the Russian soul—and that's resignation. Respect
that in your intellectual restlessness and don't let
your arrogant wisdom spoil its message to the world.
I am speaking to you now like a man with a rope
round his neck. What do you imagine I am ? A
being in revolt ? No. It's you thinkers who
are in everlasting revolt. I am one of the resigned.
When the necessity of this heavy work came to me
and I understood that it had to be done—what did
I do ? Did I exult ? Did I take pride in my purpose ? Did I try to weigh its worth and conse-

quences ? No ! I was resigned. I thought, ' God's will be done.' "

He threw himself full length on Razumov's bed, and putting the backs of his hands over his eyes remained perfectly motionless and silent. Not even the sound of his breathing could be heard. The dead stillness of the room remained undisturbed till in the darkness Razumov said gloomily :

" Haldin."

" Yes," answered the other readily, quite invisible now on the bed and without the slightest stir.

" Isn't it time for me to start ? "

" Yes, brother." The other was heard, lying still in the darkness as though he were talking in his sleep. " The time has come to put fate to the test."

He paused, then gave a few lucid directions in the quiet impersonal voice of a man in a trance. Razumov made ready without a word of answer. As he was leaving the room the voice on the bed said after him :

" Go with God, thou silent soul."

On the landing, moving softly, Razumov locked the door and put the key in his pocket.

II

The words and events of that evening must have been graven as if with a steel tool on Mr. Razumov's brain, since he was able to write his relation with such fullness and precision a good many months afterwards.

The record of the thoughts which assailed him in the street is even more minute and abundant. They seem to have rushed upon him with the greater freedom because his thinking powers were no longer crushed by Haldin's presence—the appalling presence of a great crime and the stunning force of a great fanaticism. On looking through the pages of Mr. Razumov's diary I own that a " rush of thoughts " is not an adequate image.

The more adequate description would be a tumult of thoughts—the faithful reflection of the state of his feelings. The thoughts in themselves were not numerous—they were like the thoughts of most human beings, few and simple—but they cannot be reproduced here in all their exclamatory repetitions which went on in an endless and weary turmoil—for the walk was long.

If to the Western reader they appear shocking, inappropriate, or even improper, it must be remembered that as to the first this may be the effect of my crude statement. For the rest I will only remark here that this is not a story of the West of Europe.

Nations it may be have fashioned their Governments, but the Governments have paid them back in the same coin. It is unthinkable that any young Englishman should find himself in Razumov's situation. This being so, it would be a vain enter-

prise to imagine what he would think. The only
safe surmise to make is that he would not think
as Mr. Razumov thought at this crisis of his fate.
He would not have an hereditary and personal
knowledge of the means by which a historical
autocracy represses ideas, guards its power, and
defends its existence. By an act of mental extrava-
gance he might imagine himself arbitrarily thrown
into prison, but it would never occur to him unless
he were delirious (and perhaps not even then)
that he could be beaten with whips as a practical
measure either of investigation or of punishment.

This is but a crude and obvious example of the
different conditions of Western thought. I don't
know that this danger occurred specially to Mr.
Razumov. No doubt it entered unconsciously into
the general dread and the general appallingness of
this crisis. Razumov, as has been seen, was aware
of more subtle ways in which an individual may be
undone by the proceedings of a despotic Government. A simple expulsion from the university
(the very least that could happen to him), with an
impossibility to continue his studies anywhere, was
enough to ruin utterly a young man depending
entirely upon the development of his natural abilities for his place in the world. He was a Russian :
and for him to be implicated meant simply sinking
into the lowest social depths amongst the hopeless
and the destitute—the night-birds of the city.

The peculiar circumstances of Razumov's

parentage, or rather of his lack of parentage, should be taken into the account of his thoughts. And he remembered them too. He had been lately reminded of them in a peculiarly atrocious way by this fatal Haldin. " Because I haven't that, must everything else be taken away from me ? " he thought.

He nerved himself for another effort to go on. Along the roadway sledges glided phantom-like and jingling through a fluttering whiteness on the black face of the night. " For it is a crime," he was saying to himself. " A murder is a murder. Though, of course, some sort of liberal institutions . . ."

A feeling of horrible sickness came over him. " I must be courageous," he exhorted himself mentally. All his strength was suddenly gone as if taken out by a hand. Then by a mighty effort of will it came back because he was afraid of fainting in the street and being picked up by the police with the key of his lodgings in his pocket. They would find Haldin there, and then, indeed, he would be undone.

Strangely enough it was this fear which seems to have kept him up to the end. The passers-by were rare. They came upon him suddenly, looming up black in the snowflakes close by, then vanishing all at once—without footfalls.

It was the quarter of the very poor. Razumov noticed an elderly woman tied up in ragged shawls. Under the street lamp she seemed a beggar off duty. She walked leisurely in the blizzard as though she had no home to hurry to, she hugged under one arm a round loaf of black bread with an air of guarding a priceless booty; and Razumov, averting his glance, envied her the peace of her mind and the serenity of her fate.

To one reading Mr. Razumov's narrative it is really a wonder how he managed to keep going as he did along one interminable street after another on pavements that were gradually becoming blocked with snow. It was the thought of Haldin locked up in his rooms and the desperate desire to get rid of his presence which drove him forward. No rational determination had any part in his exertions. Thus, when on arriving at the low eating-house he heard that the man of horses, Ziemianitch, was not there, he could only stare stupidly.

The waiter, a wild-haired youth in tarred boots and a pink shirt, exclaimed, uncovering his pale gums in a silly grin, that Ziemianitch had got his skinful early in the afternoon and had gone away with a bottle under each arm to keep it up amongst the horses—he supposed.

The owner of the vile den, a bony short man in a dirty cloth caftan coming down to his heels, stood by, his hands tucked into his belt, and nodded confirmation.

The reek of spirits, the greasy, rancid steam of food, got Razumov by the throat. He struck a table with his clenched hand and shouted violently:

"You lie."

Bleary unwashed faces were turned to his direction. A mild-eyed ragged tramp drinking tea at the next table moved farther away. A murmur of wonder arose with an undertone of uneasiness. A laugh was heard too, and an exclamation, " There ! there ! " jeeringly soothing. The waiter looked all round and announced to the room :

" The gentleman won't believe that Ziemianitch is drunk."

From a distant corner a hoarse voice belonging to a horrible, nondescript, shaggy being with a black face like the muzzle of a bear grunted angrily :

" The cursed driver of thieves. What do we want with his gentlemen here ? We are all honest folk in this place."

Razumov, biting his lip till blood came to keep himself from bursting into imprecations, followed the owner of the den, who, whispering " Come along, little father," led him into a tiny hole of a place behind the wooden counter, whence proceeded a sound of splashing. A wet and bedraggled creature, a sort of sexless and shivering scarecrow, washed glasses in there, bending over a wooden tub by the light of a tallow dip.

" Yes, little father," the man in the long caftan said plaintively. He had a brown, cunning little face, a thin greyish beard. Trying to light a tin lantern he hugged it to his breast and talked garrulously the while.

He would show Ziemianitch to the gentleman to

prove there were no lies told. And he would show him drunk. His woman, it seems, ran away from him last night. " Such a hag she was ! Thin ! Pfui ! " He spat. They were always running away from that driver of the devil—and he sixty years old too ; could never get used to it. But each heart knows sorrow after its own kind, and Ziemianitch was a born fool all his days. And then he would fly to the bottle. " ' Who could bear life in our land without the bottle ? ' he says. A proper Russian man—the little pig. . . . Be pleased to follow me."

Razumov crossed a quadrangle of deep snow enclosed between high walls with innumerable windows. Here and there a dim yellow light hung within the four-square mass of darkness. The house was an enormous slum, a hive of human vermin, a monumental abode of misery towering on the verge of starvation and despair.

In a corner the ground sloped sharply down, and Razumov followed the light of the lantern through a small doorway into a long cavernous place like a neglected subterranean byre. Deep within, three shaggy little horses tied up to rings hung their heads together, motionless and shadowy in the dim light of the lantern. It must have been the famous team of Haldin's escape. Razumov peered fearfully into the gloom. His guide pawed in the straw with his foot.

" Here he is. Ah ! the little pigeon. A true

3

Russian man. ' No heavy hearts for me,' he says.
' Bring out the bottle and take your ugly mug out
of my sight.' Ha, ha, ha! That's the fellow he
is."

He held the lantern over a prone form of a man,
apparently fully dressed for outdoors. His head
was lost in a pointed cloth hood. On the other
side of a heap of straw protruded a pair of feet in
monstrous thick boots.

" Always ready to drive," commented the keeper
of the eating-house. " A proper Russian driver
that. Saint or devil, night or day is all one to
Ziemianitch when his heart is free from sorrow.
' I don't ask who you are, but where you want to
go,' he says. He would drive Satan himself to his
own abode and come back chirruping to his horses.
Many a one he has driven who is clanking his
chains in the Nertchinsk mines by this time."

Razumov shuddered.

" Call him, wake him up," he faltered out.

The other set down his light, stepped back and
launched a kick at the prostrate sleeper. The
man shook at the impact but did not move. At the
third kick he grunted but remained inert as before.

The eating-house keeper desisted and fetched a
deep sigh.

" You see for yourself how it is. We have done
what we can for you."

He picked up the lantern. The intense black
spokes of shadow swung about in the circle of light.

A terrible fury—the blind rage of self-preservation—possessed Razumov.

" Ah !   The vile beast," he bellowed out in an unearthly tone which made the lantern jump and tremble !   " I shall wake you !   Give me . . . Give me . . ."

He looked round wildly, seized the handle of a stable-fork and rushing forward struck at the prostrate body with inarticulate cries.   After a time his cries ceased, and the rain of blows fell in the stillness and shadows of the cellar-like stable. Razumov belaboured Ziemianitch with an insatiable fury, in great volleys of sounding thwacks.   Except for the violent movements of Razumov nothing stirred, neither the beaten man nor the spoke-like shadows on the walls.   And only the sound of blows was heard.   It was a weird scene.

Suddenly there was a sharp crack.   The stick broke and half of it flew far away into the gloom beyond the light.   At the same time Ziemianitch sat up.   At this Razumov became as motionless as the man with the lantern—only his breast heaved for air as if ready to burst.

Some dull sensation of pain must have penetrated at last the consoling night of drunkenness enwrapping the " bright Russian soul " of Haldin's enthusiastic praise.   But Ziemianitch evidently saw nothing.   His eyeballs blinked all white in the light once, twice—then the gleam went out.   For a moment he sat in the straw with closed eyes with a strange air of weary meditation, then fell over slowly on his side without making the slightest sound. Only the straw rustled a little. Razumov stared wildly, fighting for his breath. After a second or two he heard a light snore.

He flung from him the piece of stick remaining in his grasp, and went off with great hasty strides without looking back once.

After going heedlessly for some fifty yards along the street he walked into a snowdrift and was up to his knees before he stopped.

This recalled him to himself ; and glancing about he discovered he had been going in the wrong direction. He retraced his steps, but now at a more moderate pace. When passing before the house he had just left he flourished his fist at the sombre refuge of misery and crime rearing its sinister bulk on the white ground. It had an air of brooding. He let his arm fall by his side—discouraged.

Ziemianitch's passionate surrender to sorrow and consolation had baffled him. That was the people. A true Russian man ! Razumov was glad he had beaten that brute—the " bright soul " of the other. Here they were : the people and the enthusiast.

Between the two he was done for : between the drunkenness of the peasant incapable of action and the dream-intoxication of the idealist incapable of perceiving the reason of things, and the true character of men. It was a sort of terrible childishness. But children had their masters. " Ah ! the stick, the stick, the stern hand," thought Razumov, longing for power to hurt and destroy.

He was glad he had thrashed that brute. The physical exertion had left his body in a comfortable glow. His mental agitation, too, was clarified as if all the feverishness had gone out of him in a fit of outward violence. Together with the persisting sense of terrible danger he was conscious now of a tranquil, unquenchable hate.

He walked slower and slower. And indeed, considering the guest he had in his rooms, it was no wonder he lingered on the way. It was like harbouring a pestilential disease that would not perhaps take your life, but would take from you all that made life worth living—a subtle pest that would convert earth into a hell.

What was he doing now ? Lying on the bed as if dead, with the back of his hands over his eyes ? Razumov had a morbidly vivid vision of Haldin on his bed—the white pillow hollowed by the head, the legs in long boots, the upturned feet. And in his abhorrence he said to himself, " I'll kill him when I get home." But he knew very well that that was of no use. The corpse hanging round his neck would be nearly as fatal as the living man. Nothing short of complete annihilation would do. And that was impossible. What then ? Must one kill oneself to escape this visitation ?

Razumov's despair was too profoundly tinged with hate to accept that issue.

And yet it was despair—nothing less—at the thought of having to live with Haldin for an indefinite number of days in mortal alarm at every sound. But perhaps when he heard that this " bright soul " of Ziemianitch suffered from a drunken eclipse the fellow would take his infernal resignation somewhere else. And that was not likely on the face of it.

Razumov thought : " I am being crushed—and I can't even run away." Other men had somewhere a corner of the earth—some little house in the provinces where they had a right to take their troubles. A material refuge. He had nothing. He had not even a moral refuge—the refuge of confidence. To whom could he go with this tale —in all this great, great land ?

Razumov stamped his foot—and under the soft carpet of snow felt the hard ground of Russia, inanimate, cold, inert, like a sullen and tragic mother hiding her face under a winding-sheet— his native soil !—his very own—without a fireside, without a heart !

He cast his eyes upwards and stood amazed. The snow had ceased to fall, and now, as if by a miracle, he saw above his head the clear black sky of the northern winter, decorated with the sumptuous fires of the stars. It was a canopy fit for the resplendent purity of the snows.

Razumov received an almost physical impression of endless space and of countless millions.

He responded to it with the readiness of a Russian who is born to an inheritance of space and numbers. Under the sumptuous immensity of the sky, the snow covered the endless forests, the frozen rivers, the plains of an immense country, obliterating the landmarks, the accidents of the ground, levelling everything under its uniform whiteness, like a monstrous blank page awaiting the record of an inconceivable history. It covered the passive land with its lives of countless people like Ziemianitch and its handful of agitators like this Haldin —murdering foolishly.

It was a sort of sacred inertia. Razumov felt a respect for it. A voice seemed to cry within him, " Don't touch it." It was a guarantee of duration, of safety, while the travail of maturing destiny went on—a work not of revolutions, with their passionate levity of action and their shifting impulses, but of peace. What it needed was not the conflicting aspirations of a people, but a will strong and one : it wanted not the babble of many voices, but a man—strong and one !

Razumov stood on the point of conversion. He was fascinated by its approach, by its overpowering logic. For a train of thought is never false. The falsehood lies deep in the necessities of existence, in secret fears and half-formed ambitions, in the secret confidence combined with a secret mistrust of ourselves, in the love of hope and the dread of uncertain days.

In Russia, the land of spectral ideas and disembodied aspirations, many brave minds have turned away at last from the vain and endless conflict to the one great historical fact of the land. They turned to autocracy for the peace of their patriotic conscience as a weary unbeliever, touched by grace, turns to the faith of his fathers for the blessing of spiritual rest. Like other Russians before him, Razumov, in conflict with himself, felt the touch of grace upon his forehead.

" Haldin means disruption," he thought to himself, beginning to walk again. " What is he with his indignation, with his talk of bondage— with his talk of God's justice ? All that means disruption. Better that thousands should suffer than that a people should become a disintegrated mass, helpless like dust in the wind. Obscurantism is better than the light of incendiary torches. The seed germinates in the night. Out of the dark soil springs the perfect plant. But a volcanic eruption is sterile, the ruin of the fertile ground. And am I, who love my country—who have nothing but that to love and put my faith in—am I to have my future, perhaps my usefulness, ruined by this sanguinary fanatic ? "

The grace entered into Razumov. He believed now in the man who would come at the appointed time.

What is a throne ? A few pieces of wood upholstered in velvet. But a throne is a seat of power too. The form of government is the shape of a tool—an instrument. But twenty thousand bladders inflated by the noblest sentiments and jostling against each other in the air are a miserable encumbrance of space, holding no power, possessing no will, having nothing to give.

He went on thus, heedless of the way, holding a discourse with himself with extraordinary abundance and facility. Generally his phrases came to him slowly, after a conscious and painstaking wooing. Some superior power had inspired him with a flow of masterly argument as certain converted sinners become overwhelmingly loquacious.

He felt an austere exultation.

" What are the luridly smoky lucubrations of that fellow to the clear grasp of my intellect ? " he thought. " Is not this my country ? Have I not got forty million brothers ? " he asked himself, unanswerably victorious in the silence of his breast. And the fearful thrashing he had given the inanimate Ziemianitch seemed to him a sign of intimate union, a pathetically severe necessity of brotherly love. " No ! If I must suffer let me at least suffer for my convictions, not for a crime my reason—my cool superior reason—rejects."

He ceased to think for a moment. The silence in his breast was complete. But he felt a suspicious uneasiness, such as we may experience when we enter an unlighted strange place—the irrational feeling that something may jump upon us in the dark—the absurd dread of the unseen.

Of course he was far from being a moss-grown reactionary. Everything was not for the best. Despotic bureaucracy . . . abuses . . . corruption . . . and so on. Capable men were wanted. Enlightened intelligences. Devoted hearts. But absolute power should be preserved—the tool ready for the man—for the great autocrat of the future. Razumov believed in him. The logic of history made him unavoidable. The state of the people demanded him. " What else ? " he asked himself ardently, " could move all that mass in one direction ? Nothing could. Nothing but a single will."

He was persuaded that he was sacrificing his personal longings of liberalism—rejecting the attractive error for the stern Russian truth. " That's patriotism," he observed mentally, and added, " There's no stopping midway on that road," and then remarked to himself, " I am not a coward."

And again there was a dead silence in Razumov's breast. He walked with lowered head, making room for no one. He walked slowly and his thoughts returning spoke within him with solemn slowness :

" What is this Haldin ? And what am I ? Only two grains of sand. But a great mountain is made up of just such insignificant grains. And the death of a man or of many men is an insignificant thing. Yet we combat a contagious pestilence. Do I want his death? No! I would save him if I could—but no one can do that—he is the withered member which must be cut off. If I must perish through him, let me at least not perish with him, and associated against my will with his sombre folly that understands nothing either of men or things. Why should I leave a false memory?"

It passed through his mind that there was no one in the world who cared what sort of memory he left behind him. He exclaimed to himself instantly, "Perish vainly for a falsehood! . . . What a miserable fate!"

He was now in a more animated part of the town. He did not remark the crash of two colliding sledges close to the curb. The driver of one bellowed tearfully at his fellow:

"Oh, thou vile wretch!"

This hoarse yell, let out nearly in his ear, disturbed Razumov. He shook his head impatiently and went on looking straight before him. Suddenly on the snow, stretched on his back right across his path, he saw Haldin, solid, distinct, real, with his inverted hands over his eyes, clad in a brown close-fitting coat and long boots. He was lying out of the way a little, as though he had selected that place on purpose. The snow round him was untrodden.

This hallucination had such a solidity of aspect that the first movement of Razumov was to reach for his pocket to assure himself that the key of his rooms was there. But he checked the impulse with a disdainful curve of his lips. He understood. His thought, concentrated intensely on the figure left lying on his bed, had culminated in this extraordinary illusion of the sight. Razumov tackled the phenomenon calmly. With a stern face, without a check and gazing far beyond the vision, he walked on, experiencing nothing but a slight tightening of the chest. After passing he turned his head for a glance, and saw only the unbroken track of his footsteps over the place where the breast of the phantom had been lying.

Razumov walked on and after a little time whispered his wonder to himself:

" Exactly as if alive ! Seemed to breathe ! And right in my way too ! I have had an extraordinary experience."

He made a few steps and muttered through his set teeth :

" I shall give him up."

Then for some twenty yards or more all was blank. He wrapped his cloak closer round him. He pulled his cap well forward over his eyes.

" Betray. A great word. What is betrayal ? They talk of a man betraying his country, his friends, his sweetheart. There must be a moral bond first. All a man can betray is his conscience. And how is my conscience engaged here ; by what bond of common faith, of common conviction, am I obliged to let that fanatical idiot drag me

down with him ?   On the contrary—every obligation
of true courage is the other way."

Razumov looked round from under his cap.

" What can the prejudice of the world reproach
me with ?   Have I provoked his confidence ?   No !
Have I by a single word, look, or gesture given him
reason to suppose that I accepted his trust in me ?
No !   It is true that I consented to go and see his
Ziemianitch.   Well, I have been to see him.   And
I broke a stick on his back too—the brute."

Something seemed to turn over in his head,
bringing uppermost a singularly hard, clear facet
of his brain.

" It would be better, however," he reflected, with
a quite different mental accent, " to keep that circumstance altogether to myself."

He had passed beyond the turn leading to his
lodgings, and had reached a wide and fashionable
street.   Some shops were still open, and all the
restaurants.   Lights fell on the pavement where
men in expensive fur coats, with here and there the
elegant figure of a woman, walked with an air of
leisure.   Razumov looked at them with the contempt of an austere believer for the frivolous crowd.
It was the world—those officers, dignitaries, men
of fashion, officials, members of the Yacht Club.
The event of the morning affected them all.   What
would they say if they knew what this student in a
cloak was going to do ?

" Not one of them is capable of feeling and

thinking as deeply as I can. How many of them could accomplish an act of conscience ? "

Razumov lingered in the well-lighted street. He was firmly decided. Indeed, it could hardly be called a decision. He had simply discovered what he had meant to do all along. And yet he felt the need of some other mind's sanction.

With something resembling anguish he said to himself :

" I want to be understood." The universal aspiration with all its profound and melancholy meaning assailed heavily Razumov, who, amongst eighty millions of his kith and kin, had no heart to which he could open himself.

The attorney was not to be thought of. He despised the little agent of chicane too much. One could not go and lay one's conscience before the policeman at the corner. Neither was Razumov anxious to go to the chief of his district's police— a common-looking person whom he used to see sometimes in the street in a shabby uniform and with a smouldering cigarette stuck to his lower lip. " He would begin by locking me up most probably. At any rate, he is certain to get excited and create an awful commotion," thought Razumov practically.

An act of conscience must be done with outward dignity.

Razumov longed desperately for a word of advice, for moral support. Who knows what true loneliness is—not the conventional word, but the naked terror ? To the lonely themselves it wears a mask. The most miserable outcast hugs some memory or some illusion. Now and then a fatal conjunction of events may lift the veil for an instant. For an instant only. No human being could bear a steady view of moral solitude without going mad.

Razumov had reached that point of vision. To escape from it he embraced for a whole minute the delirious purpose of rushing to his lodgings and flinging himself on his knees by the side of the bed with the dark figure stretched on it ; to pour out a full confession in passionate words that would stir the whole being of that man to its innermost depths ; that would end in embraces and tears ; in an incredible fellowship of souls—such as the world had never seen. It was sublime !

Inwardly he wept and trembled already. But to the casual eyes that were cast upon him he was aware that he appeared as a tranquil student in a cloak, out for a leisurely stroll. He noted, too, the side-long, brilliant glance of a pretty woman—with a delicate head, and covered in the hairy skins of wild beasts down to her feet, like a frail and beautiful savage—which rested for a moment with a sort of mocking tenderness on the deep abstraction of that good-looking young man.

Suddenly Razumov stood still. The glimpse of a passing grey whisker, caught and lost in the same instant, had evoked the complete image of Prince

K——, the man who once had pressed his hand as no other man had pressed it—a faint but lingering pressure like a secret sign, like a half-unwilling caress.

And Razumov marvelled at himself. Why did he not think of him before ?

" A senator, a dignitary, a great personage, the very man—He ! "

A strange softening emotion came over Razumov—made his knees shake a little. He repressed it with a newborn austerity. All that sentiment was pernicious nonsense. He couldn't be quick enough ; and when he got into a sledge he shouted to the driver :

" To the K—— Palace. Get on—you ! Fly ! "

The startled moujik, bearded up to the very whites of his eyes, answered obsequiously :

" I hear, your high Nobility."

It was lucky for Razumov that Prince K—— was not a man of timid character. On the day of Mr. de P——'s murder an extreme alarm and despondency prevailed in the high official spheres.

Prince K——, sitting sadly alone in his study, was told by his alarmed servants that a mysterious young man had forced his way into the hall, refused to tell his name and the nature of his business, and would not move from there till he had seen His Excellency in private. Instead of locking himself up and telephoning for the police, as nine out of ten high personages would have done that evening, the

prince gave way to curiosity and came quietly to
the door of his study.

In the hall, the front door standing wide open,
he recognised at once Razumov, pale as death, his
eyes blazing, and surrounded by perplexed lackeys.

The prince was vexed beyond measure, and even
indignant. But his humane instincts and a subtle
sense of self-respect could not allow him to let this
young man be thrown out into the street by base
menials. He retreated unseen into his room, and
after a little rang his bell. Razumov heard in the
hall an ominously raised harsh voice saying somewhere far away :

" Show the gentleman in here."

Razumov walked in without a tremor. He felt
himself invulnerable—raised far above the shallow-
ness of common judgment. Though he saw the
prince looking at him with black displeasure, the
lucidity of his mind, of which he was very conscious,
gave him an extraordinary assurance. He was not
asked to sit down.

Half an hour later they appeared in the hall
together. The lackeys stood up, and the prince,
moving with difficulty on his gouty feet, was helped
into his furs. The carriage had been ordered before.
When the great double door was flung open with a
crash, Razumov, who had been standing silent with
a lost gaze but with every faculty intensely on the
alert, heard the prince's voice :

" Your arm, young man."

4

The mobile, superficial mind of the ex-Guards' officer, man of showy missions, experienced in nothing but the arts of gallant intrigue and worldly success, had been equally impressed by the more obvious difficulties of such a situation and by Razumov's quiet dignity in stating them.

He had said, " No. Upon the whole I can't condemn the step you ventured to take by coming to me with your story. It is not an affair for police under-strappers. The greatest importance is attached to . . . Set your mind at rest. I shall see you through this most extraordinary and difficult situation."

Then the prince rose to ring the bell, and Razumov, making a short bow, had said with deference :

" I have trusted my instinct. A young man having no claim upon anybody in the world has in an hour of trial involving his deepest political convictions turned to an illustrious Russian—that's all."

The prince had exclaimed hastily :

" You have done well."

In the carriage—it was a small brougham on sleigh runners—Razumov broke the silence in a voice that trembled slightly.

" My gratitude surpasses the greatness of my presumption."

He gasped, feeling unexpectedly in the dark a momentary pressure on his arm.

" You have done well," repeated the prince.

When the carriage stopped the prince murmured to Razumov, who had never ventured a single question :

" The house of General T——."

In the middle of the snow-covered roadway blazed a great bonfire. Some Cossacks, the bridles of their horses over the arm, were warming themselves around it. Two sentries stood at the door, several gendarmes lounged under the great carriage gateway, and on the first floor landing two orderlies rose and stood at attention. Razumov walked at the prince's elbow.

A surprising quantity of hothouse plants in pots cumbered the floor of the anteroom. Servants came forward. A young man in civilian clothes arrived hurriedly, was whispered to, bowed low, and exclaiming zealously, " Certainly—this minute," fled within somewhere. The prince signed to Razumov.

They passed through a suite of reception-rooms all barely lit and one of them prepared for dancing. The wife of the general had put off her party. An atmosphere of consternation pervaded the place. But the general's own room, with heavy sombre hangings, two massive desks, and deep arm-chairs, had all the lights turned on. The footman shut the door behind them and they waited.

There was a coal fire in an English grate ; Razumov had never before seen such a fire ; and the silence of the room was like the silence of the grave ; perfect, measureless, for even the clock on the mantelpiece made no sound. Filling a corner, on a black pedestal, stood a quarter-life-size smooth-limbed bronze of an adolescent figure, running. The prince observed in an undertone :

" Spontini's. ' Flight of Youth.' Exquisite."

" Admirable," assented Razumov faintly.

They said nothing more after this, the prince silent with his grand air, Razumov staring at the statue. He was worried by a sensation resembling the gnawing of hunger.

He did not turn when he heard an inner door fly open, and a quick footstep muffled on the carpet.

The prince's voice immediately exclaimed, thick with excitement :

" We have got him—*ce misérable*. A worthy young man came to me—— No ! It's incredible. . . ."

Razumov held his breath before the bronze as if expecting a crash. Behind his back a voice he had never heard before insisted politely :

" *Asseyez-vous donc*."

The prince almost shrieked, " *Mais comprenez-vous, mon cher ! L'assassin !* the murderer—we have got him. . . ."

Razumov spun round. The general's smooth big cheeks rested on the stiff collar of his uniform. He must have been already looking at Razumov, because that last saw the pale blue eyes fastened on him coldly.

The prince from a chair waved an impressive hand.

" This is a most honourable young man whom Providence itself . . . Mr. Razumov."

The general acknowledged the introduction by frowning at Razumov, who did not make the slightest movement.

Sitting down before his desk the general listened with compressed lips. It was impossible to detect any sign of emotion on his face.

Razumov watched the immobility of the fleshy profile. But it lasted only a moment, till the prince had finished ; and when the general turned to the providential young man, his florid complexion, the blue, unbelieving eyes and the bright white flash of an automatic smile had an air of jovial, careless cruelty. He expressed no wonder at the extraordinary story—no pleasure or excitement—no incredulity either. He betrayed no sentiment whatever. Only with a politeness almost deferential suggested that " the bird might have flown while Mr.—Mr. Razumov was running about the streets."

Razumov advanced to the middle of the room and said, " The door is locked and I have the key in my pocket."

His loathing for the man was intense. It had come upon him so unawares that he felt he had not kept it out of his voice. The general looked up at him thoughtfully, and Razumov grinned.

All this went over the head of Prince K——seated in a deep arm-chair, very tired and impatient.

"A student called Haldin," said the general thoughtfully.

Razumov ceased to grin.

"That is his name," he said unnecessarily loud. "Victor Victorovitch Haldin—a student."

The general shifted his position a little.

"How is he dressed? Would you have the goodness to tell me?"

Razumov angrily described Haldin's clothing in a few jerky words. The general stared all the time, then addressing the prince:

"We were not without some indications," he said in French. "A good woman who was in the street described to us somebody wearing a dress of the sort as the thrower of the second bomb. We have detained her at the Secretariat, and every one in a Tcherkess coat we could lay our hands on has been brought to her to look at. She kept on crossing herself and shaking her head at them. It was exasperating. . . ."

He turned to Razumov, and in Russian, with friendly reproach:

"Take a chair, Mr. Razumov—do. Why are you standing?"

Razumov sat down carelessly and looked at the general.

" This goggle-eyed imbecile understands nothing," he thought.

The prince began to speak loftily.

" Mr. Razumov is a young man of conspicuous abilities. I have it at heart that his future should not . . ."

" Certainly," interrupted the general, with a movement of the hand. " Has he any weapons on him, do you think, Mr. Razumov ? "

The general employed a gentle musical voice. Razumov answered with suppressed irritation :

" No. But my razors are lying about—you understand."

The general lowered his head approvingly.

" Precisely."

Then to the prince, explaining courteously :

" We want that bird alive. It will be the devil if we can't make him sing a little before we are done with him."

The grave-like silence of the room with its mute clock fell upon the polite modulations of this terrible phrase. The prince, hidden in the chair, made no sound.

The general unexpectedly developed a thought.

" Fidelity to menaced institutions on which depend the safety of a throne and of a people is no child's play. We know that, *mon Prince*, and— *tenez*——" he went on with a sort of flattering harshness, " Mr. Razumov here begins to understand that too."

His eyes, which he turned upon Razumov, seemed to be starting out of his head. This grotesqueness of aspect no longer shocked Razumov. He said with gloomy conviction :

" Haldin will never speak."

" That remains to be seen," muttered the general.

" I am certain," insisted Razumov. " A man like this never speaks. . . . Do you imagine that I am here from fear ? " he added violently. He felt ready to stand by his opinion of Haldin to the last extremity.

" Certainly not," protested the general, with great simplicity of tone. " And I don't mind telling you, Mr. Razumov, that if he had not come with his tale to such a staunch and loyal Russian as you, he would have disappeared like a stone in the water . . . which would have had a detestable effect," he added, with a bright, cruel smile under his stony stare. " So you see, there can be no suspicion of any fear here."

The prince intervened, looking at Razumov round the back of the arm-chair.

" Nobody doubts the moral soundness of your action. Be at ease in that respect, pray."

He turned to the general uneasily.

" That's why I am here. You may be surprised why I should . . ."

The general hastened to interrupt :

" Not at all. Extremely natural. You saw the importance . . ."

" Yes," broke in the prince. " And I venture to ask insistently that mine and Mr. Razumov's intervention should not become public. He is a young man of promise—of remarkable aptitudes."

" I haven't a doubt of it," murmured the general. " He inspires confidence."

" All sorts of pernicious views are so widespread nowadays—they taint such unexpected quarters— that, monstrous as it seems, he might suffer. . . . His studies . . . His . . ."

The general, with his elbows on the desk, took his head between his hands.

" Yes. Yes. I am thinking it out. . . . How long is it since you left him at your rooms, Mr. Razumov ? "

Razumov mentioned the hour which nearly corresponded with the time of his distracted flight from the big slum house. He had made up his mind to keep Ziemianitch out of the affair completely. To mention him at all would mean imprisonment for the " bright soul," perhaps cruel floggings, and in the end a journey to Siberia in chains. Razumov, who had beaten Ziemianitch, felt for him now a vague, remorseful tenderness.

The general, giving way for the first time to his secret sentiments, exclaimed contemptuously :

" And you say he came in to make you this confidence like this—for nothing—*à propos des bottes*."

Razumov felt danger in the air. The merciless suspicion of despotism had spoken openly at last.

Sudden fear sealed Razumov's lips. The silence of the room resembled now the silence of a deep dungeon, where time does not count, and a suspect person is sometimes forgotten for ever. But the prince came to the rescue.

" Providence itself has led the wretch in a moment of mental aberration to seek Mr. Razumov on the strength of some old, utterly misinterpreted exchange of ideas—some sort of idle speculative conversation—months ago—I am told—and completely forgotten till now by Mr. Razumov."

" Mr. Razumov," queried the general meditatively, after a short silence, " do you often indulge in speculative conversation ? "

" No, Excellency," answered Razumov coolly, in a sudden access of self-confidence. " I am a man of deep convictions. Crude opinions are in the air. They are not always worth combating. But even the silent contempt of a serious mind may be misinterpreted by headlong Utopists."

The general stared from between his hands. Prince K—— murmured :

" A serious young man. *Un esprit supérieur*."

" I see that, *mon cher Prince*," said the general. " Mr. Razumov is quite safe with me. I am interested in him. He has, it seems, the great and useful quality of inspiring confidence. What I was wondering at is why the other should mention anything at all—I mean even the bare fact alone—if his object was only to obtain temporary shelter for a few hours. For, after all, nothing was easier than to say nothing about it unless, indeed, he were trying, under a crazy misapprehension of your true sentiments, to enlist your assistance—eh, Mr. Razumov ? "

It seemed to Razumov that the floor was moving slightly. This grotesque man in a tight uniform was terrible. It was right that he should be terrible.

" I can see what your Excellency has in your mind. But I can only answer that I don't know why."

" I have nothing in my mind," murmured the general, with gentle surprise.

" I am his prey—his helpless prey," thought Razumov. The fatigues and the disgusts of that afternoon, the need to forget, the fear which he could not keep off, reawakened his hate for Haldin.

" Then I can't help your Excellency. I don't know what he meant. I only know there was a moment when I wished to kill him. There was also a moment when I wished myself dead. I said nothing. I was overcome. I provoked no confidence—I asked for no explanations——"

Razumov seemed beside himself; but his mind was lucid. It was really a calculated outburst.

" It is rather a pity," the general said, " that you did not. Don't you know at all what he means to do ? "

Razumov calmed down and saw an opening there.

" He told me he was in hopes that a sledge would

meet him about half an hour after midnight at the seventh lamp-post on the left from the upper end of Karabelnaya. At any rate, he meant to be there at that time. He did not even ask me for a change of clothes."

"*Ah voilà!*" said the general, turning to Prince K—— with an air of satisfaction. "There is a way to keep your protégé, Mr. Razumov, quite clear of any connection with the actual arrest. We shall be ready for that gentleman in Karabelnaya."

The prince expressed his gratitude. There was real emotion in his voice. Razumov, motionless, silent, sat staring at the carpet. The general turned to him.

"Half an hour after midnight. Till then we have to depend on you, Mr. Razumov. You don't think he is likely to change his purpose?"

"How can I tell?" said Razumov. "Those men are not of the sort that ever change their purpose."

"What men do you mean?"

"Fanatical lovers of liberty in general. Liberty with a capital L, Excellency. Liberty that means nothing precise. Liberty in whose name crimes are committed."

The general murmured:

"I detest rebels of every kind. I can't help it. It's my nature!"

He clenched a fist and shook it, drawing back his arm. "They shall be destroyed, then."

" They have made a sacrifice of their lives beforehand," said Razumov with malicious pleasure
and looking the general straight in the face. " If
Haldin does change his purpose to-night, you may
depend on it that it will not be to save his life by
flight in some other way. He would have thought
then of something else to attempt. But that is
not likely."

The general repeated as if to himself, " They
shall be destroyed."

Razumov assumed an impenetrable expression.

The prince exclaimed :

" What a terrible necessity ! "

The general's arm was lowered slowly.

" One comfort there is. That brood leaves no
posterity. I've always said it ; one effort, pitiless,
persistent, steady—and we are done with them for
ever."

Razumov thought to himself that this man
entrusted with so much arbitrary power must have
believed what he said or else he could not have gone
on bearing the responsibility.

The general repeated again with extreme animosity :

" I detest rebels. These subversive minds !
These intellectual debauchees ! My existence has
been built on fidelity. It's a feeling. To defend
it I am ready to lay down my life—and even my
honour—if that were needed. But pray tell me what
honour can there be as against rebels—against people

that deny God Himself — perfect unbelievers ? Brutes ! It is horrible to think of."

During this tirade Razumov, facing the general, had nodded slightly twice. Prince K——, standing on one side with his grand air, murmured, casting up his eyes :

" *Hélas !* "

Then lowering his glance and with great decision declared :

" This young man, General, is perfectly fit to apprehend the bearing of your memorable words."

The general's whole expression changed from dull resentment to perfect urbanity.

" I would ask now Mr. Razumov," he said, " to return to his home. Note that I don't ask Mr. Razumov whether he has justified his absence to his guest. No doubt he did this sufficiently. But I don't ask. Mr. Razumov inspires confidence. It is a great gift. I only suggest that a more prolonged absence might awaken the criminal's suspicions and induce him perhaps to change his plans."

He rose and with a scrupulous courtesy escorted his visitors to the anteroom encumbered with flower-pots.

Razumov parted with the prince at the corner of a street. In the carriage he had listened to speeches where natural sentiment struggled with caution. Evidently the prince was afraid of encouraging any hopes of future intercourse. But there was a touch of tenderness in the voice uttering in the dark the guarded general phrases of goodwill. And the prince, too, said :

" I have perfect confidence in you, Mr. Razumov."

" They all, it seems, have confidence in me," thought Razumov dully. He had an indulgent contempt for the man sitting shoulder to shoulder with him in the confined space. Probably he was afraid of scenes with his wife. She was said to be proud and violent.

It seemed to him bizarre that secrecy should play such a large part in the comfort and safety of lives. But he wanted to put the prince's mind at ease ; and with a proper amount of emphasis he said that, being conscious of some small abilities and confident in his power of work, he trusted his future to his own exertions. He expressed his gratitude for the helping hand. Such dangerous situations did not occur twice in the course of one life—he added.

" And you have met this one with a firmness of mind and correctness of feeling which give me a high idea of your worth," the prince said solemnly. " You have now only to persevere—to persevere."

On getting out on the pavement Razumov saw an ungloved hand extended to him through the lowered window of the brougham. It detained his own in its grasp for a moment, while the light of a street lamp fell upon the prince's long face and old-fashioned grey whiskers.

" I hope you are perfectly reassured now as to the consequences. . . ."

" After what your Excellency has condescended to do for me, I can only rely on my conscience."

" Adieu," said the whiskered head with feeling.

Razumov bowed. The brougham glided away with a slight swish in the snow—he was alone on the edge of the pavement.

He said to himself that there was nothing to think about, and began walking towards his home.

He walked quietly. It was a common experience to walk thus home to bed after an evening spent somewhere with his fellows or in the cheaper seats of a theatre. After he had gone a little way the familiarity of things got hold of him. Nothing was changed. There was the familiar corner; and when he turned it he saw the familiar dim light of the provision shop kept by a German woman. There were loaves of stale bread, bunches of onions, and strings of sausages behind the small window-panes. They were closing it. The sickly lame fellow whom he knew so well by sight staggered out into the snow embracing a large shutter.

Nothing would change. There was the familiar gateway yawning black with feeble glimmers marking the arches of the different staircases.

The sense of life's continuity depended on trifling bodily impressions. The trivialities of daily existence were an armour for the soul. And this thought reinforced the inward quietness of Razumov as he began to climb the stairs familiar to his feet in the dark, with his hand on the familiar clammy banister. The exceptional could not prevail against the material contacts which make one day resemble another. To-morrow would be like yesterday.

It was only on the stage that the unusual was outwardly acknowledged.

" I suppose," thought Razumov, " that if I had made up my mind to blow out my brains on the landing I would be going up these stairs as quietly as I am doing it now. What's a man to do ? What must be must be. Extraordinary things do happen. But when they have happened they are done with. Thus, too, when the mind is made up. That question is done with. And the daily concerns, the familiarities of our thought swallow it up— and the life goes on as before with its mysterious and secret sides quite out of sight, as they should be. Life is a public thing."

Razumov unlocked his door and took the key out ; entered very quietly and bolted the door behind him carefully.

He thought, " He hears me," and after bolting the door he stood still, holding his breath. There was not a sound. He crossed the bare outer room, stepping deliberately in the darkness. Entering the other, he felt all over his table for the matchbox. The silence, but for the groping of his hand, was profound. Could the fellow be sleeping so soundly ?

5

He struck a light and looked at the bed. Haldin was lying on his back as before, only both his hands were under his head. His eyes were open. He stared at the ceiling.

Razumov held the match up. He saw the clear-cut features, the firm chin, the white forehead, and the top-knot of fair hair against the white pillow. There he was, lying flat on his back. Razumov thought suddenly, " I have walked over his chest."

He continued to stare till the match burnt itself out ; then struck another and lit the lamp in silence without looking towards the bed any more. He had turned his back on it and was hanging his coat on a peg when he heard Haldin sigh profoundly, then ask in a tired voice :

" Well ! And what have you arranged ? "

The emotion was so great that Razumov was glad to put his hands against the wall. A diabolical impulse to say, " I have given you up to the police," frightened him exceedingly. But he did not say that. He said, without turning round, in a muffled voice :

" It's done."

Again he heard Haldin sigh. He walked to the table, sat down with the lamp before him, and only then looked towards the bed.

In the distant corner of the large room far away from the lamp, which was small and provided with a very thick china shade, Haldin appeared like a dark and elongated shape—rigid with the immobility of death. This body seemed to have less substance than its own phantom walked over by Razumov in the street white with snow. It was more alarming in its shadowy, persistent reality than the distinct but vanishing illusion.

Haldin was heard again.

" You must have had a walk—such a walk . . ." he murmured deprecatingly. " This weather . . ."

Razumov answered with energy :

" Horrible walk. . . . A nightmare of a walk."

He shuddered audibly. Haldin sighed once more, then :

" And so you have seen Ziemianitch—brother ? "

" I've seen him."

Razumov, remembering the time he had spent with the prince, thought it prudent to add, " I had to wait some time."

" A character—eh ? It's extraordinary what a sense of the necessity of freedom there is in that man. And he has sayings too—simple, to the point, such as only the people can invent in their rough sagacity. A character that . . ."

" I, you understand, haven't had much opportunity . . ." Razumov muttered through his teeth.

Haldin continued to stare at the ceiling.

" You see, brother, I have been a good deal in that house of late. I used to take there books—leaflets. Not a few of the poor people who live there can read. And, you see, the guests for the feast of freedom must be sought for in byways and hedges. The truth is, I have almost lived in that house of late. I slept sometimes in the stable. There is a stable . . ."

" That's where I had my interview with Ziemianitch," interrupted Razumov gently. A mocking spirit entered into him and he added, " It was satisfactory in a sense. I came away from it much relieved."

" Ah ! he's a fellow," went on Haldin, talking slowly at the ceiling. " I came to know him in that way, you see. For some weeks now, ever since I resigned myself to do what had to be done, I tried to isolate myself. I gave up my rooms. What was the good of exposing a decent widow woman to the risk of being worried out of her mind by the police ? I gave up seeing any of our comrades . . ."

Razumov drew to himself a half sheet of paper and began to trace lines on it with a pencil.

" Upon my word," he thought angrily, " he seems to have thought of everybody's safety but mine."

Haldin was talking on :

" This morning—ah ! this morning—that was different. How can I explain to you ? Before the deed was done I wandered at night and lay hid in the day, thinking it out, and I felt restful. Sleepless but restful. What was there for me to torment myself about ? But this morning—after ! Then it was that I became restless. I could not have stopped in that big house full of misery. The miserable of this world can't give you peace. Then when that silly caretaker began to shout, I said to myself, ' There is a young man in this town head and shoulders above common prejudices.' "

" Is he laughing at me ? " Razumov asked himself, going on with his aimless drawing of triangles and squares. And suddenly he thought : " My behaviour must appear to him strange. Should he take fright at my manner and rush off somewhere I shall be undone completely. That infernal general . . ."

He dropped the pencil and turned abruptly towards the bed with the shadowy figure extended full length on it—so much more indistinct than the one over whose breast he had walked without faltering. Was this, too, a phantom ?

The silence had lasted a long time. " He is no longer here," was the thought against which Razumov struggled desperately, quite frightened at its absurdity. " He is already gone and this . . . only . . ."

He could resist no longer. He sprang to his feet, saying aloud, " I am intolerably anxious," and in a few headlong strides stood by the side of the bed. His hand fell lightly on Haldin's shoulder, and directly he felt its reality he was beset by an insane temptation to grip that exposed throat and squeeze the breath out of that body lest it should escape his custody, leaving only a phantom behind.

Haldin did not stir a limb, but his overshadowed eyes moving a little gazed upwards at Razumov with wistful gratitude for this manifestation of feeling.

Razumov turned away and strode up and down the room. " It would have been possibly a kindness," he muttered to himself, and was appalled by the nature of that apology for a murderous intention his mind had found somewhere within him. And all the same he could not give it up. He became lucid about it. " What can he expect ? " he thought. " The halter—in the end. And I . . ."

This argument was interrupted by Haldin's voice.

" Why be anxious for me ? They can kill my body, but they cannot exile my soul from this world. I tell you what—I believe in this world so much that I cannot conceive eternity otherwise than as a very long life. That is perhaps the reason I am so ready to die."

" H'm," muttered Razumov, and biting his lower lip he continued to walk up and down and to carry on his strange argument.

Yes, to a man in such a situation—of course it would be an act of kindness. The question, however, was not how to be kind, but how to be firm. He was a slippery customer . . .

" I too, Victor Victorovitch, believe in this world of ours," he said with force. " I too, while I live.

. . . But you seem determined to haunt it. You can't seriously mean . . ."

The voice of the motionless Haldin began :

" Haunt it ! Truly, the oppressors of thought which quickens the world, the destroyers of souls which aspire to perfection of human dignity, they shall be haunted. As to the destroyers of my mere body, I have forgiven them beforehand."

Razumov had stopped apparently to listen, but at the same time he was observing his own sensations. He was vexed with himself for attaching so much importance to what Haldin said.

" The fellow's mad," he thought firmly, but this opinion did not mollify him towards Haldin. It was a particularly impudent form of lunacy—and when it got loose in the sphere of public life of a country, it was obviously the duty of every good citizen . . .

This train of thought broke off short there and was succeeded by a paroxysm of silent hatred towards Haldin, so intense that Razumov hastened to speak at random.

" Yes. Eternity, of course. I, too, can't very well represent it to myself. . . . I imagine it, however, as something quiet and dull. There would be nothing unexpected — don't you see ? The element of time would be wanting."

He pulled out his watch and gazed at it. Haldin turned over on his side and looked on intently.

Razumov got frightened at this movement. A

slippery customer this fellow with a phantom. It was not midnight yet. He hastened on :

" And unfathomable mysteries ! Can you conceive secret places in Eternity ? Impossible. Whereas life is full of them. There are secrets of birth, for instance. One carries them on to the grave. There is something comical . . . but never mind. And there are secret motives of conduct. A man's most open actions have a secret side to them. That is interesting and so unfathomable ! For instance, a man goes out of a room for a walk. Nothing more trivial in appearance. And yet it may be momentous. He comes back—he has seen perhaps a drunken brute, taken particular notice of the snow on the ground—and behold he is no longer the same man. The most unlikely things have a secret power over one's thoughts—the grey whiskers of a particular person—the goggle eyes of another."

Razumov's forehead was moist. He took a turn or two in the room, his head low, and smiling to himself viciously.

" Have you ever reflected on the power of goggle eyes and grey whiskers ? Excuse me. You seem to think I must be crazy to talk in this vein at such a time. But I am not talking lightly. I have seen instances. It has happened to me once to be talking to a man whose fate was affected by physical facts of that kind. And the man did not know it. Of course, it was a case of conscience, but the material facts such as these brought about the solution. . . . And you tell me, Victor Victorovitch, not to be anxious ! Why ! I am responsible for you," Razumov almost shrieked.

He avoided with difficulty a burst of Mephistophelian laughter. Haldin, very pale, raised himself on his elbow.

" And the surprises of life," went on Razumov, after glancing at the other uneasily. " Just consider their astonishing nature. A mysterious impulse induces you to come here. I don't say you have done wrong. Indeed, from a certain point of view you could not have done better. You might have gone to a man with affections and family ties. You have such ties yourself. As to me, you know I have been brought up in an educational institute where they did not give us enough to eat. To talk of affection in such a connection—you perceive yourself . . . As to ties, the only ties I have in the world are social. I must get acknowledged in some way before I can act at all. I sit here working . . . And don't you think I am working for progress too ? I've got to find my own ideas of the true way. . . . Pardon me," continued Razumov, after drawing breath and with a short, throaty laugh, " but I haven't inherited a revolutionary inspiration together with a resemblance from an uncle."

He looked again at his watch and noticed with sickening disgust that there were yet a good many minutes to midnight. He tore watch and chain off his waistcoat and laid them on the table well in the circle of bright lamplight. Haldin, reclining on his elbow, did not stir. Razumov was made uneasy by this attitude. " What move is he meditating over so quietly ? " he thought. " He must be prevented. I must keep on talking to him."

He raised his voice.

" You are a son, a brother, a nephew, a cousin— I don't know what—to no end of people. I am just a man. Here I stand before you. A man with a mind. Did it ever occur to you how a man who had never heard a word of warm affection or praise in his life would think on matters on which you would think first with or against your class, your domestic tradition—your fireside prejudices ? . . . Did you ever consider how a man like that would feel ? I have no domestic tradition. I have nothing to think against. My tradition is historical. What have I to look back to but that national past from which you gentlemen want to wrench away your future ? Am I to let my intelligence, my aspirations towards a better lot, be robbed of the only thing it has to go upon at the will of violent enthusiasts ? You come from your province, but all this land is mine—or I have nothing. No doubt you shall be looked upon as a martyr some day— a sort of hero—a political saint. But I beg to be excused. I am content in fitting myself to be a worker. And what can you people do by scattering a few drops of blood on the snow ? On this Immensity. On this unhappy Immensity! I tell you," he cried, in a vibrating subdued voice, and advancing one step nearer the bed, " that what it needs is not a lot of haunting phantoms that I could walk through—but a man ! "

Haldin threw his arms forward as if to keep him off in horror.

" I understand it all now," he exclaimed with awestruck dismay. " I understand—at last."

Razumov staggered back against the table. His forehead broke out in perspiration while a cold shudder ran down his spine.

" What have I been saying ? " he asked himself. " Have I let him slip through my fingers after all ? "

He felt his lips go stiff like buckram, and instead of a reassuring smile only achieved an uncertain grimace.

" What will you have ? " he began in a conciliating voice which got steady after the first trembling word or two. " What will you have ? Consider—a man of studious, retired habits—and suddenly like this . . . I am not practised in talking delicately. But . . ."

He felt anger, a wicked anger, get hold of him again.

" What were we to do together till midnight ? Sit here opposite each other and think of your— your—shambles ? "

Haldin had a subdued, heart-broken attitude. He

bowed his head ; his hands hung between his knees. His voice was low and pained but calm.

"I see now how it is, Razumov—brother. You are a magnanimous soul, but my action is abhorrent to you—alas ! . . ."

Razumov stared. From fright he had set his teeth so hard that his whole face ached. It was impossible for him to make a sound.

"And even my person, too, is loathsome to you perhaps," Haldin added mournfully, after a short pause, looking up for a moment, then fixing his gaze on the floor. "For indeed, unless one . . ."

He broke off, evidently waiting for a word. Razumov remained silent. Haldin nodded his head dejectedly twice.

"Of course. Of course," he murmured. . . . "Ah ! weary work ! "

He remained perfectly still for a moment, then made Razumov's leaden heart strike a ponderous blow by springing up briskly.

"So be it," he cried sadly in a low, distinct tone. "Farewell then."

Razumov started forward, but the sight of Haldin's raised hand checked him before he could get away from the table. He leaned on it heavily, listening to the faint sounds of some town clock tolling the hour. Haldin, already at the door, tall and straight as an arrow, with his pale face and a hand raised attentively, might have posed for the statue of a daring youth listening to an inner voice.

Razumov mechanically glanced down at his watch. When he looked towards the door again Haldin had vanished. There was a faint rustling in the outer room, the feeble click of a bolt drawn back lightly. He was gone—almost as noiseless as a vision.

Razumov ran forward unsteadily, with parted, voiceless lips. The outer door stood open. Staggering out on the landing, he leaned far over the banister. Gazing down into the deep black shaft with a tiny glimmering flame at the bottom, he traced by ear the rapid spiral descent of some-body running down the stairs on tiptoe. It was a light, swift, pattering sound, which sank away from him into the depths ; a fleeting shadow passed over the glimmer—a wink of the tiny flame. Then stillness.

Razumov hung over, breathing the cold raw air tainted by the evil smells of the unclean staircase. All quiet.

He went back into his room slowly, shutting the doors after him. The peaceful steady light of his reading-lamp shone on the watch. Razumov stood looking down at the little white dial. It wanted yet three minutes to midnight. He took the watch into his hand fumblingly.

" Slow," he muttered, and a strange fit of nerve-lessness came over him. His knees shook, the watch and chain slipped through his fingers in an instant and fell on the floor. He was so startled that he nearly fell himself. When at last he regained enough confidence in his limbs to stoop for it he held it to his ear at once. After a while he growled :

" Stopped," and paused for quite a long time before he muttered sourly :

" It's done. . . . And now to work."

He sat down, reached haphazard for a book, opened it in the middle and began to read ; but after going conscientiously over two lines he lost his hold on the print completely and did not try to regain it. He thought :

" There was to a certainty a police agent of some sort watching the house across the street."

He imagined him lurking in a dark gateway, goggle-eyed, muffled up in a cloak to the nose and with a general's plumed, cocked hat on his head. This absurdity made him start in the chair convulsively. He literally had to shake his head violently to get rid of it. The man would be disguised perhaps as a peasant . . . a beggar. . . . Perhaps he would be just buttoned up in a dark overcoat and carrying a loaded stick—a shifty-eyed rascal, smelling of raw onions and spirits.

This evocation brought on positive nausea. " Why do I want to bother about this ? " thought Razumov with disgust. " Am I a gendarme ? Moreover, it is done."

He got up in great agitation. It was not done. Not yet. Not till half-past twelve. And the watch had stopped. This reduced him to despair. Im-

possible to know the time ! The landlady and all
the people across the landing were asleep. How
could he go and . . . God knows what they would
imagine, or how much they would guess. He dared
not go into the streets to find out. " I am a suspect
now. There's no use shirking that fact," he said
to himself bitterly. If Haldin from some cause or
another gave them the slip and failed to turn up in
the Karabelnaya the police would be invading his
lodging. . And if he were not in he could never clear
himself. Never. Razumov looked wildly about
as if for some means of seizing upon time which
seemed to have escaped him altogether. He had
never, as far as he could remember, heard the striking
of that town clock in his rooms before this night.
And he was not even sure now whether he had heard
it really on this night.

He went to the window and stood there with
slightly bent head on the watch for the faint sound.
" I will stay here till I hear something," he said to
himself. He stood still, his ear turned to the panes.
An atrocious aching numbness with shooting pains
in his back and legs tortured him. He did not
budge. His mind hovered on the borders of
delirium. He heard himself suddenly saying, " I
confess," as a person might do on the rack. " I am
on the rack," he thought. He felt ready to swoon.
The faint deep boom of the distant clock seemed to
explode in his head—he heard it so clearly. . . .
One !

If Haldin had not turned up, the police would have been already here ransacking the house. No sound reached him. This time it was done.

He dragged himself painfully to the table and dropped into the chair. He flung the book away and took a square sheet of paper. It was like the pile of sheets covered with his neat minute handwriting, only blank. He took a pen brusquely and dipped it with a vague notion of going on with the writing of his essay—but his pen remained poised over the sheet. It hung there for some time before it came down and formed long scrawly letters.

Still-faced and his lips set hard, Razumov began to write. When he wrote a large hand his neat writing lost its character altogether—became unsteady, almost childish. He wrote five lines one under the other.

> History not Theory.
> Patriotism not Internationalism.
> Evolution not Revolution.
> Direction not Destruction.
> Unity not Disruption.

He gazed at them dully. Then his eyes strayed to the bed and remained fixed there for a good many minutes, while his right hand groped all over the table for the penknife.

He rose at last, and walking up with measured steps stabbed the paper with the penknife to the lath and plaster wall at the head of the bed. This done, he stepped back a pace and flourished his hand with a glance round the room.

After that he never looked again at the bed. He took his big cloak down from its peg and, wrapping himself up closely, went to lie down on the hard horsehair sofa at the other side of his room. A leaden sleep closed his eyelids at once. Several times that night he woke up shivering from a dream of walking through drifts of snow in a Russia where he was as completely alone as any betrayed autocrat could be ; an immense, wintry Russia which, somehow, his view could embrace in all its enormous expanse as if it were a map. But after each shuddering start his heavy eyelids fell over his glazed eyes and he slept again.

III

Approaching this part of Mr. Razumov's story, my mind, the decent mind of an old teacher of languages, feels more and more the difficulty of the task.

The task is not, in truth, the writing in the narrative form a précis of a strange human document, but the rendering—I perceive it now clearly—of the moral conditions ruling over a large portion of this earth's surface : conditions not easily to be understood, much less discovered in the limits of a story, till some keyword is found ; a word that could stand at the back of all the words covering the pages ; a

6

word which, if not truth itself, may perchance hold truth enough to help the moral discovery which should be the object of every tale.

I turn over for the hundredth time the leaves of Mr. Razumov's record, I lay it aside, I take up the pen—and the pen being ready for its office of setting down black on white I hesitate. For the word that persists in creeping under its point is no other word than " cynicism."

For that is the mark of Russian autocracy and of Russian revolt. In its pride of numbers, in its strange ·pretensions of sanctity, and in the secret readiness to abase itself in suffering, the spirit of Russia is the spirit of cynicism. It informs the declarations of her statesmen, the theories of her revolutionists, and the mystic vaticinations of prophets to the point of making freedom look like a form of debauch, and the Christian virtues themselves appear actually indecent. . . . But I must apologise for the digression. It proceeds from the consideration of the course taken by the story of Mr. Razumov after his conservative convictions, diluted in a vague liberalism natural to the ardour of his age, had become crystallised by the shock of his contact with Haldin.

Razumov woke up for the tenth time perhaps with a heavy shiver. Seeing the light of day in his window, he resisted the inclination to lay himself down again. He did not remember anything, but he did not think it strange to find himself on the sofa in his cloak and chilled to the bone. The light coming through the window seemed strangely cheerless, containing no promise as the light of each new day should for a young man. It was the awakening of a man mortally ill, or of a man ninety years old. He looked at the lamp, which had burnt itself out. It stood there, the extinguished beacon of his labours, a cold object of brass and porcelain, amongst the scattered pages of his notes and small piles of books—a mere litter of blackened paper—dead matter—without significance or interest.

He got on his feet, and divesting himself of his cloak hung it on the peg, going through all the motions mechanically. An incredible dullness, a ditch-water stagnation was sensible to his perceptions, as though life had withdrawn itself from all things and even from his own thoughts. There was not a sound in the house.

Turning away from the peg, he thought in that same lifeless manner that it must be very early yet ; but when he looked at the watch on his table he saw both hands arrested at twelve o'clock.

" Ah, yes," he mumbled to himself, and as if beginning to get roused a little he took a survey of his room. The paper stabbed to the wall arrested his attention. He eyed it from the distance without approval or perplexity ; but when he heard the servant-girl beginning to bustle about in the outer room with the samovar for his morning tea, he walked up to it and took it down with an air of profound indifference.

While doing this he glanced down at the bed on which he had not slept that night. The hollow in the pillow made by the weight of Haldin's head was very noticeable.

Even his anger at this sign of the man's passage was dull. He did not try to nurse it into life. He did nothing all that day; he neglected even to brush his hair. The idea of going out never occurred to him—and if he did not start a connected train of thought it was not because he was unable to think. It was because he was not interested enough.

He yawned frequently. He drank large quantities of tea, he walked about aimlessly, and when he sat down he did not budge for a long time. He spent some time drumming on the window with his finger-tips quietly. In his listless wanderings round about the table he caught sight of his own face in the looking-glass and that arrested him. The eyes which returned his stare were the most unhappy eyes he had ever seen. And this was the first thing which disturbed the mental stagnation of that day.

He was not affected personally. He merely thought that life without happiness is impossible. What was happiness? He yawned and went on shuffling about and about between the walls of his room. Looking forward was happiness—that's all

—nothing more. To look forward to the gratification of some desire, to the gratification of some
passion, love, ambition, hate—hate, too, indubitably.
Love and hate. And to escape the dangers of
existence, to live without fear, was also happiness.
There was nothing else. Absence of fear—looking
forward. " Oh ! the miserable lot of humanity ! "
he exclaimed mentally ; and added at once in his
thought, " I ought to be happy enough as far as
that goes." But he was not excited by that assurance. On the contrary, he yawned again as he had
been yawning all day. He was mildly surprised to
discover himself being overtaken by night. The
room grew dark swiftly though time had seemed to
stand still. How was it that he had not noticed
the passing of that day ? Of course, it was the
watch being stopped. . . .

He did not light his lamp, but went over to the
bed and threw himself on it without any hesitation.
Lying on his back, he put his hands under his head
and stared upward. After a moment he thought,
" I am lying here like that man. I wonder if he
slept while I was struggling with the blizzard in
the streets. No, he did not sleep. But why should
I not sleep ? " and he felt the silence of the night
press upon all his limbs like a weight.

In the calm of the hard frost outside, the clear-
cut strokes of the town clock counting off midnight
penetrated the quietness of his suspended animation.

Again he began to think. It was twenty-four

hours since that man left his room. Razumov had a distinct feeling that Haldin in the fortress was sleeping that night. It was a certitude which made him angry because he did not want to think of Haldin, but he justified it to himself by physiological and psychological reasons. The fellow had hardly slept for weeks on his own confession, and now every incertitude was at an end for him. No doubt he was looking foward to the consummation of his martyrdom. A man who resigns himself to kill need not go very far for resignation to die. Haldin slept perhaps more soundly than General T——, whose task—weary work too—was not done, and over whose head hung the sword of revolutionary vengeance.

Razumov, remembering the thick-set man with his heavy jowl resting on the collar of his uniform, the champion of autocracy, who had let no sign of surprise, incredulity, or joy escape him, but whose goggle eyes could express a mortal hatred of all rebellion—Razumov moved uneasily on the bed.

" He suspected me," he thought. " I suppose he must suspect everybody. He would be capable of suspecting his own wife, if Haldin had gone to her boudoir with his confession."

Razumov sat up in anguish. Was he to remain a political suspect all his days ? Was he to go through life as a man not wholly to be trusted—with a bad secret police note tacked on to his record ? What sort of future could he look forward to ?

" I am now a suspect," he thought again ; but
the habit of reflection and that desire of safety, of an
ordered life, which was so strong in him came to his
assistance as the night wore on. His quiet, steady,
and laborious existence would vouch at length for
his loyalty. There were many permitted ways to
serve one's country. There was an activity that
made for progress without being revolutionary.
The field of influence was great and infinitely
varied—once one had conquered a name.

His thought, like a circling bird, reverted after
four-and-twenty hours to the silver medal, and as
it were poised itself there.

When the day broke he had not slept, not for a
moment, but he got up not very tired and quite
sufficiently self-possessed for all practical purposes.

He went out and attended three lectures in the
morning. But the work in the library was a mere
dumb show of research. He sat with many volumes
open before him trying to make notes and extracts.
His new tranquillity was like a flimsy garment, and
seemed to float at the mercy of a casual word.
Betrayal ! Why ! the fellow had done all that was
necessary to betray himself. Precious little had
been needed to deceive him.

" I have said no word to him that was not
strictly true. Not one word," Razumov argued
with himself.

Once engaged on this line of thought there could
be no question of doing useful work. The same

ideas went on passing through his mind, and he pronounced mentally the same words over and over again. He shut up all the books and rammed all his papers into his pocket with convulsive movements, raging inwardly against Haldin.

As he was leaving the library, a long bony student in a threadbare overcoat joined him, stepping moodily by his side. Razumov answered his mumbled greeting without looking at him at all.

" What does he want with me ? " he thought, with a strange dread of the unexpected which he tried to shake off lest it should fasten itself upon his life for good and all. And the other, muttering cautiously with downcast eyes, supposed that his comrade had seen the news of de P——'s executioner—that was the expression he used—having been arrested the night before last. . . .

" I've been ill—shut up in my rooms," Razumov mumbled through his teeth.

The tall student, raising his shoulders, shoved his hands deep into his pockets. He had a hairless, square, tallowy chin which trembled slightly as he spoke, and his nose nipped bright red by the sharp air looked like a false nose of painted cardboard between the sallow cheeks. His whole appearance was stamped with the mark of cold and hunger. He stalked deliberately at Razumov's elbow with his eyes on the ground.

" It's an official statement," he continued in the same cautious mutter. " It may be a lie. But

there was somebody arrested between midnight
and one in the morning on Tuesday. This is
certain."

And talking rapidly under the cover of his downcast air, he told Razumov that this was known
through an inferior Government clerk employed at
the Central Secretariat. That man belonged to one
of the revolutionary circles. " The same, in fact,
I am affiliated to," remarked the student.

They were crossing a wide quadrangle. An
infinite distress possessed Razumov, annihilated his
energy, and before his eyes everything appeared
confused and as if evanescent. He dared not leave
the fellow there. " He may be affiliated to the
police," was the thought that passed through his
mind. " Who could tell ? " But eyeing the
miserable frost-nipped, famine-struck figure of his
companion he perceived the absurdity of his suspicion.

" But I—you know—I don't belong to any circle.
I . . ."

He dared not say any more. Neither dared he
mend his pace. The other, raising and setting down
his lamentably shod feet with exact deliberation,
protested in a low tone that it was not necessary for
everybody to belong to an organisation. The most
valuable personalities remained outside. Some of
the best work was done outside the organisation.
Then very fast, with whispering, feverish lips :

" The man arrested in the street was Haldin."

And accepting Razumov's dismayed silence as natural enough, he assured him that there was no mistake. That Government clerk was on night duty at the Secretariat. Hearing a great noise of footsteps in the hall and aware that political prisoners were brought over sometimes at night from the fortress, he opened the door of the room in which he was working, suddenly. Before the gendarme on duty could push him back and slam the door in his face, he had seen a prisoner being partly carried, partly dragged along the hall by a lot of policemen. He was being used very brutally. And the clerk had recognised Haldin perfectly. Less than half an hour afterwards General T—— arrived at the Secretariat to examine that prisoner personally.

" Aren't you astonished ? " concluded the gaunt student.

" No," said Razumov roughly—and at once regretted his answer.

" Everybody supposed Haldin was in the provinces—with his people. Didn't you ? "

The student turned his big hollow eyes upon Razumov, who said unguardedly :

" His people are abroad."

He could have bitten his tongue out with vexation. The student pronounced in a tone of profound meaning :

" So ! You alone were aware . . ." and stopped.

"They have sworn my ruin," thought Razumov. "Have you spoken of this to any one else?" he asked with bitter curiosity.

The other shook his head.

"No, only to you. Our circle thought that as Haldin had been often heard expressing a warm appreciation of your character . . ."

Razumov could not restrain a gesture of angry despair which the other must have misunderstood in some way, because he ceased speaking and turned away his black, lack-lustre eyes.

They moved side by side in silence. Then the gaunt student began to whisper again, with averted gaze:

"As we have at present no one affiliated inside the fortress so as to make it possible to furnish him with a packet of poison, we have considered already some sort of retaliatory action—to follow very soon . . ."

Razumov trudging on interrupted:

"Were you acquainted with Haldin? Did he know where you live?"

"I had the happiness to hear him speak twice," his companion answered in the feverish whisper contrasting with the gloomy apathy of his face and bearing. "He did not know where I live. . . . I am lodging poorly . . . with an artisan family. . . . I have just a corner in a room. It is not very practicable to see me there, but if you should need me for anything I am ready. . . ."

Razumov trembled with rage and fear. He was beside himself, but kept his voice low.

" You are not to come near me. You are not to speak to me. Never address a single word to me. I forbid you."

" Very well," said the other submissively, showing no surprise whatever at this abrupt prohibition. " You don't wish for secret reasons . . . perfectly . . . I understand."

He edged away at once, not looking up even ; and Razumov saw his gaunt, shabby, famine-stricken figure cross the street obliquely with lowered head and that peculiar exact motion of the feet.

He watched him as one would watch a vision out of a nightmare, then he continued on his way, trying not to think. On his landing the landlady seemed to be waiting for him. She was a short, thick, shapeless woman with a large yellow face wrapped up everlastingly in a black woollen shawl. When she saw him come up the last flight of stairs she flung both her arms up excitedly, then clasped her hands before her face.

" Kirylo Sidorovitch—little father—what have you been doing ? And such a quiet young man, too ! The police have just gone this moment after searching your rooms."

Razumov gazed down at her with silent, scrutinising attention. Her puffy yellow countenance was working with emotion. She screwed up her eyes at him entreatingly.

"Such a sensible young man! Anybody can see you are sensible. And now—like this—all at once. . . . What is the good of mixing yourself up with these Nihilists? Do give over, little father. They are unlucky people."

Razumov moved his shoulders slightly.

"Or is it that some secret enemy has been calumniating you, Kirylo Sidorovitch? The world is full of black hearts and false denunciations nowadays. There is much fear about."

"Have you heard that I have been denounced by some one?" asked Razumov, without taking his eyes off her quivering face.

But she had not heard anything. She had tried to find out by asking the police captain while his men were turning the room upside down. The police captain of the district had known her for the last eleven years and was a humane person. But he said to her on the landing, looking very black and vexed:

"My good woman, do not ask questions. I don't know anything myself. The order comes from higher quarters."

And indeed there had appeared, shortly after the arrival of the policeman of the district, a very superior gentleman in a fur coat and a shiny hat, who sat down in the room and looked through all the papers himself. He came alone and went away by himself, taking nothing with him. She had been trying to put things straight a little since they left.

Razumov turned away brusquely and entered his rooms.

All his books had been shaken and thrown on the floor. His landlady followed him, and stooping painfully began to pick them up into her apron. His papers and notes, which were kept always neatly sorted (they all related to his studies), had been shuffled up and heaped together into a ragged pile in the middle of the table.

This disorder affected him profoundly, unreasonably. He sat down and stared. He had a distinct sensation of his very existence being undermined in some mysterious manner, of his moral supports falling away from him one by one. He even experienced a slight physical giddiness and made a movement as if to reach for something to steady himself with.

The old woman, rising to her feet with a low groan, shot all the books she had collected in her apron on to the sofa and left the room muttering and sighing.

It was only then that he noticed that the sheet of paper which for one night had remained stabbed to the wall above his empty bed was lying on top of the pile.

When he had taken it down the day before, he had folded it in four, absent-mindedly, before dropping it on the table. And now he saw it lying uppermost, spread out, smoothed out even and covering all the confused pile of pages, the record of his intellectual life for the last three years. It had not been flung there. It had been placed there—smoothed out, too ! He guessed in that an intention of profound meaning—or perhaps some inexplicable mockery.

He sat staring at the piece of paper till his eyes began to smart. He did not attempt to put his papers in order, either that evening or the next day—which he spent at home in a state of peculiar irresolution. This irresolution bore upon the question whether he should continue to live—neither more nor less. But its nature was very far removed from the hesitation of a man contemplating suicide. The idea of laying violent hands upon his body did not occur to Razumov. The unrelated organism bearing that label, walking, breathing, wearing these clothes, was of no importance to any one, unless maybe to the landlady. The true Razumov had his being in the willed, in the determined future—in that future menaced by the lawlessness of autocracy—for autocracy knows no law—and the lawlessness of revolution. The feeling that his moral personality was at the mercy of these lawless forces was so strong that he asked himself seriously if it were worth while to go on accomplishing the mental functions of that existence which seemed no longer his own.

" What is the good of exerting my intelligence, of pursuing the systematic development of my faculties and all my plans of work ? " he asked himself. " I want to guide my conduct by reasonable convictions, but what security have I against something—some destructive horror — walking in upon me as I sit here ? . . ."

Razumov looked apprehensively towards the door of the outer room as if expecting some shape of evil to turn the handle and appear before him silently.

" A common thief," he said to himself, " finds more guarantees in the law he is breaking, and even a brute like Ziemianitch has his consolation." Razumov envied the materialism of the thief and the passion of the incorrigible lover. The consequences of their actions were always clear and their lives remained their own.

But he slept as soundly that night as though he had been consoling himself in the manner of Ziemianitch. He dropped off suddenly, lay like a log, remembered no dream on waking. But it was as if his soul had gone out in the night to gather the flowers of wrathful wisdom. He got up in a mood of grim determination and as if with a new knowledge of his own nature. He looked mockingly on the heap of papers on his table ; and left his room to attend the lectures, muttering to himself, " We shall see."

He was in no humour to talk to anybody or hear himself questioned as to his absence from lectures the day before. But it was difficult to repulse rudely a very good comrade with a smooth pink face and fair hair, bearing the nickname amongst his fellow-students of "Madcap Kostia." He was the idolised only son of a very wealthy and illiterate Government contractor, and attended the lectures only during the periodical fits of contrition following upon tearful paternal remonstrances. Noisily blundering like a retriever puppy, his elated voice and great gestures filled the bare academy corridors with the joy of thoughtless animal life, provoking indulgent smiles at a great distance. His usual discourses treated of trotting horses, wine-parties in expensive restaurants, and the merits of persons of easy virtue, with a disarming artlessness of outlook. He pounced upon Razumov about midday, somewhat less uproariously than his habit was, and led him aside.

" Just a moment, Kirylo Sidorovitch. A few words here in this quiet corner."

He felt Razumov's reluctance, and insinuated his hand under his arm caressingly.

" No—pray do. I don't want to talk to you about any of my silly scrapes. What are my scrapes ? Absolutely nothing. Mere childishness. The other night I flung a fellow out of a certain place where I was having a fairly good time. A tyrannical little beast of a quill-driver from the Treasury department. . . . He was bullying the people of the house. I rebuked him. ' You are not behaving humanely to God's creatures that are a jolly sight more estimable than yourself,' I said. I can't bear to see any tyranny, Kirylo Sidorovitch. Upon my

7

word I can't. He didn't take it in good part at all.
' Who's that impudent puppy ? ' he begins to
shout. I was in excellent form as it happened,
and he went through the closed window very suddenly. He flew quite a long way into the yard. I
raged like—like a—minotaur. The women clung
to me and screamed, the fiddlers got under the
table. . . . Such fun ! My dad had to put his
hand pretty deep into his pocket, I can tell you."

He chuckled.

" My dad is a very useful man. Jolly good
thing it is for me, too. I do get into unholy scrapes."

His elation fell. That was just it. What was
his life ? Insignificant ; no good to any one ; a
mere festivity. It would end some fine day in his
getting his skull split with a champagne bottle in a
drunken brawl. At such times, too, when men were
sacrificing themselves to ideas. But he could never
get any ideas into his head. His head wasn't worth
anything better than to be split by a champagne
bottle.

Razumov, protesting that he had no time, made
an attempt to get away. The other's tone changed
to confidential earnestness.

" For God's sake, Kirylo, my dear soul, let me
make some sort of sacrifice. It would not be a
sacrifice really. I have my rich dad behind me.
There's positively no getting to the bottom of his
pocket."

And rejecting indignantly Razumov's suggestion

that this was drunken raving, he offered to lend him some money to escape abroad with. He could always get money from his dad. He had only to say that he had lost it at cards or something of that sort, and at the same time promise solemnly not to miss a single lecture for three months on end. That would fetch the old man ; and he, Kostia, was quite equal to the sacrifice. Though he really did not see what was the good for him to attend the lectures. It was perfectly hopeless.

" Won't you let me be of some use ? " he pleaded to the silent Razumov, who, with his eyes on the ground and utterly unable to penetrate the real drift of the other's intention, felt a strange reluctance to clear up the point.

" What makes you think I want to go abroad ? " he asked at last very quietly.

Kostia lowered his voice.

" You had the police in your rooms yesterday. There are three or four of us who have heard of that. Never mind how we know. It is sufficient that we do. So we have been consulting together."

" Ah ! You got to know that so soon," muttered Razumov negligently.

" Yes. We did. And it struck us that a man like you . . ."

" What sort of a man do you take me to be ? " Razumov interrupted him.

" A man of ideas—and a man of action too. But you are very deep, Kirylo. There's no getting to the bottom of your mind. Not for fellows like me. But we all agreed that you must be preserved for our country. Of that we have no doubt what-ever—I mean all of us who have heard Haldin speak of you on certain occasions. A man doesn't get the police ransacking his rooms without there being some devilry hanging over his head. . . . And so if you think that it would be better for you to bolt at once . . ."

Razumov tore himself away and walked down the corridor, leaving the other motionless with his mouth open. But almost at once he returned and stood before the amazed Kostia, who shut his mouth slowly. Razumov looked him straight in the eyes, before saying with marked deliberation and separat-ing his words :

" I thank—you—very—much."

He went away again rapidly. Kostia, recovering from his surprise at these manœuvres, ran up behind him pressingly.

" No ! Wait ! Listen. I really mean it. It would be like giving your compassion to a starving fellow. Do you hear, Kirylo ? And any disguise you may think of, that too I could procure from a costumier, a Jew I know. Let a fool be made serviceable according to his folly. Perhaps also a false beard or something of that kind may be needed."

Razumov turned at bay.

" There are no false beards needed in this

business, Kostia—you good-hearted lunatic, you. What do you know of my ideas? My ideas may be poison to you."

The other began to shake his head in energetic protest.

" What have you got to do with ideas? Some of them would make an end of your dad's money-bags. Leave off meddling with what you don't understand. Go back to your trotting horses and your girls, and then you'll be sure at least of doing no harm to anybody, and hardly any to yourself."

The enthusiastic youth was overcome by this disdain.

" You're sending me back to my pig's trough, Kirylo. That settles it. I am an unlucky beast— and I shall die like a beast too. But mind—it's your contempt that has done for me."

Razumov went off with long strides. That this simple and grossly festive soul should have fallen too under the revolutionary curse affected him as an ominous symptom of the time. He reproached himself for feeling troubled. Personally he ought to have felt reassured. There was an obvious advantage in this conspiracy of mistaken judgment taking him for what he was not. But was it not strange?

Again he experienced that sensation of his conduct being taken out of his hands by Haldin's revolutionary tyranny. His solitary and laborious existence had been destroyed—the only thing he could call his own on this earth. By what right ? he asked himself furiously. In what name ?

What infuriated him most was to feel that the " thinkers " of the university were evidently connecting him with Haldin—as a sort of confidant in the background apparently. A mysterious connection ! Ha, ha ! . . . He had been made a personage without knowing anything about it. How that wretch Haldin must have talked about him ! Yet it was likely that Haldin had said very little. The fellow's casual utterances were caught up and treasured and pondered over by all these imbeciles. And was not all secret revolutionary action based upon folly, self-deception, and lies ?

" Impossible to think of anything else," muttered Razumov to himself. " I'll become an idiot if this goes on. The scoundrels and the fools are murdering my intelligence."

He lost all hope of saving his future, which depended on the free use of his intelligence.

He reached the doorway of his house in a state of mental discouragement which enabled him to receive with apparent indifference an official-looking envelope from the dirty hand of the dvornik.

" A gendarme brought it," said the man. " He asked if you were at home. I told him, ' No, he's not at home.' So he left it. ' Give it into his own hand,' says he. Now you've got it—eh ? "

He went back to his sweeping, and Razumov climbed his stairs, envelope in hand. Once in his room he did not hasten to open it. Of course this official missive was from the superior direction of the police. A suspect ! A suspect !

He stared in dreary astonishment at the absurdity of his position. He thought with a sort of dry, unemotional melancholy ; three years of good work gone, the course of forty more perhaps jeopardised— turned from hope to terror, because events started by human folly link themselves into a sequence which no sagacity can foresee and no courage can break through. Fatality enters your rooms while your landlady's back is turned ; you come home and find it in possession bearing a man's name, clothed in flesh—wearing a brown cloth coat and long boots—lounging against the stove. It asks you, " Is the outer door closed ? "—and you don't know enough to take it by the throat and fling it down- stairs. You don't know. You welcome the crazy fate. " Sit down," you say. And it is all over. You cannot shake it off any more. It will cling to you for ever. Neither halter nor bullet can give you back the freedom of your life and the sanity of your thought. . . . It was enough to dash one's head against a wall.

Razumov looked slowly all round the walls as if to select a spot to dash his head against. Then he opened the letter. It directed the student Kirylo Sidorovitch Razumov to present himself without delay at the General Secretariat.

Razumov had a vision of General T——'s goggle

eyes waiting for him—the embodied power of autocracy, grotesque and terrible. He embodied the
whole power of autocracy because he was its guardian. He was the incarnate suspicion, the incarnate
anger, the incarnate ruthlessness of a political and
social régime on its defence. He loathed rebellion
by instinct. And Razumov reflected that the man
was simply unable to understand a reasonable adher-
ence to the doctrine of absolutism.

" What can he want with me precisely—I
wonder ? " he asked himself.

As if that mental question had evoked the familiar
phantom, Haldin stood suddenly before him in the
room with an extraordinary completeness of detail.
Though the short winter day had passed already
into the sinister twilight of a land buried in snow,
Razumov saw plainly the narrow leather strap round
the Tcherkess coat. The illusion of that hateful
presence was so perfect that he half expected it to
ask, " Is the outer door closed ? " He looked at
it with hatred and contempt. Souls do not take a
shape of clothing. Moreover, Haldin could not be
dead yet. Razumov stepped forward menacingly ;
the vision vanished—and turning short on his heel
he walked out of his room with infinite disdain.

But after going down the first flight of stairs it
occurred to him that perhaps the superior authorities
of police meant to confront him with Haldin in the
flesh. This thought struck him like a bullet, and
had he not clung with both hands to the banister he

would have rolled down to the next landing most
likely. His legs were of no use for a considerable time. . . . But why ? For what conceivable
reason ? To what end ?

There could be no rational answer to these
questions ; but Razumov remembered the promise
made by the general to Prince K——. His action
was to remain unknown.

He got down to the bottom of the stairs, lowering himself as it were from step to step, by the
banister. Under the gate he regained much of his
firmness of thought and limb. He went out into
the street without staggering visibly. Every moment
he felt steadier mentally. And yet he was saying to
himself that General T—— was perfectly capable
of shutting him up in the fortress for an indefinite
time. His temperament fitted his remorseless task,
and his omnipotence made him inaccessible to
reasonable argument.

But when Razumov arrived at the Secretariat
he discovered that he would have nothing to do with
General T——. It is evident from Mr. Razumov's
diary that this dreaded personality was to remain
in the background. A civilian of superior rank
received him in a private room after a period of
waiting in outer offices where a lot of scribbling
went on at many tables in a heated and stuffy atmosphere.

The clerk in uniform who conducted him said in
the corridor :

"You are going before Gregory Matvieitch Mikulin."

There was nothing formidable about the man bearing that name. His mild, expectant glance was turned on the door already when Razumov entered. At once, with the penholder he was holding in his hand, he pointed to a deep sofa between two windows. He followed Razumov with his eyes while that last crossed the room and sat down. The mild gaze rested on him, not curious, not inquisitive—certainly not suspicious—almost without expression. In its passionless persistence there was something resembling sympathy.

Razumov, who had prepared his will and his intelligence to encounter General T—— himself, was profoundly troubled. All the moral bracing up against the possible excesses of power and passion went for nothing before this sallow man, who wore a full unclipped beard. It was fair, thin, and very fine. The light fell in coppery gleams on the protuberances of a high, rugged forehead. And the aspect of the broad, soft physiognomy was so homely and rustic that the careful middle parting of the hair seemed a pretentious affectation.

The diary of Mr. Razumov testifies to some irritation on his part. I may remark here that the diary proper, consisting of the more or less daily entries, seems to have been begun on that very evening after Mr. Razumov had returned home.

Mr. Razumov, then, was irritated. His strung-up individuality had gone to pieces within him very suddenly.

" I must be very prudent with him," he warned himself in the silence during which they sat gazing at each other. It lasted some little time, and was characterised (for silences have their character) by a sort of sadness imparted to it perhaps by the mild and thoughtful manner of the bearded official. Razumov learned later that he was the chief of a department in the General Secretariat, with a rank in the Civil Service equivalent to that of a colonel in the Army.

Razumov's mistrust became acute. The main point was, not to be drawn into saying too much. He had been called there for some reason. What reason ? To be given to understand that he was a suspect—and also no doubt to be pumped. As to what precisely ? There was nothing. Or perhaps Haldin had been telling lies. . . . Every alarming uncertainty beset Razumov. He could bear the silence no longer, and cursing himself for his weakness spoke first, though he had promised himself not to do so on any account.

" I haven't lost a moment's time," he began in a hoarse, provoking tone ; and then the faculty of speech seemed to leave him and enter the body of Councillor Mikulin, who chimed in approvingly :

" Very proper. Very proper. Though as a matter of fact . . ."

But the spell was broken, and Razumov interrupted him boldly, under a sudden conviction that this was the safest attitude to take. With a great flow of words he complained of being totally misunderstood. Even as he talked with a perception of his own audacity he thought that the word " misunderstood " was better than the word " mistrusted," and he repeated it again with insistence. Suddenly he ceased, being seized with fright before the attentive immobility of the official. " What am I talking about ? " he thought, eyeing him with a vague gaze. Mistrusted—not misunderstood—was the right symbol for these people. Misunderstood was the other kind of curse. Both had been brought on his head by that fellow Haldin. And his head ached terribly. He passed his hand over his brow—an involuntary gesture of suffering, which he was too careless to restrain. At that moment Razumov beheld his own brain suffering on the rack—a long, pale figure drawn asunder horizontally with terrific force in the darkness of a vault, whose face he failed to see. It was as though he had dreamed for an infinitesimal fraction of time of some dark print of the Inquisition. . . .

It is not to be seriously supposed that Razumov had actually dozed off and had dreamed in the presence of Councillor Mikulin, of an old print of the Inquisition. He was indeed extremely exhausted, and he records a remarkably dreamlike experience of anguish at the circumstance that there was no one whatever near the pale and extended figure. The solitude of the racked victim was particularly horrible to behold. The mysterious impossibility to see the face, he also notes, inspired a sort of terror. All these characteristics of an ugly dream were present. Yet he is certain that he never lost the consciousness of himself on the sofa, leaning forward with his hands between his knees and turning his cap round and round in his fingers. But everything vanished at the voice of Councillor Mikulin. Razumov felt profoundly grateful for the even simplicity of its tone.

" Yes. I have listened with interest. I comprehend in a measure your . . . But, indeed, you are mistaken in what you . . ." Councillor Mikulin uttered a series of broken sentences. Instead of finishing them he glanced down his beard. It was a deliberate curtailment which somehow made the phrases more impressive. But he could talk fluently enough, as became apparent when changing his tone to persuasiveness he went on : " By listening to you as I did, I think I have proved that I do not regard our intercourse as strictly official. In fact, I don't want it to have that character at all. . . . Oh yes ! I admit that the request for your presence here had an official form. But I put it to you whether it was a form which would have been used to secure the attendance of a . . ."

" Suspect," exclaimed Razumov, looking straight into the official's eyes. They were big with heavy eyelids, and met his boldness with a dim, steadfast

gaze. " A suspect." The open repetition of that
word which had been haunting all his waking
hours gave Razumov a strange sort of satisfaction. Councillor Mikulin shook his head slightly.
" Surely you do know that I've had my rooms
searched by the police ? "

" I was about to say a ' misunderstood person,'
when you interrupted me," insinuated quietly
Councillor Mikulin.

Razumov smiled without bitterness. The renewed sense of his intellectual superiority sustained
him in the hour of danger. He said a little disdainfully :

" I know I am but a reed. But I beg you to
allow me the superiority of the thinking reed over
the unthinking forces that are about to crush him out
of existence. Practical thinking in the last instance
is but criticism. I may perhaps be allowed to
express my wonder at this action of the police being
delayed for two full days during which, of course,
I could have annihilated everything compromising
by burning it—let us say—and getting rid of the
very ashes, for that matter."

" You are angry," remarked the official, with an
unutterable simplicity of tone and manner. " Is
that reasonable ? "

Razumov felt himself colouring with annoyance.

" I am reasonable. I am even—permit me to
say—a thinker, though, to be sure, this name nowa-

days seems to be the monopoly of hawkers of
revolutionary wares, the slaves of some French or
German thought—devil knows what foreign notions.
But I am not an intellectual mongrel. I think like
a Russian. I think faithfully—and I take the
liberty to call myself a thinker. It is not a forbidden word, as far as I know."

"No. Why should it be a forbidden word?"
Councillor Mikulin turned in his seat with crossed
legs, and resting his elbow on the table propped his
head on the knuckles of a half-closed hand. Razumov noticed a thick forefinger clasped by a massive
gold band set with a blood-red stone—a signet
ring that, looking as if it could weigh half a pound,
was an appropriate ornament for that ponderous
man with the accurate middle-parting of glossy
hair above a rugged Socratic forehead.

"Could it be a wig?" Razumov detected himself
wondering with an unexpected detachment. His
self-confidence was much shaken. He resolved to
chatter no more. Reserve! Reserve! All he had
to do was to keep the Ziemianitch episode secret
with absolute determination, when the question
came. Keep Ziemianitch strictly out of all the
answers.

Councillor Mikulin looked at him dimly.
Razumov's self-confidence abandoned him completely. It seemed impossible to keep Ziemianitch
out. Every question would lead to that, because,
of course, there was nothing else. He made an

effort to brace himself up. It was a failure. But
Councillor Mikulin was surprisingly detached too.

"Why should it be forbidden?" he repeated.
"I too consider myself a thinking man, I assure you.
The principal condition is to think correctly. I
admit it is difficult sometimes at first for a young
man abandoned to himself—with his generous
impulses undisciplined, so to speak—at the mercy
of every wild wind that blows. Religious belief, of
course, is a great . . ."

Councillor Mikulin glanced down his beard, and
Razumov, whose tension was relaxed by that unexpected and discursive turn, murmured with gloomy
discontent:

"That man, Haldin, believed in God."

"Ah! You are aware," breathed out Councillor
Mikulin, making the point softly, as if with discretion,
but making it nevertheless plainly enough, as if he
too were put off his guard by Razumov's remark.
The young man preserved an impassive, moody
countenance, though he reproached himself bitterly
for a pernicious fool, to have given thus an utterly
false impression of intimacy. He kept his eyes
on the floor. "I must positively hold my tongue
unless I am obliged to speak," he admonished
himself. And at once against his will the question,
"Hadn't I better tell him everything?" presented
itself with such force that he had to bite his lower
lip. Councillor Mikulin could not, however, have
nourished any hope of confession. He went on:

" You tell me more than his judges were able to get out of him. He was judged by a commission of three. He would tell them absolutely nothing. I have the report of the interrogatories here, by me. After every question there stands ' Refuses to answer—refuses to answer.' It's like that, page after page. You see, I have been entrusted with some further investigations around and about this affair. He has left me nothing to begin my investigations on. A hardened miscreant. And so, you say, he believed in . . ."

Again Councillor Mikulin glanced down his beard with a faint grimace ; but he did not pause for long. Remarking with a shade of scorn that blasphemers also had that sort of belief, he concluded by supposing that Mr. Razumov had conversed frequently with Haldin on the subject.

" No," said Razumov loudly, without looking up. " He talked and I listened. That is not a conversation."

" Listening is a great art," observed Mikulin parenthetically.

" And getting people to talk is another," mumbled Razumov.

" Well, no—that is not very difficult," Mikulin said innocently, " except, of course, in special cases. For instance, this Haldin. Nothing could induce him to talk. He was brought four times before the delegated judges. Four secret interrogatories—and

8

even during the last, when your personality was put forward . . ."

" My personality put forward ? " repeated Razumov, raising his head brusquely. " I don't understand."

Councillor Mikulin turned squarely to the table, and taking up some sheets of grey foolscap dropped them one after another, retaining only the last in his hand. He held it before his eyes while speaking.

" It was—you see—judged necessary. In a case of that gravity no means of action upon the culprit should be neglected. You understand that yourself, I am certain."

Razumov stared with enormous wide eyes at the side view of Councillor Mikulin, who now was not looking at him at all.

" So it was decided (I was consulted by General T——) that a certain question should be put to the accused. But in deference to the earnest wishes of Prince K—— your name has been kept out of the documents and even from the very knowledge of the judges themselves. Prince K—— recognised the propriety, the necessity of what we proposed to do, but he was concerned for your safety. Things do leak out—that we can't deny. One cannot always answer for the discretion of inferior officials. There was, of course, the secretary of the special tribunal —one or two gendarmes in the room. Moreover, as I have said, in deference to Prince K—— even the judges themselves were to be left in ignorance.

The question ready framed was sent to them by General T—— (I wrote it out with my own hand) with instructions to put it to the prisoner the very last of all.   Here it is."

Councillor Mikulin threw back his head into proper focus and went on reading monotonously : " Question—Was the man well known to you, in whose rooms you remained for several hours on Monday and on whose information you have been arrested—has he had any previous knowledge of your intention to commit a political murder ? . . . Prisoner refuses to reply.

" Question repeated. Prisoner preserves the same stubborn silence.

" The venerable Chaplain of the Fortress being then admitted and exhorting the prisoner to repentance, entreating him also to atone for his crime by an unreserved and full confession which should help to liberate from the sin of rebellion against the Divine laws and the sacred Majesty of the Ruler of our Christ-loving land—the prisoner opens his lips for the first time during this morning's audience and in a loud, clear voice rejects the venerable Chaplain's ministrations.

" At eleven o'clock the Court pronounces in summary form the death sentence.

" The execution is fixed for four o'clock in the afternoon, subject to further instructions from superior authorities."

Councillor Mikulin dropped the page of foolscap,

glanced down his beard, and turning to Razumov, added in an easy, explanatory tone :

" We saw no object in delaying the execution. The order to carry out the sentence was sent by telegraph at noon. I wrote out the telegram myself He was hanged at four o'clock this afternoon."

The definite information of Haldin's death gave Razumov the feeling of general lassitude which follows a great exertion or a great excitement. He kept very still on the sofa, but a murmur escaped him :

" He had a belief in a future existence."

Councillor Mikulin shrugged his shoulders slightly, and Razumov got up with an effort. There was nothing now to stay for in that room. Haldin had been hanged at four o'clock. There could be no doubt of that. He had, it seemed, entered upon his future existence, long boots, Astrakhan fur cap and all, down to the very leather strap round his waist. A flickering, vanishing sort of existence. It was not his soul, it was his mere phantom he had left behind on this earth—thought Razumov, smiling caustically to himself while he crossed the room, utterly forgetful of where he was and of Councillor Mikulin's existence. The official could have set a lot of bells ringing all over the building without leaving his chair. He let Razumov go quite up to the door before he spoke :

" Come, Kirylo Sidorovitch—what are you doing ? "

Razumov turned his head and looked at him in silence. He was not in the least disconcerted. Councillor Mikulin's arms were stretched out on the table before him and his body leaned forward a little with an effort of his dim gaze.

" Was I actually going to clear out like this ? " Razumov wondered at himself with an impassive countenance. And he was aware of this impassive-' ness concealing a lucid astonishment.

" Evidently I was going out if he had not spoken," he thought. " What would he have done then ? I must end this affair one way or another. I must make him show his hand."

For a moment longer he reflected behind the mask as it were, then let go the door-handle and came back to the middle of the room.

" I'll tell you what you think," he said explosively, but not raising his voice. " You think that you are dealing with a secret accomplice of that unhappy man. No, I do not know that he was unhappy. He did not tell me. He was a wretch from my point of view, because to keep alive a false idea is a greater crime than to kill a man. I suppose you will not deny that ? I hated him ! Visionaries work everlasting evil on earth. Their Utopias inspire in the mass of mediocre minds a disgust of reality and a contempt for the secular logic of human development."

Razumov shrugged his shoulders and stared. " What a tirade ! " he thought. The silence and

immobility of Councillor Mikulin impressed him.
The bearded bureaucrat sat at his post, mysteriously
self-possessed like an idol with dim, unreadable
eyes.   Razumov's voice changed involuntarily.

" If you were to ask me where is the necessity
of my hate for such as Haldin, I would answer you—
there is nothing sentimental in it.   I did not hate
him because he had committed the crime of murder.
Abhorrence is not hate.   I hated him simply because
I am sane.   It is in that character that he outraged
me.   His death . . ."

Razumov felt his voice growing thick in his
throat.   The dimness of Councillor Mikulin's eyes
seemed to spread all over his face and made it indistinct to Razumov's sight.   He tried to disregard
these phenomena.

" Indeed," he pursued, pronouncing each word
carefully, " what is his death to me ?   If he were
lying here on the floor I could walk over his breast.
. . . The fellow is a mere phantom. . . ."

Razumov's voice died out very much against his
will.   Mikulin behind the table did not allow himself the slightest movement.   The silence lasted for
some little time before Razumov could go on again.

" He went about talking of me. . . . Those
intellectual fellows sit in each other's rooms and get
drunk on foreign ideas in the same way young
Guards' officers treat each other with foreign wines.
Merest debauchery. . . . Upon my word,"—Razumov, enraged by a sudden recollection of Ziemian-

itch, lowered his voice forcibly,—" upon my word, we Russians are a drunken lot. Intoxication of some sort we must have : to get ourselves wild with sorrow or maudlin with resignation ; to lie inert like a log or set fire to the house. What is a sober man to do, I should like to know ? To cut oneself entirely from one's kind is impossible. To live in a desert one must be a saint. But if a drunken man runs out of the grog-shop, falls on your neck and kisses you on both cheeks because something about your appearance has taken his fancy, what then—kindly tell me ? You may break, perhaps, a cudgel on his back and yet not succeed in beating him off. . . ."

Councillor Mikulin raised his hand and passed it down his face deliberately.

" That's . . . of course," he said in an under-tone.

The quiet gravity of that gesture made Razumov pause. It was so unexpected too. What did it mean ? It had an alarming aloofness. Razumov remembered his intention of making him show his hand.

" I have said all this to Prince K——," he began, with assumed indifference, but lost it on seeing Councillor Mikulin's slow nod of assent. " You know it ? You've heard . . . Then why should I be called here to be told of Haldin's execution ? Did you want to confront me with his silence now that the man is dead ? What is his silence to me ?

This is incomprehensible. You want in some way to shake my moral balance."

" No. Not that," murmured Councillor Mikulin, just audibly. " The service you have rendered is appreciated . . ."

" Is it ? " interrupted Razumov ironically.

" . . . and your position too." Councillor Mikulin did not raise his voice. " But only think ! You fall into Prince K——'s study as if from the sky with your startling information. . . . You are studying yet, Mr. Razumov, but we are serving already — don't forget that. . . . And naturally some curiosity was bound to . . ."

Councillor Mikulin looked down his beard. Razumov's lips trembled.

" An occurrence of that sort marks a man," the homely murmur went on. " I admit I was curious to see you. General T—— thought it would be useful too. . . . Don't think I am incapable of understanding your sentiments. When I was young like you I studied . . ."

" Yes—you wished to see me," said Razumov in a tone of profound distaste. " Naturally you have the right—-I mean the power. It all amounts to the same thing. But it is perfectly useless, if you were to look at me and listen to me for a year. I begin to think there is something about me which people don't seem able to make out. It's unfortunate. I imagine, however, that Prince K—— understands. He seems to."

Councillor Mikulin moved slightly and spoke.

" Prince K—— is aware of everything that is being done, and I don't mind informing you that he approved my intention of becoming personally acquainted with you."

Razumov concealed an immense disappointment under the accents of railing surprise.

" So he is curious too ! . . . Well—after all, Prince K—— knows me very little. It is really very unfortunate for me, but—it is not exactly my fault."

Councillor Mikulin raised a hasty deprecatory hand and inclined his head slightly over his shoulder.

" Now, Mr. Razumov—is it necessary to take it in that way ? Everybody I am sure can . . ."

He glanced rapidly down his beard, and when he looked up again there was for a moment an interested expression in his misty gaze. Razumov discouraged it with a cold, repellent smile.

" No. That's of no importance, to be sure—except that in respect of all this curiosity being aroused by a very simple matter. . . . What is to be done with it ? It is unappeasable. I mean to say there is nothing to appease it with. I happen to have been born a Russian with patriotic instincts —whether inherited or not I am not in a position to say."

Razumov spoke consciously with elaborate steadiness.

"Yes, patriotic instincts developed by a faculty of independent thinking—of detached thinking. In that respect I am more free than any social democratic revolution could make me. It is more than probable that I don't think exactly as you are thinking. Indeed, how could it be? You would think most likely at this moment that I am elaborately lying to cover up the track of my repentance."

Razumov stopped. His heart had grown too big for his breast. Councillor Mikulin did not flinch.

"Why so?" he said simply. "I assisted personally at the search of your rooms. I looked through all the papers myself. I have been greatly impressed by a sort of political confession of faith. A very remarkable document. Now may I ask for what purpose . . ."

"To deceive the police naturally," said Razumov savagely. . . . "What is all this mockery? Of course, you can send me straight from this room to Siberia. That would be intelligible. To what is intelligible I can submit. But I protest against this comedy of persecution. The whole affair is becoming too comical altogether for my taste. A comedy of errors, phantoms, and suspicions. It's positively indecent . . ."

Councillor Mikulin turned an attentive ear.

"Did you say phantoms?" he murmured.

"I could walk over dozens of them." Razumov, with an impatient wave of his hand, went on headlong, " But, really, I must claim the right to be done once for all with that man.   And in order to accomplish this I shall take the liberty . . ."

Razumov on his side of the table bowed slightly to the seated bureaucrat.

" . . . To retire—simply to retire," he finished with great resolution.

He walked to the door, thinking, " Now he must show his hand.   He must ring and have me arrested before I am out of the building, or he must let me go.   And either way . . ."

An unhurried voice said :

" Kirylo Sidorovitch."

Razumov at the door turned his head.

" To retire," he repeated.

" Where to ? " asked Councillor Mikulin softly.

PART SECOND

I

IN the conduct of an invented story there are,
no doubt, certain proprieties to be observed
for the sake of clearness and effect. A man
of imagination, however inexperienced in the art of
narrative, has his instinct to guide him in the choice
of his words, and in the development of the action.
A grain of talent excuses many mistakes. But this
is not a work of imagination ; I have no talent ;
my excuse for this undertaking lies not in its art,
but in its artlessness. Aware of my limitations and
strong in the sincerity of my purpose, I would not
try (were I able) to invent anything. I push my
scruples so far that I would not even invent a
transition.

Dropping then Mr. Razumov's record at the
point where Councillor Mikulin's question, " Where
to ? " comes in with the force of an insoluble problem, I shall simply say that I made the acquaintance
of these ladies about six months before that time.
By " these ladies " I mean, of course, the mother
and the sister of the unfortunate Haldin.

By what arguments he had induced his mother

to sell their little property and go abroad for an indefinite time, I cannot tell precisely. I have an idea that Mrs. Haldin, at her son's wish, would have set fire to her house and emigrated to the moon without any sign of surprise or apprehension ; and that Miss Haldin—Nathalie, caressingly Natalia— would have given her assent to the scheme.

Their proud devotion to that young man became clear to me in a very short time. Following his directions they went straight to Switzerland—to Zurich—where they remained the best part of a year. From Zurich, which they did not like, they came to Geneva. A friend of mine in Lausanne, a lecturer in history at the university (he had married a Russian lady, a distant connection of Mrs. Haldin's), wrote to me suggesting I should call on these ladies. It was a very kindly meant business suggestion. Miss Haldin wished to go through a course of reading the best English authors with a competent teacher.

Mrs. Haldin received me very kindly. Her bad French, of which she was smilingly conscious, did away with the formality of the first interview. She was a tall woman in a black silk dress. A wide brow, regular features, and delicately cut lips testified to her past beauty. She sat upright in an easy-chair, and in a rather weak, gentle voice told me that her Natalia simply thirsted after knowledge. Her thin hands were lying on her lap, her facial immobility had in it something monachal. " In

Russia," she went on, " all knowledge was tainted with falsehood. Not chemistry and all that, but education generally," she explained. The Government corrupted the teaching for its own purposes. Both her children felt that. Her Natalia had obtained a diploma of a superior school for women, and her son was a student at the St. Petersburg University. He had a brilliant intellect, a most noble unselfish nature, and he was the oracle of his comrades. Early next year, she hoped, he would join them and they would then go to Italy together. In any other country but their own she would have been certain of a great future for a man with the extraordinary abilities and the lofty character of her son—but in Russia . . .

The young lady sitting by the window turned her head and said :

" Come, mother. Even with us things change with years."

Her voice was deep, almost harsh, and yet caressing in its harshness. She had a dark complexion, with red lips and a full figure. She gave the impression of strong vitality. The old lady sighed.

" You are both young—you two. It is easy for you to hope. But I, too, am not hopeless. Indeed, how could I be with a son like this ? "

I addressed Miss Haldin, asking her what authors she wished to read. She directed upon me her grey eyes shaded by black eyelashes, and

I became aware, notwithstanding my years, how attractive physically her personality could be to a man capable of appreciating in a woman something else than the mere grace of femininity. Her glance was as direct and trustful as that of a young man yet unspoiled by the world's wise lessons. And it was intrepid, but in this intrepidity there was nothing aggressive. A naïve yet thoughtful assurance is a better definition. She had reflected already (in Russia the young begin to think early), but she had never known deception as yet, because obviously she had never yet fallen under the sway of passion. She was—to look at her was enough—very capable of being roused by an idea or simply by a person. At least, so I judged with I believe an unbiased mind ; for clearly my person could not be the person —and as to my ideas ! . . .

We became excellent friends in the course of our reading. It was very pleasant. Without fear of provoking a smile, I will confess that I became very much attached to that young girl. At the end of four months I told her that now she could very well go on reading English by herself. It was time for the teacher to depart. My pupil looked unpleasantly surprised.

Mrs. Haldin, with her immobility of feature and kindly expression of the eyes, uttered from her arm-chair in her uncertain French, " *Mais l'ami reviendra.*" And so it was settled. I returned— not four times a week as before, but pretty frequently.

In the autumn we made some short excursions together in company with other Russians. My friendship with these ladies gave me a standing in the Russian colony which otherwise I could not have had.

The day I saw in the papers the news of Mr. de P——'s assassination—it was a Sunday—I met the two ladies in the street and walked with them for some distance. Mrs. Haldin wore a heavy grey cloak, I remember, over her black silk dress, and her fine eyes met mine with a very quiet expression.

" We have been to the late service," she said. " Natalia came with me. Her girl-friends, the students here, of course don't. . . . With us in Russia the Church is so identified with oppression, that it seems almost necessary when one wishes to be free in this life, to give up all hope of a future existence. But I cannot give up praying for my son."

She added with a sort of stony grimness, colouring slightly, and in French, " *Ce n'est peut-être qu'une habitude*." (" It may be only habit.")

Miss Haldin was carrying the prayer-book. She did not glance at her mother.

" You and Victor are both profound believers," she said.

I communicated to them the news from their country which I had just read in a café. For a whole minute we walked together fairly briskly in silence. Then Mrs. Haldin murmured :

" There will be more trouble, more persecutions for this. They may be even closing the university. There is neither peace nor rest in Russia for one but in the grave."

" Yes. The way is hard," came from the daughter, looking straight before her at the Chain of Jura covered with snow, like a white wall closing the end of the street. " But concord is not so very far off."

" That is what my children think," observed Mrs. Haldin to me.

I did not conceal my feeling that these were strange times to talk of concord. Nathalie Haldin surprised me by saying, as if she had thought very much on the subject, that the Occidentals did not understand the situation. She was very calm and youthfully superior.

" You think it is a class conflict, or a conflict of interests, as social contests are with you in Europe. But it is not that at all. It is something quite different."

" It is quite possible that I don't understand," I admitted.

That propensity of lifting every problem from the plane of the understandable by means of some sort of mystic expression, is very Russian. I knew her well enough to have discovered her scorn for all the practical forms of political liberty known to the Western world. I suppose one must be a Russian to understand Russian simplicity, a terrible corroding

9

simplicity in which mystic phrases clothe a naïve and hopeless cynicism. I think sometimes that the psychological secret of the profound difference of that people consists in this, that they detest life, the irremediable life of the earth as it is, whereas we Westerners cherish it with perhaps an equal exaggeration of its sentimental value. But this is a digression indeed. . . .

I helped these ladies into the tramcar, and they asked me to call in the afternoon. At least Mrs. Haldin asked me as she climbed up, and her Natalia smiled down at the dense Westerner indulgently from the rear platform of the moving car. The light of the clear wintry forenoon was softened in her grey eyes.

Mr. Razumov's record, like the open book of fate, revives for me the memory of that day as something startlingly pitiless in its freedom from all forebodings. Victor Haldin was still with the living, but with the living whose only contact with life is the expectation of death. He must have been already referring to the last of his earthly affections, the hours of that obstinate silence, which for him was to be prolonged into eternity. That afternoon the ladies entertained a good many of their compatriots—more than was usual for them to receive at one time ; and the drawing-room on the ground floor of a large house on the Boulevard des Philosophes was very much crowded.

I outstayed everybody ; and when I rose Miss

Haldin stood up too. I took her hand and was moved to revert to that morning's conversation in the street.

" Admitting that we Occidentals do not understand the character of your people . . ." I began.

It was as if she had been prepared for me by some mysterious foreknowledge. She checked me gently :

" Their impulses—their . . ." she sought the proper expression and found it, but in French . . . " their *mouvements d'âme*."

Her voice was not much above a whisper.

" Very well," I said. " But still we are looking at a conflict. You say it is not a conflict of classes and not a conflict of interests. Suppose I admitted that. Are antagonistic ideas then to be reconciled more easily—can they be cemented with blood and violence into that concord which you proclaim to be so near ? "

She looked at me searchingly with her clear grey eyes, without answering my reasonable question— my obvious, my unanswerable question.

" It is inconceivable," I added, with something like annoyance.

" Everything is inconceivable," she said. " The whole world is inconceivable to the strict logic of ideas. And yet the world exists to our senses, and we exist in it. There must be a necessity superior to our conceptions. It is a very miserable and a very false thing to belong to the majority. We Russians shall find some better form of national freedom than an artificial conflict of parties—which is wrong because it is a conflict and contemptible because it is artificial. It is left for us Russians to discover a better way."

Mrs. Haldin had been looking out of the window. She turned upon me the almost lifeless beauty of her face, and the living benign glance of her big dark eyes.

"That's what my children think," she declared.

"I suppose," I addressed Miss Haldin, "that you will be shocked if I tell you that I haven't understood—I won't say a single word; I've understood all the words. . . . But what can be this era of disembodied concord you are looking forward to? Life is a thing of form. It has its plastic shape and a definite intellectual aspect. The most idealistic conceptions of love and forbearance must be clothed in flesh as it were before they can be made understandable."

I took my leave of Mrs. Haldin, whose beautiful lips never stirred. She smiled with her eyes only. Nathalie Haldin went with me as far as the door, very amiable.

"Mother imagines that I am the slavish echo of my brother Victor. It is not so. He understands me better than I can understand him. When he joins us and you come to know him you will see what an exceptional soul it is." She paused. "He is not a strong man in the conventional sense, you know," she added. " But his character is without a flaw."

" I believe that it will not be difficult for me to make friends with your brother Victor."

" Don't expect to understand him quite," she said, a little maliciously. " He is not at all—at all —Western at bottom."

And on this unnecessary warning I left the room with another bow in the doorway to Mrs. Haldin in her arm-chair by the window. The shadow of autocracy all unperceived by me had already fallen upon the Boulevard des Philosophes, in the free, independent, and democratic city of Geneva, where there is a quarter called " La Petite Russie." Whenever two Russians come together, the shadow of autocracy is with them, tinging their thoughts, their views, their most intimate feelings, their private life, their public utterances—haunting the secret of their silences.

What struck me next in the course of a week or so was the silence of these ladies. I used to meet them walking in the public garden near the university. They greeted me with their usual friendliness, but I could not help noticing their taciturnity. By that time it was generally known that the assassin of Mr. de P—— had been caught, judged, and executed. So much had been declared officially to the news agencies. But for the world at large he remained anonymous. The official secrecy had withheld his name from the public. I really cannot imagine for what reason.

One day I saw Miss Haldin walking alone in the main valley of the Bastions under the naked trees.

" Mother is not very well," she explained.

As Mrs. Haldin had, it seemed, never had a day's illness in her life, this indisposition was disquieting. It was nothing definite, too.

" I think she is fretting because we have not heard from my brother for rather a long time."

" No news—good news," I said cheerfully, and we began to walk slowly side by side.

" Not in Russia," she breathed out so low that I only just caught the words. I looked at her with more attention.

" You too are anxious ? "

She admitted after a moment of hesitation that she was.

" It is really such a long time since we heard . . ."

And before I could offer the usual banal suggestions she confided in me.

" Oh ! But it is much worse than that. I wrote to a family we know in Petersburg. They had not seen him for more than a month. They thought he was already with us. They were even offended a little that he should have left Petersburg without calling on them. The husband of the lady went at once to his lodgings. Victor had left there and they did not know his address."

I remember her catching her breath rather piti-fully. Her brother had not been seen at lectures for a very long time either. He only turned up now and then at the university gate to ask the porter for his letters. And the gentleman friend was told that the student Haldin did not come to claim the last two letters for him. But the police came to inquire if the student Haldin ever received any corre-spondence at the university and took them away.

" My last two letters," she said.

We faced each other. A few snowflakes fluttered under the naked boughs. The sky was dark.

" What do you think could have happened ? " I asked.

Her shoulders moved slightly.

" One can never tell—in Russia."

I saw then the shadow of autocracy lying upon Russian lives in their submission or their revolt. I saw it touch her handsome open face nestled in a fur collar and darken her clear eyes that shone upon me brilliantly grey in the murky light of a beclouded, inclement afternoon.

" Let us move on," she said. " It is cold standing—to-day."

She shuddered a little and stamped her little feet. We moved briskly to the end of the alley and back to the great gates of the garden.

" Have you told your mother ? " I ventured to ask.

"No. Not yet. I came out to walk off the impression of this letter."

I heard a rustle of paper somewhere. It came from her muff. She had the letter with her in there.

"What is it that you are afraid of?" I asked.

To us Europeans of the West, all ideas of political plots and conspiracies seem childish, crude inventions for the theatre or a novel. I did not like to be more definite in my inquiry.

"For us—for my mother specially, what I am afraid of is incertitude. People do disappear. Yes, they do disappear. I leave you to imagine what it is—the cruelty of the dumb weeks—months —years! This friend of ours has abandoned his inquiries when he heard of the police getting hold of the letters. I suppose he was afraid of compromising himself. He has a wife and children— and why should he, after all? . . . Moreover, he is without influential connections and not rich. What could he do? . . . Yes, I am afraid of silence—for my poor mother. She won't be able to bear it. For my brother I am afraid of . . ." she became almost indistinct, "of anything."

We were now near the gate opposite the theatre. She raised her voice.

"But lost people do turn up even in Russia. Do you know what my last hope is? Perhaps the next thing we know, we shall see him walking into our rooms."

I raised my hat and she passed out of the gardens, graceful and strong, after a slight movement of the head to me, her hands in the muff, crumpling the cruel Petersburg letter.

On returning home I opened the newspaper I receive from London, and glancing down the correspondence from Russia—not the telegrams but the correspondence—the first thing that caught my eye was the name of Haldin. Mr. de P——'s death was no longer an actuality, but the enterprising correspondent was proud of having ferreted out some unofficial information about that fact of modern history. He had got hold of Haldin's name, and had picked up the story of the midnight arrest in the street. But the sensation from a journalistic point of view was already well in the past. He did not allot to it more than twenty lines out of a full column. It was quite enough to give me a sleepless night. I perceived that it would have been a sort of treason to let Miss Haldin come without preparation upon that journalistic discovery which would infallibly be reproduced on the morrow by French and Swiss newspapers. I had a very bad time of it till the morning, wakeful with nervous worry and nightmarish with the feeling of being mixed up with something theatrical and morbidly affected. The incongruity of such a complication in those two women's lives was sensible to me all night in the form of absolute anguish. It seemed due to their refined simplicity that it should remain concealed from them for ever. Arriving at an unconscionably early hour at the door of their apartment, I felt as if I were about to commit an act of vandalism. . . .

The middle-aged servant-woman led me into the drawing-room, where there was a duster on a chair and a broom leaning against the centre table. The motes danced in the sunshine. I regretted I had not written a letter instead of coming myself, and was thankful for the brightness of the day. Miss Haldin, in a plain black dress, came lightly out of her mother's room with a fixed uncertain smile on her lips.

I pulled the paper out of my pocket. I did not imagine that a number of the *Standard* could have the effect of Medusa's head. Her face went stony in a moment—her eyes—her limbs. The most terrible thing was that being stony she remained alive. One was conscious of her palpitating heart. I hope she forgave me the delay of my clumsy circumlocution. It was not very prolonged ; she could not have kept so still from head to foot for more than a second or two ; and then I heard her draw a breath. As if the shock had paralysed her moral resistance and affected the firmness of her muscles, the contours of her face seemed to have given way. She was frightfully altered. She looked aged—ruined. But only for a moment. She said with decision :

" I am going to tell my mother at once."

" Would that be safe in her state ? " I objected.

" What can be worse than the state she has been in for the last month ? We understand this in another way. The crime is not at his door. Don't imagine I am defending him before you."

She went to the bedroom door, then came back to ask me in a low murmur not to go till she returned. For twenty interminable minutes not a sound reached me. At last Miss Haldin came out and walked across the room with her quick light step. When she reached the arm-chair she dropped into it heavily as if completely exhausted.

Mrs. Haldin, she told me, had not shed a tear. She was sitting up in bed, and her immobility, her silence, were very alarming. At last she lay down gently and had motioned her daughter away.

. " She will call me in presently," added Miss Haldin. " I left a bell near the bed."

I confess that my very real sympathy had no standpoint. The Western readers for whom this story is written will understand what I mean. It was, if I may say so, the want of experience. Death is a remorseless spoliator. The anguish of irreparable loss is familiar to us all. There is no life so lonely as to be safe against that experience. But the grief I had brought to these two ladies had gruesome associations. It had the associations of bombs and gallows—a lurid, Russian colouring which made the complexion of my sympathy uncertain.

I was grateful to Miss Haldin for not embarrassing me by an outward display of deep feeling. I admired her for that wonderful command over herself, even while I was a little frightened at it. It was the stillness of a great tension. What if it should suddenly snap ? Even the door of Mrs. Haldin's room, with the old mother alone in there, had a rather awful aspect.

Nathalie Haldin murmured sadly :

" I suppose you are wondering what my feelings are ? "

Essentially that was true. It was that very wonder which unsettled my sympathy of a dense Occidental. I could get hold of nothing but of some commonplace phrases, those futile phrases that give the measure of our impotence before each other's trials. I mumbled something to the effect that, for the young, life held its hopes and compensations. It held duties too—but of that I was certain it was not necessary to remind her.

She had a handkerchief in her hands and pulled at it nervously.

" I am not likely to forget my mother," she said. " We used to be three. Now we are two—two women. She's not so very old. She may live quite a long time yet. What have we to look for in the future ? For what hope and what consolation ? "

" You must take a wider view," I said resolutely, thinking that with this exceptional creature this was the right note to strike. She looked at me steadily for a moment, and then the tears she had been keeping down flowed unrestrained. She jumped up and stood in the window with her back to me.

I slipped away without attempting even to approach her. Next day I was told at the door that Mrs. Haldin was better. The middle-aged servant remarked that a lot of people—Russians—had called that day, but Miss Haldin had not seen anybody. A fortnight later, when making my daily call, I was asked in and found Mrs. Haldin sitting in her usual place by the window.

At first one would have thought that nothing was changed. I saw across the room the familiar profile, a little sharper in outline and overspread by a uniform pallor as might have been expected in an invalid. But no disease could have accounted for the change in her black eyes, smiling no longer with gentle irony. She raised them as she gave me her hand. I observed the three weeks' old number of the *Standard* folded with the correspondence from Russia uppermost, lying on a little table by the side of the arm-chair. Mrs. Haldin's voice was startlingly weak and colourless. Her first words to me framed a question :

" Has there been anything more in your newspapers ? "

I released her long, emaciated hand, shook my head negatively, and sat down.

" The English Press is wonderful. Nothing can be kept secret from it, and all the world must hear. Only our Russian news is not always easy to understand. Not always easy. . . . But English mothers do not look for news like that . . ."

She laid her hand on the newspaper and took it away again. I said :

" We too have had tragic times in our history."

" A long time ago. A very long time ago."

" Yes."

" There are nations that have made their bargain with Fate," said Miss Haldin, who had approached us. " We need not envy them."

" Why this scorn ? " I asked gently. " It may be that our bargain was not a very lofty one. But the terms men and nations obtain from Fate are hallowed by the price."

Mrs. Haldin turned her head away and looked out of the window for a time, with that new, sombre, extinct gaze of her sunken eyes which so completely made another woman of her.

" That Englishman, this correspondent," she addressed me suddenly, " do you think it is possible that he knew my son ? "

To this strange question I could only say that it was possible, of course. She saw my surprise.

" If one knew what sort of man he was one could perhaps write to him," she murmured.

" Mother thinks," explained Miss Haldin, standing between us, with one hand resting on the back of my chair, " that my poor brother perhaps did not try to save himself."

I looked up at Miss Haldin in sympathetic consternation, but Miss Haldin was looking down calmly at her mother. The latter said :

" We do not know the address of any of his friends. Indeed, we know nothing of his Petersburg comrades. He had a multitude of young friends, only he never spoke much of them. One could guess that they were his disciples and that they idolised him. But he was so modest. One would think that with so many devoted . . ."

She averted her head again and looked down the Boulevard des Philosophes, a singularly arid and dusty thoroughfare, where nothing could be seen at the moment but two dogs, a little girl in a pinafore hopping on one leg, and in the distance a workman wheeling a bicycle.

" Even amongst the Apostles of Christ there was found a Judas," she whispered as if to herself, but with the evident intention to be heard by me.

The Russian visitors assembled in little knots, conversed amongst themselves meantime, in low murmurs, and with brief glances in our direction. It was a great contrast to the usual loud volubility of these gatherings. Miss Haldin followed me into the anteroom.

" People will come," she said. " We cannot shut the door in their faces."

While I was putting on my overcoat she began to talk to me of her mother. Poor Mrs. Haldin was fretting after more news. She wanted to go on hearing about her unfortunate son. She could not make up her mind to abandon him quietly to the dumb unknown. She would persist in pursuing him in there through the long days of motionless silence face to face with the empty Boulevard des Philosophes. She could not understand why he had not escaped—as so many other revolutionists and conspirators had managed to escape in other instances of that kind. It was really inconceivable that the means of secret revolutionary organisations should have failed so inexcusably to preserve her son. But in reality the inconceivable that staggered her mind was nothing but the cruel audacity of Death passing over her head to strike at that young and precious heart.

Miss Haldin mechanically, with an absorbed look, handed me my hat. I understood from her that the poor woman was possessed by the sombre and simple idea that her son must have perished because he did not want to be saved. It could not have been that he despaired of his country's future. That was impossible. Was it possible that his mother and sister had not known how to merit his confidence ; and that, after having done what he was compelled to do, his spirit became crushed by an intolerable doubt, his mind distracted by a sudden mistrust ?

I was very much shocked by this piece of ingenuity.

" Our three lives were like that ! " Miss Haldin

twined the fingers of both her hands together in
demonstration, then separated them slowly, looking
straight into my face. " That's what poor mother
found to torment herself and me with, for all the
years to come," added the strange girl. At that
moment her indefinable charm was revealed to me
in the conjunction of passion and stoicism. I
imagined what her life was likely to be by the side
of Mrs. Haldin's terrible immobility, inhabited by
that fixed idea. But my concern was reduced to
silence by my ignorance of her modes of feeling.
Difference of nationality is a terrible obstacle for
our complex Western natures. But Miss Haldin
probably was too simple to suspect my embarrass-
ment. She did not wait for me to say anything,
but as if reading my thoughts on my face she went
on courageously :

" At first poor mother went numb, as our
peasants say ; then she began to think, and she
will go on now thinking and thinking in that unfortunate strain. You see yourself how cruel that
is. . . ."

I never spoke with greater sincerity than when
I agreed with her that it would be deplorable
in the highest degree. She took an anxious
breath.

" But all these strange details in the English
paper," she exclaimed suddenly. " What is the
meaning of them ? I suppose they are true ? But
is it not terrible that my poor brother should be

10

caught wandering alone, as if in despair, about the streets at night? . . ."

We stood so close to each other in the dark anteroom that I could see her biting her lower lip to suppress a dry sob. After a short pause she said :

" I suggested to mother that he may have been betrayed by some false friend or simply by some cowardly creature. It may be easier for her to believe that."

I understood now the poor woman's whispered allusion to Judas.

" It may be easier," I admitted, admiring inwardly the directness and the subtlety of the girl's outlook. She was dealing with life as it was made for her by the political conditions of her country. She faced cruel realities, not morbid imaginings of her own making. I could not defend myself from a certain feeling of respect when she added simply :

" Time they say can soften every sort of bitterness. But I cannot believe that it has any power over remorse. It is better that mother should think some person guilty of Victor's death, than that she should connect it with a weakness of her son or a shortcoming of her own."

" But you, yourself, don't suppose that ? . . ." I began.

She compressed her lips and shook her head. She harboured no evil thought against any one, she declared—and perhaps nothing that happened was

unnecessary. On these words, pronounced low
and sounding mysterious in the half obscurity of
the anteroom, we parted with an expressive and
warm handshake. The grip of her strong, shapely
hand had a seductive frankness, a sort of exquisite
virility. I do not know why she should have felt
so friendly to me. It may be that she thought I
understood her much better than I was able to do.
The most precise of her sayings seemed always to
me to have enigmatical prolongations vanishing
somewhere beyond my reach. I am reduced to
suppose that she appreciated my attention and my
silence. The attention she could see was quite
sincere, so that the silence could not be suspected of
coldness. It seemed to satisfy her. And it is to
be noted that if she confided in me it was clearly
not with the expectation of receiving advice, for
which, indeed, she never asked.

II

Our daily relations were interrupted at this
period for something like a fortnight. I had to
absent myself unexpectedly from Geneva. On my
return I lost no time in directing my steps up the
Boulevard des Philosophes.

Through the open door of the drawing-room I
was annoyed to hear a visitor holding forth steadily
in an unctuous deep voice.

Mrs. Haldin's arm-chair by the window stood

empty. On the sofa, Nathalie Haldin raised her charming grey eyes in a glance of greeting accompanied by the merest hint of a welcoming smile. But she made no movement. With her strong white hands lying inverted in the lap of her mourning dress she faced a man who presented to me a robust back covered with black broadcloth, and well in keeping with the deep voice. He turned his head sharply over his shoulder, but only for a moment.

" Ah ! your English friend. I know. I know. That's nothing."

He wore spectacles with smoked glasses, a tall silk hat stood on the floor by the side of his chair. Flourishing slightly a big soft hand he went on with his discourse, precipitating his delivery a little more.

" I have never changed the faith I held while wandering in the forests and bogs of Siberia. It sustained me then—it sustains me now. The Great Powers of Europe are bound to disappear— and the cause of their collapse will be very simple. They will exhaust themselves struggling against their proletariat. In Russia it is different. In Russia we have no classes to combat each other, one holding the power of wealth, and the other mighty with the strength of numbers. We have only an unclean bureaucracy in the face of a people as great and as incorruptible as the ocean. No, we have no classes. But we have the Russian woman. The admirable Russian woman ! I receive most re-

markable letters signed by women. So elevated in
tone, so courageous, breathing such a noble ardour
of service ! The greatest part of our hopes rests
on women. I behold their thirst for knowledge.
It is admirable. Look how they absorb, how
they are making it their own. It is miraculous.
But what is knowledge ? . . . I understand that
you have not been studying anything especially—
medicine, for instance. No ? That's right. Had
I been honoured by being asked to advise you
on the use of your time when you arrived here, I
would have been strongly opposed to such a course.
Knowledge in itself is mere dross."

He had one of those bearded Russian faces without shape, a mere appearance of flesh and hair with
not a single feature having any sort of character.
His eyes being hidden by the dark glasses, there
was an utter absence of all expression. I knew him
by sight. He was a Russian refugee of mark. All
Geneva knew his burly, black-coated figure. At one
time all Europe was aware of the story of his life
written by himself and translated into seven or more
languages. In his youth he had led an idle, dis-
solute life. Then a society girl he was about to
marry died suddenly, and thereupon he abandoned
the world of fashion and began to conspire in
a spirit of repentance, and, after that, his native
autocracy took good care that the usual things should
happen to him. He was imprisoned in fortresses,
beaten within an inch of his life, and condemned

to work in mines with common criminals. The great success of his book, however, was the chain.

I do not remember now the details of the weight and length of the fetters riveted on his limbs by an " Administrative " order, but it was in the number of pounds and the thickness of links an appalling assertion of the divine right of autocracy. Appalling and futile too, because this big man managed to carry off that simple engine of government with him into the woods. The sensational clink of these fetters is heard all through the chapters describing his escape—a subject of wonder to two continents. He had begun by concealing himself successfully from his guard in a hole on a river bank. It was the end of the day ; with infinite labour he managed to free one of his legs. Meantime night fell. He was going to begin on his other leg when he was overtaken by a terrible misfortune. He dropped his file.

All this is precise yet symbolic ; and the file had its pathetic history. It was given to him unexpectedly one evening, by a quiet, pale-faced girl. The poor creature had come out to the mines to join one of his fellow-convicts, a delicate young man, a mechanic and a social democrat, with broad cheekbones and large staring eyes. She had worked her way across half Russia and nearly the whole of Siberia to be near him, and, as it seems, with the hope of helping him to escape. But she arrived too late. Her lover had died only a week before.

Through that obscure episode, as he says, in the history of ideas in Russia, the file came into his hands, and inspired him with an ardent resolution to regain his liberty. When it slipped through his fingers it was as if it had gone straight into the earth. He could by no manner of means put his hand on it again in the dark. He groped systematically in the loose earth, in the mud, in the water ; the night was passing meantime, the precious night on which he counted to get away into the forests, his only chance of escape. For a moment he was tempted by despair to give up ; but recalling the quiet, sad face of the heroic girl, he felt profoundly ashamed of his weakness. She had selected him for the gift of liberty and he must show himself worthy of the favour conferred by her feminine, indomitable soul. It appeared to be a sacred trust. To fail would have been a sort of treason against the sacredness of self-sacrifice and womanly love.

There are in his book whole pages of self-analysis whence emerges like a white figure from a dark confused sea the conviction of woman's spiritual superiority—his new faith confessed since in several volumes. His first tribute to it, the great act of his conversion, was his extraordinary existence in the endless forests of the Okhotsk Province, with the loose end of the chain wound about his waist. A strip torn off his convict shirt secured the end firmly. Other strips fastened it at intervals up his left leg to deaden the clanking

and to prevent the slack links from getting hooked
in the bushes. He became very fierce. He developed an unsuspected genius for the arts of a
wild and hunted existence. He learned to creep
into villages without betraying his presence by
anything more than an occasional faint jingle. He
broke into outhouses with an axe he managed to
purloin in a woodcutters' camp. In the deserted
tracts of country he lived on wild berries and
hunted for honey. His clothing dropped off him
gradually. His naked, tawny figure, glimpsed
vaguely through the bushes with a cloud of mosquitoes and flies hovering about the shaggy head,
spread tales of terror through whole districts. His
temper grew savage as the days went by, and he
was glad to discover that there was so much of a
brute in him. He had nothing else to put his trust
in. For it was as though there had been two
human beings indissolubly joined in that enterprise.
The civilised man, the enthusiast of advanced
humanitarian ideals thirsting for the triumph of
spiritual love and political liberty ; and the stealthy,
primeval savage, pitilessly cunning in the preservation of his freedom from day to day, like a tracked
wild beast.

The wild beast was making its way instinctively
eastward to the Pacific coast, and the civilised
humanitarian in fearful anxious dependence watched
the proceedings with awe. Through all these weeks
he could never make up his mind to appeal to

human compassion. In the wary primeval savage this shyness might have been natural, but the other too, the civilised creature, the thinker, the escaping " political," had developed an absurd form of morbid pessimism, a form of temporary insanity, originating perhaps in the physical worry and discomfort of the chain. These links, he fancied, made him odious to the rest of mankind. It was a repugnant and suggestive load. Nobody could feel any pity at the disgusting sight of a man escaping with a broken chain. His imagination became affected by his fetters in a precise, matter-of-fact manner. It seemed to him impossible that people could resist the temptation of fastening the loose end to a staple in the wall while they went for the nearest police official. Crouching in holes or hidden in thickets, he had tried to read the faces of unsuspecting free settlers working in the clearings or passing along the paths within a foot or two of his eyes. His feeling was that no man on earth could be trusted with the temptation of the chain.

One day, however, he chanced to come upon a solitary woman. It was on an open slope of rough grass outside the forest. She sat on the bank of a narrow stream ; she had a red handkerchief on her head and a small basket was lying on the ground near her hand. At a little distance could be seen a cluster of log cabins, with a water-mill over a dammed pool shaded by birch trees and looking

bright as glass in the twilight. He approached
her silently, his hatchet stuck in his iron belt, a
thick cudgel in his hand ; there were leaves and
bits of twig in his tangled hair, in his matted beard ;
bunches of rags he had wound round the links
fluttered from his waist. A faint clink of his fetters
made the woman turn her head. Too terrified by
this savage apparition to jump up or even to scream,
she was yet too stout-hearted to faint. . . . Expecting nothing less than to be murdered on the spot,
she covered her eyes with her hands to avoid the
sight of the descending axe. When at last she
found courage to look again, she saw the shaggy
wild man sitting on the bank six feet away from
her. His thin, sinewy arms hugged his naked legs ;
the long beard covered the knees on which he rested
his chin ; all these clasped, folded limbs, the bare
shoulders, the wild head with red staring eyes,
shook and trembled violently while the bestial
creature was making efforts to speak. It was six
weeks since he had heard the sound of his own
voice. It seemed as though he had lost the faculty
of speech. He had become a dumb and despairing
brute, till the woman's sudden, unexpected cry of
profound pity, the insight of her feminine compassion discovering the complex misery of the
man under the terrifying aspect of the monster,
restored him to the ranks of humanity. This
point of view is presented in his book with a very
effective eloquence. She ended, he says, by shed-

ding tears over him, sacred, redeeming tears, while
he also wept with joy in the manner of a converted
sinner. Directing him to hide in the bushes
and wait patiently (a police patrol was expected in
the Settlement) she went away towards the houses,
promising to return at night.

As if providentially appointed to be the newly
wedded wife of the village blacksmith, the woman
persuaded her husband to come out with her,
bringing some tools of his trade, a hammer, a
chisel, a small anvil. . . . " My fetters "—the book
says—" were struck off on the banks of the stream,
in the starlight of a calm night by an athletic,
taciturn young man of the people, kneeling at my
feet, while the woman like a liberating genius stood
by with clasped hands." Obviously a symbolic
couple. At the same time they furnished his
regained humanity with some decent clothing, and
put heart into the new man by the information that
the seacoast of the Pacific was only a very few miles
away. It could be seen, in fact, from the top of
the next ridge. . . .

The rest of his escape does not lend itself to
mystic treatment and symbolic interpretation. He
ended by finding his way to the West by the Suez
Canal route in the usual manner. Reaching the
shores of South Europe he sat down to write his
autobiography—the great literary success of its
year. This book was followed by other books
written with the declared purpose of elevating

humanity. In these works he preached generally
the cult of the woman. For his own part he
practised it under the rites of special devotion
to the transcendental merits of a certain Madame
de S——, a lady of advanced views, no longer
very young, once upon a time the intriguing wife
of a now dead and forgotten diplomat. Her loud
pretensions to be one of the leaders of modern
thought and of modern sentiment, she sheltered
(like Voltaire and Mme de Staël) on the republican
territory of Geneva. Driving through the streets
in her big landau she exhibited to the indifference
of the natives and the stares of the tourists a long-
waisted, youthful figure of hieratic stiffness, with
a pair of big gleaming eyes, rolling restlessly behind
a short veil of black lace, which, coming down no
farther than her vividly red lips, resembled a mask.
Usually the " heroic fugitive " (this name was
bestowed upon him in a review of the English
edition of his book)—the " heroic fugitive " accompanied her, sitting, portentously bearded and
darkly bespectacled, not by her side, but opposite
her, with his back to the horses. Thus, facing each
other, with no one else in the roomy carriage, their
airings suggested a conscious public manifestation.
Or it may have been unconscious. Russian simplicity often marches innocently on the edge of
cynicism for some lofty purpose. But it is a vain
enterprise for sophisticated Europe to try and
understand these doings. Considering the air of

gravity extending even to the physiognomy of the coachman and the action of the showy horses, this quaint display might have possessed a mystic significance, but to the corrupt frivolity of a Western mind, like my own, it seemed hardly decent.

However, it is not becoming for an obscure teacher of languages to criticise a " heroic fugitive " of world-wide celebrity. I was aware from hearsay that he was an industrious busybody, hunting up his compatriots in hotels, in private lodgings, and —I was told—conferring upon them the honour of his notice in public gardens when a suitable opening presented itself. I was under the impression that after a visit or two, several months before, he had given up the ladies Haldin—no doubt reluctantly, for there could be no question of his being a determined person. It was perhaps to be expected that he should reappear again on this terrible occasion, as a Russian and a revolutionist, to say the right thing, to strike the true, perhaps a comforting, note. But I did not like to see him sitting there. I trust that an unbecoming jealousy of my privileged position had nothing to do with it. I made no claim to a special standing for my silent friendship. Removed by the difference of age and nationality as if into the sphere of another existence, I produced, even upon myself, the effect of a dumb, helpless ghost, of an anxious immaterial thing that could only hover about without the power to protect or guide by as much as a whisper. Since Miss Haldin with her sure instinct had refrained from introducing me to the burly celebrity, I would have retired quietly and returned later on, had I not met a peculiar expression in her eyes which I interpreted as a request to stay, with the view, perhaps, of shortening an unwelcome visit.

He picked up his hat, but only to deposit it on his knees.

" We shall meet again, Natalia Victorovna. To-day I have called only to mark those feelings towards your honoured mother and yourself, the nature of which you cannot doubt. I needed no urging, but Eleanor—Madame de S—— herself has in a way sent me. She extends to you the hand of feminine fellowship. There is positively in all the range of human sentiments no joy and no sorrow that woman cannot understand, elevate, and spiritualise by her interpretation. That young man newly arrived from St. Petersburg, I have mentioned to you, is already under the charm."

At this point Miss Haldin got up abruptly. I was glad. He did not evidently expect anything so decisive, and, at first, throwing his head back, he tilted up his dark glasses with bland curiosity. At last, recollecting himself, he stood up hastily, seizing his hat off his knees with great adroitness.

" How is it, Natalia Victorovna, that you have kept aloof so long, from what after all is—let disparaging tongues say what they like—a unique centre of intellectual freedom and of effort to shape

a high conception of our future ? In the case of
your honoured mother I understand in a measure.
At her age new ideas—new faces—are not perhaps . . .
But you ! Was it mistrust—or indifference ? You
must come out of your reserve. We Russians
have no right to be reserved with each other. In
our circumstances it is almost a crime against
humanity. The luxury of private grief is not for
us. Nowadays the devil is not combated by prayers
and fasting. And what is fasting, after all, but
starvation ? You must not starve yourself, Natalia
Victorovna. Strength is what we want—spiritual
strength, I mean. As to the other kind, what could
withstand us Russians if we only put it forth ?
Sin is different in our day, and the way of salvation
for pure souls is different too. It is no longer to be
found in monasteries, but in the world, in the . . ."

The deep sound seemed to rise from under the
floor, and one felt steeped in it to the lips. Miss
Haldin's interruption resembled the effort of a
drowning person to keep above water. She struck
in with an accent of impatience :

" But, Peter Ivanovitch, I don't mean to retire
into a monastery. Who would look for salvation
there ? "

" I spoke figuratively," he boomed.

" Well, then, I am speaking figuratively too.
But sorrow is sorrow and pain is pain in the old way.
They make their demands upon people. One has
got to face them the best way one can. I know that

the blow which has fallen upon us so unexpectedly is only an episode in the fate of a people. You may rest assured that I don't forget that. But just now I have to think of my mother. How can you expect me to leave her to herself ? . . . "

" That is putting it in a very crude way," he protested in his great, effortless voice.

Miss Haldin did not wait for the vibration to die out.

" And run about visiting amongst a lot of strange people ? The idea is distasteful for me ; and I do not know what else you may mean."

He towered before her, enormous, deferential, cropped as close as a convict ; and this big pinkish poll evoked for me the vision of a wild head with matted locks peering through parted bushes, glimpses of naked, tawny limbs slinking behind the masses of sodden foliage under a cloud of flies and mosquitoes. It was an involuntary tribute to the vigour of his writing. Nobody could doubt that he had wandered in Siberian forests, naked and girt with a chain. The black broadcloth coat invested his person with a character of austere decency —something recalling a missionary.

" Do you know what I want, Natalia Victorovna?" he uttered solemnly. " I want you to be a fanatic."

" A fanatic ? "

" Yes. Faith alone won't do."

His voice dropped to a still lower tone. He raised for a moment one thick arm ; the other remained hanging down against his thigh, with the fragile silk hat at the end.

" I shall tell you now something which I entreat you to ponder over carefully. Listen, we need a force that would move heaven and earth—nothing less."

The profound, subterranean note of this " nothing less " made one shudder, almost, like the deep muttering of wind in the pipes of an organ.

" And are we to find that force in the salon of Madame de S—— ? Excuse me, Peter Ivanovitch, if I permit myself to doubt it. Is not that lady a woman of the great world, an aristocrat ? "

" Prejudice ! " he cried. " You astonish me. And suppose she was all that ! She is also a woman of flesh and blood. There is always something to weigh down the spiritual side in all of us. But to make of it a reproach is what I did not expect from you. No ! I did not expect that. One would think you have listened to some malevolent scandal."

" I have heard no gossip, I assure you. In our province how could we ? But the world speaks of her. What can there be in common in a lady of that sort and an obscure country girl like me ? "

" She is a perpetual manifestation of a noble and peerless spirit," he broke in. " Her charm—no, I shall not speak of her charm. But, of course, everybody who approaches her falls under the spell. . . . Contradictions vanish, trouble falls away from one. . . . Unless I am mistaken—but I never make

II

a mistake in spiritual matters—you are troubled in your soul, Natalia Victorovna."

Miss Haldin's clear eyes looked straight at his soft, enormous face ; I received the impression that behind these dark spectacles of his he could be as impudent as he chose.

" Only the other evening walking back to town from Château Borel with our latest interesting arrival from Petersburg, I could notice the powerful soothing influence—I may say reconciling influence. . . . There he was, all these kilometres along the shores of the lake, silent, like a man who has been shown the way of peace. I could feel the leaven working in his soul, you understand. For one thing, he listened to me patiently. I myself was inspired that evening by the firm and exquisite genius of Eleanor—Madame de S——, you know. It was a full moon and I could observe his face. I cannot be deceived. . . ."

Miss Haldin, looking down, seemed to hesitate.

" Well ! I will think of what you said, Peter Ivanovitch. I shall try to call as soon as I can leave mother for an hour or two safely."

Coldly as these words were said I was amazed at the concession. He snatched her right hand with such fervour that I thought he was going to press it to his lips or his breast. But he only held it by the finger-tips in his great paw and shook it a little up and down while he delivered his last volley of words.

" That's right. That's right. I haven't obtained your full confidence as yet, Natalia Victorovna, but that will come. All in good time. The
sister of Victor Haldin cannot be without importance. . . . It's simply impossible. And no woman
can remain sitting on the steps. Flowers, tears,
applause—that has had its time ; it's a mediæval
conception. The arena, the arena itself is the place
for women ! "

He relinquished her hand with a flourish, as if
giving it to her for a gift, and remained still, his head
bowed in dignified submission before her femininity.

" The arena ! . . . You must descend into the
arena, Natalia."

He made one step backwards, inclined his
enormous body, and was gone swiftly. The door
fell to behind him. But immediately the powerful
resonance of his voice was heard addressing in
the anteroom the middle-aged servant-woman who
was letting him out. Whether he exhorted her too
to descend into the arena I cannot tell. The thing
sounded like a lecture, and the slight crash of the
outer door cut it short suddenly.

III

We remained looking at each other for a time.
" Do you know who he is ? "

Miss Haldin, coming forward, put this question
to me in English.

I took her offered hand.

"Everybody knows. He is a revolutionary feminist, a great writer, if you like, and—how shall I say it?—the—the familiar guest of Madame de S——'s mystic revolutionary salon."

Miss Haldin passed her hand over her forehead.

"You know, he was with me for more than an hour before you came in. I was so glad mother was lying down. She has many nights without sleep, and then sometimes in the middle of the day she gets a rest of several hours. It is sheer exhaustion— but still, I am thankful. . . . If it were not for these intervals . . ."

She looked at me and, with that extraordinary penetration which used to disconcert me, shook her head.

"No. She would not go mad."

"My dear young lady," I cried, by way of protest, the more shocked because in my heart I was far from thinking Mrs. Haldin quite sane.

"You don't know what a fine, lucid intellect mother had," continued Nathalie Haldin, with her calm, clear-eyed simplicity, which seemed to me always to have a quality of heroism.

"I am sure . . ." I murmured.

"I darkened mother's room and came out here. I've wanted for so long to think quietly."

She paused, then, without giving any sign of distress, added, "It's so difficult," and looked at me with a strange fixity, as if watching for a sign of dissent or surprise.

I gave neither. I was irresistibly impelled to say :

" The visit from that gentleman has not made it any easier, I fear."

Miss Haldin stood before me with a peculiar expression in her eyes.

" I don't pretend to understand Peter Ivanovitch completely. Some guide one must have, even if one does not wholly give up the direction of one's conduct to him. I am an inexperienced girl, but I am not slavish. There has been too much of that in Russia. Why should I not listen to him ? There is no harm in having one's thoughts directed. But I don't mind confessing to you that I have not been completely candid with Peter Ivanovitch. I don't quite know what prevented me at the moment . . ."

She walked away suddenly from me to a distant part of the room ; but it was only to open and shut a drawer in a bureau. She returned with a piece of paper in her hand. It was thin and blackened with close handwriting. It was obviously a letter.

" I wanted to read you the very words," she said. " This is one of my poor brother's letters. He never doubted. How could he doubt ? They make only such a small handful, these miserable oppressors, before the unanimous will of our people."

" Your brother believed in the power of a people's will to achieve anything ? "

" It was his religion," declared Miss Haldin.

I looked at her calm face and her animated eyes.

" Of course the will must be awakened, inspired, concentrated," she went on. " That is the true task of real agitators. One has got to give up one's life to it. The degradation of servitude, the absolutist lies must be uprooted and swept out. Reform is impossible. There is nothing to reform. There is no legality, there are no institutions. There are only arbitrary decrees. There is only a handful of cruel—perhaps blind—officials against a nation."

The letter rustled slightly in her hand. I glanced down at the flimsy blackened pages whose very handwriting seemed cabalistic, incomprehensible to the experience of Western Europe.

" Stated like this," I confessed, " the problem seems simple enough. But I fear I shall not see it solved. And if you go back to Russia I know that I shall not see you again. Yet once more I say : go back ! Don't suppose that I am thinking of your preservation. No ! I know that you will not be returning to personal safety. But I had much rather think of you in danger there than see you exposed to what may be met here."

" I tell you what," said Miss Haldin, after a moment of reflection. " I believe that you hate revolution ; you fancy it's not quite honest. You belong to a people which has made a bargain with

Fate and wouldn't like to be rude to it. But we have made no bargain. It was never offered to us —so much liberty for so much hard cash. You shrink from the idea of revolutionary action for those you think well of as if it were something— how shall I say it ?—not quite decent."

I bowed my head.

" You are quite right," I said. " I think very highly of you."

" Don't suppose I do not know it," she began hurriedly. " Your friendship has been very valuable."

" I have done little else but look on."

She was a little flushed under the eyes.

" There is a way of looking on which is valuable. I have felt less lonely because of it. It's difficult to explain."

" Really ? Well, I too have felt less lonely. That's easy to explain, though. But it won't go on much longer. The last thing I want to tell you is this : in a real revolution—not a simple dynastic change or a mere reform of institutions—in a real revolution the best characters do not come to the front. A violent revolution falls into the hands of narrow-minded fanatics and of tyrannical hypo-crites at first. Afterwards comes the turn of all the pretentious intellectual failures of the time. Such are the chiefs and the leaders. You will notice that I have left out the mere rogues. The scrupulous and the just, the noble, humane, and

devoted natures ; the unselfish and the intelligent
may begin a movement—but it passes away from
them. They are not the leaders of a revolution.
They are its victims : the victims of disgust, of
disenchantment—often of remorse. Hopes grotesquely betrayed, ideals caricatured—that is the
definition of revolutionary success. There have
been in every revolution hearts broken by such
successes. But enough of that. My meaning is
that I don't want you to be a victim."

"If I could believe all you have said I still
wouldn't think of myself," protested Miss Haldin.
"I would take liberty from any hand as a hungry
man would snatch at a piece of bread. The true
progress must begin after. And for that the right
men shall be found. They are already amongst
us. One comes upon them in their obscurity,
unknown, preparing themselves. . . ."

She spread out the letter she had kept in her
hand all the time, and looking down at it :

"Yes ! One comes upon such men !" she
repeated, and then read out the words, "Unstained,
lofty, and solitary existences."

Folding up the letter, while I looked at her
interrogatively, she explained :

"These are the words which my brother applies
to a young man he came to know in St. Petersburg.
An intimate friend, I suppose. It must be. His
is the only name my brother mentions in all his
correspondence with me. Absolutely the only one,

and—would you believe it ?—the man is here. He arrived recently in Geneva."

" Have you seen him ? " I inquired. " But, of course, you must have seen him."

" No ! No ! I haven't ! I didn't know he was here. It's Peter Ivanovitch himself who told me. You have heard him yourself mentioning a new arrival from Petersburg. . . . Well, that is the man of ' unstained, lofty, and solitary existence.' My brother's friend ! "

" Compromised politically, I suppose," I remarked.

" I don't know. Yes. It must be so. Who knows ! Perhaps it was this very friendship with my brother which . . . But no ! It is scarcely possible. Really, I know nothing except what Peter Ivanovitch told me of him. He has brought a letter of introduction from Father Zosim—you know, the priest-democrat ; you have heard of Father Zosim ? "

" Oh yes. The famous Father Zosim was staying here in Geneva for some two months about a year ago," I said. " When he left here he seems to have disappeared from the world."

" It appears that he is at work in Russia again. Somewhere in the centre," Miss Haldin said, with animation. " But please don't mention that to any one—don't let it slip from you, because if it got into the papers it would be dangerous for him."

" You are anxious, of course, to meet that friend of your brother ? " I asked.

Miss Haldin put the letter into her pocket. Her eyes looked beyond my shoulder at the door of her mother's room.

" Not here," she murmured. " Not for the first time, at least."

After a moment of silence I said good-bye, but Miss Haldin followed me into the anteroom, closing the door behind us carefully.

" I suppose you guess where I mean to go to-morrow ? "

" You have made up your mind to call on Madame de S——."

" Yes. I am going to the Château Borel. I must."

" What do you expect to hear there ? " I asked, in a low voice.

I wondered if she were not deluding herself with some impossible hope. It was not that, however.

" Only think—such a friend. The only man mentioned in his letters. He would have something to give me, if nothing more than a few poor words. It may be something said and thought in those last days. Would you want me to turn my back on what is left of my poor brother—a friend ? "

" Certainly not," I said. " I quite understand your pious curiosity."

" ' Unstained, lofty, and solitary existences,' " she murmured to herself. " There are ! There are! Well, let me question one of them about the loved dead."

"How do you know, though, that you will meet him there? Is he staying in the château as a guest—do you suppose?"

"I can't really tell," she confessed. "He brought a written introduction from Father Zosim—who, it seems, is a friend of Madame de S—— too. She can't be such a worthless woman after all."

"There were all sorts of rumours afloat about Father Zosim himself," I observed.

She shrugged her shoulders.

"Calumny is a weapon of our government too. It's well known. Oh yes! It is a fact that Father Zosim had the protection of the Governor-General of a certain province. We talked on the subject with my brother two years ago, I remember. But his work was good. And now he is proscribed. What better proof can one require? But no matter what that priest was or is. All that cannot affect my brother's friend. If I don't meet him there I shall ask these people for his address. And, of course, mother must see him too, later on. There is no guessing what he may have to tell us. It would be a mercy if mamma could be soothed. You know what she imagines. Some explanation perhaps may be found, or—or even made up, perhaps. It would be no sin."

"Certainly," I said, "it would be no sin. It may be a mistake, though."

" I want her only to recover some of her old spirit. While she is like this I cannot think of anything calmly."

" Do you mean to invent some sort of pious fraud for your mother's sake ? " I asked.

" Why fraud ? Such a friend is sure to know something of my brother in these last days. He could tell us. . . . There is something in the facts which will not let me rest. I am certain he meant to join us abroad—that he had some plans—some great patriotic action in view ; not only for himself, but for both of us. I trusted in that. I looked forward to the time, oh ! with such hope and impatience. . . . I could have helped. And now suddenly this appearance of recklessness—as if he had not cared. . . ."

She remained silent for a time, then obstinately she concluded :

" I want to know . . ."

Thinking it over, later on, while I walked slowly away from the Boulevard des Philosophes, I asked myself critically, what precisely was it that she wanted to know ? What I had heard of her history was enough to give me a clue. In the educational establishment for girls where Miss Haldin finished her studies she was looked upon rather unfavourably. She was suspected of holding independent views on matters settled by official teaching. Afterwards, when the two ladies returned to their country place, both mother and daughter, by speaking their minds openly on public events, had earned for themselves a reputation of liberalism. The three-horse trap of the district police captain began to be seen frequently in their village. " I must keep an eye on the peasants "—so he explained his visits up at the house. " Two lonely ladies must be looked after a little." He would inspect the walls as though he wanted to pierce them with his eyes, peer at the photographs, turn over the books in the drawing-room negligently, and after the usual re-freshments, would depart. But the old priest of the village came one evening in the greatest distress and agitation, to confess that he—the priest—had been ordered to watch and ascertain in other ways too (such as using his spiritual power with the ser-vants) all that was going on in the house, and especially in respect of the visitors these ladies received, who they were, the length of their stay, whether any of them were strangers to that part of the country, and so on. The poor, simple old man was in an agony of humiliation and terror. " I came to warn you. Be cautious in your conduct, for the love of God. I am burning with shame, but there is no getting out from under the net. I shall have to tell them what I see, because if I did not there is my deacon. He would make the worst of things to curry favour. And then my son-in-law, the husband of my Parasha, who is a writer in the Government Domain office ; they would soon kick him out—and maybe send him away somewhere."

The old man lamented the necessities of the times—
" when people do not agree somehow," and wiped
his eyes. He did not wish to spend the evening
of his days with a shaven head in the penitent's
cell of some monastery—" and subjected to all
the severities of ecclesiastical discipline ; for they
would show no mercy to an old man," he groaned.
He became almost hysterical, and the two ladies,
full of commiseration, soothed him the best they
could before they let him go back to his cottage.
But, as a matter of fact, they had very few visitors.
The neighbours—some of them old friends—began
to keep away ; a few from timidity, others with
marked disdain, being grand people that came only
for the summer—Miss Haldin explained to me—
aristocrats, reactionaries. It was a solitary existence
for a young girl. Her relations with her mother
were of the tenderest and most open kind ; but Mrs.
Haldin had seen the experiences of her own generation, its sufferings, its deceptions, its apostasies too.
Her affection for her children was expressed by the
suppression of all signs of anxiety. She maintained
a heroic reserve. To Nathalie Haldin, her brother
with his Petersburg existence, not enigmatical in the
least (there could be no doubt of what he felt or
thought) but conducted a little mysteriously, was
the only visible representative of a proscribed liberty.
All the significance of freedom, its indefinite pro-
mises, lived in their long discussions, which breathed
the loftiest hope of action and faith in success.

Then, suddenly, the action, the hopes, came to an end with the details ferreted out by the English journalist. The concrete fact, the fact of his death, remained ; but it remained obscure in its deeper causes. She felt herself abandoned without explanation. But she did not suspect him. What she wanted was to learn almost at any cost how she could remain faithful to his departed spirit.

IV

Several days elapsed before I met Nathalie Haldin again. I was crossing the place in front of the theatre when I made out her shapely figure in the very act of turning between the gate pillars of the unattractive public promenade of the Bastions. She walked away from me, but I knew we should meet as she returned down the main alley—unless, indeed, she were going home. In that case, I don't think I should have called on her yet. My desire to keep her away from these people was as strong as ever, but I had no illusions as to my power. I was but a Westerner, and it was clear that Miss Haldin would not, could not, listen to my wisdom ; and as to my desire of listening to her voice, it were better, I thought, not to indulge overmuch in that pleasure. No, I should not have gone to the Boulevard des Philosophes ; but when at about the middle of the principal alley I saw Miss Haldin coming towards me, I was too curious, and too honest, perhaps, to run away.

There was something of the spring harshness in the air. The blue sky was hard, but the young leaves clung like soft mist about the uninteresting range of trees ; and the clear sun put little points of gold into the grey of Miss Haldin's frank eyes, turned to me with a friendly greeting.

I inquired after the health of her mother.

She had a slight movement of the shoulders and a little sad sigh.

" But, you see, I did come out for a walk . . . for exercise, as you English say."

I smiled approvingly, and she added an unexpected remark :

" It is a glorious day."

Her voice, slightly harsh, but fascinating with its masculine and bird-like quality, had the accent of spontaneous conviction. I was glad of it. It was as though she had become aware of her youth— for there was but little of spring-like glory in the rectangular railed space of grass and trees, framed visibly by the orderly roof-slopes of that town, comely without grace, and hospitable without sympathy. In the very air through which she moved there was but little warmth ; and the sky, the sky of a land without horizons, swept and washed clean by the April showers, extended a cold, cruel blue, without elevation, narrowed suddenly by the ugly, dark wall of the Jura, where, here and there, lingered yet a few miserable trails and patches of snow. All the glory of the season must have been within herself—and I was glad this feeling had come into her life, if only for a little time.

" I am pleased to hear you say these words."

She gave me a quick look—quick, not stealthy. If there was one thing of which she was absolutely incapable, it was stealthiness. Her sincerity was expressed in the very rhythm of her walk. It was I who was looking at her covertly—if I may say so. I knew where she had been, but I did not know what she had seen and heard in that nest of aristocratic conspiracies. I use the word aristocratic for want of a better term. The Château Borel, embowered in the trees and thickets of its neglected grounds, had its fame in our day, like the residence of that other dangerous and exiled woman, Madame de Staël, in the Napoleonic era. Only the Napoleonic despotism, the booted heir of the Revolution, which counted that intellectual woman for an enemy worthy to be watched, was something quite unlike the autocracy in mystic vestments, engendered by the slavery of a Tartar conquest. And Madame de S—— was very far from resembling the gifted author of *Corinne*. She made a great noise about being persecuted. I don't know if she were regarded in certain circles as dangerous. As to being watched, I imagine that the Château Borel could be subjected only to a most distant observation. It was in its exclusiveness an ideal abode for hatching superior

12

plots—whether serious or futile. But all this did not interest me. I wanted to know the effect its extraordinary inhabitants and its special atmosphere had produced on a girl like Miss Haldin, so true, so honest, but so dangerously inexperienced! Her unconsciously lofty ignorance of the baser instincts of mankind left her disarmed before her own impulses. And there was also that friend of her brother, the significant new arrival from Russia. . . . I wondered whether she had managed to meet him.

We walked for some time, slowly and in silence.

"You know," I attacked her suddenly, "if you don't intend to tell me anything, you must say so distinctly, and then, of course, it shall be final. But I won't play at delicacy. I ask you point-blank for all the details."

She smiled faintly at my threatening tone.

"You are as curious as a child."

"No. I am only an anxious old man," I replied earnestly.

She rested her glance on me as if to ascertain the degree of my anxiety or the number of my years. My physiognomy has never been expressive, I believe, and as to my years I am not ancient enough as yet to be strikingly decrepit. I have no long beard like the good hermit of a romantic ballad ; my footsteps are not tottering, my aspect not that of a slow, venerable sage. Those picturesque advantages are not mine. I am old, alas ! in a brisk, commonplace way. And it seemed to me as though there were some pity for me in Miss Haldin's prolonged glance. She stepped out a little quicker.

"You ask for all the details. Let me see. I ought to remember them. It was novel enough for a—a village girl like me."

After a moment of silence she began by saying that the Château Borel was almost as neglected inside as outside. It was nothing to wonder at. A Hamburg banker, I believe, retired from business, had it built to cheer his remaining days by the view of that lake whose precise, orderly, and well-to-do beauty must have been attractive to the unromantic imagination of a business man. But he died soon. His wife departed too (but only to Italy), and this house of moneyed ease, presumably unsaleable, had stood empty for several years. One went to it up a gravel drive, round a large, coarse grass-plot, with plenty of time to observe the degradation of its stuccoed front. Miss Haldin said that the impression was unpleasant. It grew more depressing as one came nearer.

She observed green stains of moss on the steps of the terrace. The front door stood wide open. There was no one about. She found herself in a wide, lofty, and absolutely empty hall, with a good many doors. These doors were all shut. A broad, bare stone staircase faced her, and the effect of the whole was of an untenanted house. She stood still, disconcerted by the solitude, but after a while she became aware of a voice speaking continuously somewhere.

" You were probably being observed all the time," I suggested. " There must have been eyes."

" I don't see how that could be," she retorted. " I haven't seen even a bird in the grounds. I don't remember hearing a single twitter in the trees. The whole place appeared utterly deserted except for the voice."

She could not make out the language—Russian, French, or German. No one seemed to answer it. It was as though the voice had been left behind by the departed inhabitants to talk to the bare walls. It went on volubly, with a pause now and then. It was lonely and sad. The time seemed very long to Miss Haldin. An invincible repugnance prevented her from opening one of the doors in the hall. It was so hopeless. No one would come, the voice would never stop. She confessed to me that she had to resist an impulse to turn round and go away unseen, as she had come.

" Really ? You had that impulse ? " I cried, full of regret. " What a pity you did not obey it."

She shook her head.

" What a strange memory it would have been for one. Those deserted grounds, that empty hall, that impersonal, voluble voice, and—nobody, nothing, not a soul."

The memory would have been unique and

harmless. But she was not a girl to run away from
an intimidating impression of solitude and mystery.
" No, I did not run away," she said. " I stayed
where I was—and I did see a soul. Such a strange
soul."

As she was gazing up the broad staircase, and
had concluded that the voice came from somewhere
above, a rustle of a dress attracted her attention. She
looked down and saw a woman crossing the hall,
having issued apparently through one of the many
doors. Her face was averted, so that at first she
was not aware of Miss Haldin.

On turning her head and seeing a stranger, she
appeared very much startled. From her slender
figure Miss Haldin had taken her for a young girl ;
but if her face was almost childishly round, it was
also sallow and wrinkled, with dark rings under the
eyes. A thick crop of dusty brown hair was parted
boyishly on the side with a lateral wave above the
dry, furrowed forehead. After a moment of dumb
blinking, she suddenly squatted down on the floor.

" What do you mean by squatted down ? " I
asked, astonished. " This is a very strange detail."

Miss Haldin explained the reason. This person
when first seen was carrying a small bowl in her
hand. She had squatted down to put it on the
floor for the benefit of a large cat, which appeared
then from behind her skirts, and hid its head into
the bowl greedily. She got up, and approaching
Miss Haldin asked with nervous bluntness :

" What do you want ?   Who are you ? "

Miss Haldin mentioned her name and also the name of Peter Ivanovitch. The girlish, elderly woman nodded and puckered her face into a momentary expression of sympathy. Her black silk blouse was old and even frayed in places ; the black serge skirt was short and shabby. She continued to blink at close quarters, and her eye-lashes and eyebrows seemed shabby too. Miss Haldin, speaking gently to her, as if to an unhappy and sensitive person, explained how it was that her visit could not be an altogether unexpected event to Madame de S——.

" Ah ! Peter Ivanovitch brought you an in-vitation. How was I to know ? A *dame de com-pagnie* is not consulted, as you may imagine."

The shabby woman laughed a little. Her teeth, splendidly white and admirably even, looked ab-surdly out of place, like a string of pearls on the neck of a ragged tramp. " Peter Ivanovitch is the greatest genius of the century perhaps, but he is the most inconsiderate man living. So if you have an appointment with him you must not be surprised to hear that he is not here."

Miss Haldin explained that she had no appoint-ment with Peter Ivanovitch. She became inter-ested at once in that bizarre person.

" Why should he put himself out for you or any one else ? Oh, these geniuses ! If you only knew ! Yes ! And their books—I mean, of course, the

books that the world admires, the inspired books.
But you have not been behind the scenes. Wait
till you have to sit at a table for half a day
with a pen in your hand. He can walk up and
down his rooms for hours and hours. I used to
get so stiff and numb that I was afraid I would
lose my balance and fall off the chair all at
once."

She kept her hands folded in front of her, and
her eyes, fixed on Miss Haldin's face, betrayed no
animation whatever. Miss Haldin, gathering that
the lady who called herself a *dame de compagnie*
was proud of having acted as secretary to Peter
Ivanovitch, made an amiable remark.

" You could not imagine a more trying experience," ·declared the lady. " There is an Anglo-
American journalist interviewing Madame de S——
now, or I would take you up," she continued in a
changed tone and glancing towards the staircase.
" I act as master of ceremonies."

It appeared that Madame de S—— could not
bear Swiss servants about her person ; and, indeed,
servants would not stay for very long in the Château Borel. There were always difficulties. Miss
Haldin had already noticed that the hall was like a
dusty barn of marble and stucco with cobwebs in
the corners and faint tracks of mud on the black
and white tessellated floor.

" I look also after this animal," continued the
dame de compagnie, keeping her hands folded quietly

in front of her ; and she bent her worn gaze upon the cat. " I don't mind a bit. Animals have their rights ; though, strictly speaking, I see no reason why they should not suffer as well as human beings. Do you ? But of course they never suffer so much. That is impossible. Only, in their case it is more pitiful because they cannot make a revolution. I used to be a Republican. I suppose you are a Republican ? "

Miss Haldin confessed to me that she did not know what to say. But she nodded slightly, and asked in her turn :

" And are you no longer a Republican ? "

" After taking down Peter Ivanovitch from dictation for two years, it is difficult for me to be anything. First of all, you have to sit perfectly motionless. The slightest movement you make puts to flight the ideas of Peter Ivanovitch. You hardly dare to breathe. And as to coughing— God forbid ! Peter Ivanovitch changed the position of the table to the wall because at first I could not help raising my eyes to look out of the window, while waiting for him to go on with his dictation. That was not allowed. He said I stared so stupidly. I was likewise not permitted to look at him over my shoulder. Instantly Peter Ivanovitch stamped his foot, and would roar, ' Look down on the paper ! ' It seems my expression, my face, put him off. Well, I know that I am not beautiful, and that my expression is not hopeful either. He said that my air of unintelligent expectation irritated him. These are his own words."

Miss Haldin was shocked, but admitted to me that she was not altogether surprised.

" Is it possible that Peter Ivanovitch could treat any woman so rudely ? " she cried.

The *dame de compagnie* nodded several times with an air of discretion, then assured Miss Haldin that she did not mind in the least. The trying part of it was to have the secret of the composition laid bare before her ; to see the great author of the revolutionary gospels grope for words as if he were in the dark as to what he meant to say.

" I am quite willing to be the blind instrument of higher ends. To give one's life for the cause is nothing. But to have one's illusions destroyed— that is really almost more than one can bear. I really don't exaggerate," she insisted. " It seemed to freeze my very beliefs in me—the more so that when we worked in winter Peter Ivanovitch, walking up and down the room, required no artificial heat to keep himself warm. Even when we move to the South of France there are bitterly cold days, especially when you have to sit still for six hours at a stretch. The walls of these villas on the Riviera are so flimsy. Peter Ivanovitch did not seem to be aware of anything. It is true that I kept down my shivers from fear of putting him out. I used to set my teeth till my jaws felt absolutely locked. In the moments when Peter Ivanovitch interrupted his dictation, and sometimes these intervals were very long—often twenty minutes, no less, while he walked to and fro behind my back muttering to himself—I felt I was dying by inches, I assure you. Perhaps if I had let my teeth rattle Peter Ivanovitch might have noticed my distress, but I don't think it would have had any practical effect. He's very miserly in such matters."

The *dame de compagnie* glanced up the staircase. The big cat had finished the milk and was rubbing its whiskered cheek sinuously against her skirt. She dived to snatch it up from the floor.

" Miserliness is rather a quality than otherwise, you know," she continued, holding the cat in her folded arms. " With us it is misers who can spare money for worthy objects—not the so-called generous natures. But pray don't think I am a sybarite. My father was a clerk in the Ministry of Finances with no position at all. You may guess by this that our home was far from luxurious, though, of course, we did not actually suffer from cold. I ran away from my parents, you know, directly I began to think by myself. It is not very easy, such thinking. One has got to be put in the way of it—awakened to the truth. I am indebted for my salvation to an old apple-woman, who had her stall under the gateway of the house we lived in. She had a kind, wrinkled face, and the most friendly voice imaginable. One day, casually, we began to talk about a child, a ragged little girl we had seen begging from men in the streets at dusk ; and from one thing to another my eyes began to open gradually to the horrors from which innocent people are made to suffer in this world, only in order that Governments might exist. After I once understood the crime of the upper classes, I could not go on living with my parents. Not a single charitable word was to be heard in our home from year's end to year's end ; there was nothing but the talk of vile office intrigues, and of promotion and of salaries, and of courting the favour of the chiefs. The mere idea of marrying one day such another man as my father made me shudder. I don't mean that there was any one wanting to marry me. There was not the slightest prospect of anything of the kind. But was it not sin enough to live on a Government salary while half Russia was dying of hunger ? The Ministry of Finances ! What a grotesque horror it is ! What does the starving, ignorant people want with a Ministry of Finances ? I kissed my old folks on both cheeks, and went away from them to live in cellars with the proletariat. I tried to make myself useful to the utterly hopeless. I suppose you understand what I mean ? I mean the people who have no-where to go and nothing to look forward to in this life. Do you understand how frightful that is— nothing to look forward to ! Sometimes I think that it is only in Russia that there are such people and such a depth of misery can be reached. Well, I plunged into it, and—do you know ?—there isn't much that one can do in there. No, indeed—at least as long as there are Ministries of Finances and such-like grotesque horrors to stand in the way. I suppose I would have gone mad there just trying to fight the vermin, if it had not been for a man. It was my old friend and teacher, the poor saintly apple-woman, who discovered him for me, quite accidentally. She came to fetch me late one evening in her quiet way. I followed her where she would lead ; that part of my life was in her hands altogether, and without her my spirit would have perished miserably. The man was a young workman, a lithographer by trade, and he had got into trouble in connection with that affair of temperance tracts—you remember. There was a lot of people put in prison for that. The Ministry of Finances again ! What would become of it if the poor folk ceased making beasts of themselves with drink ? Upon my word, I would think that finances and all the rest of it are an invention of the devil—only that a belief in a supernatural source of evil is not necessary ; men alone are quite capable of every wickedness. Finances indeed ! "

Hatred and contempt hissed in her utterance of the word " finances," but at the very moment she gently stroked the cat reposing in her arms. She even raised them slightly, and inclining her head rubbed her cheek against the fur of the animal, which received this caress with the complete detachment so characteristic of its kind. Then looking

at Miss Haldin she excused herself once more for
not taking her upstairs to Madame S——. The
interview could not be interrupted. Presently the
journalist would be seen coming down the stairs.
The best thing was to remain in the hall ; and
besides, all these rooms (she glanced all round at
the many doors), all these rooms on the ground
floor were unfurnished.

" Positively there is no chair down here to offer
you," she continued. " But if you prefer your own
thoughts to my chatter, I will sit down on the
bottom step here and keep silent."

Miss Haldin hastened to assure her that, on the
contrary, she was very much interested in the story
of the journeyman lithographer. He was a revolutionist, of course.

" A martyr, a simple man," said the *dame de
compagnie*, with a faint sigh, and gazing through the
open front door dreamily. She turned her misty
brown eyes on Miss Haldin.

" I lived with him for four months. It was like
a nightmare."

As Miss Haldin looked at her inquisitively she
began to describe the emaciated face of the man,
his fleshless limbs, his destitution. The room into
which the apple-woman had led her was a tiny
garret, a miserable den under the roof of a sordid
house. The plaster fallen off the walls covered the
floor, and when the door was opened a horrible
tapestry of black cobwebs waved in the draught.

He had been liberated a few days before—flung out of prison into the streets. And Miss Haldin seemed to see for the first time a name and a face upon the body of that suffering people whose hard fate had been the subject of so many conversations, between her and her brother, in the garden of their country house.

He had been arrested with scores and scores of other people in that affair of the lithographed temperance tracts. Unluckily, having got hold of a great many suspected persons, the police thought they could extract from some of them other information relating to the revolutionist propaganda.

"They beat him so cruelly in the course of investigation," went on the *dame de compagnie*, "that they injured him internally. When they had done with him he was doomed. He could do nothing for himself. I beheld him lying on a wooden bedstead without any bedding, with his head on a bundle of dirty rags, lent to him out of charity by an old ragpicker who happened to live in the basement of the house. There he was, uncovered, burning with fever, and there was not even a jug in the room for the water to quench his thirst with. There was nothing whatever—just that bedstead and the bare floor."

"Was there no one in all that great town amongst the liberals and revolutionaries to extend a helping hand to a brother?" asked Miss Haldin indignantly.

"Yes. But you do not know the most terrible

part of that man's misery. Listen. It seems that
they ill-used him so atrociously that, at last, his
firmness gave way, and he did let out some information. Poor soul, the flesh is weak, you know.
What it was he did not tell me. There was a
crushed spirit in that mangled body. Nothing I
found to say could make him whole. When they
let him out, he crept into that hole, and bore his
remorse stoically. He would not go near any
one he knew. I would have sought assistance for
him, but, indeed, where could I have gone looking
for it ? Where was I to look for any one who had
anything to spare or any power to help ? The people
living round us were all starving and drunken.
They were the victims of the Ministry of Finances.
Don't ask me how we lived. I couldn't tell you.
It was like a miracle of wretchedness. I had
nothing to sell, and I assure you my clothes were
in such a state that it was impossible for me to go
out in the daytime. I was indecent. I had to wait
till it was dark before I ventured into the streets to
beg for a crust of bread, or whatever I could get,
to keep him and me alive. Often I got nothing,
and then I would crawl back and lie on the floor by
the side of his couch. Oh yes, I can sleep quite
soundly on bare boards. That is nothing, and I
am only mentioning it to you so that you should not
think I am a sybarite. It was infinitely less killing
than the task of sitting for hours at a table in a cold
study to take the books of Peter Ivanovitch from

dictation. But you shall see yourself what that is like, so I needn't say any more about it."

" It is by no means certain that I will ever take Peter Ivanovitch from dictation," said Miss Haldin.

" No ! " cried the other incredulously. " Not certain ? You mean to say that you have not made up your mind ? "

When Miss Haldin assured her that there never had been any question of that between her and Peter Ivanovitch, the woman with the cat compressed her lips tightly for a moment.

" Oh, you will find yourself settled at the table before you know that you have made up your mind. Don't make a mistake, it is disenchanting to hear Peter Ivanovitch dictate, but at the same time there is a fascination about it. He is a man of genius. Your face is certain not to irritate him ; you may perhaps even help his inspiration, make it easier for him to deliver his message. As I look at you, I feel certain that you are the kind of woman who is not likely to check the flow of his inspiration."

Miss Haldin thought it useless to protest against all these assumptions.

" But this man—this workman—did he die under your care ? " she said, after a short silence.

The *dame de compagnie*, listening up the stairs where now two voices were alternating with some animation, made no answer for a time. When the loud sounds of the discussion had sunk into an almost inaudible murmur, she turned to Miss Haldin.

" Yes, he died, but not, literally speaking, in my arms, as you might suppose. As a matter of fact, I was asleep when he breathed his last. So even now I cannot say I have seen anybody die. A few days before the end, some young men found us out in our extremity. They were revolutionists, as you might guess. He ought to have trusted in his political friends when he came out of prison. He had been liked and respected before, and nobody would have dreamed of reproaching him with his indiscretion before the police. Everybody knows how they go to work, and the strongest man has his moments of weakness before pain. Why, even hunger alone is enough to give one queer ideas as to what may be done. A doctor came, our lot was alleviated as far as physical comforts go, but otherwise he could not be consoled—poor man. I assure you, Miss Haldin, that he was very lovable, but I had not the strength to weep. I was nearly dead myself. But there were kind hearts to take care of me. A dress was found to clothe my nakedness. I tell you, I was not decent—and after a time the revolutionists placed me with a Jewish family going abroad, as governess. Of course I could teach the children, I finished the sixth class of the Lyceum ; but the real object was, that I should carry some important papers across the frontier. I was entrusted with a packet which I carried next my heart. The gendarmes at the station did not suspect the governess of a Jewish family, busy looking after three children. I don't suppose those Hebrews knew what I had on me, for I had been introduced to them in a very round-about way by persons who did not belong to the revolutionary movement, and naturally I had been instructed to accept a very small salary. When we reached Germany I left that family and delivered my papers to a revolutionist in Stuttgart; after this I was employed in various ways. But you do not want to hear all that. I have never felt that I was very useful, but I live in hopes of seeing all the Ministries destroyed, finances and all. The greatest joy of my life has been to hear what your brother has done."

She directed her round eyes again to the sunshine outside, while the cat reposed within her folded arms in lordly beatitude and sphinx-like meditation.

"Yes, I rejoiced," she began again. "For me there is a heroic ring about the very name of Haldin. They must have been trembling with fear in their Ministries—all those men with fiendish hearts. Here I stand talking to you, and when I think of all the cruelties, oppressions, and injustices that are going on at this very moment, my head begins to swim. I have looked closely at what would seem inconceivable if one's own eyes had not to be trusted. I have looked at things that made me hate myself for my helplessness. I hated my hands that had no power, my voice that could not be heard, my very mind that would not become unhinged. Ah! I have seen things. And you ? "

Miss Haldin was moved. She shook her head slightly.

" No, I have seen nothing for myself as yet," she murmured. " We have always lived in the country. It was my brother's wish."

" It is a curious meeting—this—between you and me," continued the other. " Do you believe in chance, Miss Haldin ? How could I have expected to see you, his sister, with my own eyes ? Do you know that when the news came the revolutionaries here were as much surprised as pleased, every bit ? No one seemed to know anything about your brother. Peter Ivanovitch himself had not foreseen that such a blow was going to be struck. I suppose your brother was simply inspired. I myself think that such deeds should be done by inspiration. It is a great privilege to have the inspiration and the opportunity. Did he resemble you at all ? Don't you rejoice, Miss Haldin ? "

" You must not expect too much from me," said Miss Haldin, repressing an inclination to cry which came over her suddenly. She succeeded, then added calmly, " I am not an heroic person ! "

" You think you couldn't have done such a thing yourself, perhaps ? "

" I don't know. I must not even ask myself till I have lived a little longer, seen more . . ."

The other moved her head appreciatively. The purring of the cat had a loud complacency in the empty hall. No sound of voices came from upstairs. Miss Haldin broke the silence.

" What is it precisely that you heard people say about my brother? You said that they were surprised. Yes, I suppose they were. Did it not seem strange to them that my brother should have failed to save himself after the most difficult part—that is, getting away from the spot—was over? Conspirators should understand these things well. There are reasons why I am very anxious to know how it is he failed to escape."

The *dame de compagnie* had advanced to the open hall door. She glanced rapidly over her shoulder at Miss Haldin, who remained within the hall.

" Failed to escape," she repeated absently. " Didn't he make the sacrifice of his life? Wasn't he just simply inspired? Wasn't it an act of abnegation? Aren't you certain? "

" What I am certain of," said Miss Haldin, " is that it was not an act of despair. Have you not heard some opinion expressed here upon his miserable capture? "

The *dame de compagnie* mused for a while in the doorway.

" Did I hear? Of course, everything is dis-

cussed here. Has not all the world been speaking
about your brother ? For my part, the mere mention of his achievement plunges me into an envious
ecstasy. Why should a man certain of immortality
think of his life at all ? "

She kept her back turned to Miss Haldin.
Upstairs from behind a great, dingy, white-and-gold
door, visible behind the balustrade of the first floor
landing, a deep voice began to drone formally, as if
reading over notes or something of the sort. It
paused frequently, and then ceased altogether.

" I don't think I can stay any longer now," said
Miss Haldin. " I may return another day."

She waited for the *dame de compagnie* to make
room for her exit ; but the woman appeared lost in
the contemplation of sunshine and shadows, sharing
between themselves the stillness of the deserted
grounds. She concealed the view of the drive from
Miss Haldin. Suddenly she said :

" It will not be necessary ; here is Peter Ivanovitch himself coming up. But he is not alone.
He is seldom alone now."

Hearing that Peter Ivanovitch was approaching,
Miss Haldin was not so pleased as she might have
been expected to be. Somehow she had lost the
desire to see either the heroic captive or Madame
de S——, and the reason of that shrinking which
came upon her at the very last minute is accounted
for by the feeling that those two people had not been
treating the woman with the cat kindly.

"Would you please let me pass?" said Miss Haldin at last, touching lightly the shoulder of the *dame de compagnie*.

But the other, pressing the cat to her breast, did not budge.

"I know who is with him," she said, without even looking back.

More unaccountably than ever Miss Haldin felt a strong impulse to leave the house.

"Madame de S—— may be engaged for some time yet, and what I have got to say to Peter Ivanovitch is just a simple question which I might put to him when I meet him in the grounds on my way down. I really think I must go. I have been some time here, and I am anxious to get back to my mother. Will you let me pass, please?"

The *dame de compagnie* turned her head at last.

"I never supposed that you really wanted to see Madame de S——," she said, with unexpected insight. "Not for a moment." There was something confidential and mysterious in her tone. She passed through the door, with Miss Haldin following her, on to the terrace, and they descended side by side the moss-grown stone steps. There was no one to be seen on the part of the drive visible from the front of the house.

"They are hidden by the trees over there," explained Miss Haldin's new acquaintance, "but you shall see them directly. I don't know who that young man is to whom Peter Ivanovitch has taken

such a fancy. He must be one of us, or he would
not be admitted here when the others come. You
know what I mean by the others. But I must say
that he is not at all mystically inclined. I don't
know that I have made him out yet. Naturally
I am never for very long in the drawing-room.
There is always something for me to do, though the
establishment here is not so extensive as the villa
on the Riviera. But still there are plenty of oppor-
tunities for me to make myself useful."

To the left, passing by the ivy-grown end of the
stables, appeared Peter Ivanovitch and his companion. They walked very slowly, conversing with
some animation. They stopped for a moment,
and Peter Ivanovitch was seen to gesticulate, while
the young man listened motionless, with his arms
hanging down and his head bowed a little. He was
dressed in a dark brown suit and a black hat. The
round eyes of the *dame de compagnie* remained fixed
on the two figures, which had resumed their leisurely
approach.

"An extremely polite young man," she said.
"You shall see what a bow he will make ; and it
won't altogether be so exceptional either. He bows
in the same way when he meets me alone in the
hall."

She moved on a few steps, with Miss Haldin
by her side, and things happened just as she had
foretold. The young man took off his hat, bowed
and fell back, while Peter Ivanovitch advanced

quicker, his black, thick arms extended heartily, and seized hold of both Miss Haldin's hands, shook them, and peered at her through his dark glasses.

" That's right, that's right ! " he exclaimed twice, approvingly. " And so you have been looked after by . . ." He frowned slightly at the *dame de compagnie*, who was still nursing the cat. " I conclude Eleanor—Madame de S—— is engaged. I know she expected somebody to-day. So the newspaper man did turn up, eh ? She is engaged ? "

For all answer the *dame de compagnie* turned away her head.

" It is very unfortunate — very unfortunate indeed. I very much regret that you should have been . . ." He lowered suddenly his voice. " But what is it—surely you are not departing, Natalia Victorovna ? You got bored waiting, didn't you ? "

" Not in the least," Miss Haldin protested. " Only I have been here some time, and I am anxious to get back to my mother."

" The time seemed long, eh ? I am afraid our worthy friend here "—(Peter Ivanovitch suddenly jerked his head sideways towards his right shoulder and jerked it up again)—" our worthy friend here has not the art of shortening the moments of waiting. No, distinctly she has not the art ; and in that respect good intentions alone count for nothing."

The *dame de compagnie* dropped her arms, and the cat found itself suddenly on the ground. It remained quite still after alighting, one hind leg stretched backwards. Miss Haldin was extremely indignant on behalf of the lady companion.

"Believe me, Peter Ivanovitch, that the moments I have passed in the hall of this house have been not a little interesting, and very instructive too. They are memorable. I do not regret the waiting, but I see that the object of my call here can be attained without taking up Madame de S——'s time."

At this point I interrupted Miss Haldin. The above relation is founded on her narrative, which I have not so much dramatised as might be supposed. She had rendered, with extraordinary feeling and animation, the very accent almost of the disciple of the old apple-woman, the irreconcilable hater of Ministries, the voluntary servant of the poor. Miss Haldin's true and delicate humanity had been extremely shocked by the uncongenial fate of her new acquaintance, that lady companion, secretary, whatever she was. For my own part, I was pleased to discover in it one more obstacle to intimacy with Madame de S——. I had a positive abhorrence for the painted, bedizened, dead-faced, glassy-eyed Egeria of Peter Ivanovitch. I do not know what was her attitude to the unseen, but I know that in the affairs of this world she was avaricious, greedy, and unscrupulous. It was within my knowledge that she had been worsted in a sordid and desperate quarrel about money matters with the family of her late husband, the diplomatist. Some very august personages indeed (whom in her fury she had insisted upon scandalously involving in her affairs) had incurred her animosity. I find it perfectly easy to believe that she had come to within an ace of being spirited away, for reasons of State, into some discreet *maison de santé*—a madhouse of sorts, to be plain. It appears, however, that certain high-placed personages opposed it for reasons which . . .

But it is no use to go into details.

Wonder may be expressed at a man in the position of a teacher of languages knowing all this with such definiteness. A novelist says this and that of his personages, and if only he knows how to say it earnestly enough he may not be questioned upon the inventions of his brain in which his own belief is made sufficiently manifest by a telling phrase, a poetic image, the accent of emotion. Art is great ? But I have no art, and not having invented Madame de S——, I feel bound to explain how I came to know so much about her.

My informant was the Russian wife of a friend of mine already mentioned, the professor of Lausanne University. It was from her that I learned the last fact of Madame de S——'s history, with which I intend to trouble my readers. She told me, speaking positively, as a person who trusts her sources, of the cause of Madame de S——'s flight from Russia, some years before. It was neither more nor less than this : that she became suspect to the police in connection with the assassination of the Emperor Alexander. The ground of this suspicion was either some unguarded expressions that escaped her in public, or some talk overheard in her salon—overheard, we must believe, by some guest, perhaps a friend, who hastened to play the informer, I suppose. At any rate, the overheard matter seemed to imply her foreknowledge of that event, and I think she was wise in not waiting for the investigation of such a charge. Some of my readers may remember a little book from her pen, published in Paris, a mystically bad-tempered, declamatory, and frightfully disconnected piece of writing, in which she all but admits the foreknowledge, more than hints at its supernatural origin, and plainly suggests in venomous innuendoes that the guilt of the act was not with the terrorists, but with a palace intrigue. When I observed to my friend, the professor's wife, that the life of Madame de S——, with its unofficial diplomacy, its intrigues, lawsuits, favours, disgrace, expulsions, its atmosphere of scandal, occultism, and charlatanism, was more fit for the eighteenth century than for the conditions of our own time, she assented with a smile, but a moment after went on in a reflective tone : " Charlatanism ? —yes, in a certain measure. Still, times are changed. There are forces now which were non-existent in the eighteenth century. I should not be surprised if she were more dangerous than an Englishman would be willing to believe. And what's more, she is looked upon as really dangerous by certain people—*chez nous*."

Chez nous in this connection meant Russia in general, and the Russian political police in particular. The object of my digression from the straight course of Miss Haldin's relation (in my own words) of her visit to the Château Borel, was to bring forward that statement of my friend, the professor's wife. I wanted to bring it forward simply to make what I have to say presently of Mr. Razumov's presence in Geneva a little more credible—for this is a Russian story for Western ears, which, as I have observed already, are not attuned to certain tones of cynicism and cruelty, of moral negation, and even of moral distress already silenced at our end of Europe. And this I state as my excuse for having left Miss Haldin standing, one of the little group of two women and two men who had come together below the terrace of the Château Borel.

The knowledge which I have just stated was in my mind when, as I have said, I interrupted Miss Haldin. I interrupted her with the cry of profound satisfaction :

" So you never saw Madame de S—— after all ? "

Miss Haldin shook her head. It was very satisfactory to me. She had not seen Madame de S—— ! That was excellent, excellent ! I welcomed the conviction that she would never know Madame de S—— now. I could not explain the reason of the conviction but by the knowledge

that Miss Haldin was standing face to face with her
brother's wonderful friend. I preferred him to
Madame de S—— as the companion and guide of
that young girl, abandoned to her inexperience by
the miserable end of her brother. But, at any rate,
that life now ended had been sincere, and perhaps
its thoughts might have been lofty, its moral sufferings profound, its last act a true sacrifice. It is
not for us, the staid lovers calmed by the possession
of a conquered liberty, to condemn without appeal
the fierceness of thwarted desire.

I am not ashamed of the warmth of my regard
for Miss Haldin. It was, it must be admitted, an
unselfish sentiment, being its own reward. The
late Victor Haldin —in the light of that sentiment—
appeared to me not as a sinister conspirator, but as
a pure enthusiast. I did not wish indeed to judge
him, but the very fact that he did not escape, that
fact which brought so much trouble to both his
mother and his sister, spoke to me in his favour.
Meantime, in my fear of seeing the girl surrender
to the influence of the Château Borel revolutionary
feminism, I was more than willing to put my trust
in that friend of the late Victor Haldin. He was
nothing but a name, you will say. Exactly ! A
name ! And what's more, the only name ; the
only name to be found in the correspondence
between brother and sister. The young man had
turned up ; they had come face to face, and, fortunately, without the direct interference of Madame

de S——. What will come of it ? what will she tell me presently ? I was asking myself.

It was only natural that my thought should turn to the young man, the bearer of the only name uttered in all the dream-talk of a future to be brought about by a revolution. And my thought took the shape of asking myself why this young man had not called upon these ladies. He had been in Geneva for some days before Miss Haldin heard of him first in my presence from Peter Ivanovitch. I regretted that last's presence at their meeting. I would rather have had it happen somewhere out of his spectacled sight. But I supposed that, having both these young people there, he introduced them to each other.

I broke the silence by beginning a question on that point :

" I suppose Peter Ivanovitch . . ."

Miss Haldin gave vent to her indignation. Peter Ivanovitch directly he had got his answer from her had turned upon the *dame de compagnie* in a shameful manner.

" Turned upon her ? " I wondered. " What about ? For what reason ? "

" It was unheard of ; it was shameful," Miss Haldin pursued, with angry eyes. " *Il lui a fait une scène*—like this, before strangers. And for what ? You would never guess. For some eggs. . . . Oh ! "

I was astonished. " Eggs, did you say ? "

"For Madame de S——. That lady observes a special diet, or something of the sort. It seems she complained the day before to Peter Ivanovitch that the eggs were not rightly prepared. Peter Ivanovitch suddenly remembered this against the poor woman, and flew out at her. It was most astonishing. I stood as if rooted."

"Do you mean to say that the great feminist allowed himself to be abusive to a woman?" I asked.

"Oh, not that! It was something you have no conception of. It was an odious performance. Imagine, he raised his hat to begin with. He made his voice soft and deprecatory. 'Ah! you are not kind to us—you will not deign to remember . . .' This sort of phrases, that sort of tone. The poor creature was terribly upset. Her eyes ran full of tears. She did not know where to look. I shouldn't wonder if she would have preferred abuse, or even a blow."

I did not remark that very possibly she was familiar with both on occasions when no one was by. Miss Haldin walked by my side, her head up in scornful and angry silence.

"Great men have their surprising peculiarities," I observed inanely. "Exactly like men who are not great. But that sort of thing cannot be kept up for ever. How did the great feminist wind up this very characteristic episode?"

Miss Haldin, without turning her face my way,

told me that the end was brought about by the appearance of the interviewer, who had been closeted with Madame de S——.

He came up rapidly, unnoticed, lifted his hat slightly, and paused to say in French : " The Baroness has asked me, in case I met a lady on my way out, to desire her to come in at once."

After delivering this message, he hurried down the drive. The *dame de compagnie* flew towards the house, and Peter Ivanovitch followed her hastily, looking uneasy. In a moment Miss Haldin found herself alone with the young man, who undoubtedly must have been the new arrival from Russia. She wondered whether her brother's friend had not already guessed who she was.

I am in a position to say that, as a matter of fact, he had guessed. It is clear to me that Peter Ivanovitch, for some reason or other, had refrained from alluding to these ladies' presence in Geneva. But Razumov had guessed. The trustful girl ! Every word uttered by Haldin lived in Razumov's memory. They were like haunting shapes ; they could not be exorcised. The most vivid amongst them was the mention of the sister. The girl had existed for him ever since. But he did not recognise her at once. Coming up with Peter Ivanovitch, he did observe her ; their eyes had met, even. He had responded, as no one could help responding, to the harmonious charm of her whole person, its strength, its grace, its tranquil frankness—and then he had turned his gaze away. He said to himself that all this was not for him ; the beauty of women and the friendship of men were not for him. He accepted that feeling with a purposeful sternness, and tried to pass on. It was only her outstretched hand which brought about the recognition. It stands recorded in the pages of his self-confession, that it nearly suffocated him physically with an emotional reaction of hate and dismay, as though her appearance had been a piece of accomplished treachery.

He faced about. The considerable elevation of the terrace concealed them from any one lingering in the doorway of the house ; and even from the upstairs windows they could not have been seen. Through the thickets run wild, and the trees of the gently sloping grounds, he had cold, placid glimpses of the lake. A moment of perfect privacy had been vouchsafed to them at this juncture. I wondered to myself what use they had made of that fortunate circumstance.

" Did you have time for more than a few words ? " I asked.

That animation with which she had related to me the incidents of her visit to the Château Borel had left her completely. Strolling by my side, she looked straight before her ; but I noticed a little colour on her cheek. She did not answer me.

After some little time I observed that they could not have hoped to remain forgotten for very long,

unless the other two had discovered Madame de
S—— swooning with fatigue, perhaps, or in a state
of morbid exaltation after the long interview. Either
would require their devoted ministrations. I could
depict to myself Peter Ivanovitch rushing busily
out of the house again, bareheaded, perhaps, and
on across the terrace with his swinging gait, the
black skirts of the frock-coat floating clear of his
stout light-grey legs. I confess to having looked
upon these young people as the quarry of the
" heroic fugitive." I had the notion that they
would not be allowed to escape capture. But of
that I said nothing to Miss Haldin, only as she still
remained uncommunicative, I pressed her a little.

" Well—but you can tell me at least your impression."

She turned her head to look at me, and turned
away again.

" Impression ? " she repeated slowly, almost
dreamily ; then in a quicker tone :

" He seems to be a man who has suffered more
from his thoughts than from evil fortune."

" From his thoughts, you say ? "

" And that is natural enough in a Russian," she
took me up. " In a young Russian ; so many of
them are unfit for action, and yet unable to rest."

" And you think he is that sort of man ? "

" No, I do not judge him. How could I, so
suddenly ? You asked for my impression—I explain
my impression. I—I—don't know the world, nor

yet the people in it ; I have been too solitary—I am too young to trust my own opinions."

" Trust your instinct," I advised her. " Most women trust to that, and make no worse mistakes than men. In this case you have your brother's letter to help you."

She drew a deep breath like a light sigh.

" ' Unstained, lofty, and solitary existences,' " she quoted as if to herself. But I caught the wistful murmur distinctly.

" High praise," I whispered to her.

" The highest possible."

" So high that, like the award of happiness, it is more fit to come only at the end of a life. But still no common or altogether unworthy personality could have suggested such a confident exaggeration of praise and . . ."

" Ah ! " She interrupted me ardently. " And if you had only known the heart from which that judgment has come ! "

She ceased on that note, and for a space I reflected on the character of the words which I perceived very well must tip the scale of the girl's feelings in that young man's favour. They had not the sound of a casual utterance. Vague they were to my Western mind and to my Western sentiment, but I could not forget that, standing by Miss Haldin's side, I was like a traveller in a strange country. It had also become clear to me that Miss Haldin was unwilling to enter into the details of the only material part of their visit to the Château Borel. But I was not hurt. Somehow I didn't feel it to be a want of confidence. It was some other difficulty—a difficulty I could not resent. And it was without the slightest resentment that I said :

" Very well. But on that high ground, which I will not dispute, you, like any one else in such circumstances, you must have made for yourself a representation of that exceptional friend, a mental image of him, and—please tell me—you were not disappointed ? "

" What do you mean ? His personal appearance ? "

" I don't mean precisely his good looks, or otherwise."

We turned at the end of the alley and made a few steps without looking at each other.

" His appearance is not ordinary," said Miss Haldin at last.

" No, I should have thought not—from the little you've said of your first impression. After all, one has to fall back on that word. Impression ! What I mean is that something indescribable which is likely to mark a ' not ordinary ' person."

I perceived that she was not listening. There was no mistaking her expression ; and once more I had the sense of being out of it—not because of my age, which at any rate could draw inferences— but altogether out of it, on another plane whence I could only watch her from afar. And so ceasing to speak I watched her stepping out by my side.

"No," she exclaimed suddenly, "I could not have been disappointed with a man of such strong feeling."

"Aha! Strong feeling," I muttered, thinking to myself censoriously : like this, at once, all in a moment!

"What did you say?" inquired Miss Haldin innocently.

"Oh, nothing. I beg your pardon. Strong feeling. I am not surprised."

"And you don't know how abruptly I behaved to him!" she cried remorsefully.

I suppose I must have appeared surprised, for, looking at me with a still more heightened colour, she said she was ashamed to admit that she had not been sufficiently collected ; she had failed to control her words and actions as the situation demanded. She lost the fortitude worthy of both the men, the dead and the living—the fortitude which should have been the note of the meeting of Victor Haldin's sister with Victor Haldin's only known friend. He was looking at her keenly, but said nothing, and she was—she confessed—painfully affected by his want of comprehension. All she could say was : "You are Mr. Razumov." A slight frown passed over his forehead. After a short, watchful pause, he made a little bow of assent, and waited.

At the thought that she had before her the man

so highly regarded by her brother, the man who had known his value, spoken to him, understood him, had listened to his confidences, perhaps had encouraged him—her lips trembled, her eyes ran full of tears ; she put out her hand, made a step towards him impulsively, saying with an effort to restrain her emotion, " Can't you guess who I am ? " He did not take the proffered hand. He even recoiled a pace, and Miss Haldin imagined that he was unpleasantly affected. Miss Haldin excused him, directing her displeasure at herself. She had behaved unworthily, like an emotional French girl. A manifestation of that kind could not be welcomed by a man of stern, self-contained character.

He must have been stern indeed, or perhaps very timid with women, not to respond in a more human way to the advances of a girl like Nathalie Haldin— I thought to myself. Those " lofty and solitary existences " (I remembered the words suddenly) make a young man shy and an old man savage—often.

" Well ? " I encouraged Miss Haldin to proceed. She was still very dissatisfied with herself.

" I went from bad to worse," she said, with an air of discouragement very foreign to her. " I did everything foolish except actually bursting into tears. I am thankful to say I did not do that. But I was unable to speak for quite a long time."

She had stood before him, speechless, swallowing her sobs, and when she managed at last to utter something, it was only her brother's name—" Victor

—Victor Haldin ! " she gasped out, and again her voice failed her.

" Of course," she commented to me, " this distressed him. He was quite overcome. I have told you my opinion that he is a man of deep feeling —it is impossible to doubt it. You should have seen his face. He positively reeled. He leaned against the wall of the terrace. Their friendship must have been the very brotherhood of souls ! I was grateful to him for that emotion, which made me feel less ashamed of my own lack of self-control. Of course I had regained the power of speech at once, almost. All this lasted not more than a few seconds. ' I am his sister,' I said. ' Maybe you have heard of me.' "

" And had he ? " I interrupted.

" I don't know. How could it have been otherwise ? And yet . . . But what does that matter ? I stood there before him, near enough to be touched and surely not looking like an impostor. All I know is, that he put out both his hands then to me, I may say flung them out at me, with the greatest readiness and warmth, and that I seized and pressed them, feeling that I was finding again a little of what I thought was lost to me for ever, with the loss of my brother—some of that hope, inspiration, and support which I used to get from my dear dead . . ."

I understood quite well what she meant. We strolled on slowly. I refrained from looking at her.

And it was as if answering my own thoughts that I murmured :

"No doubt it was a great friendship—as you say. And that young man ended by welcoming your name, so to speak, with both hands. After that, of course, you would understand each other. Yes, you would understand each other quickly."

It was a moment before I heard her voice.

"Mr. Razumov seems to be a man of few words. A reserved man—even when he is strongly moved."

Unable to forget—or even to forgive—the bass-toned expansiveness of Peter Ivanovitch, the arch-patron of revolutionary parties, I said that I took this for a favourable trait of character. It was associated with sincerity—in my mind.

"And, besides, we had not much time," she added.

"No, you would not have, of course." My suspicion and even dread of the feminist and his Egeria was so ineradicable that I could not help asking with real anxiety, which I made smiling :

"But you escaped all right ? "

She understood me, and smiled too, at my uneasiness.

"Oh yes ! I escaped, if you like to call it that. I walked away quickly. There was no need to run. I am neither frightened nor yet fascinated, like that poor woman who received me so strangely."

"And Mr.—Mr. Razumov . . . ? "

"He remained there, of course. I suppose he

went into the house after I left him.   You remember
that he came here strongly recommended to Peter
Ivanovitch — possibly entrusted with important
messages for him."

" Ah yes !   From that priest who . . ."

" Father Zosim—yes. Or from others, perhaps."

" You left him, then. But have you seen him
since, may I ask ? "

For some time Miss Haldin made no answer to
this very direct question, then :

" I have been expecting to see him here to-day,"
she said quietly.

" You   have ! Do you meet, then, in this
garden ? In that case I had better leave you at
once."

" No ; why leave me ? And we don't meet in
this garden. I have not seen Mr. Razumov since
that first time. Not once. But I have been expecting him . . ."

She paused. I wondered to myself why that
young revolutionist should show so little alacrity.

" Before we parted I told Mr. Razumov that I
walked here for an hour every day at this time. I
could not explain to him then why I did not ask
him to come and see us at once. Mother must be
prepared for such a visit. And then, you see, I
do not know myself what Mr. Razumov has to tell
us. He, too, must be told first how it is with poor
mother. All these thoughts flashed through my

mind at once. So I told him hurriedly that there was a reason why I could not ask him to see us at home, but that I was in the habit of walking here. . . . This is a public place, but there are never many people about at this hour. I thought it would be very well. And it is so near our apartments. I don't like to be very far away from mother. Our servant knows where I am in case I should be wanted suddenly."

" Yes. It is very convenient from that point of view," I agreed.

In fact, I thought the Bastions a very convenient place, since the girl did not think it prudent as yet to introduce that young man to her mother. It is here, then, I thought, looking round at that plot of ground of deplorable banality, that their acquaintance will begin and go on in the exchange of generous indignations and of extreme sentiments, too poignant, perhaps, for a non-Russian mind to conceive. I saw these two, escaped out of fourscore millions of human beings ground between the upper and nether millstone, walking under these trees, their young heads close together. Yes, an excellent place to stroll and talk in. It even occurred to me, while we turned once more away from the wide iron gates, that when tired they would have plenty of accommodation to rest themselves. There was a quantity of tables and chairs displayed between the restaurant chalet and the bandstand, a whole raft of painted deals spread out under the trees.

In the very middle of it I observed a solitary Swiss couple, whose fate was made secure from the cradle to the grave by the perfected mechanism of democratic institutions in a republic that could almost be held in the palm of one's hand. The man, colourlessly uncouth, was drinking beer out of a glittering glass ; the woman, rustic and placid, leaning back in the rough chair, gazed idly around.

There is little logic to be expected on this earth, not only in the matter of thought, but also of sentiment. I was surprised to discover myself displeased with that unknown young man. A week had gone by since they met. Was he callous, or shy, or very stupid ? I could not make it out.

" Do you think," I asked Miss Haldin, after we had gone some distance up the great alley, " that Mr. Razumov understood your intention ? "

" Understood what I meant ? " she wondered. " He was greatly moved. That I know ! In my own agitation I could see it. But I spoke distinctly. He heard me ; he seemed, indeed, to hang on my words . . ."

Unconsciously she had hastened her pace. Her utterance, too, became quicker.

I waited a little before I observed thoughtfully :

" And yet he allowed all these days to pass."

" How can we tell what work he may have to do here ? He is not an idler travelling for his pleasure. His time may not be his own—nor yet his thoughts, perhaps."

She slowed her pace suddenly, and in a lowered voice added :

" Or his very life "—then paused and stood still. " For all I know, he may have had to leave Geneva the very day he saw me."

" Without telling you ! " I exclaimed incredulously.

" I did not give him time. I left him quite abruptly. I behaved emotionally to the end. I am sorry for it. Even if I had given him the opportunity he would have been justified in taking me for a person not to be trusted. An emotional, tearful girl is not a person to confide in. But even if he has left Geneva for a time, I am confident that we shall meet again."

" Ah ! you are confident. . . . I dare say. But on what ground ? "

" Because I've told him that I was in great need of some one, a fellow-countryman, a fellow-believer, to whom I could give my confidence in a certain matter."

" I see. I don't ask you what answer he made. I confess that this is good ground for your belief in Mr. Razumov's appearance before long. But he has not turned up to-day ? "

" No," she said quietly, " not to-day " ; and we stood for a time in silence, like people that have nothing more to say to each other and let their thoughts run widely asunder before their bodies go off their different ways. Miss Haldin glanced at

the watch on her wrist and made a brusque movement. She had already overstayed her time, it
seemed.

" I don't like to be away from mother," she
murmured, shaking her head. " It is not that she is
very ill now. But somehow when I am not with her
I am more uneasy than ever."

Mrs. Haldin had not made the slightest allusion
to her son for the last week or more. She sat, as
usual, in the arm-chair by the window, looking out
silently on that hopeless stretch of the Boulevard
des Philosophes. When she spoke, a few lifeless
words, it was of indifferent, trivial things.

" For any one who knows what the poor soul is
thinking of, that sort of talk is more painful than her
silence. But that is bad too ; I can hardly endure
it, and I dare not break it."

Miss Haldin sighed, refastening a button of her
glove which had come undone. I knew well enough
what a hard time of it she must be having. The
stress, its causes, its nature, would have undermined
the health of an Occidental girl ; but Russian natures
have a singular power of resistance against the
unfair strains of life. Straight and supple, with a
short jacket open on her black dress, which made
her figure appear more slender and her fresh but
colourless face more pale, she compelled my wonder
and admiration.

" I can't stay a moment longer. You ought to
come soon to see mother. You know she calls you

' *L'ami.*' It is an excellent name, and she really means it. And now au revoir, I must run.''

She glanced vaguely down the broad walk—the hand she put out to me eluded my grasp by an unexpected upward movement, and rested upon my shoulder. Her red lips were slightly parted, not in a smile, however, but expressing a sort of startled pleasure. She gazed towards the gates and said quickly, with a gasp :

'' There ! I knew it. Here he comes ! ''

I understood that she must mean Mr. Razumov. A young man was walking up the alley, without haste. His clothes were some dull shade of brown, and he carried a stick. When my eyes first fell on him, his head was hanging on his breast as if in deep thought. While I was looking at him he raised it sharply, and at once stopped. I am certain he did, but that pause was nothing more perceptible than a faltering check in his gait, instantaneously overcome. Then he continued his approach, looking at us steadily. Miss Haldin signed to me to remain, and advanced a step or two to meet him.

I turned my head away from that meeting, and did not look at them again till I heard Miss Haldin's voice uttering his name in the way of introduction. Mr. Razumov was informed, in a warm, low tone, that, besides being a wonderful teacher, I was a great support '' in our sorrow and distress.''

Of course I was described also as an Englishman.

Miss Haldin spoke rapidly, faster than I have ever heard her speak, and that by contrast made the quietness of her eyes more expressive.

" I have given him my confidence," she added, looking all the time at Mr. Razumov. That young man did, indeed, rest his gaze on Miss Haldin, but certainly did not look into her eyes which were so ready for him. Afterwards he glanced backwards and forwards at us both, while the faint commencement of a forced smile, followed by the suspicion of a frown, vanished one after another ; I detected them, though neither could have been noticed by a person less intensely bent upon divining him than myself. I don't know what Nathalie Haldin had observed, but my attention seized the very shades of these movements. The attempted smile was given up, the incipient frown was checked, and smoothed so that there should be no sign ; but I imagined him exclaiming inwardly :

" Her confidence ! To this elderly person—this foreigner ! "

I imagined this because he looked foreign enough to me. I was upon the whole favourably impressed. He had an air of intelligence and even some distinction quite above the average of the students and other inhabitants of the *Petite Russie*. His features were more decided than in the generality of Russian faces ; he had a line of the jaw, a clean-shaven, sallow cheek ; his nose was a ridge, and not a mere protuberance. He wore the hat well down over his eyes, his dark hair curled low on the nape of his neck ; in the ill-fitting brown clothes there were sturdy limbs ; a slight stoop brought out a satisfactory breadth of shoulders. Upon the whole I was not disappointed. Studious—robust— shy. . . .

Before Miss Haldin had ceased speaking I felt the grip of his hand on mine, a muscular, firm grip, but unexpectedly hot and dry. Not a word or even a mutter assisted this short and arid handshake.

I intended to leave them to themselves, but Miss Haldin touched me lightly on the forearm with a significant contact, conveying a distinct wish. Let him smile who likes, but I was only too ready to stay near Nathalie Haldin, and I am not ashamed to say that it was no smiling matter to me. I stayed, not as a youth would have stayed, uplifted, as it were poised in the air, but soberly, with my feet on the ground and my mind trying to penetrate her intention. She had turned to Razumov.

" Well. This is the place. Yes, it is here that I meant you to come. I have been walking every day. . . . Don't excuse yourself — I understand. I am grateful to you for coming to-day, but all the same I cannot stay now. It is impossible. I must hurry off home. Yes, even with you standing before me, I must run off. I have been too long away. . . . You know how it is ? "

These last words were addressed to me. I noticed that Mr. Razumov passed the tip of his tongue over his lips just as a parched, feverish man might do. He took her hand in its black glove, which closed on his, and held it—detained it quite visibly to me against a drawing-back movement.

" Thank you once more for—for understanding me," she went on warmly. He interrupted her with a certain effect of roughness. I didn't like him speaking to this frank creature so much from under the brim of his hat, as it were. And he produced a faint, rasping voice quite like a man with a parched throat.

" What is there to thank me for ? Understand you ? . . . How did I understand you ? . . . You had better know that I understand nothing. I was aware that you wanted to see me in this garden. I could not come before. I was hindered. And even to-day, you see . . . late."

She still held his hand.

" I can, at any rate, thank you for not dismissing me from your mind as a weak, emotional girl. No doubt I want sustaining. I am very ignorant. But I can be trusted. Indeed I can ! "

" You are ignorant," he repeated thoughtfully. He had raised his head, and was looking straight into her face now, while she held his hand. They stood like this for a long moment. She released his hand.

" Yes. You did come late. It was good of you to come on the chance of me having loitered beyond my time. I was talking with this good friend here.

15

I was talking of you. Yes, Kirylo Sidorovitch, of you. He was with me when I first heard of your being here in Geneva. He can tell you what comfort it was to my bewildered spirit to hear that news. He knew I meant to seek you out. It was the only object of my accepting the invitation of Peter Ivanovitch . . ."

" Peter Ivanovitch talked to you of me ? " he interrupted, in that wavering, hoarse voice which suggested a horribly dry throat.

" Very little. Just told me your name, and that you had arrived here. Why should I have asked for more ? What could he have told me that I did not know already from my brother's letter ? Three lines ! And how much they meant to me ! I will show them to you one day, Kirylo Sidorovitch. But now I must go. The first talk between us cannot be a matter of five minutes, so we had better not begin. . . ."

I had been standing a little aside, seeing them both in profile. At that moment it occurred to me that Mr. Razumov's face was older than his age.

" If mother "—the girl had turned suddenly to me—" were to wake up in my absence (so much longer than usual) she would perhaps question me. She seems to miss me more, you know, of late. She would want to know what delayed me—and, you see, it would be painful for me to dissemble before her."

I understood the point very well. For the same

reason she checked what seemed to be on Mr. Razumov's part a movement to accompany her.

" No, no ! I go alone, but meet me here as soon as possible." Then to me in a lower, significant tone :

" Mother may be sitting at the window at this moment, looking down the street. She must not know anything of Mr. Razumov's presence here till —till something is arranged." She paused before she added a little louder, but still speaking to me, " Mr. Razumov does not quite understand my difficulty, but you know what it is."

V

With a quick inclination of the head for us both, and an earnest, friendly glance at the young man, Miss Haldin left us covering our heads and looking after her straight, supple figure receding rapidly. Her walk was not that hybrid and uncertain gliding affected by some women, but a frank, strong, healthy movement forward. Rapidly she increased the distance—disappeared with suddenness at last. I discovered only then that Mr. Razumov, after ramming his hat well over his brow, was looking me over from head to foot. I dare say I was a very unexpected fact for that young Russian to stumble upon. I caught in his physiognomy, in his whole bearing, an expression compounded of curiosity and scorn, tempered by alarm—as though he had been holding his breath while I was not looking. But his eyes met mine with a gaze direct enough. I saw then for the first time that they were of a clear brown colour and fringed with thick black eyelashes. They were the youngest feature of his face. Not at all unpleasant eyes. He swayed slightly, leaning on his stick and generally hung in the wind. It flashed upon me that in leaving us together Miss Haldin had an intention— that something was entrusted to me, since by a mere accident I had been found at hand. On this assumed ground I put all possible friendliness into my manner. I cast about for some right thing to say, and suddenly in Miss Haldin's last words I perceived the clue to the nature of my mission.

" No," I said gravely, if with a smile, " you cannot be expected to understand."

His clean-shaven lip quivered ever so little before he said, as if wickedly amused :

" But haven't you heard just now ? I was thanked by that young lady for understanding so well."

I looked at him rather hard. Was there a hidden and inexplicable sneer in this retort ? No. It was not that. It might have been resentment. Yes. But what had he to resent ? He looked as though he had not slept very well of late. I could almost feel on me the weight of his unrefreshed, motionless stare, the stare of a man who lies unwinking in the dark, angrily passive in the toils of disastrous thoughts. Now, when I know how true it was, I can honestly affirm that this *was* the effect he produced on me. It was painful in a curiously indefinite way—for, of course, the definition comes to me now while I sit writing in the fullness of my knowledge. But this is what the effect was at that time of absolute ignorance. This new sort of uneasiness which he seemed to be forcing upon me I attempted to put down by assuming a conversational, easy familiarity.

" That extremely charming and essentially admirable young girl (I am—as you see—old enough to be frank in my expressions) was referring to her own feelings. Surely you must have understood that much ? "

He made such a brusque movement that he even tottered a little.

" Must understand this ! Not expected to understand that ! I may have other things to do. And the girl is charming and admirable. Well— and if she is ! I suppose I can see that for myself."

This sally would have been insulting if his voice had not been practically extinct, dried up in his throat ; and the rustling effort of his speech too painful to give real offence.

I remained silent, checked between the obvious fact and the subtle impression. It was open to me to leave him there and then ; but the sense of having been entrusted with a mission, the suggestion of

Miss Haldin's last glance, was strong upon me. After a moment of reflection I said :

" Shall we walk together a little ? "

He shrugged his shoulders so violently that he tottered again. I saw it out of the corner of my eye as I moved on, with him at my elbow. He had fallen back a little and was practically out of my sight, unless I turned my head to look at him. I did not wish to indispose him still further by an appearance of marked curiosity. It might have been distasteful to such a young and secret refugee from under the pestilential shadow hiding the true, kindly face of his land. And the shadow, the attendant of his countrymen, stretching across the middle of Europe, was lying on him too, darkening his figure to my mental vision. " Without doubt," I said to myself, " he seems a sombre, even a desperate revolutionist ; but he is young, he may be unselfish and humane, capable of compassion, of . . ."

I heard him clear gratingly his parched throat, and became all attention.

" This is beyond everything," were his first words. " It is beyond everything ! I find you here, for no reason that I can understand, in possession of something I cannot be expected to understand ! A confidant ! A foreigner ! Talking about an admirable Russian girl. Is the admirable girl a fool, I begin to wonder ? What are you at ? What is your object ? "

He was barely audible, as if his throat had no

more resonance than a dry rag, a piece of tinder. It was so pitiful that I found it extremely easy to control my indignation.

" When you have lived a little longer, Mr. Razumov, you will discover that no woman is an absolute fool.   I am not a feminist, like that illustrious author, Peter Ivanovitch, who, to say the truth, is not a little suspect to me. . . ."

He interrupted me, in a surprising note of whispering astonishment :

" Suspect to you !   Peter Ivanovitch suspect to you !   To you ! . . ."

" Yes, in a certain aspect he is," I said, dismissing my remark lightly. " As I was saying, Mr. Razumov, when you have lived long enough, you will learn to discriminate between the noble trustfulness of a nature foreign to every meanness and the flattered credulity of some women ; though even the credulous, silly as they may be, unhappy as they are sure to be, are never absolute fools. It is my belief that no woman is ever completely deceived. Those that are lost leap into the abyss with their eyes open, if all the truth were known."

" Upon my word," he cried at my elbow, " what is it to me whether women are fools or lunatics ?   I really don't care what you think of them.   I—I am not interested in them.   I let them be.   I am not a young man in a novel.   How do you know that I want to learn anything about women ? . . . What is the meaning of all this ? "

" The object, you mean, of this conversation, which I admit I have forced upon you in a measure ? "

" Forced ! Object ! " he repeated, still keeping half a pace or so behind me. " You wanted to talk about women apparently. That's a subject. But I don't care for it. I have never . . . In fact, I have had other subjects to think about."

" I am concerned here with one woman only—a young girl—the sister of your dead friend—Miss Haldin. Surely you can think a little of her. What I meant from the first was that there is a situation which you cannot be expected to understand."

I listened to his unsteady footfalls by my side for the space of several strides.

" I think that it may prepare the ground for your next interview with Miss Haldin if I tell you of it. I imagine that she might have had something of the kind in her mind when she left us together. I believe myself authorised to speak. The peculiar situation I have alluded to has arisen in the first grief and distress of Victor Haldin's execution. There was something peculiar in the circumstances of his arrest. You no doubt know the whole truth. . . ."

I felt my arm seized above the elbow, and next instant found myself swung so as to face Mr. Razumov.

" You spring up from the ground before me with this talk. Who the devil are you ? This is not to be borne ! Why ? What for ? What do you know what is or is not peculiar ? What have you to do with any confounded circumstances, or with anything that happens in Russia, anyway ? "

He leaned on his stick with his other hand heavily ; and when he let go my arm, I was certain in my mind that he was hardly able to keep on his feet.

" Let us sit down at one of these vacant tables," I proposed, disregarding this display of unexpectedly profound emotion. It was not without its effect on me, I confess. I was sorry for him.

" What tables ? What are you talking about ? Oh—the empty tables... The tables there. Certainly. I will sit at one of the empty tables."

I led him away from the path to the very centre of the raft of deals before the chalet. The Swiss couple were gone by that time. We were alone on the raft, so to speak. Mr. Razumov dropped into a chair, let fall his stick, and propped on his elbows, his head between his hands, stared at me persistently, openly, and continuously, while I signalled the waiter and ordered some beer. I could not quarrel with this silent inspection very well, because, truth to tell, I felt somewhat guilty of having been sprung on him with some abruptness—of having " sprung from the ground," as he expressed it.

While waiting to be served I mentioned that, born from parents settled in St. Petersburg, I had acquired the language as a child. The town I did not remember, having left it for good as a boy of nine, but in later years I had renewed my acquaintance with the language. He listened, without as much as moving his eyes the least little bit. He had to change his position when the beer came, and the instant draining of his glass revived him. He leaned back in his chair and, folding his arms across his chest, continued to stare at me squarely. It occurred to me that his clean-shaven, almost swarthy face was really of the very mobile sort, and that the absolute stillness of it was the acquired habit of a revolutionist, of a conspirator everlastingly on his guard against self-betrayal in a world of secret spies.

" But you are an Englishman—a teacher of English literature," he murmured, in a voice that was no longer issuing from a parched throat. " I have heard of you. People told me you have lived here for years."

" Quite true. More than twenty years. And I have been assisting Miss Haldin with her English studies."

" You have been reading English poetry with her," he said, immovable now, like another man altogether, a complete stranger to the man of the heavy and uncertain footfalls a little while ago— at my elbow.

" Yes, English poetry," I said. " But the trouble of which I speak was caused by an English newspaper."

He continued to stare at me. I don't think he

was aware that the story of the midnight arrest had been ferreted out by an English journalist and given to the world. When I explained this to him he muttered contemptuously, " It may have been altogether a lie."

" I should think you are the best judge of that," I retorted, a little disconcerted. " I must confess that to me it looks to be true in the main."

" How can you tell truth from lies ? " he queried in his new, immovable manner.

" I don't know how you do it in Russia," I began, rather nettled by his attitude. He interrupted me.

" In Russia, and in general everywhere—in a newspaper, for instance. The colour of the ink and the shapes of the letters are the same."

" Well, there are other trifles one can go by. The character of the publication, the general verisimilitude of the news, the consideration of the motive, and so on. I don't trust blindly the accuracy of special correspondents—but why should this one have gone to the trouble of concocting a circumstantial falsehood on a matter of no importance to the world ? "

" That's what it is," he grumbled. " What's going on with us is of no importance—a mere sensational story to amuse the readers of the papers— the superior contemptuous Europe. It is hateful to think of.   But let them wait a bit ! "

He broke off on this sort of threat addressed to

the Western world. Disregarding the anger in his stare, I pointed out that whether the journalist was well- or ill-informed, the concern of the friends of these ladies was with the effect the few lines of print in question had produced—the effect alone. And surely he must be counted as one of the friends —if only for the sake of his late comrade and intimate fellow-revolutionist. At that point I thought he was going to speak vehemently ; but he only astounded me by the convulsive start of his whole body. He restrained himself, folded his loosened arms tighter across his chest, and sat back with a smile in which there was a twitch of scorn and malice.

" Yes, a comrade and an intimate. . . . Very well," he said.

" I ventured to speak to you on that assumption. And I cannot be mistaken. I was present when Peter Ivanovitch announced your arrival here to Miss Haldin, and I saw her relief and thankfulness when your name was mentioned. Afterwards she showed me her brother's letter, and read out the few words in which he alludes to you. What else but a friend could you have been ? "

" Obviously. That's perfectly well known. A friend. Quite correct. . . . Go on. You were talking of some effect."

I said to myself : " He puts on the callousness of a stern revolutionist, the insensibility to common emotions of a man devoted to a destructive idea.

He is young, and his sincerity assumes a pose before a stranger, a foreigner, an old man. Youth must assert itself. . . ." As concisely as possible I exposed to him the state of mind poor Mrs. Haldin had been thrown into by the news of her son's untimely end.

He listened—I felt it—with profound attention. His level stare deflected gradually downwards, left my face, and rested at last on the ground at his feet.

" You can enter into the sister's feelings. As you said, I have only read a little English poetry with her, and I won't make myself ridiculous in your eyes by trying to speak of her. But you have seen her. She is one of those rare human beings that do not want explaining. At least I think so. They had only that son, that brother, for a link with the wider world, with the future. The very ground-work of active existence for Nathalie Haldin is gone with him. Can you wonder then that she turns with eagerness to the only man her brother mentions in his letters? Your name is a sort of legacy."

" What could he have written of me ? " he cried, in a low, exasperated tone.

" Only a few words. It is not for me to repeat them to you, Mr. Razumov ; but you may believe my assertion that these words are forcible enough to make both his mother and his sister believe implicitly in the worth of your judgment and in the truth of anything you may have to say to them.

It's impossible for you now to pass them by like strangers."

I paused, and for a moment sat listening to the footsteps of the few people passing up and down the broad central walk. While I was speaking his head had sunk upon his breast above his folded arms. He raised it sharply.

" Must I go then and lie to that old woman ? "

It was not anger ; it was something else, something more poignant, and not so simple. I was aware of it sympathetically, while I was profoundly concerned at the nature of that exclamation.

" Dear me ! Won't the truth do, then ? I hoped you could have told them something consoling. I am thinking of the poor mother now. Your Russia *is* a cruel country."

He moved a little in his chair.

" Yes," I repeated. " I thought you would have had something authentic to tell."

The twitching of his lips before he spoke was curious.

" What if it is not worth telling ? "

" Not worth ? From what point of view ? I don't understand."

" From every point of view."

I spoke with some asperity.

" I should think that anything which could explain the circumstances of that midnight arrest . . ."

" Reported by a journalist for the amusement of the civilised Europe," he broke in scornfully.

" Yes, reported. . . . But aren't they true ?   I can't make out your attitude in this.   Either the man is a hero to you, or . . ."

He approached his face with fiercely distended nostrils close to mine so suddenly that I had the greatest difficulty in not starting back.

" You ask me !   I suppose it amuses you, all this.   Look here !   I am a worker.   I studied. Yes, I studied very hard.   There is intelligence here."   (He tapped his forehead with his finger-tips.)   " Don't you think a Russian may have sane ambitions ?   Yes—I had even prospects.   Certainly !   I had.   And now you see me here, abroad, everything gone, lost, sacrificed.   You see me here—and you ask !   You see me, don't you ?—sitting before you."

He threw himself back violently.   I kept outwardly calm.

" Yes, I see you here ; and I assume you are here on account of the Haldin affair ? "

His manner changed.

" You call it the Haldin affair—do you ? " he observed indifferently.

" I have no right to ask you anything," I said. " I wouldn't presume.   But in that case the mother and the sister of him who must be a hero in your eyes cannot be indifferent to you.   The girl is a frank and generous creature, having the noblest—well—illusions.   You will tell her nothing—or you will tell her everything.   But speaking now of the object with which I've approached you : first, we have to deal with the morbid state of the mother. Perhaps something could be invented under your authority as a cure for a distracted and suffering soul filled with maternal affection."

His air of weary indifference was accentuated, I could not help thinking, wilfully.

" Oh yes. Something might," he mumbled carelessly.

He put his hand over his mouth to conceal a yawn. When he uncovered his lips they were smiling faintly.

" Pardon me. This has been a long conversation, and I have not had much sleep the last two nights."

This unexpected, somewhat insolent sort of apology had the merit of being perfectly true. He had had no nightly rest to speak of since that day when, in the grounds of the Château Borel, the sister of Victor Haldin had appeared before him. The perplexities and the complex terrors—I may say—of this sleeplessness are recorded in the document I was to see later—the document which is the main source of this narrative. At the moment he looked to me convincingly tired, gone slack all over, like a man who has passed through some sort of crisis.

" I have had a lot of urgent writing to do," he added.

I rose from my chair at once, and he followed my example, without haste, a little heavily.

" I must apologise for detaining you so long," I said.

" Why apologise ? One can't very well go to bed before night. And you did not detain me. I could have left you at any time."

I had not stayed with him to be offended.

" I am glad you have been sufficiently interested," I said calmly. " No merit of mine, though —the commonest sort of regard for the mother of your friend was enough. . . . As to Miss Haldin herself, she at one time was disposed to think that her brother had been betrayed to the police in some way."

To my great surprise Mr. Razumov sat down again suddenly. I stared at him, and I must say that he returned my stare without winking for quite a considerable time.

" In some way," he mumbled, as if he had not understood or could not believe his ears.

" Some unforeseen event, a sheer accident might have done that," I went on. " Or, as she characteristically put it to me, the folly or weakness of some unhappy fellow-revolutionist."

" Folly or weakness," he repeated bitterly.

" She is a very generous creature," I observed after a time. The man admired by Victor Haldin fixed his eyes on the ground. I turned away and moved off, apparently unnoticed by him. I nourished no resentment of the moody brusqueness with which he had treated me. The sentiment

16

I was carrying away from that conversation was that of hopelessness. Before I had got fairly clear of the raft of chairs and tables he had rejoined me.

" H'm, yes ! " I heard him at my elbow again. " But what do you think ? "

I did not even look round.

" I think that you people are under a curse."

He made no sound. It was only on the pavement outside the gate that I heard him again.

" I should like to walk with you a little."

After all, I preferred this enigmatical young man to his celebrated compatriot, the great Peter Ivanovitch. But I saw no reason for being particularly gracious.

" I am going now to the railway station, by the shortest way from here, to meet a friend from England," I said, for all answer to his unexpected proposal. I hoped that something informing could come of it. As we stood on the curbstone waiting for a tramcar to pass, he remarked gloomily :

" I like what you said just now."

" Do you ? "

We stepped off the pavement together.

" The great problem," he went on, " is to understand thoroughly the nature of the curse."

" That's not very difficult, I think."

" I think so too," he agreed with me, and his readiness, strangely enough, did not make him less enigmatical in the least.

" A curse is an evil spell," I tried him again.

" And the important, the great, problem is to find the means to break it."

" Yes. To find the means."

That was also an assent, but he seemed to be thinking of something else. We had crossed diagonally the open space before the theatre, and began to descend a broad, sparely frequented street in the direction of one of the smaller bridges. He kept on by my side without speaking for a long time.

" You are not thinking of leaving Geneva soon ? " I asked.

He was silent for so long that I began to think I had been indiscreet, and should get no answer at all. Yet on looking at him I almost believed that my question had caused him something in the nature of positive anguish. I detected it mainly in the clasping of his hands, in which he put a great force stealthily. Once, however, he had overcome that sort of agonising hesitation sufficiently to tell me that he had no such intention, he became rather communicative—at least relatively to the former off-hand curtness of his speeches. The tone, too, was more amiable. He informed me that he intended to study and also to write. He went even so far as to tell me he had been to Stuttgart. Stuttgart, I was aware, was one of the revolutionary centres. The directing committee of one of the Russian parties (I can't tell now which) was located in that town. It was there that he got into touch with the active work of the revolutionists outside Russia.

" I have never been abroad before," he explained, in a rather inanimate voice now. Then, after a slight hesitation, altogether different from the agonising irresolution my first simple question " whether he meant to stay in Geneva " had aroused, he made me an unexpected confidence :

" The fact is, I have received a sort of mission from them."

" Which will keep you here in Geneva ? "

" Yes. Here. In this odious . . ."

I was satisfied with my faculty for putting two and two together when I drew the inference that the mission had something to do with the person of the great Peter Ivanovitch. But I kept that surmise to myself naturally, and Mr. Razumov said nothing more for some considerable time. It was only when we were nearly on the bridge we had been making for that he opened his lips again abruptly :

" Could I see that precious article anywhere ? "

I had to think for a moment before I saw what he was referring to.

" It has been reproduced in parts by the Press here. There are files to be seen in various places. My copy of the English newspaper I left with Miss Haldin, I remember, on the day after it reached me. I was sufficiently worried by seeing it lying on a table by the side of the poor mother's chair for weeks. Then it disappeared. It was a relief, I assure you."

He had stopped short.

"I trust," I continued, "that you will find time to see these ladies fairly often—that you will make time."

He stared at me so queerly that I hardly knew how to define his aspect. I could not understand it in this connection at all. What ailed him? I asked myself. What strange thought had come into his head? What vision of all the horrors that can be seen in his hopeless country had come suddenly to haunt his brain? If it were anything connected with the fate of Victor Haldin, then I hoped earnestly he would keep it to himself for ever. I was, to speak plainly, so shocked that I tried to conceal my impression by—Heaven forgive me—a smile and the assumption of a light manner.

"Surely," I exclaimed, "that needn't cost you a great effort."

He turned away from me and leaned over the parapet of the bridge. For a moment I waited, looking at his back. And yet, I assure you, I was not anxious just then to look at his face again. He did not move at all. He did not mean to move. I walked on slowly on my way towards the station, and at the end of the bridge I glanced over my shoulder. No, he had not moved. He hung well over the parapet, as if captivated by the smooth rush of the blue water under the arch. The current there is swift, extremely swift ; it makes some people dizzy ; I myself can never look at it for any length of time without experiencing a dread of being suddenly snatched away by its destructive force. Some brains cannot resist the suggestion of irresistible power and of headlong motion.

It apparently had a charm for Mr. Razumov. I left him hanging far over the parapet of the bridge. The way he had behaved to me could not be put down to mere boorishness. There was something else under his scorn and impatience. Perhaps, I thought, with sudden approach to hidden truth, it was the same thing which had kept him over a week, nearly ten days indeed, from coming near Miss Haldin. But what it was I could not tell.

PART THIRD

I

THE water under the bridge ran violent and deep. Its slightly undulating rush seemed capable of scouring out a channel for itself through solid granite while you looked. But had it flowed through Razumov's breast, it could not have washed away the accumulated bitterness the wrecking of his life had deposited there.

"What is the meaning of all this?" he thought, staring downwards at the headlong flow so smooth and clean that only the passage of a faint air-bubble, or a thin vanishing streak of foam like a white hair, disclosed its vertiginous rapidity, its terrible force. "Why has that meddlesome old Englishman blundered against me? And what is this silly tale of a crazy old woman?"

He was trying to think brutally on purpose, but he avoided any mental reference to the young girl. "A crazy old woman," he repeated to himself. "It is a fatality! Or ought I to despise all this as absurd? But no! I am wrong! I can't afford to despise anything. An absurdity may be the starting-point of the most dangerous complica-

tions. How is one to guard against it ? It puts
to rout one's intelligence. The more intelligent
one is, the less one suspects an absurdity."

A wave of wrath choked his thoughts for a
moment. It even made his body leaning over the
parapet quiver ; then he resumed his silent thinking, like a secret dialogue with himself. And even
in that privacy, his thought had some reservations
of which he was vaguely conscious.

" After all, this is not absurd. It is insignificant. It is absolutely insignificant — absolutely.
The craze of an old woman—the fussy officiousness
of a blundering elderly Englishman. What devil
put him in the way ? Haven't I treated him
cavalierly enough ? Haven't I just ? That's the
way to treat these meddlesome persons. Is it
possible that he still stands behind my back, waiting ? "

Razumov felt a faint chill run down his spine.
It was not fear. He was certain that it was not
fear—not fear for himself—but it was, all the same,
a sort of apprehension as if for another, for some one
he knew without being able to put a name on the
personality. But the recollection that the officious
Englishman had a train to meet tranquillised him for
a time. It was too stupid to suppose that he should
be wasting his time in waiting. It was unnecessary
to look round and make sure.

But what did the man mean by his extraordinary
rigmarole about the newspaper, and that crazy old

woman ? he thought suddenly. It was a damnable presumption, anyhow, something that only an Englishman could be capable of. All this was a sort of sport for him—the sport of revolution—a game to look at from the height of his superiority. And what on earth did he mean by his exclamation, " Won't the truth do ? "

Razumov pressed his folded arms to the stone coping over which he was leaning with force. " Won't the truth do ? The truth for the crazy old mother of the——"

The young man shuddered again. Yes. The truth would do ! Apparently it would do. Exactly. And receive thanks, he thought, formulating the unspoken words cynically. " Fall on my neck in gratitude, no doubt," he jeered mentally. But this mood abandoned him at once. He felt sad, as if his heart had become empty suddenly. " Well, I must be cautious," he concluded, coming to himself as though his brain had been awakened from a trance. " There is nothing, no one, too insignificant, too absurd to be disregarded," he thought wearily. " I must be cautious."

Razumov pushed himself with his hand away from the balustrade, and, retracing his steps along the bridge, walked straight to his lodgings, where, for a few days, he led a solitary and retired existence. He neglected Peter Ivanovitch, to whom he was accredited by the Stuttgart group ; he never went near the refugee revolutionists, to whom he had been introduced on his arrival. He kept out of that world altogether. And he felt that such conduct, causing surprise and arousing suspicion, contained an element of danger for himself.

This is not to say that during these few days he never went out. I met him several times in the streets, but he gave me no recognition. Once, going home after an evening call on the ladies Haldin, I saw him crossing the dark roadway of the Boulevard des Philosophes. He had a broad-brimmed soft hat, and the collar of his coat turned up. I watched him make straight for the house, but, instead of going in, he stopped opposite the still lighted windows, and after a time went away down a side-street.

I knew that he had not been to see Mrs. Haldin yet. Miss Haldin told me he was reluctant ; moreover, the mental condition of Mrs. Haldin had changed. She seemed to think now that her son was living, and she perhaps awaited his arrival. Her immobility in the great arm-chair in front of the window had an air of expectancy, even when the blind was down and the lamps lighted.

For my part, I was convinced that she had received her death-stroke ; Miss Haldin, to whom, of course, I said nothing of my forebodings, thought that no good would come from introducing Mr. Razumov just then, an opinion which I shared fully. I knew that she met the young man on the Bastions. Once or twice I saw them strolling

slowly up the main alley. They met every day for
weeks. I avoided passing that way during the
hour when Miss Haldin took her exercise there.
One day, however, in a fit of absent-mindedness, I
entered the gates and came upon her walking alone.
I stopped to exchange a few words. Mr. Razumov
failed to turn up, and we began to talk about him—
naturally.

" Did he tell you anything definite about your
brother's activities—his end ? " I ventured to ask.

" No," admitted Miss Haldin, with some hesitation. " Nothing definite."

I understood well enough that all their conversations must have been referred mentally to that
dead man who had brought them together. That
was unavoidable. But it was in the living man that
she was interested. That was unavoidable too, I
suppose. And as I pushed my inquiries I discovered that he had disclosed himself to her as
a by no means conventional revolutionist, contemptuous of catchwords, of theories, of men too.
I was rather pleased at that—but I was a little
puzzled.

" His mind goes forward, far ahead of the
struggle," Miss Haldin explained. " Of course,
he is an actual worker too," she added.

" And do you understand him ? " I inquired
point-blank.

She hesitated again. " Not altogether," she
murmured.

I perceived that he had fascinated her by an assumption of mysterious reserve.

" Do you know what I think ? " she went on, breaking through her reserved, almost reluctant attitude : " I think that he is observing, studying me, to discover whether I am worthy of his trust . . ."

" And that pleases you ? "

She kept mysteriously silent for a moment. Then with energy, but in a confidential tone :

" I am convinced," she declared, " that this extraordinary man is meditating some vast plan, some great undertaking ; he is possessed by it—he suffers from it—and from being alone in the world."

" And so he's looking for helpers ? " I commented, turning away my head.

Again there was a silence.

" Why not ? " she said at last.

The dead brother, the dying mother, the foreign friend, had fallen into a distant background. But, at the same time, Peter Ivanovitch was absolutely nowhere now. And this thought consoled me. Yet I saw the gigantic shadow of Russian life deepening around her like the darkness of an advancing night. It would devour her presently. I inquired after Mrs. Haldin—that other victim of the deadly shade.

A remorseful uneasiness appeared in her frank eyes. Mother seemed no worse, but if I only

knew what strange fancies she had sometimes!
Then Miss Haldin, glancing at her watch, declared
that she could not stay a moment longer, and with
a hasty hand-shake ran off lightly.

Decidedly, Mr. Razumov was not to turn up
that day. Incomprehensible youth! . . .

But less than an hour afterwards, while crossing
the Place Mollard, I caught sight of him boarding
a South Shore tramcar.

" He's going to the Château Borel," I thought.

. . . .

After depositing Razumov at the gates of the
Château Borel, some half a mile or so from the town,
the car continued its journey between two straight
lines of shady trees. Across the roadway in the
sunshine a short wooden pier jutted into the shallow
pale water, which farther out had an intense blue
tint contrasting unpleasantly with the green orderly
slopes on the opposite shore. The whole view,
with the harbour jetties of white stone underlining
lividly the dark front of the town to the left, and the
expanding space of water to the right with jutting
promontories of no particular character, had the
uninspiring, glittering quality of a very fresh oleo-
graph. Razumov turned his back on it with contempt. He thought it odious—oppressively odious
—in its unsuggestive finish: the very perfection
of mediocrity attained at last after centuries of toil
and culture. And turning his back on it, he faced
the entrance to the grounds of the Château Borel.

The bars of the central way and the wrought-iron arch between the dark weather-stained stone piers were very rusty ; and, though fresh tracks of wheels ran under it, the gate looked as if it had not been opened for a very long time. But close against the lodge, built of the same grey stone as the piers (its windows were all boarded up), there was a small side entrance. The bars of that were rusty too ; it stood ajar and looked as though it had not been closed for a long time. In fact, Razumov, trying to push it open a little wider, discovered it was immovable.

" Democratic virtue. There are no thieves here apparently," he muttered to himself, with displeasure. Before advancing into the grounds he looked back sourly at an idle working man lounging on a bench in the clean, broad avenue. The fellow had thrown his feet up ; one of his arms hung over the low back of the public seat ; he was taking a day off in lordly repose, as if everything in sight belonged to him.

" Elector ! Eligible ! Enlightened ! " Razumov muttered to himself. " A brute, all the same."

Razumov entered the grounds and walked fast up the wide sweep of the drive, trying to think of nothing—to rest his head, to rest his emotions too. But arriving at the foot of the terrace before the house he faltered, affected physically by some invisible interference. The mysteriousness of his quickened heart-beats startled him. He stopped short and looked at the brick wall of the terrace, faced with shallow arches, meagrely clothed by a few unthriving creepers, with an ill-kept narrow flower-bed along its foot.

" It is here ! " he thought, with a sort of awe. " It is here—on this very spot . . ."

He was tempted to flight at the mere recollection of his first meeting with Nathalie Haldin. He confessed it to himself ; but he did not move, and that not because he wished to resist an unworthy weakness, but because he knew that he had no place to fly to. Moreover, he could not leave Geneva. He recognised, even without thinking, that it was impossible. It would have been a fatal admission, an act of moral suicide. It would have been also physically dangerous. Slowly he ascended the stairs of the terrace, flanked by two stained greenish stone urns of funereal aspect.

Across the broad platform, where a few blades of grass sprouted on the discoloured gravel, the door of the house, with its ground-floor windows shuttered, faced him, wide open. He believed that his approach had been noted, because, framed in the doorway, without his tall hat, Peter Ivanovitch seemed to be waiting for his approach.

The ceremonious black frock-coat and the bared head of Europe's greatest feminist accentuated the dubiousness of his status in the house rented by Madame de S——, his Egeria. His aspect combined the formality of the caller with the freedom of the proprietor. Florid and bearded and masked by the dark blue glasses, he met the visitor, and at once took him familiarly under the arm.

Razumov suppressed every sign of repugnance by an effort which the constant necessity of prudence had rendered almost mechanical. And this necessity had settled his expression in a cast of austere, almost fanatical, aloofness. The "heroic fugitive," impressed afresh by the severe detachment of this new arrival from revolutionary Russia, took a conciliatory, even a confidential tone. Madame de S—— was resting after a bad night. She often had bad nights. He had left his hat upstairs on the landing and had come down to suggest to his young friend a stroll and a good open-hearted talk in one of the shady alleys behind the house. After voicing this proposal, the great man glanced at the unmoved face by his side, and could not restrain himself from exclaiming :

"On my word, young man, you are an extraordinary person."

"I fancy you are mistaken, Peter Ivanovitch. If I were really an extraordinary person, I would not be here, walking with you in a garden in Switzerland, Canton of Geneva, Commune of—what's the name of the Commune this place belongs to ? . . . Never mind—the heart of democracy, anyhow. A fit heart for it ; no bigger than a parched pea and about as much value. I am no more extraordinary than the rest of us Russians wandering abroad."

But Peter Ivanovitch dissented emphatically :

" No, no ! You are not ordinary. I have some experience of Russians who are—well—living abroad. You appear to me, and to others too, a marked personality."

" What does he mean by this ? " Razumov asked himself, turning his eyes fully on his companion. The face of Peter Ivanovitch expressed a meditative seriousness.

" You don't suppose, Kirylo Sidorovitch, that I have not heard of you from various points where you made yourself known on your way here ? I have had letters."

" Oh, we are great in talking about each other," interjected Razumov, who had listened with great attention. " Gossip, tales, suspicions, and all that sort of thing, we know how to deal in to perfection. Calumny, even."

In indulging in this sally, Razumov managed very well to conceal the feeling of anxiety which had come over him. At the same time he was saying to himself that there could be no earthly reason for anxiety. He was relieved by the evident sincerity of the protesting voice.

" Heavens ! " cried Peter Ivanovitch. " What are you talking about ? What reason can *you* have to . . . ? "

The great exile flung up his arms as if words had failed him in sober truth. Razumov was satisfied. Yet he was moved to continue in the same vein.

17

" I am talking of the poisonous plants which flourish in the world of conspirators, like evil mushrooms in a dark cellar."

" You are casting aspersions," remonstrated Peter Ivanovitch, " which as far as you are concerned——"

" No ! " Razumov interrupted without heat. " Indeed, I don't want to cast aspersions, but it's just as well to have no illusions."

Peter Ivanovitch gave him an inscrutable glance of his dark spectacles, accompanied by a faint smile.

" The man who says that he has no illusions has at least that one," he said, in a very friendly tone. " But I see how it is, Kirylo Sidorovitch. You aim at stoicism."

" Stoicism ! That's a pose of the Greeks and the Romans. Let's leave it to them. We are Russians, that is—children ; that is—sincere ; that is—cynical, if you like. But that's not a pose."

A long silence ensued. They strolled slowly under the lime trees. Peter Ivanovitch had put his hands behind his back. Razumov felt the ungravelled ground of the deeply shaded walk damp and as if slippery under his feet. He asked himself, with uneasiness, if he were saying the right things. The direction of the conversation ought to have been more under his control, he reflected. The great man appeared to be reflecting on his side too. He cleared his throat slightly, and Razumov felt at once a painful reawakening of scorn and fear.

" I am astonished," began Peter Ivanovitch
gently. " Supposing you are right in your indict-
ment, how can you raise any question of calumny
or gossip, in your case ? It is unreasonable. The
fact is, Kirylo Sidorovitch, there is not enough
known of you to give hold to gossip or even calumny.
Just now you are a man associated with a great deed,
which had been hoped for, and tried for too, without
success. People have perished for attempting that
which you and Haldin have done at last. You come
to us out of Russia with that prestige. But you
cannot deny that you have not been communicative,
Kirylo Sidorovitch. People you have met imparted their impressions to me ; one wrote this,
another that, but I form my own opinions. I
waited to see you first. You are a man out of the
common. That's positively so. You are close,
very close. This taciturnity, this severe brow, this
something inflexible and secret in you, inspires
hopes and a little wonder as to what you may mean.
There is something of a Brutus . . ."

" Pray spare me those classical allusions ! "
burst out Razumov nervously. " What comes
Junius Brutus to do here ? It is ridiculous ! Do
you mean to say," he added sarcastically, but lowering his voice, " that the Russian revolutionists are
all patricians and that I am an aristocrat ? "

Peter Ivanovitch, who had been helping himself
with a few gestures, clasped his hands again behind
his back and made a few steps, pondering.

" Not *all* patricians," he muttered at last. " But you, at any rate, are one of *us*."

Razumov smiled bitterly.

" To be sure my name is not Gugenheimer," he said in a sneering tone. "I am not a democratic Jew. How can I help it? Not everybody has such luck. I have no name, I have no . . ."

The European celebrity showed a great concern. He stepped back a pace and his arms flew in front of his person, extended, deprecatory, almost entreating. His deep bass voice was full of pain.

" But, my dear young friend ! " he cried. " My dear Kirylo Sidorovitch . . ."

Razumov shook his head.

" The very patronymic you are so civil as to use when addressing me I have no legal right to— but what of that ? I don't wish to claim it. I have no father. So much the better. But I will tell you what : my mother's grandfather was a peasant— a serf. See how much I am one of *you*. I don't want any one to claim me. But Russia *can't* disown me. She cannot ! "

Razumov struck his breast with his fist.

" I am *it* ! "

Peter Ivanovitch walked on slowly, his head lowered. Razumov followed, vexed with himself. That was not the right sort of talk. All sincerity was an imprudence. Yet one could not renounce truth altogether, he thought, with despair. Peter Ivanovitch, meditating behind his dark glasses,

became to him suddenly so odious that if he had
had a knife, he fancied he could have stabbed
him not only without compunction, but with a
horrible, triumphant satisfaction. His imagination
dwelt on that atrocity in spite of himself. It was as
if he were becoming light-headed. " It is not what
is expected of me," he repeated to himself. " It
is not what is—I could get away by breaking the
fastening on the little gate I see there in the back
wall. It is a flimsy lock. Nobody in the house
seems to know he is here with me. Oh yes. The
hat ! These women would discover presently the
hat he has left on the landing. They would come
upon him, lying dead in this damp, gloomy shade—
but I would be gone and no one could ever . . .
Lord ! Am I going mad ? " he asked himself in a
fright.

The great man was heard—musing in an undertone.

" H'm, yes ! That—no doubt—in a certain
sense . . ." He raised his voice. " There is a
deal of pride about you . . ."

The intonation of Peter Ivanovitch took on a
homely, familiar ring, acknowledging, in a way,
Razumov's claim to peasant descent.

" A great deal of pride, brother Kirylo. And
I don't say that you have no justification for it.
I have admitted you had. I have ventured to
allude to the facts of your birth simply because
I attach no mean importance to it. You are one

of us—*un des nôtres*. I reflect on that with satisfaction."

"I attach some importance to it also," said Razumov quietly. "I won't even deny that it may have some importance for you too," he continued, after a slight pause and with a touch of grimness of which he was himself aware, with some annoyance. He hoped it had escaped the perception of Peter Ivanovitch. "But suppose we talk no more about it?"

"Well, we shall not—not after this one time, Kirylo Sidorovitch," persisted the noble archpriest of revolution. "This shall be the last occasion. You cannot believe for a moment that I had the slightest idea of wounding your feelings. You are clearly a superior nature—that's how I read you. Quite above the common—h'm—susceptibilities. But the fact is, Kirylo Sidorovitch, I don't know your susceptibilities. Nobody, out of Russia, knows much of you—as yet!"

"You have been watching me?" suggested Razumov.

"Yes."

The great man had spoken in a tone of perfect frankness, but as they turned their faces to each other Razumov felt baffled by the dark spectacles. Under their cover, Peter Ivanovitch hinted that he had felt for some time the need of meeting a man of energy and character, in view of a certain project. He said nothing more precise, however; and after some critical remarks upon the personalities of the various members of the committee of revolutionary action in Stuttgart, he let the conversation lapse for quite a long while. They paced the alley from end to end. Razumov, silent too, raised his eyes from time to time to cast a glance at the back of the house. It offered no sign of being inhabited. With its grimy, weather-stained walls and all the windows shuttered from top to bottom, it looked damp and gloomy and deserted. It might very well have been haunted in traditional style by some doleful, groaning, futile ghost of a middle-class order. The shades evoked, as worldly rumour had it, by Madame de S—— to meet statesmen, diplomatists, deputies of various European Parliaments, must have been of another sort. Razumov had never seen Madame de S—— but in the carriage.

Peter Ivanovitch came out of his abstraction.

"Two things I may say to you at once. I believe, first, that neither a leader nor any decisive action can come out of the dregs of a people. Now, if you ask me what are the dregs of a people—h'm— it would take too long to tell. You would be surprised at the variety of ingredients that for me go to the making up of these dregs—of that which ought, *must* remain at the bottom. Moreover, such a statement might be subject to discussion. But I can tell you what is *not* the dregs. On that it is impossible for us to disagree. The peasantry of a people is not the dregs ; neither is its highest class—

well—the nobility. Reflect on that, Kirylo Sidorovitch ! I believe you are well fitted for reflection.
Everything in a people that is not genuine, not
its own by origin or development, is—well—dirt !
Intelligence in the wrong place is that. Foreign-
bred doctrines are that. Dirt ! Dregs ! The
second thing I would offer to your meditation is
this : that for us at this moment there yawns a
chasm between the past and the future. It can
never be bridged by foreign liberalism. All attempts at it are either folly or cheating. Bridged
it can never be ! It has to be filled up."

A sort of sinister jocularity had crept into the
tones of the burly feminist. He seized Razumov's
arm above the elbow, and gave it a slight shake.

" Do you understand, enigmatical young man ?
It has got to be just filled up."

Razumov kept an unmoved countenance.

" Don't you think that I have already gone
beyond meditation on that subject ? " he said,
freeing his arm by a quiet movement which increased the distance a little between himself and
Peter Ivanovitch, as they went on strolling abreast.
And he added that surely whole cartloads of words
and theories could never fill that chasm. No
meditation was necessary. A sacrifice of many
lives could alone—— He fell silent without finishing the phrase.

Peter Ivanovitch inclined his big hairy head
slowly. After a moment he proposed that they

should go and see if Madame de S—— was now visible.

"We shall get some tea," he said, turning out of the shaded gloomy walk with a brisker step.

The lady companion had been on the look out. Her dark skirt whisked into the doorway as the two men came in sight round the corner. She ran off somewhere altogether, and had disappeared when they entered the hall. In the crude light falling from the dusty glass skylight upon the black-and-white tessellated floor, covered with muddy tracks, their footsteps echoed faintly. The great feminist led the way up the stairs. On the balustrade of the first-floor landing a shiny tall hat reposed, rim upwards, opposite the double door of the drawing-room, haunted, it was said, by evoked ghosts, and frequented, it was to be supposed, by fugitive revolutionists. The cracked white paint of the panels, the tarnished gilt of the mouldings, permitted one to imagine nothing but dust and emptiness within. Before turning the massive brass handle, Peter Ivanovitch gave his young companion a sharp, partly critical, partly preparatory glance.

"No one is perfect," he murmured discreetly. Thus, the possessor of a rare jewel might, before opening the casket, warn the profane that no gem perhaps is flawless.

He remained with his hand on the door-handle so long that Razumov assented by a moody "No."

" Perfection itself would not produce that effect," pursued Peter Ivanovitch, " in a world not meant for it. But you shall find there a mind— no !—the quintessence of feminine intuition which will understand any perplexity you may be suffering from by the irresistible, enlightening force of sympathy. Nothing can remain obscure before that—that—inspired, yes, inspired penetration, this true light of femininity."

The gaze of the dark spectacles in its glossy steadfastness gave his face an air of absolute conviction. Razumov felt a momentary shrinking before that closed door.

" Penetration ? Light ? " he stammered out. " Do you mean some sort of thought-reading ? "

Peter Ivanovitch seemed shocked.

" I mean something utterly different," he retorted, with a faint, pitying smile.

Razumov began to feel angry, very much against his wish.

" This is very mysterious," he muttered through his teeth.

" You don't object to being understood, to being guided ? " queried the great feminist.

Razumov exploded in a fierce whisper :

" In what sense ? Be pleased to understand that I am a serious person. Who do you take me for ? "

They looked at each other very closely. Razumov's temper was cooled by the impenetrable

earnestness of the blue glasses meeting his stare.
Peter Ivanovitch turned the handle at last.

" You shall know directly," he said, pushing
the door open.

A low-pitched grating voice was heard within the
room :

" *Enfin. Vous voilà.*"

In the doorway, his black-coated bulk blocking
the view, Peter Ivanovitch boomed in a hearty
tone with something boastful in it.

" Yes. Here I am ! "

He glanced over his shoulder at Razumov, who
waited for him to move on.

" And I am bringing you a proved conspirator—
a real one this time. *Un vrai celui-là.*"

This pause in the doorway gave the " proved
conspirator " time to make sure that his face did not
betray his angry curiosity and his mental disgust.

These sentiments stand confessed in Mr.
Razumov's memorandum of his first interview with
Madame de S——. The very words I used in my
narrative are written where their sincerity cannot be
suspected. The record, which could not have been
meant for any one's eyes but his own, was not, I
think, the outcome of that strange impulse of indiscretion common to men who lead secret lives, and
accounting for the invariable existence of " compromising documents " in all the plots and conspiracies of history. Mr. Razumov looked at it, I
suppose, as a man looks at himself in a mirror,

with wonder, perhaps with anguish, with anger or despair. Yes, as a threatened man may look fearfully at his own face in the glass, formulating to himself reassuring excuses for his appearance marked by the taint of some insidious hereditary disease.

II

The Egeria of the " Russian Mazzini " produced, at first view, a strong effect by the death-like immobility of an obviously painted face. The eyes appeared extraordinarily brilliant. The figure, in a close-fitting dress, admirably made, but by no means fresh, had an elegant stiffness. The rasping voice inviting him to sit down ; the rigidity of the upright attitude with one arm extended along the back of the sofa, the white gleam of the big eyeballs setting off the black, fathomless stare of the enlarged pupils, impressed Razumov more than anything he had seen since his hasty and secret departure from St. Petersburg. A witch in Parisian clothes, he thought. A portent ! He actually hesitated in his advance, and did not even comprehend, at first, what the rasping voice was saying.

" Sit down. Draw your chair nearer me. There——"

He sat down. At close quarters the rouged cheek-bones, the wrinkles, the fine lines on each side of the vivid lips, astounded him. He was being received graciously, with a smile which made him think of a grinning skull.

" We have been hearing about you for some time."

He did not know what to say, and murmured some disconnected words. The grinning-skull effect vanished.

" And do you know that the general complaint is that you have shown yourself very reserved everywhere ? "

Razumov remained silent for a time, thinking of his answer.

" I, don't you see, am a man of action," he said huskily, glancing upwards.

Peter Ivanovitch stood in portentous expectant silence by the side of his chair. A slight feeling of nausea came over Razumov. What could be the relations of these two people to each other ? She like a galvanised corpse out of some Hoffmann's Tale ; he the preacher of feminist gospel for all the world, and a super-revolutionist besides ! This ancient, painted mummy with unfathomable eyes, and this burly, bull-necked, deferential . . . what was it ? Witchcraft, fascination. . . . " It's for her money," he thought. " She has millions ! "

The walls, the floor of the room were bare like a barn. The few pieces of furniture had been discovered in the garrets and dragged down into service without even having been properly dusted. It was the refuse the banker's widow had left behind her. The windows without curtains had an indigent, sleepless look. In two of them the dirty yellowy-white blinds had been pulled down. All this spoke, not of poverty, but of sordid penuriousness.

The hoarse voice on the sofa uttered angrily :

" You are looking round, Kirylo Sidorovitch. I have been shamefully robbed, positively ruined."

A rattling laugh, which seemed beyond her control, interrupted her for a moment.

" A slavish nature would find consolation in the fact that the principal robber was an exalted and almost a sacrosanct person—a Grand Duke, in fact. Do you understand, Mr. Razumov ? A Grand Duke—No ! You have no idea what thieves those people are ! Downright thieves ! "

Her bosom heaved, but her left arm remained rigidly extended along the back of the couch.

" You will only upset yourself," breathed out a deep voice, which, to Razumov's startled glance, seemed to proceed from under the steady spectacles of Peter Ivanovitch, rather than from his lips, which had hardly moved.

" What of that ? I say thieves ! *Voleurs ! Voleurs !* "

Razumov was quite confounded by this unexpected clamour, which had in it something of wailing and croaking, and more than a suspicion of hysteria.

" *Voleurs ! Voleurs ! Vol . . .*"

" No power on earth can rob you of your

genius," shouted Peter Ivanovitch in an overpowering bass, but without stirring, without a gesture of
any kind. A profound silence fell.

Razumov remained outwardly impassive. "What
is the meaning of this performance?" he was
asking himself. But with a preliminary sound
of bumping outside some door behind him, the
lady companion, in a threadbare black skirt and
frayed blouse, came in rapidly, walking on her
heels, and carrying in both hands a big Russian
samovar, obviously too heavy for her. Razumov
made an instinctive movement to help, which
startled her so much that she nearly dropped her
hissing burden. She managed, however, to land
it on the table, and looked so frightened that Razumov hastened to sit down. She produced then,
from an adjacent room, four glass tumblers, a
teapot, and a sugar-basin, on a black iron tray.

The rasping voice asked from the sofa abruptly:
" *Les gâteaux?* Have you remembered to bring
the cakes?"

Peter Ivanovitch, without a word, marched out
on to the landing and returned instantly with a
parcel wrapped up in white glazed paper, which he
must have extracted from the interior of his hat.
With imperturbable gravity he undid the string
and smoothed the paper open on a part of the table
within reach of Madame de S——'s hand. The
lady companion poured out the tea, then retired
into a distant corner out of everybody's sight. From

time to time Madame de S—— extended a claw-
like hand, glittering with costly rings, towards
the paper of cakes, took up one and devoured it,
displaying her big false teeth ghoulishly. Meantime she talked in a hoarse tone of the political
situation in the Balkans. She built great hopes
on some complication in the peninsula for arousing
a great movement of national indignation in Russia
against " these thieves—thieves—thieves ! "

" You will only upset yourself," Peter Ivanovitch interposed, raising his glassy gaze. He smoked
cigarettes and drank tea in silence, continuously.
When he had finished a glass, he flourished his hand
above his shoulder. At that signal the lady companion, ensconced in her corner, with round eyes
like a watchful animal, would dart out to the table
and pour him out another tumblerful.

Razumov looked at her once or twice. She was
anxious, tremulous, though neither Madame de
S—— nor Peter Ivanovitch paid the slightest attention to her. "What have they done between them
to that forlorn creature ? " Razumov asked himself.
" Have they terrified her out of her senses with
ghosts, or simply have they only been beating
her ? " When she gave him his second glass of
tea, he noticed that her lips trembled in the manner
of a scared person about to burst into speech. But,
of course, she said nothing, and retired into her
corner, as if hugging to herself the smile of thanks
he gave her.

" She may be worth cultivating," thought Razumov suddenly.

He was calming down, getting hold of the actuality into which he had been thrown—for the first time perhaps since Victor Haldin had entered his room . . . and had gone out again. He was distinctly aware of being the object of the famous —or notorious — Madame de S——'s ghastly graciousness.

Madame de S—— was pleased to discover that this young man was different from the other types of revolutionist members of committees, secret emissaries, vulgar and unmannerly fugitive professors, rough students, ex-cobblers with apostolic faces, consumptive and ragged enthusiasts, Hebrew youths, common fellows of all sorts that used to come and go around Peter Ivanovitch—fanatics, pedants, proletarians all. It was pleasant to talk to this young man of notably good appearance— for Madame de S—— was not always in a mystical state of mind. Razumov's taciturnity only excited her to a quicker, more voluble utterance. It still dealt with the Balkans. She knew all the statesmen of that region, Turks, Bulgarians, Montenegrins, Roumanians, Greeks, Armenians, and nondescripts, young and old, the living and the dead. With some money an intrigue could be started which would set the peninsula in a blaze, and outrage the sentiment of the Russian people. A cry of abandoned brothers could be raised, and then, with the

18

nation seething with indignation, a couple of regiments or so would be enough to begin a military revolution in St. Petersburg and make an end of these thieves. . . .

"Apparently I've got only to sit still and listen," the silent Razumov thought to himself. "As to that hairy and obscene brute" (in such terms did Mr. Razumov refer mentally to the popular expounder of a feministic conception of social state), "as to him, for all his cunning he too shall speak out some day."

Razumov ceased to think for a moment. Then a sombre-toned reflection formulated itself in his mind, ironical and bitter. "I have the gift of inspiring confidence." He heard himself laughing aloud. It was like a goad to the painted, shiny-eyed harridan on the sofa.

"You may well laugh!" she cried hoarsely. "What else can one do? Perfect swindlers—and what base swindlers at that! Cheap Germans—Holstein-Gottorps! Though, indeed, it's hardly safe to say who and what they are. A family that counts a creature like Catherine the Great in its ancestry—you understand!"

"You are only upsetting yourself," said Peter Ivanovitch, patiently but in a firm tone. This admonition had its usual effect on the Egeria. She dropped her thick, discoloured eyelids and changed her position on the sofa. All her angular and lifeless movements seemed completely automatic now that her eyes were closed. Presently she opened them very full. Peter Ivanovitch drank tea steadily, without haste.

" Well, I declare ! " She addressed Razumov directly. " The people who have seen you on your way here are right. You are very reserved. You haven't said twenty words altogether since you came in. You let nothing of your thoughts be seen in your face either."

" I have been listening, Madame," said Razumov, using French for the first time hesitatingly, not being certain of his accent. But it seemed to produce an excellent impression. Madame de S—— looked meaningly into Peter Ivanovitch's spectacles, as if to convey her conviction of this young man's merit. She even nodded the least bit in his direction, and Razumov heard her murmur under her breath the words, " Later on in the diplomatic service," which could not but refer to the favourable impression he had made. The fantastic absurdity of it revolted him,; because it seemed to outrage his ruined hopes with the vision of a mock-career. Peter Ivanovitch, impassive as though he were deaf, drank some more tea. Razumov felt that he must say something.

" Yes," he began deliberately, as if uttering a meditated opinion. " Clearly. Even in planning a purely military revolution the temper of the people should be taken into account."

" You have understood me perfectly. The dis-

content should be spiritualised. That is what the
ordinary heads of revolutionary committees will
not understand. They are incapable of it. For
instance, Mordatiev was in Geneva last month.
Peter Ivanovitch brought him here. You know
Mordatiev ? Well, yes—you have heard of him.
They call him an eagle—a hero ! He has never
done half as much as you have. Never attempted
—not half. . . ."

Madame de S—— agitated herself angularly
on the sofa.

" We, of course, talked to him. And do you
know what he said to me ? ' What have we to do
with Balkan intrigues ? We must simply extirpate
the scoundrels.' Extirpate is all very well—but
what then ? The imbecile ! I screamed at him,
' But you must spiritualise—don't you understand ?
—spiritualise the discontent.' . . ."

She felt nervously in her pocket for a handkerchief ; she pressed it to her lips.

" Spiritualise ? " said Razumov interrogatively,
watching her heaving breast. The long ends of an
old black lace scarf she wore over her head slipped
off her shoulders and hung down on each side of her
ghastly rosy cheeks.

" An odious creature," she burst out again.
" Imagine a man who takes five lumps of sugar in
his tea. . . . Yes, I said spiritualise ! How else
can you make discontent effective and universal ? "

" Listen to this, young man." Peter Ivanovitch

made himself heard solemnly. " Effective and universal."

Razumov looked at him suspiciously.

" Some say hunger will do that," he remarked.

" Yes. I know. Our people are starving in heaps. But you can't make famine universal. And it is not despair that we want to create. There is no moral support to be got out of that. It is indignation . . ."

Madame de S—— let her thin, extended arm sink on her knees.

" I am not a Mordatiev," began Razumov.

" *Bien sûr !* " murmured Madame de S——.

" Though I too am ready to say extirpate, extirpate ! But in my ignorance of political work, permit me to ask : A Balkan—well—intrigue, wouldn't that take a very long time ? "

Peter Ivanovitch got up and moved off quietly, to stand with his face to the window. Razumov heard a door close ; he turned his head and perceived that the lady companion had scuttled out of the room.

" In matters of politics I am a supernaturalist." Madame de S—— broke the silence harshly.

Peter Ivanovitch moved away from the window and struck Razumov lightly on the shoulder. This was a signal for leaving, but at the same time he addressed Madame de S—— in a peculiar reminding tone :

" Eleanor ! "

Whatever it meant, she did not seem to hear him. She leaned back in the corner of the sofa like a wooden figure. The immovable peevishness of the face, framed in the limp, rusty lace, had a character of cruelty.

" As to extirpating," she croaked at the attentive Razumov, " there is only one class in Russia which must be extirpated. Only one. And that class consists of only one family. You understand me ? That one family must be extirpated."

Her rigidity was frightful, like the rigor of a corpse galvanised into harsh speech and glittering stare by the force of murderous hate. The sight fascinated Razumov—yet he felt more self-possessed than at any other time since he had entered this weirdly bare room. He was interested. But the great feminist by his side again uttered his appeal :

" Eleanor ! "

She disregarded it. Her carmine lips vaticinated with an extraordinary rapidity. The liberating spirit would use arms before which rivers would part like Jordan, and ramparts fall down like the walls of Jericho. The deliverance from bondage would be effected by plagues and by signs, by wonders and by war. The women . . .

" Eleanor ! "

She ceased ; she had heard him at last. She pressed her hand to her forehead.

" What is it ? Ah yes ! That girl—the sister of . . ."

It was Miss Haldin that she meant. That young girl and her mother had been leading a very retired life. They were provincial ladies—were they not? The mother had been very beautiful—traces were left yet. Peter Ivanovitch, when he called there for the first time, was greatly struck. . . . But the cold way they received him was really surprising.

" He is one of our national glories," Madame de S—— cried out, with sudden vehemence. " All the world listens to him."

" I don't know these ladies," said Razumov loudly, rising from his chair.

" What are you saying, Kirylo Sidorovitch? I understand that she was talking to you here, in the garden, the other day."

" Yes, in the garden," said Razumov gloomily. Then, with an effort, " She made herself known to me."

" And then ran away from us all," Madame de S—— continued, with ghastly vivacity. " After coming to the very door! What a peculiar proceeding! Well, I have been a shy little provincial girl at one time. Yes, Razumov " (she fell into this familiarity intentionally, with an appalling grimace of graciousness. Razumov gave a perceptible start), " yes, that's my origin. A simple provincial family."

" You are a marvel," Peter Ivanovitch uttered in his deepest voice.

But it was to Razumov that she gave her death's-head smile. Her tone was quite imperious.

" You must bring the wild young thing here. She is wanted. I reckon upon your success—mind ! "

" She is not a wild young thing," muttered Razumov, in a surly voice.

" Well, then—that's all the same. She may be one of those young conceited democrats. Do you know what I think ? I think she is very much like you in character. There is a smouldering fire of scorn in you. You are darkly self-sufficient, but I can see your very soul."

Her shiny eyes had a dry, intense stare, which, missing Razumov, gave him an absurd notion that she was looking at something which was visible to her behind him. He cursed himself for an impressionable fool, and asked with forced calmness :

" What is it you see ? Anything resembling me ? "

She moved her rigidly set face from left to right negatively.

" Some sort of phantom in my image ? " pursued Razumov slowly. " For, I suppose, a soul when it is seen is just that. A vain thing. There are phantoms of the living as well as of the dead."

The tenseness of Madame de S——'s stare had relaxed, and now she looked at Razumov in a silence that became disconcerting.

" I myself have had an experience," he stammered out, as if compelled. " I've seen a phantom once."

The unnaturally red lips moved to frame a question harshly.

" Of a dead person ? "

" No. Living."

" A friend ? "

" No."

" An enemy ? "

" I hated him."

" Ah ! It was not a woman, then ? "

" A woman ! " repeated Razumov, his eyes looking straight into the eyes of Madame de S——. " Why should it have been a woman ? And why this conclusion ? Why should I not have been able to hate a woman ? "

As a matter of fact, the idea of hating a woman was new to him. At that moment he hated Madame de S——. But it was not exactly hate. It was more like the abhorrence that may be caused by a wooden or plaster figure of a repulsive kind. She moved no more than if she were such a figure ; even her eyes, whose unwinking stare plunged into his own, though shining, were lifeless, as though they were as artificial as her teeth. For the first time Razumov became aware of a faint perfume, but faint as it was it nauseated him exceedingly. Again Peter Ivanovitch tapped him slightly on the shoulder. Thereupon he bowed, and was about to turn away when he received the unexpected favour of a bony, inanimate hand extended to him, with the two words in hoarse French :

" Au revoir ! "

He bowed over the skeleton hand and left the room, escorted by the great man, who made him go out first. The voice from the sofa cried after them :

" You remain here, Pierre."

" Certainly, *ma chère amie*."

But he left the room with Razumov, shutting the door behind him. The landing was prolonged into a bare corridor, right and left, desolate perspectives of white-and-gold decoration without a strip of carpet. The very light, pouring through a large window at the end, seemed dusty ; and a solitary speck reposing on the balustrade of white marble—the silk top-hat of the great feminist—asserted itself extremely, black and glossy in all that crude whiteness.

Peter Ivanovitch escorted the visitor without opening his lips. Even when they had reached the head of the stairs, Peter Ivanovitch did not break the silence. Razumov's impulse to continue down the flight and out of the house without as much as a nod abandoned him suddenly. He stopped on the first step and leaned his back against the wall. Below him the great hall with its checkered floor of black and white seemed absurdly large and like some public place where a great power of resonance awaits the provocation of footfalls and voices. As

if afraid of awakening the loud echoes of that empty
house, Razumov adopted a low tone.

" I really have no mind to turn into a dilettante
spiritualist."

Peter Ivanovitch shook his head slightly, very
serious.

" Or spend my time in spiritual ecstasies or
sublime meditations upon the gospel of feminism,"
continued Razumov. " I made my way here for
my share of action—action, most respected Peter
Ivanovitch ! It was not the great European writer
who attracted me, here, to this odious town of
liberty. It was somebody much greater. It was
the idea of the chief which attracted me. There
are starving young men in Russia who believe in
you so much that it seems the only thing that keeps
them alive in their misery. Think of that, Peter
Ivanovitch ! No ! But only think of that ! "

The great man, thus entreated, perfectly motionless and silent, was the very image of patient,
placid respectability.

" Of course I don't speak of the people. They
are brutes," added Razumov, in the same subdued
but forcible tone. At this, a protesting murmur
issued from the " heroic fugitive's " beard—a
murmur of authority :

" Say—children."

" No ! Brutes ! " Razumov insisted bluntly.

" But they are sound, they are innocent," the
great man pleaded in a whisper.

" As far as that goes, a brute is sound enough."
Razumov raised his voice at last. " And you can't
deny the natural innocence of a brute. But what's
the use of disputing about names ? You just try
to give these children the power and stature of men
and see what they will be like. You just give it
to them and see. . . . But never mind. I tell
you, Peter Ivanovitch, that half a dozen young men
do not come together nowadays in a shabby student's
room without your name being whispered, not as
a leader of thought, but as a centre of revolutionary
energies—the centre of action. What else has
drawn me near you, do you think ? It is not what
all the world knows of you surely. It's precisely
what the world at large does not know. I was
irresistibly drawn—let us say impelled, yes, impelled ; or, rather, compelled, driven—driven,"
repeated Razumov loudly, and ceased, as if startled
by the hollow reverberation of the word " driven "
along two bare corridors and in the great empty
hall.

Peter Ivanovitch did not seem startled in the least.
The young man could not control a dry, uneasy
laugh. The great revolutionist remained unmoved
with an effect of commonplace, homely superiority.

" Curse him," said Razumov to himself, " he is
waiting behind his spectacles for me to give myself
away." Then aloud, with a satanic enjoyment of
the scorn prompting him to play with the greatness
of the great man :

" Ah, Peter Ivanovitch, if you only knew the
force which drew—no, which *drove* me towards
you !   The irresistible force."

He did not feel any desire to laugh now. This
time Peter Ivanovitch moved his head sideways,
knowingly, as much as to say, " Don't I ? " This
expressive movement was almost imperceptible.
Razumov went on in secret derision :

" All these days you have been trying to read me,
Peter Ivanovitch. That is natural. I have perceived it and I have been frank. Perhaps you may
think I have not been very expansive ? But with
a man like you it was not needed ; it would have
looked like an impertinence, perhaps. And besides,
we Russians are prone to talk too much, as a rule.
I have always felt that. And yet, as a nation, we
are dumb. I assure you that I am not likely to
talk to you so much again—ha, ha !——"

Razumov, still keeping on the lower step, came
a little nearer to the great man.

" You have been condescending enough. I
quite understood it was to lead me on. You must
render me the justice that I have not tried to please.
I have been impelled, compelled, or rather sent—
let us say sent—towards you for a work that no
one but myself can do. You would call it a
harmless delusion : a ridiculous delusion at which
you don't even smile. It is absurd of me to talk
like this, yet some day you will remember these
words, I hope. Enough of this. Here I stand

before you—confessed ! But one thing more I must add to complete it : a mere blind tool I can never consent to be."

Whatever acknowledgment Razumov was prepared for, he was not prepared to have both his hands seized in the great man's grasp. The swiftness of the movement was aggressive enough to startle. The burly feminist could not have been quicker had his purpose been to jerk Razumov treacherously up on the landing and bundle him behind one of the numerous closed doors near by. This idea actually occurred to Razumov ; his hands being released after a darkly eloquent squeeze, he smiled, with a beating heart, straight at the beard and the spectacles hiding that impenetrable man.

He thought to himself (it stands confessed in his handwriting), " I won't move from here till he either speaks or turns away. This is a duel." Many seconds passed without a sign or sound.

" Yes, yes," the great man said hurriedly, in subdued tones, as if the whole thing had been a stolen, breathless interview. " Exactly. Come to see us here in a few days. This must be gone into deeply—deeply, between you and me. Quite to the bottom. To the . . . And, by-the-bye, you must bring along Natalia Victorovna—you know, the Haldin girl . . ."

" Am I to take this as my first instruction from you ? " inquired Razumov stiffly.

Peter Ivanovitch seemed perplexed by this new attitude.

" Ah ! h'm ! You are naturally the proper person—*la personne indiquée*. Every one shall be wanted presently. Every one."

He bent down from the landing over Razumov, who had lowered his eyes.

" The moment of action approaches," he murmured.

Razumov did not look up. He did not move till he heard the door of the drawing-room close behind the greatest of feminists returning to his painted Egeria. Then he walked down slowly into the hall. The door stood open, and the shadow of the house was lying aslant over the greatest part of the terrace. While crossing it slowly, he lifted his hat and wiped his damp forehead, expelling his breath with force to get rid of the last vestiges of the air he had been breathing inside. He looked at the palms of his hands, and rubbed them gently against his thighs.

He felt, bizarre as it may seem, as though another self, an independent sharer, of his mind, had been able to view his whole person very distinctly indeed. " This is curious," he thought. After a while he formulated his opinion of it in the mental ejaculation : " Beastly ! " This disgust vanished before a marked uneasiness. " This is an effect of nervous exhaustion," he reflected with weary sagacity. " How am I to go on day after day

if I have no more power of resistance—moral
resistance ? "

He followed the path at the foot of the terrace.
" Moral resistance, moral resistance "; he kept
on repeating these words mentally. Moral endurance. Yes, that was the necessity of the situation. An immense longing to make his way out of
these grounds and to the other end of the town, of
throwing himself on his bed and going to sleep for
hours, swept everything clean out of his mind for a
moment. " Is it possible that I am but a weak
creature after all ? " he asked himself, in sudden
alarm. " Eh ! What's that ? "

He gave a start as if awakened from a dream.
He even swayed a little before recovering himself.

" Ah ! You stole away from us quietly to walk
about here," he said.

The lady companion stood before him, but how
she came there he had not the slightest idea. Her
folded arms were closely cherishing the cat.

" I have been unconscious as I walked, it's a
positive fact," said Razumov to himself in wonder.
He raised his hat with marked civility.

The sallow woman blushed duskily. She had
her invariably scared expression, as if somebody
had just disclosed to her some terrible news. But
she held her ground, Razumov noticed, without
timidity. " She is incredibly shabby," he thought.
In the sunlight her black costume looked greenish,
with here and there threadbare patches where the

stuff seemed decomposed by age into a velvety, black, furry state. Her very hair and eyebrows looked shabby. Razumov wondered whether she were sixty years old. Her figure, though, was young enough. He observed that she did not appear starved, but rather as if she had been fed on unwholesome scraps and leavings of plates.

Razumov smiled amiably and moved out of her way. She turned her head to keep her scared eyes on him.

" I know what you have been told in there," she affirmed, without preliminaries. Her tone, in contrast with her manner, had an unexpectedly assured character which put Razumov at his ease.

" Do you ? You must have heard all sorts of talk on many occasions in there."

She varied her phrase, with the same incongruous effect of positiveness.

" I know to a certainty what you have been told to do."

" Really ? " Razumov shrugged his shoulders a little. He was about to pass on with a bow, when a sudden thought struck him. " Yes. To be sure ! In your confidential position you are aware of many things," he murmured, looking at the cat.

That animal got a momentary convulsive hug from the lady companion.

" Everything was disclosed to me a long time ago," she said.

" Everything," Razumov repeated absently.

19

" Peter Ivanovitch is an awful despot," she jerked out.

Razumov went on studying the stripes on the grey fur of the cat.

" An iron will is an integral part of such a temperament. How else could he be a leader ? And I think that you are mistaken in——"

" There ! " she cried. " You tell me that I am mistaken. But I tell you all the same that he cares for no one." She jerked her head up. " Don't you bring that girl here. That's what you have been told to do—to bring that girl here. Listen to me ; you had better tie a stone round her neck and throw her into the lake."

Razumov had a sensation of chill and gloom, as if a heavy cloud had passed over the sun.

" The girl ? " he said. " What have I to do with her ? "

" But you have been told to bring Nathalie Haldin here. Am I not right ? Of course I am right. I was not in the room, but I know. I know Peter Ivanovitch sufficiently well. He is a great man. Great men are horrible. Well, that's it. Have nothing to do with her. That's the best you can do, unless you want her to become like me—disillusioned ! Disillusioned ! "

" Like you," repeated Razumov, glaring at her face, as devoid of all comeliness of feature and complexion as the most miserable beggar is of money. He smiled, still feeling chilly—a peculiar sensation which annoyed him. " Disillusioned as to Peter Ivanovitch ! Is that all you have lost ? "

She declared, looking frightened, but with immense conviction, " Peter Ivanovitch stands for everything." Then she added, in another tone, " Keep the girl away from this house."

" And are you absolutely inciting me to disobey Peter Ivanovitch just because—because you are disillusioned ? "

She began to blink.

" Directly I saw you for the first time I was comforted. You took your hat off to me. You looked as if one could trust you. Oh ! "

She shrank before Razumov's savage snarl of, " I have heard something like this before."

She was so confounded that she could do nothing but blink for a long time.

" It was your humane manner," she explained plaintively. " I have been starving for, I won't say kindness, but just for a little civility, for I don't know how long. And now you are angry . . ."

" But no, on the contrary," he protested. " I am very glad you trust me. It's possible that later on I may . . ."

" Yes, if you were to get ill," she interrupted eagerly, " or meet some bitter trouble, you would find I am not a useless fool. You have only to let me know. I will come to you. I will indeed. And I will stick to you. Misery and I are old acquaintances—but this life here is worse than starving."

She paused anxiously, then in a voice for the first time sounding really timid, she added :

" Or if you were engaged in some dangerous work. Sometimes a humble companion—I would not want to know anything. I would follow you with joy. I could carry out orders. I have the courage."

Razumov looked attentively at the scared round eyes, at the withered, sallow, round cheeks. They were quivering about the corners of the mouth.

" She wants to escape from here," he thought.

" Suppose I were to tell you that I am engaged in dangerous work ? " he uttered slowly.

She pressed the cat to her threadbare bosom with a breathless exclamation. " Ah ! " Then not much above a whisper : " Under Peter Ivanovitch ? "

" No, not under Peter Ivanovitch."

He read admiration in her eyes, and made an effort to smile.

" Then—alone ? "

He held up his closed hand with the index raised.

" Like this finger," he said.

She was trembling slightly. But it occurred to Razumov that they might have been observed from the house, and he became anxious to be gone. She blinked, raising up to him her puckered face, and seemed to beg mutely to be told something more, to be given a word of encouragement for her starving, grotesque, and pathetic devotion.

"Can we be seen from the house?" asked Razumov confidentially.

She answered, without showing the slightest surprise at the question :

"No, we can't, on account of this end of the stables." And she added, with an acuteness which surprised Razumov, "But anybody looking out of an upstairs window would know that you have not passed through the gates yet."

"Who's likely to spy out of the window?" queried Razumov. "Peter Ivanovitch?"

She nodded.

"Why should he trouble his head?"

"He expects somebody this afternoon."

"You know the person?"

"There's more than one."

She had lowered her eyelids. Razumov looked at her curiously.

"Of course. You hear everything they say."

She murmured without any animosity :

"So do the tables and chairs."

He understood that the bitterness accumulated in the heart of that helpless creature had got into her veins, and, like some subtle poison, had decomposed her fidelity to that hateful pair. It was a great piece of luck for him, he reflected ; because women are seldom venal after the manner of men, who can be bought for material considerations. She would be a good ally, though it was not likely that she was allowed to hear as much as the tables and chairs of the Château Borel. That could not be expected. But still . . . And, at any rate, she could be made to talk.

When she looked up, her eyes met the fixed stare of Razumov, who began to speak at once.

" Well, well, dear . . . but, upon my word, I haven't the pleasure of knowing your name yet. Isn't it strange ? "

For the first time she made a movement of the shoulders.

" Is it strange ? No one is told my name. No one cares. No one talks to me, no one writes to me. My parents don't even know if I'm alive. I have no use for a name, and I have almost forgotten it myself."

Razumov murmured gravely, " Yes, but still . . ."

She went on much slower, with indifference :

" You may call me Tekla, then. My poor Andrei called me so. I was devoted to him. He lived in wretchedness and suffering, and died in misery. That is the lot of all us Russians, nameless Russians. There is nothing else for us, and no hope anywhere, unless . . ."

" Unless what ? "

" Unless all these people with names are done away with," she finished, blinking and pursing up her lips.

" It will be easier to call you Tekla, as you direct me," said Razumov, " if you consent to call me Kirylo, when we are talking like this—quietly—only you and me."

And he said to himself, " Here's a being who must be terribly afraid of the world, else she would have run away from this situation before." Then he reflected that the mere fact of leaving the great man abruptly would make her a suspect. She could expect no support or countenance from any one. This revolutionist was not fit for an independent existence.

She moved with him a few steps, blinking and nursing the cat with a small balancing movement of her arms.

" Yes—only you and I. That's how I was with my poor Andrei, only he was dying, killed by these official brutes—while you ! You are strong. You kill the monsters. You have done a great deed. Peter Ivanovitch himself must consider you. Well—don't forget me—especially if you are going back to work in Russia. I could follow you, carrying anything that was wanted—at a distance, you know. Or I could watch for hours at the corner of a street if necessary,—in wet or snow—yes, I could—all day long. Or I could write for you dangerous documents, lists of names or instructions, so that in case of mischance the handwriting could not compromise you. And you need not be afraid if they were to catch me. I would know how to keep dumb. We women are not so easily daunted by pain. I heard Peter Ivanovitch say it is our blunt nerves or something. We can stand it better. And it's true ; I would just as soon bite my tongue out and throw it at them as not. What's the good of speech to me ? Who would ever want to hear what I could say ? Ever since I closed the eyes of my poor Andrei I haven't met a man who seemed to care for the sound of my voice. I should never have spoken to you if the very first time you appeared here you had not taken notice of me so nicely. I could not help speaking of you to that charming dear girl. Oh, the sweet creature ! And strong ! One can see that at once. If you have a heart don't let her set her foot in here. Good-bye ! "

Razumov caught her by the arm. Her emotion at being thus seized manifested itself by a short struggle, after which she stood still, not looking at him.

" But you can tell me," he spoke in her ear, " why they—those people in that house there—are so anxious to get hold of her ? "

She freed herself to turn upon him, as if made angry by the question.

" Don't you understand that Peter Ivanovitch must direct, inspire, influence ? It is the breath of his life. There can never be too many disciples. He can't bear thinking of any one escaping him. And a woman, too ! There is nothing to be done without women, he says. He has written it. He——"

The young man was staring at her passion when she broke off suddenly and ran away behind the stable.

III

Razumov, thus left to himself, took the direction of the gate. But on this day of many conversations, he discovered that very probably he could not leave the grounds without having to hold another one.

Stepping in view from beyond the lodge appeared the expected visitors of Peter Ivanovitch : a small party composed of two men and a woman. They noticed him too, immediately, and stopped short as if to consult. But in a moment the woman, moving aside, motioned with her arm to the two men, who, leaving the drive at once, struck across the large neglected lawn, or rather grass-plot, and made directly for the house. The woman remained on the path waiting for Razumov's approach. She had recognised him. He, too, had recognised her at the first glance. He had been made known to her at Zurich, where he had broken his journey while on his way from Dresden. They had been much together for the two days of his stay.

She was wearing the very same costume in which he had seen her first. A blouse of crimson silk made her noticeable at a distance. With that she wore a short brown skirt and a leather belt. Her complexion was the colour of coffee and milk, but very clear ; her eyes black and glittering, her figure erect. A lot of thick hair, nearly white, was done up loosely under a dusty Tyrolese hat of dark cloth, which seemed to have lost some of its trimmings.

The expression of her face was grave, intent ; so grave that Razumov, after approaching her close, felt obliged to smile. She greeted him with a manly handgrasp.

" What ! Are you going away ? " she exclaimed. " How is that, Razumov ? "

" I am going away because I haven't been asked to stay," Razumov answered, returning the pressure of her hand with much less force than she had put into it.

She jerked her head sideways like one who understands. Meantime Razumov's eyes had strayed after the two men. They were crossing the grass - plot obliquely, without haste. The shorter of the two was buttoned up in a narrow overcoat of some thin grey material, which came nearly to his heels. His companion, much taller and broader, wore a short, close-fitting jacket and tight trousers tucked into shabby top-boots.

The woman, who had sent them out of Razumov's way apparently, spoke in a businesslike voice :

" I had to come rushing from Zurich on purpose to meet the train and take these two along here to see Peter Ivanovitch. I've just managed it."

" Ah, indeed ! " Razumov said perfunctorily, and very vexed at her staying behind to talk to him. " From Zurich—yes, of course. And these two, they come from . . ."

She interrupted, without emphasis :

" From quite another direction. From a distance, too. A considerable distance."

Razumov shrugged his shoulders. The two men from a distance, after having reached the wall of the terrace, disappeared suddenly at its foot as if the earth had opened to swallow them up.

" Oh, well, they have just come from America." The woman in the crimson blouse shrugged her shoulders too a little before making that statement. " The time is drawing near," she interjected, as if speaking to herself. " I did not tell them who you were. Yakovlitch would have wanted to embrace you."

" Is that he with the wisp of hair hanging from his chin, in the long coat ? "

" You've guessed aright. That's Yakovlitch."

" And they could not find their way here from the station without you coming on purpose from Zurich to show it to them ? Verily, without women we can do nothing. So it stands written, and apparently so it is."

He was conscious of an immense lassitude under his effort to be sarcastic. And he could see that she had detected it with those steady, brilliant black eyes.

" What is the matter with you ? "

" I don't know. Nothing. I've had a devil of a day."

She waited, with her black eyes fixed on his face.
Then :

" What of that ? You men are so impressionable and self-conscious. One day is like another,
hard, hard—and there's an end of it, till the great
day comes. I came over for a very good reason.
They wrote to warn Peter Ivanovitch of their
arrival. But where from ? Only from Cherbourg
on a bit of ship's notepaper. Anybody could have
done that. Yakovlitch has lived for years and years
in America. I am the only one at hand who had
known him well in the old days. I knew him
very well indeed. So Peter Ivanovitch telegraphed,
asking me to come. It's natural enough, is it
not ? "

" You came to vouch for his identity ? "
inquired Razumov.

" Yes. Something of the kind. Fifteen years
of a life like his make changes in a man. Lonely,
like a crow in a strange country. When I think of
Yakovlitch before he went to America——"

The softness of the low tone caused Razumov to
glance at her sideways. She sighed : her black eyes
were looking away ; she had plunged the fingers of
her right hand deep into the mass of nearly white
hair, and stirred them there absently. When she
withdrew her hand the little hat perched on the
top of her head remained slightly tilted, with a
queer inquisitive effect, contrasting strongly with
the reminiscent murmur that escaped her.

" We were not in our first youth even then. But a man is a child always."

Razumov thought suddenly, " They have been living together." Then aloud :

" Why didn't you follow him to America ? " he asked point-blank.

She looked up at him with a perturbed air.

" Don't you remember what was going on fifteen years ago ? It was a time of activity. The Revolution has its history by this time. You are in it and yet you don't seem to know it. Yakovlitch went away then on a mission ; I went back to Russia. It had to be so. Afterwards there was nothing for him to come back to."

" Ah, indeed ! " muttered Razumov, with affected surprise. " Nothing ! "

" What are you trying to insinuate ? " she exclaimed quickly. " Well, and what then if he did get discouraged a little ? . . ."

" He looks like a Yankee, with that goatee hanging from his chin. A regular Uncle Sam," growled Razumov. " Well, and you ? You who went to Russia ? You did not get discouraged."

" Never mind. Yakovlitch is a man who cannot be doubted. He, at any rate, is the right sort."

Her black, penetrating gaze remained fixed upon Razumov while she spoke, and for a moment afterwards.

" Pardon me," Razumov inquired coldly, " but

does it mean that you, for instance, think that I am not the right sort ? "

She made no protest, gave no sign of having heard the question ; she continued looking at him in a manner which he judged not to be absolutely unfriendly. In Zurich when he passed through she had taken him under her charge, in a way, and was with him from morning till night during his stay of two days. She took him round to see several people. At first she talked to him a great deal and rather unreservedly, but always avoiding all reference to herself ; towards the middle of the second day she fell silent, attending him zealously as before, and even seeing him off at the railway station, where she pressed his hand firmly through the lowered carriage window, and, stepping back without a word, waited till the train moved. He had noticed that she was treated with quiet regard. He knew nothing of her parentage, nothing of her private history or political record ; he judged her from his own private point of view, as being a distinct danger in his path. " Judged " is not perhaps the right word. It was more of a feeling, the summing up of slight impressions aided by the discovery that he could not despise her as he despised all the others. He had not expected to see her again so soon.

No, decidedly ; her expression was not unfriendly. Yet he perceived an acceleration in the beat of his heart. The conversation could not be

abandoned at that point.   He went on in accents of
scrupulous inquiry :

" Is it perhaps because I don't seem to accept
blindly every development of the general doctrine—
such, for instance, as the feminism of our great Peter
·Ivanovitch ?   If that is what makes me suspect,
then I can only say I would scorn to be a slave even
to an idea."

She had been looking at him all the time, not
as a listener looks at one, but as if the words he chose
to say were only of secondary interest.   When he
finished she slipped her hand, by a sudden and
decided movement, under his arm and impelled him
gently towards the gate of the grounds.   He felt
her firmness and obeyed the impulsion at once,
just as the other two men had, a moment before,
obeyed unquestioningly the wave of her hand.

They made a few steps like this.

" No, Razumov, your ideas are probably all
right," she said.   " You may be valuable—very
valuable.   What's the matter with you is that you
don't like us."

She released him.   He met her with a frosty
smile.

" Am I expected, then, to have love as well as
convictions ? "

She shrugged her shoulders.

" You know very well what I mean.   People
have been thinking you not quite whole-hearted.
I have heard that opinion from one side and another.

But I have understood you at the end of the first day . . ."

Razumov interrupted her, speaking steadily.

" I assure you that your perspicacity is at fault here."

" What phrases he uses ! " she exclaimed parenthetically. " Ah ! Kirylo Sidorovitch, you, like other men, are fastidious, full of self-love, and afraid of trifles. Moreover, you had no training. What you want is to be taken in hand by some woman. I am sorry I am not staying here a few days. I am going back to Zurich to-morrow, and shall take Yakovlitch with me most likely."

This information relieved Razumov.

" I am sorry too," he said. " But, all the same, I don't think you understand me."

He breathed more freely ; she did not protest, but asked, " And how did you get on with Peter Ivanovitch ? You have seen a good deal of each other. How is it between you two ? "

Not knowing what answer to make, the young man inclined his head slowly.

Her lips had been parted in expectation. She pressed them together, and seemed to reflect.

" That's all right."

This had a sound of finality, but she did not leave him. It was impossible to guess what she had in her mind. Razumov muttered :

" It is not of me that you should have asked that question. In a moment you shall see Peter Ivano-

vitch himself, and the subject will come up naturally. He will be curious to know what has delayed
you so long in this garden."

" No doubt Peter Ivanovitch will have something
to say to me. Several things. He may even speak
of you—question me. Peter Ivanovitch is inclined
to trust me generally."

" Question you ? That's very likely."

She smiled, half serious.

" Well—and what shall I say to him ? "

" I don't know. You may tell him of your discovery."

" What's that ? "

" Why—my lack of love for . . ."

" Oh ! That's between ourselves," she interrupted, it was hard to say whether in jest or earnest.

" I see that you want to tell Peter Ivanovitch
something in my favour," said Razumov, with grim
playfulness. " Well, then, you can tell him that
I am very much in earnest about my mission. I
mean to succeed." ,

" You have been given a mission ! " she exclaimed quickly.

" It amounts to that. I have been told to bring
about a certain event."

She looked at him searchingly.

" A mission," she repeated, very grave and
interested all at once. " What sort of mission ? "

" Something in the nature of propaganda work."

" Ah ! Far away from here ? "

20

" No. Not very far," said Razumov, restraining a sudden desire to laugh, though he did not feel joyous in the least.

" So ! " she said thoughtfully. " Well, I am not asking questions. It's sufficient that Peter Ivanovitch should know what each of us is doing. Everything is bound to come right in the end."

" You think so ? "

" I don't think, young man. I just simply believe it."

" And is it to Peter Ivanovitch that you owe that faith ? "

She did not answer the question, and they stood idle, silent, as if reluctant to part with each other.

" That's just like a man," she murmured at last. " As if it were possible to tell how a belief comes to one." Her thin Mephistophelian eyebrows moved a little. " Truly there are millions of people in Russia who would envy the life of dogs in this country. It is a horror and a shame to confess this even between ourselves. One must believe for very pity. This can't go on. No ! It can't go on. For twenty years I have been coming and going, looking neither to the left nor to the right. . . . What are you smiling to yourself for ? You are only at the beginning. You have begun well, but you just wait till you have trodden every particle of yourself under your feet in your comings and goings. For that is what it comes to. You've got to trample down every particle of your own feelings ; for stop you cannot, you must not. I have been young, too—but perhaps you think that I am complaining—eh ? "

" I don't think anything of the sort," protested Razumov indifferently.

" I dare say you don't, you dear superior creature. You don't care."

She plunged her fingers into the bunch of hair on the left side, and that brusque movement had the effect of setting the Tyrolese hat straight on her head. She frowned under it without animosity, in the manner of an investigator. Razumov averted his face carelessly.

" You men are all alike. You mistake luck for merit. You do it in good faith too ! I would not be too hard on you. It's masculine nature. You men are ridiculously pitiful in your aptitude to cherish childish illusions down to the very grave. There are a lot of us who have been at work for fifteen years—I mean constantly—trying one way after another, underground and above-ground, looking neither to the right nor to the left ! I can talk about it. I have been one of those that never rested. . . . There ! What's the use of talking ? . . . Look at my grey hairs ! And here two babies come along—I mean you and Haldin—you come along and manage to strike a blow at the very first try."

At the name of Haldin falling from the rapid and energetic lips of the woman revolutionist, Razumov

had the usual brusque consciousness of the irrevoc-
able. But in all the months which had passed over
his head he had become hardened to the experience.
The consciousness was no longer accompanied by
the blank dismay and the blind anger of the early
days. He had argued himself into new beliefs ;
and he had made for himself a mental atmosphere
of gloomy and sardonic reverie, a sort of murky
medium through which the event appeared like a
featureless shadow having vaguely the shape of
a man—a shape extremely familiar, yet utterly
inexpressive, except for its air of discreet waiting
in the dusk. It was not alarming.

" What was *he* like ? " the woman revolutionist
asked unexpectedly.

" What was he like ? " echoed Razumov, making
a painful effort not to turn upon her savagely.
But he relieved himself by laughing a little while he
stole a glance at her out of the corners of his eyes.
This reception of her inquiry disturbed her.

" How like a woman," he went on. " What is
the good of concerning yourself with his appearance ? Whatever it was, he is removed beyond all
feminine influences now."

A frown, making three folds at the root of her
nose, accentuated the Mephistophelian slant of her
eyebrows.

" You suffer, Razumov," she suggested, in her
low, confident voice.

" What nonsense ! " Razumov faced the

woman fairly. " But now I think of it, I am not sure that he is beyond the influence of one woman at least ; the one over there—Madame de S——, you know. Formerly the dead were allowed to rest, but now it seems they are at the beck and call of a crazy old harridan. We revolutionists make wonderful discoveries. It is true that they are not exactly our own. We have nothing of our own. But couldn't the friend of Peter Ivanovitch satisfy your feminine curiosity ? Couldn't she conjure him up for you ? "—he jested like a man in pain.

Her concentrated frowning expression relaxed, and she said, a little wearily, " Let us hope she will make an effort and conjure up some tea for us. But that is by no means certain. I am tired, Razumov."

" You tired ! What a confession ! Well, there has been tea up there. I had some. If you hurry on after Yakovlitch, instead of wasting your time with such an unsatisfactory sceptical person as myself, you may find the ghost of it—the cold ghost of it—still lingering in the temple. But as to you being tired I can hardly believe it. We are not supposed to be. We mustn't. We can't. The other day I read in some paper or other an alarmist article on the tireless activity of the revolutionary parties. It impresses the world. It's our prestige."

" He flings out continually these flouts and sneers " ; the woman in the crimson blouse spoke as if appealing quietly to a third person, but her black eyes never left Razumov's face. " And what for, pray? Simply because some of his conventional notions are shocked, some of his petty masculine standards. You might think he was one of those nervous sensitives that come to a bad end. And yet," she went on, after a short, reflective pause and changing the mode of her address, " and yet I have just learned something which makes me think that you are a man of character, Kirylo Sidorovitch. Yes, indeed!—you are."

The mysterious positiveness of this assertion startled Razumov. Their eyes met. He looked away and, through the bars of the rusty gate, stared at the clean, wide road shaded by the leafy trees. An electric tramcar, quite empty, ran along the avenue with a metallic rustle. It seemed to him he would have given anything to be sitting inside all alone. He was inexpressibly weary, weary in every fibre of his body, but he had a reason for not being the first to break off the conversation. At any instant, in the visionary and criminal babble of revolutionists, some momentous words might fall on his ear; from her lips, from anybody's lips. As long as he managed to preserve a clear mind and to keep down his irritability there was nothing to fear. The only condition of success and safety was indomitable will-power, he reminded himself.

He longed to be on the other side of the bars, as though he were actually a prisoner within the grounds of this centre of revolutionary plots, of this house of folly, of blindness, of villainy and crime. Silently he indulged his wounded spirit in a feeling of immense moral and mental remoteness. He did not even smile when he heard her repeat the words :

"Yes ! A strong character."

He continued to gaze through the bars like a moody prisoner, not thinking of escape, but merely pondering upon the faded memories of freedom.

"If you don't look out," he mumbled, still looking away, "you will certainly miss seeing as much as the mere ghost of that tea."

She was not to be shaken off in such a way. As a matter of fact he had not expected to succeed.

"Never mind, it will be no great loss. I mean the missing of her tea and only the ghost of it at that. As to the lady, you must understand that she has her positive uses. See *that*, Razumov."

He turned his head at this imperative appeal and saw the woman revolutionist making the motions of counting money into the palm of her hand.

"That's what it is. You see ? "

Razumov uttered a slow " I see," and returned to his prisoner-like gazing upon the neat and shady road.

"Material means must be obtained in some way, and this is easier than breaking into banks. More certain too. There ! I am joking. . . . What is he muttering to himself now ? " she cried under her breath.

"My admiration of Peter Ivanovitch's devoted

self-sacrifice, that's all. It's enough to make one sick."

" Oh, you squeamish, masculine creature. Sick! Makes him sick! And what do you know of the truth of it? There's no looking into the secrets of the heart. Peter Ivanovitch knew her years ago, in his worldly days, when he was a young officer in the Guards. It is not for us to judge an inspired person. That's where you men have an advantage. You are inspired sometimes both in thought and action. I have always admitted that when you *are* inspired, when you manage to throw off your masculine cowardice and prudishness, you are not to be equalled by us. Only, how seldom . . . Whereas the silliest woman can always be made of use. And why? Because we have passion, unappeasable passion. . . . I should like to know what he is smiling at?"

" I am not smiling," protested Razumov gloomily.

" Well! How is one to call it? You made some sort of face. Yes, I know! You men can love here and hate there and desire something or other— and you make a great to-do about it, and you call it passion! Yes! While it lasts! But we women are in love with love, and with hate, with these very things I tell you, and with desire itself. That's why we can't be bribed off so easily as you men. In life, you see, there is not much choice. You have either to rot or to burn. And there is not one of us, painted or unpainted, that would not rather burn than rot."

She spoke with energy, but in a matter-of-fact tone. Razumov's attention had wandered away on a track of its own—outside the bars of the gate—but not out of earshot. He stuck his hands into the pockets of his coat.

" Rot or burn ! Powerfully stated. Painted or unpainted. Very vigorous. Painted or . . . Do tell me—she would be infernally jealous of him, wouldn't she ? "

" Who ? What ? The Baroness ? Eleanor Maximovna ? Jealous of Peter Ivanovitch ? Heavens ! Are these the questions the man's mind is running on ? Such a thing is not to be thought of."

" Why ? Can't a wealthy old woman be jealous ? Or, are they all pure spirits together ? "

" But what put it into your head to ask such a question ? " she wondered.

" Nothing. I just asked. Masculine frivolity, if you like."

" I don't like," she retorted at once. " It is not the time to be frivolous. What are you flinging your very heart against ? Or, perhaps, you are only playing a part."

Razumov had felt that woman's observation of him like a physical contact, like a hand resting lightly on his shoulder. At that moment he received the mysterious impression of her having made up her mind for a closer grip. He stiffened himself inwardly to bear it without betraying himself.

" Playing a part," he repeated, presenting to her an unmoved profile. " It must be done very badly since you see through the assumption."

She watched him, her forehead drawn into perpendicular folds, the thin black eyebrows diverging upwards like the antennæ of an insect. He added hardly audibly :

" You are mistaken. I am doing it no more than the rest of us."

" Who is doing it ? " she snapped out.

" Who ? Everybody," he said impatiently. " You are a materialist, aren't you ? "

" Eh ! My dear soul, I have outlived all that nonsense."

" But you must remember the definition of Cabanis : ' Man is a digestive tube.' I imagine now . . ."

" I spit on him."

" What ? On Cabanis ? All right. But you can't ignore the importance of a good digestion. The joy of life—you know the joy of life ?—depends on a sound stomach, whereas a bad digestion inclines one to scepticism, breeds black fancies and thoughts of death. These are facts ascertained by physiologists. Well, I assure you that ever since I came over from Russia I have been stuffed with indigestible foreign concoctions of the most nauseating kind— pah ! "

" You are joking," she murmured incredulously. He assented in a detached way.

" Yes. It is all a joke. It's hardly worth while talking to a man like me. Yet for that very reason men have been known to take their own life."

" On the contrary, I think it *is* worth while talking to you."

He kept her in the corner of his eye. She seemed to be thinking out some scathing retort, but ended by only shrugging her shoulders slightly.

" Shallow talk ! I suppose one must pardon this weakness in you," she said, putting a special accent on the last word. There was something anxious in her indulgent conclusion.

Razumov noted the slightest shades in this conversation, which he had not expected, for which he was not prepared. That was it. " I was not prepared," he said to himself. " It has taken me unawares." It seemed to him that if he only could allow himself to pant openly like a dog for a time this oppression would pass away. " I shall never be found prepared," he thought, with despair. He laughed a little, saying as lightly as he could :

" Thanks. I don't ask for mercy." Then affecting a playful uneasiness, " But aren't you afraid Peter Ivanovitch might suspect us of plotting something unauthorised together by the gates here ? "

" No, I am not afraid. You are quite safe from

suspicions while you are with me, my dear young man." The humorous gleam in her black eyes went out. " Peter Ivanovitch trusts me," she went on, quite austerely. " He takes my advice. I am his right hand, as it were, in certain most important things. . . . That amuses you—what? Do you think I am boasting ? "

" God forbid. I was just only saying to myself that Peter Ivanovitch seems to have solved the woman question pretty completely."

Even as he spoke he reproached himself for his words, for his tone. All day long he had been saying the wrong things. It was folly, worse than folly. It was weakness ; it was this disease of perversity overcoming his will. Was this the way to meet speeches which certainly contained the promise of future confidences from that woman who apparently had a great store of secret knowledge and so much influence ? Why give her this puzzling impression ? But she did not seem inimical. There was no anger in her voice. It was strangely speculative.

" One does not know what to think, Razumov. You must have bitten something bitter in your cradle."

Razumov gave her a sidelong glance.

" H'm ! Something bitter ? That's an explanation," he muttered. " Only it was much later. And don't you think, Sophia Antonovna, that you and I come from the same cradle ? "

The woman, whose name he had forced himself
at last to pronounce (he had experienced a strong
repugnance in letting it pass his lips), the woman
revolutionist murmured, after a pause :

" You mean—Russia ? "

He disdained even to nod.   She seemed
softened, her black eyes very still, as though she
were pursuing the simile in her thoughts to all its
tender associations. · But suddenly she knitted her
brows in a Mephistophelian frown.

" Yes. Perhaps no wonder, then. Yes. One
lies there lapped up in evils, watched over by beings
that are worse than ogres, ghouls, and vampires.
They must be driven away, destroyed utterly. In
regard of that task nothing else matters if men and
women are determined and faithful. That's how
I came to feel in the end. The great thing is not
to quarrel amongst ourselves about all sorts of conventional trifles. Remember that, Razumov."

Razumov was not listening. He had even lost
the sense of being watched in a sort of heavy tranquillity. His uneasiness, his exasperation, his scorn
were blunted at last by all these trying hours. It
seemed to him that now they were blunted for ever.
" I am a match for them all," he thought, with a
conviction too firm to be exulting. The woman
revolutionist had ceased speaking ; he was not
looking at her ; there was no one passing along the
road. He almost forgot that he was not alone.
He heard her voice again, curt, businesslike, and yet

betraying the hesitation which had been the real reason of her prolonged silence.

" I say, Razumov ! "

Razumov, whose face was turned away from her, made a grimace like a man who hears a false note.

" Tell me : is it true that on the very morning of the deed you actually attended the lectures at the university ? "

An appreciable fraction of a second elapsed before the real import of the question reached him, like a bullet which strikes some time after the flash of the fired shot. Luckily his disengaged hand was ready to grip a bar of the gate. He held it with a terrible force, but his presence of mind was gone. He could make only a sort of gurgling, grumpy sound.

" Come, Kirylo Sidorovitch ! " she urged him. " I know you are not a boastful man. *That* one must say for you. You are a silent man. Too silent, perhaps. You are feeding on some bitterness of your own. You are not an enthusiast. You are, perhaps, all the stronger for that. But you might tell me. One would like to understand you a little more. I was so immensely struck . . . Have you really done it ? "

He got his voice back. The shot had missed him. It had been fired at random, altogether, more like a signal for coming to close quarters. It was to be a plain struggle for self-preservation. And she

was a dangerous adversary too. But he was ready
for battle ; he was so ready that when he turned
towards her not a muscle of his face moved.

" Certainly," he said, without animation, secretly
strung up but perfectly sure of himself. " Lectures
—certainly. But what makes you ask ? "

It was she who was animated.

" I had it in a letter, written by a young man in
Petersburg ; one of us, of course. You were seen
—you were observed with your notebook, impassible,
taking notes . . ."

He enveloped her with his fixed stare.

" What of that ? "

" I call such coolness superb—that's all. It is
a proof of uncommon strength of character. The
young man writes that nobody could have guessed
from your face and manner the part you had played
only some two hours before—the great, momentous,
glorious part . . ."

" Oh no. Nobody could have guessed,"
assented Razumov gravely, " because, don't you
see, nobody at that time . . ."

" Yes, yes. But all the same you are a man of
exceptional fortitude, it seems. You looked exactly
as usual. It was remembered afterwards with
wonder . . ."

" It cost me no effort," Razumov declared, with
the same staring gravity.

" Then it's almost more wonderful still ! " she
exclaimed, and fell silent while Razumov asked

himself whether he had not said there something utterly unnecessary—or even worse.

She raised her head eagerly.

" Your intention was to stay in Russia ? You had planned . . ."

" No," interrupted Razumov without haste. " I had made no plans of any sort."

" You just simply walked away ? " she struck in.

He bowed his head in slow assent. " Simply—yes." He had gradually released his hold on the bar of the gate, as though he had acquired the conviction that no random shot could knock him over now. And suddenly he was inspired to add, " The snow was coming down very thick, you know."

She had a slight appreciative movement of the head, like an expert in such enterprises, very interested, capable of taking every point professionally. Razumov remembered something he had heard.

" I turned into a narrow side street, you understand," he went on negligently, and paused as if it were not worth talking about. Then he remembered another detail and dropped it before her, like a disdainful dole to her curiosity.

" I felt inclined to lie down and go to sleep there."

She clicked her tongue at that symptom, very struck indeed. Then :

" But the notebook ! The amazing notebook, man. You don't mean to say you had put it in your pocket beforehand ! " she cried.

Razumov gave a start. It might have been a sign of impatience.

" I went home. Straight home to my rooms," he said distinctly.

" The coolness of the man ! You dared ? "

" Why not ? I assure you I was perfectly calm. Ha ! Calmer than I am now perhaps."

" I like you much better as you are now than when you indulge that bitter vein of yours, Razumov. And nobody in the house saw you return— eh ? That might have appeared queer."

" No one," Razumov said firmly. " Dvornik, landlady, girl, all out of the way. I went up like a shadow. It was a murky morning. The stairs were dark. I glided up like a phantom. Fate ? Luck ? What do you think ? "

" I just see it ! " The eyes of the woman revolutionist snapped darkly. " Well—and then you considered . . ."

Razumov had it all ready in his head.

" No. I looked at my watch, since you want to know. There was just time. I took that notebook and ran down the stairs on tiptoe. Have you ever listened to the pit-pat of a man running round and round the shaft of a deep staircase ? They have a gaslight at the bottom burning night and day. I suppose it's gleaming down there now. . . . The sound dies out—the flame winks . . ."

He noticed the vacillation of surprise passing over the steady curiosity of the black eyes fastened

on his face as if the woman revolutionist received the
sound of his voice into her pupils instead of her
ears. He checked himself, passed his hand over his
forehead, confused, like a man who has been dream-
ing aloud.

"Where could a student be running if not to
his lectures in the morning ? At night it's another
matter. I did not care if all the house had been
there to look at me. But I don't suppose there was
any one. It's best not to be seen or heard. Aha !
The people that are neither seen nor heard are the
lucky ones—in Russia. Don't you admire my
luck ? "

"Astonishing," she said. "If you have luck
as well as determination, then indeed you are likely
to turn out an invaluable acquisition for the work in
hand."

Her tone was earnest ; and it seemed to Razumov
that it was speculative, even as though she were
already apportioning him, in her mind, his share of
the work. Her eyes were cast down. He waited,
not very alert now, but with the grip of the ever-
present danger giving him an air of attentive gravity.
Who could have written about him in that letter
from Petersburg ? A fellow-student, surely—some
imbecile victim of revolutionary propaganda, some
foolish slave of foreign, subversive ideals. A long,
famine-stricken, red-nosed figure presented itself
to his mental search. That must have been
the fellow !

He smiled inwardly at the absolute wrong-headedness of the whole thing, the self-deception of a criminal idealist shattering his existence like a thunder-clap out of a clear sky, and re-echoing amongst the wreckage in the false assumptions of those other fools. Fancy that hungry and piteous imbecile furnishing to the curiosity of the revolutionist refugees this utterly fantastic detail! He appreciated it as by no means constituting a danger. On the contrary. As things stood it was for his advantage rather, a piece of sinister luck which had only to be accepted with proper caution.

"And yet, Razumov," he heard the musing voice of the woman, "you have not the face of a lucky man." She raised her eyes with renewed interest. "And so that was the way of it. After doing your work you simply walked off and made for your rooms. That sort of thing succeeds sometimes. I suppose it was agreed beforehand that, once the business over, each of you would go his own way?"

Razumov preserved the seriousness of his expression and the deliberate, if cautious, manner of speaking.

"Was not that the best thing to do?" he asked, in a dispassionate tone. "And anyway," he added, after waiting a moment, "we did not give much thought to what would come after. We never discussed formally any line of conduct. It was understood, I think."

She approved his statement with slight nods.

" You, of course, wished to remain in Russia ? "

" In St. Petersburg itself," emphasised Razumov. " It was the only safe course for me. And, moreover, I had nowhere else to go."

" Yes, yes ! I know. Clearly. And the other —this wonderful Haldin appearing only to be regretted—you don't know what he intended ? "

Razumov had foreseen that such a question would certainly come to meet him sooner or later. He raised his hands a little and let them fall helplessly by his side—nothing more.

It was the white-haired woman conspirator who was the first to break the silence.

" Very curious," she pronounced slowly. " And you did not think, Kirylo Sidorovitch, that he might perhaps wish to get in touch with you again ? "

Razumov discovered that he could not suppress the trembling of his lips. But he thought that he owed it to himself to speak. A negative sign would not do again. Speak he must, if only to get at the bottom of what that St. Petersburg letter might have contained.

" I stayed at home next day," he said, bending down a little and plunging his glance into the black eyes of the woman so that she should not observe the trembling of his lips. " Yes, I stayed at home. As my actions are remembered and written about, then perhaps you are aware that I was *not* seen at the lectures next day. Eh? You didn't know? Well, I stopped at home—the livelong day."

As if moved by his agitated tone, she murmured a sympathetic " I see! It must have been trying enough."

" You seem to understand one's feelings," said Razumov steadily. " It was trying. It was horrible; it was an atrocious day. It was not the last."

" Yes, I understand. Afterwards, when you heard they had got him. Don't I know how one feels after losing a comrade in the good fight? One's ashamed of being left. And I can remember so many. Never mind. They shall be avenged before long. And what is death? At any rate, it is not a shameful thing like some kinds of life."

Razumov felt something stir in his breast, a sort of feeble and unpleasant tremor.

" Some kinds of life? " he repeated, looking at her searchingly.

" The subservient, submissive life. Life? No! Vegetation on the filthy heap of iniquity which the world is. Life, Razumov, not to be vile must be a revolt—a pitiless protest—all the time."

She calmed down, the gleam of suffused tears in her eyes dried out instantly by the heat of her passion, and it was in her capable, businesslike manner that she went on :

" You understand me, Razumov. You are not an enthusiast, but there is an immense force of revolt in you. I felt it from the first, directly I set my eyes on you—you remember—in Zurich. Oh ! You are full of bitter revolt. That is good. Indignation flags sometimes, revenge itself may become a weariness, but that uncompromising sense of necessity and justice which armed your and Haldin's hands to strike down that fanatical brute . . . for it was that—nothing but that ! I have been thinking it out. It could have been nothing else but that."

Razumov made a slight bow, the irony of which was concealed by an almost sinister immobility of feature.

" I can't speak for the dead. As for myself, I can assure you that my conduct was dictated by necessity and by the sense of—well—retributive justice."

" Good, that," he said to himself, while her eyes rested upon him, black and impenetrable like the mental caverns where revolutionary thought should sit plotting the violent way of its dream of changes. As if anything could be changed ! In this world of men nothing can be changed—neither happiness nor misery. They can only be displaced at the cost of corrupted consciences and broken lives— a futile game for arrogant philosophers and sanguinary triflers. Those thoughts darted through Razumov's head while he stood facing the old revolutionary hand, the respected, trusted, and influential Sophia Antonovna, whose word had

such a weight in the " active " section of every
party. She was much more representative than
the great Peter Ivanovitch. Stripped of rhetoric,
mysticism, and theories, she was the true spirit of
destructive revolution. And she was the personal
adversary he had to meet. It gave him a feeling of
triumphant pleasure to deceive her out of her own
mouth. The epigrammatic saying that speech has
been given to us for the purpose of concealing our
thought came into his mind. Of that cynical
theory this was a very subtle and a very scornful
application, flouting in its own words the very
spirit of ruthless revolution, embodied in that
woman with her white hair and black eyebrows,
like slightly sinuous lines of Indian ink, drawn
together by the perpendicular folds of a thoughtful
frown.

" That's it. Retributive. No pity ! " was the
conclusion of her silence. And this once broken,
she went on impulsively in short, vibrating sentences :

" Listen to my story, Razumov ! . . ." Her
father was a clever but unlucky artisan. No joy
had lighted up his laborious days. He died at
fifty ; all the years of his life he had panted under
the thumb of masters whose rapacity exacted from
him the price of the water, of the salt, of the very
air he breathed—taxed the sweat of his brow and
claimed the blood of his sons. No protection, no
guidance ! What had society to say to him ? Be

submissive and be honest. If you rebel I shall kill you. If you steal I shall imprison you. But if you suffer I have nothing for you—nothing except perhaps a beggarly dole of bread—but no consolation for your trouble, no respect for your manhood, no pity for the sorrows of your miserable life.

And so he laboured, he suffered, and he died. He died in the hospital. Standing by the common grave she thought of his tormented existence—she saw it whole. She reckoned the simple joys of life, the birthright of the humblest, of which his gentle heart had been robbed by the crime of a society which nothing can absolve.

" Yes, Razumov," she continued, in an impressive, lowered voice, " it was like a lurid light in which I stood, still almost a child, and cursed not the toil, not the misery which had been his lot, but the great social iniquity of the system resting on unrequited toil and unpitied sufferings. From that moment I was a revolutionist."

Razumov, trying to raise himself above the dangerous weaknesses of contempt or compassion, had preserved an impassive countenance. She, with an unaffected touch of mere bitterness, the first he could notice since he had come in contact with the woman, went on :

" As I could not go to the Church where the priests of the system exhorted such unconsidered vermin as I to resignation, I went to the secret societies as soon as I knew how to find my way. I

was sixteen years old—no more, Razumov ! And—
look at my white hair."

In these last words there was neither pride nor
sadness. The bitterness, too, was gone.

" There is a lot of it. I had always magnificent
hair, even as a chit of a girl. Only, at that time we
were cutting it short and thinking that there was
the first step towards crushing the social infamy.
Crush the Infamy ! A fine watchword ! I would
placard it on the walls of prisons and palaces, carve
it on hard rocks, hang it out in letters of fire on that
empty sky for a sign of hope and terror—a portent
of the end . . ."

" You are eloquent, Sophia Antonovna," Razumov interrupted suddenly. " Only, so far you
seem to have been writing it in water . . ."

She was checked but not offended. " Who
knows ? Very soon it may become a fact written
all over that great land of ours," she hinted meaningly. " And then one would have lived long
enough. White hair won't matter."

Razumov looked at her white hair : and this
mark of so many uneasy years seemed nothing but
a testimony to the invincible vigour of revolt. It
threw out into an astonishing relief the unwrinkled
face, the brilliant black glance, the upright compact
figure, the simple, brisk self-possession of the mature
personality—as though in her revolutionary pil-
grimage she had discovered the secret, not of everlasting youth, but of everlasting endurance.

How un-Russian she looked, thought Razumov. Her mother might have been a Jewess or an Armenian or—devil knew what. He reflected that a revolutionist is seldom true to the settled type. All revolt is the expression of strong individualism—ran his thought vaguely. One can tell them a mile off in any society, in any surroundings. It was astonishing that the police . . .

" We shall not meet again very soon, I think," she was saying, " I am leaving to-morrow."

" For Zurich ? " Razumov asked casually, but feeling relieved, not from any distinct apprehension, but from a feeling of stress as if after a wrestling match.

" Yes, Zurich—and farther on, perhaps, much farther. Another journey. When I think of all my journeys ! The last must come some day. Never mind, Razumov. We had to have a good long talk. I would have certainly tried to see you if we had not met. Peter Ivanovitch knows where you live ? Yes. I meant to have asked him—but it's better like this. You see, we expect two more men ; and I had much rather wait here talking with you than up there at the house with . . ."

Having cast a glance beyond the gate, she interrupted herself. " Here they are," she said rapidly. " Well, Kirylo Sidorovitch, we shall have to say good-bye presently."

IV

In his incertitude of the ground on which he stood, Razumov felt perturbed. Turning his head quickly, he saw two men on the opposite side of the road. Seeing themselves noticed by Sophia Antonovna, they crossed over at once, and passed one after another through the little gate by the side of the empty lodge. They looked hard at the stranger, but without mistrust, the crimson blouse being a flaring safety signal. The first, great white hairless face, double chin, prominent stomach, which he seemed to carry forward consciously within a strongly distended overcoat, only nodded and averted his eyes peevishly ; his companion— lean, flushed cheek-bones, a military red moustache below a sharp, salient nose—at once approached Sophia Antonovna, greeting her warmly. His voice was very strong but inarticulate. It sounded like a deep buzzing. The woman revolutionist was quietly cordial. . . .

" This is Razumov," she announced in a clear voice.

The lean newcomer made an eager half-turn. " He will want to embrace me," thought our young man with a deep recoil of all his being, while his limbs seemed too heavy to move. But it was a groundless alarm. He had to do now with a genera- tion of conspirators who did not kiss each other on both cheeks ; and raising an arm that felt like lead he dropped his hand into a largely-outstretched palm, fleshless and hot as if dried up by fever, giving a bony pressure, expressive, seeming to say, " Between us there's no need of words."

The man had big, wide-open eyes. Razumov fancied he could see a smile behind their sadness.

" This is Razumov," Sophia Antonovna repeated loudly for the benefit of the fat man, who at some distance displayed the profile of his stomach.

No one moved. Everything, sounds, attitudes, movements, and immobility, seemed to be part of an experiment, the result of which was a thin voice piping with comic peevishness :

" Oh yes ! Razumov. We have been hearing of nothing but Mr. Razumov for months. For my part, I confess I would rather have seen Haldin on this spot instead of Mr. Razumov."

The squeaky stress put on the name " Razumov —Mr. Razumov " pierced the ear ridiculously, like the falsetto of a circus clown beginning an elaborate joke. Astonishment was Razumov's first response, followed by sudden indignation.

" What's the meaning of this ? " he asked in a stern tone.

" Tut ! Silliness. He's always like that."

Sophia Antonovna was obviously vexed. But she dropped the information, " Necator," from her lips just loud enough to be heard by Razumov. The abrupt squeaks of the fat man seemed to proceed from that thing like a balloon he carried under his overcoat. The solidity of his attitude, the big feet, the lifeless, hanging hands, the enormous bloodless cheek, the thin wisps of hair straggling down the fat nape of the neck, fascinated Razumov into a stare on the verge of horror and laughter.

Nikita, surnamed Necator, with a sinister aptness of alliteration ! Razumov had heard of him. He had heard so much since crossing the frontier of these celebrities of the militant revolution ; the legends, the stories, the authentic chronicle which now and then peeps out before a half-incredulous world. Razumov had heard of him. He was supposed to have killed more gendarmes and police agents than any revolutionist living. He had been entrusted with executions.

The paper with the letters N.N., the very pseudonym of murder, found pinned on the stabbed breast of a certain notorious spy (this picturesque detail of a sensational murder case had got into the newspapers), was the mark of his handiwork. " By order of the Committee.—N.N." A corner of the curtain lifted to strike the imagination of the gaping world. He was said to have been innumerable times in and out of Russia, the Necator of bureaucrats or provincial governors, of obscure informers. He lived between whiles, Razumov had heard, on the shores of the Lake of Como, with a charming wife, devoted to the cause, and two young children. But how could that creature, so grotesque as to set town dogs barking at its mere sight, go about on those deadly errands and slip through the meshes of the police ?

" What now ? what now ? " the voice squeaked. " I am only sincere. It's not denied that the other was the leading spirit. Well, it would have been better if he had been the one spared to us. More useful. I am not a sentimentalist. Say what I think . . . only natural."

Squeak, squeak, squeak, without a gesture, without a stir—the horrible squeaky burlesque of professional jealousy—this man of a sinister alliterative nickname, this executioner of revolutionary verdicts, the terrifying N.N. exasperated like a fashionable tenor by the attention attracted to the performance of an obscure amateur. Sophia Antonovna shrugged her shoulders. The comrade with the martial red moustache hurried towards Razumov full of conciliatory intentions in his strong, buzzing voice.

" Devil take it ! And in this place, too, in the public street, so to speak. But you can see yourself how it is. One of his fantastic sallies. Absolutely of no consequence."

" Pray don't concern yourself," cried Razumov, going off into a long fit of laughter. " Don't mention it."

The other, his hectic flush like a pair of burns on his cheek-bones, stared for a moment and burst out laughing too. Razumov, whose hilarity died out all at once, made a step forward.

"Enough of this," he began in a clear, incisive voice, though he could hardly control the trembling of his legs. "I will have no more of it. I shall not permit any one. . . . I can see very well what you are at with those allusions. . . . Inquire, investigate! I defy you, but I will not be played with."

He had spoken such words before. He had been driven to cry them out in the face of other suspicions. It was an infernal cycle bringing round that protest like a fatal necessity of his existence. But it was no use. He would be always played with. Luckily life does not last for ever.

"I won't have it!" he shouted, striking his fist into the palm of his other hand.

"Kirylo Sidorovitch—what has come to you?" The woman revolutionist interfered with authority. They were all looking at Razumov now; the slayer of spies and gendarmes had turned about, presenting his enormous stomach in full, like a shield.

"Don't shout. There are people passing." Sophia Antonovna was apprehensive of another outburst. A steam-launch from Monrepos had come to the landing-stage opposite the gate, its hoarse whistle and the churning noise alongside all unnoticed, had landed a small bunch of local passengers who were dispersing their several ways. Only a specimen of early tourist in knickerbockers, conspicuous by a brand-new yellow leather glass-case, hung about for a moment, scenting something unusual about these four people within the rusty iron gates of what looked like the grounds run wild of an unoccupied private house. Ah! If he had only known what the chance of commonplace travelling had suddenly put in his way! But he was a well-bred person; he averted his gaze and moved off with short steps along the avenue, on the watch for a tramcar.

A gesture from Sophia Antonovna, " Leave him to me," had sent the two men away—the buzzing of the inarticulate voice growing fainter and fainter, and the thin pipe of " What now? what's the matter? " reduced to the proportions of a squeaking toy by the distance. They had left him to her. So many things could be left safely to the experience of Sophia Antonovna. And at once, her black eyes turned to Razumov, her mind tried to get at the heart of that outburst. It had some meaning. No one is born an active revolutionist. The change comes disturbingly, with the force of a sudden vocation, bringing in its train agonising doubts, assertive violences, an unstable state of the soul, till the final appeasement of the convert in the perfect fierceness of conviction. She had seen—often had only divined—scores of these young men and young women going through an emotional crisis. This young man looked like a moody egotist. And besides, it was a special—a unique case. She had never met an individuality which interested and puzzled her so much.

" Take care, Razumov, my good friend. If you carry on like this you will go mad. You are angry with everybody and bitter with yourself, and on the look out for something to torment yourself with."

" It's intolerable ! " Razumov could only speak in gasps. " You must admit that I can have no illusions on the attitude which . . . it isn't clear . . . or rather . . . only too clear."

He made a gesture of despair. It was not his courage that failed him. The choking fumes of falsehood had taken him by the throat—the thought of being condemned to struggle on and on in that tainted atmosphere without the hope of ever renewing his strength by a breath of fresh air.

" A glass of cold water is what you want." Sophia Antonovna glanced up the grounds at the house and shook her head, then out of the gate at the brimful placidity of the lake. With a half-comical shrug of the shoulders, she gave the remedy up in the face of that abundance.

" It is you, my dear soul, who are flinging yourself at something which does not exist. What is it ? Self-reproach, or what ? It's absurd. You couldn't have gone and given yourself up because your comrade was taken."

She remonstrated with him reasonably, at some length too. He had nothing to complain of in his reception. Every newcomer was discussed more or less. Everybody had to be thoroughly understood before being accepted. No one that she could

22

remember had been shown from the first so much
confidence. Soon, very soon, perhaps sooner than
he expected, he would be given an opportunity of
showing his devotion to the sacred task of crushing
the Infamy.

Razumov, listening quietly, thought : " It may
be that she is trying to lull my suspicions to sleep.
On the other hand, it is obvious that most of them
are fools." He moved aside a couple of paces, and,
folding his arms on his breast, leaned back against
the stone pillar of the gate.

" As to what remains obscure in the fate of that
poor Haldin," Sophia Antonovna dropped into a
slowness of utterance which was to Razumov like
the falling of molten lead drop by drop ; " as to
that—though no one ever hinted that either from
fear or neglect your conduct has not been what
it should have been—well, I have a bit of intelligence . . ."

Razumov could not prevent himself from raising
his head, and Sophia Antonovna nodded slightly.

" I have. You remember that letter from St.
Petersburg I mentioned to you a moment ago ? "

" The letter ? Perfectly. Some busybody has
been reporting my conduct on a certain day. It's
rather sickening. I suppose our police are greatly
edified when they open these interesting and—and—
superfluous letters."

" Oh dear, no ! The police do not get hold of
our letters as easily as you imagine. The letter in

question did not leave St. Petersburg till the ice
broke up. It went by the first English steamer
which left the Neva this spring. They have a fire-
man on board—one of us, in fact. It has reached
me from Hull . . ."

She paused as if she were surprised at the sullen
fixity of Razumov's gaze, but went on at once, and
much faster.

" We have some of our people there who . . .
but never mind. The writer of the letter relates an
incident which he thinks may possibly be connected
with Haldin's arrest. I was just going to tell you
when those two men came along."

" That also was an incident," muttered Razumov,
" of a very charming kind—for me."

" Leave off that ! " cried Sophia Antonovna.
" Nobody cares for Nikita's barking. There's no
malice in him. Listen to what I have to say. You
may be able to throw a light. There was in St.
Petersburg a sort of town-peasant—a man who
owned horses. He came to town years ago to work
for some relation as a driver and ended by owning
a cab or two."

She might have well spared herself the slight
effort of the gesture : " Wait ! " Razumov did
not mean to speak ; he could not have interrupted
her now, not to save his life. The contraction of
his facial muscles had been involuntary, a mere
surface stir, leaving him sullenly attentive as
before.

" He was not a quite ordinary man of his class —it seems," she went on. " The people of the house—my informant talked with many of them— you know, one of those enormous houses of shame and misery . . ."

Sophia Antonovna need not have enlarged on the character of the house. Razumov saw clearly, towering at her back, a dark mass of masonry veiled in snowflakes, with the long row of windows of the eating-shop shining greasily very near the ground. The ghost of that night pursued him. He stood up to it with rage and with weariness.

" Did the late Haldin ever by chance speak to you of that house ? " Sophia Antonovna was anxious to know.

" Yes." Razumov, making that answer, wondered whether he were falling into a trap. It was so humiliating to lie to these people that he probably could not have said no. " He mentioned to me once," he added, as if making an effort of memory, " a house of that sort. He used to visit some workmen there."

" Exactly."

Sophia Antonovna triumphed. Her correspondent had discovered that fact quite accidentally from the talk of the people of the house, having made friends with a workman who occupied a room there. They described Haldin's appearance perfectly. He brought comforting words of hope into their misery. He came irregularly, but he came very often, and—her correspondent wrote—sometimes he spent a night in the house, sleeping, they thought, in a stable which opened upon the inner yard.

" Note that, Razumov ! In a stable."

Razumov had listened with a sort of ferocious but amused acquiescence.

" Yes. In the straw. It was probably the cleanest spot in the whole house."

" No doubt," assented the woman with that deep frown which seemed to draw closer together her black eyes in a sinister fashion. No four-footed beast could stand the filth and wretchedness so many human beings were condemned to suffer from in Russia. The point of this discovery was that it proved Haldin to have been familiar with that horse-owning peasant—a reckless, independent, free-living fellow not much liked by the other inhabitants of the house. He was believed to have been the associate of a band of housebreakers. Some of these got captured. Not while he was driving them, however ; but still there was a suspicion against the fellow of having given a hint to the police and . . .

The woman revolutionist checked herself suddenly.

" And you ? Have you ever heard your friend refer to a certain Ziemianitch ? "

Razumov was ready for the name. He had

been looking out for the question. " When it comes I shall own up," he had said to himself. But he took his time.

" To be sure ! " he began slowly. " Ziemianitch, a peasant owning a team of horses. Yes. On one occasion. Ziemianitch ! Certainly ! Ziemianitch of the horses. . . . How could it have slipped my memory like this ? One of the last conversations we had together."

" That means,"—Sophia Antonovna looked very grave,—" that means, Razumov, it was very shortly before—eh ? "

" Before what ? " shouted Razumov, advancing at the woman, who looked astonished but stood her ground. " Before . . . Oh ! Of course, it was before ! How could it have been after ? Only a few hours before."

" And he spoke of him favourably ? "

" With enthusiasm ! The horses of Ziemianitch ! The free soul of Ziemianitch ! "

Razumov took a savage delight in the loud utterance of that name, which had never before crossed his lips audibly. He fixed his blazing eyes on the woman till at last her fascinated expression recalled him to himself.

" The late Haldin," he said, holding himself in, with downcast eyes, " was inclined to take sudden fancies to people on—on—what shall I say ?—insufficient grounds."

" There ! " Sophia Antonovna clapped her

hands. "That, to my mind, settles it. The suspicions of my correspondent were aroused . . ."

"Aha! Your correspondent," Razumov said in an almost openly mocking tone. "What suspicions? How aroused? By this Ziemianitch? Probably some drunken, gabbling, plausible . . ."

"You talk as if you had known him."

Razumov looked up.

"No. But I knew Haldin."

Sophia Antonovna nodded gravely.

"I see. Every word you say confirms to my mind the suspicion communicated to me in that very interesting letter. This Ziemianitch was found one morning hanging from a hook in the stable—dead."

Razumov felt a profound trouble. It was visible, because Sophia Antonovna was moved to observe vivaciously:

"Aha! You begin to see."

He saw it clearly enough—in the light of a lantern casting spokes of shadow in a cellar-like stable, the body in a sheepskin coat and long boots hanging against the wall. A pointed hood, with the ends wound about up to the eyes, hid the face. "But that does not concern me," he reflected. "It does not affect my position at all. He never knew who had thrashed him. He could not have known." Razumov felt sorry for the old lover of the bottle and women.

"Yes. Some of them end like that," he

muttered. " What is your idea, Sophia Antonovna ? "

It was really the idea of her correspondent, but
Sophia Antonovna had adopted it fully. She stated
it in one word—" Remorse." Razumov opened
his eyes very wide at that. Sophia Antonovna's
informant, by listening to the talk of the house, by
putting this and that together, had managed to
come very near to the truth of Haldin's relation
to Ziemianitch.

" It is I who can tell you what you were not
certain of—that your friend had some plan for
saving himself afterwards, for getting out of St.
Petersburg, at any rate. Perhaps that and no
more, trusting to luck for the rest. And that
fellow's horses were part of the plan."

" They have actually got at the truth," Razumov
marvelled to himself, while he nodded judicially.
" Yes, that's possible, very possible." But the
woman revolutionist was very positive that it was so.
First of all, a conversation about horses between
Haldin and Ziemianitch had been partly overheard.
Then there were the suspicions of the people in the
house when their " young gentleman " (they did not
know Haldin by his name) ceased to call at the
house. Some of them used to charge Ziemianitch
with knowing something of this absence. He
denied it with exasperation ; but the fact was that
ever since Haldin's disappearance he was not
himself, growing moody and thin. Finally, during

a quarrel with some woman (to whom he was making up), in which most of the inmates of the house took part apparently, he was openly abused by his chief enemy, an athletic pedlar, for an informer, and for having driven " our young gentleman to Siberia, the same as you did those young fellows who broke into houses." In consequence of this there was a fight, and Ziemianitch got flung down a flight of stairs. Thereupon he drank and moped for a week, and then hanged himself.

Sophia Antonovna drew her conclusions from the tale. She charged Ziemianitch either with drunken indiscretion as to a driving job on a certain date, overheard by some spy in some low grog-shop— perhaps in the very eating-shop on the ground floor of the house—or, maybe, a downright denunciation, followed by remorse. A man like that would be capable of anything. People said he was a flighty old chap. And if he had been once before mixed up with the police—as seemed certain, though he always denied it—in connection with these thieves, he would be sure to be acquainted with some police underlings, always on the look out for something to report. Possibly at first his tale was not made anything of till the day that scoundrel de P—— got his deserts. Ah ! But then every bit and scrap of hint and information would be acted on, and fatally they were bound to get Haldin.

Sophia Antonovna spread out her hands— " Fatally."

Fatality—chance ! Razumov meditated in silent astonishment upon the queer verisimilitude of these inferences. They were obviously to his advantage.

" It is right now to make this conclusive evidence known generally." Sophia Antonovna was very calm and deliberate again. She had received the letter three days ago, but did not write at once to Peter Ivanovitch. She knew then that she would have the opportunity presently of meeting several men of action assembled for an important purpose.

" I thought it would be more effective if I could show the letter itself at large. I have it in my pocket now. You understand how pleased I was to come upon you."

Razumov was saying to himself, " She won't offer to show the letter to me. Not likely. Has she told me everything that correspondent of hers has found out ? " He longed to see the letter, but he felt he must not ask.

" Tell me, please, was this an investigation ordered, as it were ? "

" No, no," she protested. " There you are again with your sensitiveness. It makes you stupid. Don't you see, there was no starting-point for an investigation even if any one had thought of it. A perfect blank ! That's exactly what some people were pointing out as the reason for receiving you cautiously. It was all perfectly accidental, arising from my informant striking an acquaintance with an intelligent skin-dresser lodging in that particular slum-house. A wonderful coincidence ! "

" A pious person," suggested Razumov, with a pale smile, " would say that the hand of God had done it all."

" My poor father would have said that." Sophia Antonovna did not smile. She dropped her eyes. " Not that his God ever helped him. It's a long time since God has done anything for the people. Anyway, it's done."

" All this would be quite final," said Razumov, with every appearance of reflective impartiality, " if there was any certitude that the ' our young gentleman ' of these people was Victor Haldin. Have we got that ? "

" Yes. There's no mistake. My correspondent was as familiar with Haldin's personal appearance as with your own," the woman affirmed decisively.

" It's the red-nosed fellow beyond a doubt," Razumov said to himself, with reawakened uneasiness. Had his own visit to that accursed house passed unnoticed ? It was barely possible. Yet it was hardly probable. It was just the right sort of food for the popular gossip that gaunt busybody had been picking up. But the letter did not seem to contain any allusion to that. Unless she had suppressed it. And, if so, why ? If it had really escaped the prying of that hunger-stricken democrat with a confounded genius for recognising people from description, it could only be for a time. He would come upon it presently and hasten to write another letter—and then !

For all the envenomed recklessness of his temper, fed on hate and disdain, Razumov shuddered inwardly. It guarded him from common fear, but it could not defend him from disgust at being dealt with in any way by these people. It was a sort of superstitious dread. Now, since his position had been made more secure by their own folly at the cost of Ziemianitch, he felt the need of perfect safety, with its freedom from direct lying, with its power of moving amongst them silent, unquestioning, listening, impenetrable, like the very fate of their crimes and their folly. Was this advantage his already ? Or not yet ? Or never would be ?

" Well, Sophia Antonovna," his air of reluctant concession was genuine in so far that he was really loath to part with her without testing her sincerity by a question it was impossible to bring about in any way ; " well, Sophia Antonovna, if that is so, then——"

" The creature has done justice to himself," the woman observed, as if thinking aloud.

" What ? Ah yes ! Remorse," Razumov muttered, with equivocal contempt.

" Don't be harsh, Kirylo Sidorovitch, if you have lost a friend." There was no hint of softness in her tone, only the black glitter of her eyes seemed detached for an instant from vengeful visions. " He was a man of the people. The simple Russian soul is never wholly impenitent.   It's something to know that."

" Consoling ? " insinuated Razumov, in a tone of inquiry.

" Leave off railing," she checked him explosively. " Remember, Razumov, that women, children, and revolutionists hate irony, which is the negation of all saving instincts, of all faith, of all devotion, of all action. Don't rail ! Leave off. . . . I don't know how it is, but there are moments when you are abhorrent to me. . . ."

She averted her face.   A languid silence, as if all the electricity of the situation had been discharged in this flash of passion, lasted for some time.   Razumov had not flinched.   Suddenly she laid the tips of her fingers on his sleeve.

" Don't mind."

" I don't mind," he said very quietly.

He was proud to feel that she could read nothing on his face.   He was really mollified, relieved, if only for a moment, from an obscure oppression. And suddenly he asked himself, " Why the devil did I go to that house ?   It was an imbecile thing to do."

A profound disgust came over him.   Sophia Antonovna lingered, talking in a friendly manner with an evident conciliatory intention.   And it was still about the famous letter, referring to various minute details given by her informant, who had never seen Ziemianitch.   The " victim of remorse "

had been buried several weeks before her correspondent began frequenting the house. It—the
house—contained very good revolutionary material.
The spirit of the heroic Haldin had passed through
these dens of black wretchedness with a promise
of universal redemption from all the miseries that
oppress mankind. Razumov listened without hearing, gnawed by the newborn desire of safety with its
independence from that degrading method of direct
lying which at times he found it almost impossible
to practise.

No. The point he wanted to hear about could
never come into this conversation. There was no
way of bringing it forward. He regretted not having
composed a perfect story for use abroad, in which
his fatal connection with the house might have been
owned up to. But when he left Russia he did not
know that Ziemianitch had hanged himself. And,
anyway, who could have foreseen this woman's
" informant " stumbling upon that particular slum,
of all the slums awaiting destruction in the purifying
flame of social revolution ? Who could have foreseen ? Nobody ! " It's a perfect, diabolic surprise," thought Razumov, calm-faced in his attitude
of inscrutable superiority, nodding assent to Sophia
Antonovna's remarks upon the psychology of " the
people." " Oh yes—certainly," rather coldly, but
with a nervous longing in his fingers to tear some
sort of confession out of her throat.

Then, at the very last, on the point of separating,

the feeling of relaxed tension already upon him, he heard Sophia Antonovna allude to the subject of his uneasiness. How it came about he could only guess, his mind being absent at the moment, but it must have sprung from Sophia Antonovna's complaints of the illogical absurdity of the people. For instance—that Ziemianitch was notoriously irreligious, and yet, in the last weeks of his life, he suffered from the notion that he had been beaten by the devil.

" The devil," repeated Razamov, as though he had not heard aright.

" The actual devil. The devil in person. You may well look astonished, Kirylo Sidorovitch. Early on the very night poor Haldin was taken, a complete stranger turned up and gave Ziemianitch a most fearful thrashing while he was lying dead-drunk in the stable. The wretched creature's body was one mass of bruises. He showed them to the people in the house."

" But you, Sophia Antonovna, you don't believe in the actual devil ? "

" Do you ? " retorted the woman curtly. " Not but that there are plenty of men worse than devils to make a hell of this earth," she muttered to herself.

Razumov watched her, vigorous and white-haired, with the deep fold between her thin eyebrows, and her black glance turned idly away. It was obvious that she did not make much of the story—unless, indeed, this was the perfection of duplicity. " A dark young man," she explained further. " Never seen there before, never seen afterwards. Why are you smiling, Razumov ? "

" At the devil being still young after all these ages," he answered composedly. " But who was able to describe him, since the victim, you say, was dead-drunk at the time ? "

" Oh ! The eating-house keeper has described him. An overbearing, swarthy young man in a student's cloak, who came rushing in, demanded Ziemianitch, beat him furiously, and rushed away without a word, leaving the eating-house keeper paralysed with astonishment."

" Does he, too, believe it was the devil ? "

" That I can't say. I am told he's very reserved on the matter. Those sellers of spirits are great scoundrels generally. I should think he knows more of it than anybody."

" Well, and you, Sophia Antonovna, what's your theory ? " asked Razumov, in a tone of great interest. " Yours and your informant's, who is on the spot."

" I agree with him. Some police-hound in disguise. Who else could beat a helpless man so unmercifully ? As for the rest, if they were out that day on every trail, old and new, it is probable enough that they might have thought it just as well to have Ziemianitch at hand for more information, or for identification, or what not. Some scoundrelly detective was sent to fetch him along, and being vexed at finding him so drunk broke a stable fork over his ribs. Later on, after they had the big game safe in the net, they troubled their heads no more about that peasant."

Such were the last words of the woman revolutionist in this conversation, keeping so close to the truth, departing from it so far in the verisimilitude of thoughts and conclusions as to give one the notion of the invincible nature of human error, a glimpse into the utmost depths of self-deception. Razumov, after shaking hands with Sophia Antonovna, left the grounds, crossed the road, and walking out on the little steamboat pier, leaned over the rail.

His mind was at ease—ease such as he had not known for many days, ever since that night . . . the night. The conversation with the woman revolutionist had given him the view of his danger at the very moment this danger vanished, characteristically enough. " I ought to have foreseen the doubts that would arise in those people's minds," he thought. Then his attention being attracted by a stone of a peculiar shape, which he could see clearly lying at the bottom, he began to speculate as to the depth of water in that spot. But very soon, with a start of wonder at this extraordinary instance of ill-timed detachment, he returned to his train of thought. " I ought to have told very circumstantial lies from the first," he said to himself, with a mortal distaste of the mere idea which silenced his mental utterance for quite a perceptible interval. " Luckily, that's all right now," he reflected, and after a time

23

spoke to himself, half aloud, " Thanks to the devil," and laughed a little.

The end of Ziemianitch then arrested his wandering thoughts. He was not exactly amused at the interpretation, but he could not help detecting in it a certain piquancy. He owned to himself that, had he known of that suicide before leaving Russia, he would have been incapable of making such excellent use of it for his own purposes. He ought to be infinitely obliged to the fellow with the red nose for his patience and ingenuity. " A wonderful psychologist apparently," he said to himself sarcastically. Remorse, indeed ! It was a striking example of your true conspirator's blindness, of the stupid subtlety of people with one idea. This was a drama of love, not of conscience, Razumov continued to himself mockingly. A woman the old fellow was making up to ! A robust pedlar, clearly a rival, throwing him down a flight of stairs. . . . And at sixty, for a lifelong lover, it was not an easy matter to get over. That was a feminist of a different stamp from Peter Ivanovitch. Even the comfort of the bottle might conceivably fail him in this supreme crisis. At such an age nothing but a halter could cure the pangs of an unquenchable passion. And, besides, there was the wild exasperation aroused by the unjust aspersions and the contumely of the house, with the maddening impossibility to account for that mysterious thrashing, added to these simple and bitter sorrows. " Devil, eh ? " Razumov exclaimed, with mental excitement, as if he had made an interesting discovery. " Ziemianitch ended by falling into mysticism. So many of our true Russian souls end in that way ! Very characteristic." He felt pity for Ziemianitch, a large, neutral pity, such as one may feel for an unconscious multitude, a great people seen from above—like a community of crawling ants working out its destiny. It was as if this Ziemianitch could not possibly have done anything else. And Sophia Antonovna's cocksure and contemptuous " some police-hound " was characteristically Russian in another way. But there was no tragedy there. This was a comedy of errors. It was as if the devil himself were playing a game with all of them in turn. First with him, then with Ziemianitch, then with those revolutionists. The devil's own game this. . . . He interrupted his earnest mental soliloquy with a jocular thought at his own expense. " Hullo ! I am falling into mysticism too."

His mind was more at ease than ever. Turning about, he put his back against the rail comfortably. " All this fits with marvellous aptness," he continued to think. " The brilliance of my reputed exploit is no longer darkened by the fate of my supposed colleague. The mystic Ziemianitch accounts for that. An incredible chance has served me. No more need of lies. I shall have only to listen and to keep my scorn from getting the upper hand of my caution."

He sighed, folded his arms, his chin dropped on his breast, and it was a long time before he started forward from that pose, with the recollection that he had made up his mind to do something important that day. What it was he could not immediately recall, yet he made no effort of memory, for he was uneasily certain that he would remember presently.

He had not gone more than a hundred yards towards the town when he slowed down, almost faltered in his walk, at the sight of a figure walking in the contrary direction, draped in a cloak, under a soft, broad-brimmed hat, picturesque but diminutive, as if seen through the big end of an opera-glass. It was impossible to avoid that tiny man, for there was no issue for retreat.

" Another one going to that mysterious meeting," thought Razumov. He was right in his surmise, only *this* one, unlike the others who came from a distance, was known to him personally. Still, he hoped to pass on with a mere bow, but it was impossible to ignore the little thin hand with hairy wrist and knuckles protruded in a friendly wave from under the folds of the cloak, worn Spanish-wise, in disregard of a fairly warm day, a corner flung over the shoulder.

" And how is Herr Razumov ? " sounded the greeting in German, by that alone made more odious to the object of the affable recognition. At closer quarters the diminutive personage looked like a reduction of an ordinary-sized man, with a lofty brow bared for a moment by the raising of the hat, the great pepper-and-salt full beard spread over the proportionally broad chest. A fine bold nose jutted over a thin mouth hidden in the mass of fine hair. All this, accented features, strong limbs in their relative smallness, appeared delicate without the slightest sign of debility. The eyes alone, almond-shaped and brown, were too big, with the whites slightly bloodshot by much pen labour under a lamp. The obscure celebrity of the tiny man was well known to Razumov. Polyglot, of unknown parentage, of indefinite nationality, anarchist, with a pedantic and ferocious temperament, and an amazingly inflammatory capacity for invective, he was a power in the background, this violent pamphleteer clamouring for revolutionary justice, this Julius Laspara, editor of the *Living Word*, confidant of conspirators, inditer of sanguinary menaces and manifestoes, suspected of being in the secret of every plot. Laspara lived in the old town in a sombre, narrow house presented to him by a naïve middle-class admirer of his humanitarian eloquence. With him lived his two daughters, who overtopped him head and shoulders, and a pasty-faced, lean boy of six, languishing in the dark rooms in blue cotton overalls and clumsy boots, who might have belonged to either one of them or to neither. No stranger could tell. Julius Laspara no doubt knew which of his girls it was who, after casually vanishing for a few years, had as casually returned to him possessed of that child ; but, with admirable pedantry, he had refrained from asking her for details—no, not so much as the name of the father, because maternity should be an anarchist function. Razumov had been admitted twice to that suite of several small dark rooms on the top floor : dusty window-panes, litter of all sorts of sweepings all over the place, half-full glasses of tea forgotten on every table, the two Laspara daughters prowling about enigmatically silent, sleepy-eyed, corsetless, and generally, in their want of shape and the disorder of their rumpled attire, resembling old dolls ; the great but obscure Julius, his feet twisted round his three-legged stool, always ready to receive the visitors, the pen instantly dropped, the body screwed round with a striking display of the lofty brow and of the great austere beard. When he got down from his stool it was as though he had descended from the heights of Olympus. He was dwarfed by his daughters, by the furniture, by any caller of ordinary stature. But he very seldom left it, and still more rarely was seen walking in broad daylight.

It must have been some matter of serious importance which had driven him out in that direction that afternoon. Evidently he wished to be amiable to that young man whose arrival had made some sensation in the world of political refugees. In Russian now, which he spoke, as he spoke and wrote four or five other European languages, without distinction and without force (other than that of invective), he inquired if Razumov had taken his inscriptions at the university as yet. And the young man shaking his head negatively :

" There's plenty of time for that. But, meantime, are you not going to write something for us ? "

He could not understand how any one could refrain from writing on anything, social, economic, historical—anything. Any subject could be treated in the right spirit, and for the ends of social revolution. And, as it happened, a friend of his in London had got in touch with a review of advanced ideas. " We must educate, educate everybody—develop the great thought of absolute liberty and of revolutionary justice."

Razumov muttered rather surlily that he did not even know English.

" Write in Russian. We'll have it translated. There can be no difficulty. Why, without seeking further, there is Miss Haldin. My daughters go to see her sometimes." He nodded significantly. " She does nothing, has never done anything in her life. She would be quite competent, with a little assistance. Only write. You know you must. And so good-bye for the present."

He raised his arm and went on. Razumov backed against the low wall, looked after him, spat violently, and went on his way with an angry mutter :

" Cursed Jew ! "

He did not know anything about it. Julius Laspara might have been a Transylvanian, a Turk, an Andalusian, or a citizen of one of the Hanse towns for anything he could tell to the contrary. But this is not a story of the West, and this exclamation must be recorded, accompanied by the comment that it was merely an expression of hate and contempt, best adapted to the nature of the feelings Razumov suffered from at the time. He was boiling with rage, as though he had been grossly insulted. He walked as if blind, following instinctively the shore of the diminutive harbour along the quay, through a pretty, dull garden, where dull people sat on chairs under the trees, till, his fury abandoning him, he discovered himself in the middle of a long, broad bridge. He slowed down at once. To his right, beyond the toy-like jetties, he saw the green slopes framing the Petit Lac in all the marvellous banality of the picturesque made of painted cardboard, with the more distant stretch of water inanimate and shining like a piece of tin.

He turned his head away from that view for the tourists, and walked on slowly, his eyes fixed on the ground. One or two persons had to get out of his way, and then turned round to give a surprised stare at his profound absorption. The insistence of the celebrated subversive journalist rankled in his mind strangely. Write! Must write! He! Write! A sudden light flashed upon him. To

write was the very thing he had made up his mind
to do that day.   He had made up his mind irrevoc-
ably to that step and then had forgotten all about
it.   That incorrigible tendency to escape from the
grip of the situation was fraught with serious danger.
He was ready to despise himself for it.   What
was it ?   Levity, or deep-seated weakness ?   Or an
unconscious dread ?

" Is it that I am shrinking ?   It can't be !   It's
impossible.   To shrink now would be worse than
moral suicide ; it would be nothing less than moral
damnation," he thought.   " Is it possible that I
have a conventional conscience ? "

He rejected that hypothesis with scorn, and,
checked on the edge of the pavement, made ready to
cross the road and proceed up the wide street facing
the head of the bridge ; and that for no other reason
except that it was there before him.   But at the
moment a couple of carriages and a slow-moving
cart interposed, and suddenly he turned sharp to
the left, following the quay again, but now away
from the lake.

" It may be just my health," he thought, allow-
ing himself a very unusual doubt of his soundness ;
for, with the exception of a childish ailment or two,
he had never been ill in his life.   But that was a
danger too.   Only, it seemed as though he were
being looked after in a specially remarkable way.
" If I believed in an active Providence," Razumov
said to himself, amused grimly, " I would see here

the working of an ironical finger. To have a Julius Laspara put in my way as if expressly to remind me of my purpose is—— Write, he had said. I must write—I must, indeed! I shall write—never fear. Certainly. That's why I am here. And for the future I shall have something to write about."

He was exciting himself by this mental soliloquy. But the idea of writing evoked the thought of a place to write in, of shelter, of privacy, and naturally of his lodgings, mingled with a distaste for the necessary exertion of getting there, with a mistrust as of some hostile influence awaiting him within those odious four walls.

" Suppose one of those revolutionists," he asked himself, " were to take a fancy to call on me while I am writing ? " The mere prospect of such an interruption made him shudder. One could lock one's door, or ask the tobacconist downstairs (some sort of a refugee himself) to tell inquirers that one was not in. Not very good precautions these. The manner of his life, he felt, must be kept clear of every cause for suspicion or even occasion for wonder, down to such trifling occurrences as a delay in opening a locked door. " I wish I were in the middle of some field miles away from every-where," he thought.

He had unconsciously turned to the left once more and now was aware of being on a bridge again. This one was much narrower than the other, and instead of being straight, made a sort of elbow or angle. At the point of that angle a short arm joined it to a hexagonal islet with a soil of gravel and its shores faced with dressed stone, a perfection of puerile neatness. A couple of tall poplars and a few other trees stood grouped on the clean, dark gravel, and under them a few garden benches and a bronzed effigy of Jean Jacques Rousseau seated on its pedestal.

On setting his foot on it Razumov became aware that, except for the woman in charge of the refreshment chalet, he would be alone on the island. There was something of naïve, odious, and inane simplicity about that unfrequented tiny crumb of earth named after Jean Jacques Rousseau. Something pretentious and shabby too. He asked for a glass of milk, which he drank, standing, at one draught (nothing but tea had passed his lips since the morning), and was going away with a weary, lagging step when a thought stopped him short. He had found precisely what he needed. If solitude could ever be secured in the open air in the middle of a town, he would have it there on this absurd island, together with the faculty of watching the only approach.

He went back heavily to a garden seat, dropped into it. This was the place for making a beginning of that writing which had to be done. The materials he had on him. " I shall always come here," he said to himself, and afterwards sat for quite a long time motionless, without thought and sight and hearing, almost without life. He sat long enough for the declining sun to dip behind the roofs of the town at his back, and throw the shadow of the houses on the lake front over the islet, before he pulled out of his pocket a fountain pen, opened a small notebook on his knee, and began to write quickly, raising his eyes now and then at the connecting arm of the bridge. These glances were needless ; the people crossing over in the distance seemed unwilling even to look at the islet where the exiled effigy of the author of the *Social Contract* sat enthroned above the bowed head of Razumov in the sombre immobility of bronze. After finishing his scribbling, Razumov, with a sort of feverish haste, put away the pen, then rammed the notebook into his pocket, first tearing out the written pages with an almost convulsive brusqueness. But the folding of the flimsy batch on his knee was executed with thoughtful nicety. That done, he leaned back in his seat and remained motionless, holding the papers in his left hand. The twilight had deepened. He got up and began to pace to and fro slowly under the trees.

" There can be no doubt that now I am safe," he thought. His fine ear could detect the faintly accentuated murmurs of the current breaking against the point of the island, and he forgot himself in listening to them with interest. But even to his acute sense of hearing the sound was too elusive.

" Extraordinary occupation I am giving myself up to," he murmured.   And it occurred to him that this was about the only sound he could listen to innocently, and for his own pleasure, as it were. Yes, the sound of water, the voice of the wind— completely foreign to human passions. All the other sounds of this earth brought contamination to the solitude of a soul.

This was Mr. Razumov's feeling—the soul, of course, being his own, and the word being used not in the theological sense, but standing, as far as I can understand it, for that part of Mr. Razumov which was not his body, and more specially in danger from the fires of this earth. And it must be admitted that in Mr. Razumov's case the bitterness of solitude from which he suffered was not an altogether morbid phenomenon.

PART FOURTH

I

THAT I should, at the beginning of this retrospect, mention again that Mr. Razumov's youth had no one in the world, as literally no one as it can be honestly affirmed of any human being, is but a statement of fact from a man who believes in the psychological value of facts. There is also, perhaps, a desire of punctilious fairness. Unidentified with any one in this narrative where the aspects of honour and shame are remote from the ideas of the Western world, and taking my stand on the ground of common humanity, it is for that very reason that I feel a strange reluctance to state baldly here what every reader has most likely already discovered himself. Such reluctance may appear absurd if it were not for the thought that because of the imperfection of language there is always something ungracious (and even disgraceful) in the exhibition of naked truth. But the time has come when Councillor of State Mikulin can no longer be ignored. His simple question, " Where to ? " on which we left Mr. Razumov in St. Petersburg, throws a light on the general meaning of this individual case.

" Where to ? " was the answer in the form of a gentle question to what we may call Mr. Razumov's declaration of independence. The question was not menacing in the least, and, indeed, had the ring of innocent inquiry. Had it been taken in a merely topographical sense, the only answer to it would have appeared sufficiently appalling to Mr. Razumov. Where to ? Back to his rooms, where the Revolution had sought him out to put to a sudden test his dormant instincts, his half-conscious thoughts and almost wholly unconscious ambitions, by the touch as of some furious and dogmatic religion, with its call to frantic sacrifices, its tender resignations, its dreams and hopes uplifting the soul by the side of the most sombre moods of despair. And Mr. Razumov had let go the door-handle and had come back to the middle of the room, asking Councillor Mikulin angrily, " What do you mean by it ? "

As far as I can tell, Councillor Mikulin did not answer that question. He drew Mr. Razumov into familiar conversation. It is the peculiarity of Russian natures that, however strongly engaged in the drama of action, they are still turning their ear to the murmur of abstract ideas. This conversation (and others later on) need not be recorded. Suffice it to say that it brought Mr. Razumov as we know him to the test of another faith. There was nothing official in its expression, and Mr. Razumov was led to defend his attitude of detachment. But Councillor Mikulin would have none of his arguments. "For a man like you," were his last weighty words in the discussion, "such a position is impossible. Don't forget that I have seen that interesting piece of paper. I understand your liberalism. I have an intellect of that kind myself. Reform for me is mainly a question of method. But the principle of revolt is a physical intoxication, a sort of hysteria which must be kept away from the masses. You agree to this without reserve, don't you? Because, you see, Kirylo Sidorovitch, abstention, reserve, in certain situations, come very near to political crime. The ancient Greeks understood that very well."

Mr. Razumov, listening with a faint smile, asked Councillor Mikulin point-blank if this meant that he was going to have him watched.

The high official took no offence at the cynical inquiry.

"No, Kirylo Sidorovitch," he answered gravely. "I don't mean to have you watched."

Razumov, suspecting a lie, affected yet the greatest liberty of mind during the short remainder of that interview. The older man expressed himself throughout in familiar terms, and with a sort of shrewd simplicity. Razumov concluded that to get to the bottom of that mind was an impossible feat. A great disquiet made his heart beat quicker. The high official, issuing from behind the desk, was actually offering to shake hands with him.

" Good-bye, Mr. Razumov. An understanding between intelligent men is always a satisfactory occurrence. Is it not ? And, of course, these rebel gentlemen have not the monopoly of intelligence."

" I presume that I shall not be wanted any more ? " Razumov brought out that question while his hand was still being grasped. Councillor Mikulin released it slowly.

" That, Mr. Razumov," he said with great earnestness, " is as it may be. God alone knows the future. But you may rest assured that I never thought of having you watched. You are a young man of great independence. Yes. You are going away free as air, but you will end by coming back to us."

" I ! I ! " Razumov exclaimed, in an appalled murmur of protest. " What for ? " he added feebly.

" Yes ! You yourself, Kirylo Sidorovitch," the high police functionary insisted in a low, severe tone of conviction. " You will be coming back to us. Some of our greatest minds had to do that in the end."

" Our greatest minds ? " repeated Razumov in a dazed voice.

" Yes, indeed ! Our greatest minds. . . . Good-bye."

Razumov, shown out of the room, walked away from the door. But before he got to the end of the passage he heard heavy footsteps, and a voice calling

24

upon him to stop. He turned his head and was startled to see Councillor Mikulin pursuing him in person. The high functionary hurried up, very simple, slightly out of breath.

" One minute. As to what we were talking about just now, it shall be as God wills it. But I may have occasion to require you again. You look surprised, Kirylo Sidorovitch. Yes, again . . . to clear up any further point that may turn up."

" But I don't know anything," stammered out Razumov. " I couldn't possibly know anything."

" Who can tell ? Things are ordered in a wonderful manner. Who can tell what *may* become disclosed to you before this day is out ? You have been already the instrument of Providence. You smile, Kirylo Sidorovitch ; you are an *esprit fort*." (Razumov was not conscious of having smiled.) " But I believe firmly in Providence. Such a confession on the lips of an old hardened official like me may sound to you funny. But you yourself yet some day will recognise . . . Or else what happened to you cannot be accounted for at all. Yes, decidedly I shall have occasion to see you again, but not here. This wouldn't be quite—h'm . . . Some convenient place shall be made known to you. And even the written communications between us in *that* respect or in any other had better pass through the intermediacy of our—if I may express myself so—common friend, Prince K——. Now I beg you, Kirylo Sidorovitch—don't ! I am

certain he'll consent.   You must give me the credit
of being aware of what I am saying.   You have no
better friend than Prince K——, and as to myself,
it is a long time now since I've been honoured by
his . . ."

He glanced down his beard.

" I won't detain you any longer.   We live in
difficult times, in times of monstrous chimeras and
evil dreams and criminal follies.   We shall certainly
meet once more.   It may be some little time, though,
before we do.   Till then may Heaven send you
fruitful reflections ! "

Once in the street, Razumov started off rapidly,
without caring for the direction.   At first he thought
of nothing ; but in a little while the consciousness
of his position presented itself to him as something
so ugly, dangerous, and absurd, the difficulty of
ever freeing himself from the toils of that complication so insoluble, that the idea of going back
and, as he termed it to himself, *confessing* to Councillor Mikulin, flashed through his mind.

Go back !   What for ?   Confess !   To what ?
" I have been speaking to him with the greatest
openness," he said to himself with perfect truth.
" What else could I tell him ?   That I have undertaken to carry a message to that brute Ziemianitch ?
Establish a false complicity and destroy what chance
of safety I have won for nothing—what folly ! "

Yet he could not defend himself from fancying
that Councillor Mikulin was, perhaps, the only man

in the world able to understand his conduct. To be understood appeared extremely fascinating.

On the way home he had to stop several times ; all his strength seemed to run out of his limbs ; and in the movement of the busy streets, isolated as if in a desert, he remained suddenly motionless for a minute or so before he could proceed on his way. He reached his rooms at last.

Then came an illness, something in the nature of a low fever, which all at once removed him to a great distance from the perplexing actualities, from his very room, even. He never lost consciousness ; he only seemed to himself to be existing languidly somewhere very far away from everything that had ever happened to him. He came out of this state slowly, with an effect, that is to say, of extreme slowness, though the actual number of days was not very great. And when he had got back into the middle of things they were all changed, subtly and provokingly, in their nature : inanimate objects, human faces, the landlady, the rustic servant-girl, the staircase, the streets, the very air. He tackled these changed conditions in a spirit of severity. He walked to and fro to the university, ascended stairs, paced the passages, listened to lectures, took notes, crossed courtyards in angry aloofness, his teeth set hard till his jaws ached.

He was perfectly aware of Madcap Kostia gazing like a young retriever from a distance, of the famished student with the red drooping nose, keeping scrupulously away as desired ; of twenty others, perhaps, he knew well enough to speak to. And they all had an air of curiosity and concern as if they expected something to happen. " This can't last much longer," thought Razumov more than once. On certain days he was afraid that any one addressing him suddenly in a certain way would make him scream out insanely a lot of filthy abuse. Often, after returning home, he would drop into a chair in his cap and cloak and remain still for hours holding some book he had got from the library in his hand ; or he would pick up the little penknife and sit there scraping his nails endlessly and feeling furious all the time—simply furious. " This is impossible," he would mutter suddenly to the empty room.

Fact to be noted : this room might conceivably have become physically repugnant to him, emotionally intolerable, morally uninhabitable. But no. Nothing of the sort (and he had himself dreaded it at first), nothing of the sort happened. On the contrary, he liked his lodgings better than any other shelter he, who had never known a home, had ever hired before. He liked his lodgings so well that often, on that very account, he found a certain difficulty in making up his mind to go out. It resembled a physical seduction such as, for instance, makes a man reluctant to leave the neighbourhood of a fire on a cold day.

For as, at that time, he seldom stirred except to

go to the university (what else was there to do ?)
it followed that whenever he went abroad he felt
himself at once closely involved in the moral consequences of his act. It was there that the dark
prestige of the Haldin mystery fell on him, clung
to him like a poisoned robe it was impossible to
fling off. He suffered from it exceedingly, as well
as from the conversational, commonplace, unavoidable intercourse with the other kind of students.
" They must be wondering at the change in me,"
he reflected anxiously. He had an uneasy recollection of having savagely told one or two innocent,
nice enough fellows to go to the devil. Once a
married professor he used to call upon formerly
addressed him in passing : " How is it we never
see you at our Wednesdays now, Kirylo Sidorovitch ? " Razumov was conscious of meeting this
advance with odious, muttering boorishness. The
professor was obviously too astonished to be offended.
All this was bad. And all this was Haldin, always
Haldin—nothing but Haldin—everywhere Haldin :
a moral spectre infinitely more effective than any
visible apparition of the dead. It was only the room
through which that man had blundered on his way
from crime to death that his spectre did not seem
to be able to haunt. Not, to be exact, that he was
ever completely absent from it, but that there he
had no sort of power. There it was Razumov who
had the upper hand, in a composed sense of his own
superiority. A vanquished phantom—nothing more.

Often in the evening, his repaired watch faintly ticking on the table by the side of the lighted lamp, Razumov would look up from his writing and stare at the bed with an expectant, dispassionate attention. Nothing was to be seen there. He never really supposed that anything ever could be seen there. After a while he would shrug his shoulders slightly and bend again over his work. For he had gone to work, and, at first, with some success. His unwillingness to leave that place where he was safe from Haldin grew so strong that at last he ceased to go out at all. From early morning till far into the night he wrote, he wrote for nearly a week ; never looking at the time, and only throwing himself on the bed when he could keep his eyes open no longer. Then, one afternoon, quite casually, he happened to glance at his watch. He laid down his pen slowly.

" At this very hour," was his thought, " the fellow stole unseen into this room while I was out. And there he sat quiet as a mouse—perhaps in this very chair."

Razumov got up and began to pace the floor steadily, glancing at the watch now and then. " This is the time when I returned and found him standing against the stove," he observed to himself. When it grew dark he lit his lamp. Later on he interrupted his tramping once more, only to wave away angrily the girl who attempted to enter the room with tea and something to eat on a tray. And presently he noted the watch pointing at the hour of his own going forth into the falling snow on that terrible errand.

" Complicity," he muttered faintly, and resumed his pacing, keeping his eye on the hands as they crept on slowly to the time of his return.

" And, after all," he thought suddenly, " I might have been the chosen instrument of Providence. This is a manner of speaking, but there may be truth in every manner of speaking. What if that absurd saying were true in its essence ? "

He meditated for a while, then sat down, his legs stretched out, with stony eyes, and with his arms hanging down on each side of the chair like a man totally abandoned by Providence—desolate.

He noted the time of Haldin's departure and continued to sit still for another half-hour ; then muttering, " And now to work," drew up to the table, seized the pen and instantly dropped it under the influence of a profoundly disquieting reflection : " There's three weeks gone by and no word from Mikulin."

What did it mean ? Was he forgotten ? Possibly. Then why not remain forgotten—creep in somewhere ? Hide. But where ? How ? With whom ? In what hole ? And was it to be for ever, or what ?

But a retreat was big with shadowy dangers. The eye of the social revolution was on him, and Razumov for a moment felt an unnamed and despairing dread, mingled with an odious sense of humiliation. Was it possible that he no longer belonged to himself? This was damnable. But why not simply keep on as before? Study. Advance. Work hard as if nothing had happened (and first of all win the Silver Medal), acquire distinction, become a great reforming servant of the greatest of States. Servant, too, of the mightiest homogeneous mass of mankind with a capability for logical, guided development in a brotherly solidarity of force and aim such as the world had never dreamt of . . . the Russian nation!

Calm, resolved, steady in his great purpose, he was stretching his hand towards the pen when he happened to glance towards the bed. He rushed at it, enraged, with a mental scream: "It's you, crazy fanatic, who stand in the way!" He flung the pillow on the floor violently, tore the blankets aside. . . . Nothing there. And, turning away, he caught for an instant in the air, like a vivid detail in a dissolving view of two heads, the eyes of General T—— and of Privy Councillor Mikulin side by side fixed upon him, quite different in character, but with the same unflinching and weary and yet purposeful expression . . . servants of the nation!

Razumov tottered to the washstand very alarmed about himself, drank some water and bathed his forehead. "This will pass and leave no trace," he thought confidently. "I am all right." But as to supposing that he had been forgotten it was perfect nonsense. He was a marked man on that side. And that was nothing. It was what that miserable phantom stood for which had to be got out of the way. . . . " If one only could go and spit it all out at some of them—and take the consequences."

He imagined himself accosting the red-nosed student and suddenly shaking his fist in his face. " From that one, though," he reflected, " there's nothing to be got, because he has no mind of his own. He's living in a red democratic trance. Ah ! you want to smash your way into universal happiness, my boy. I will give you universal happiness, you silly, hypnotised ghoul, you ! And what about my own happiness, eh ? Haven't I got any right to it, just because I can think for myself ? . . ."

And again, but with a different mental accent, Razumov said to himself, " I am young. Everything can be lived down." At that moment he was crossing the room slowly, intending to sit down on the sofa and try to compose his thoughts. But before he had got so far everything abandoned him —hope, courage, belief in himself, trust in men. His heart had, as it were, suddenly emptied itself. It was no use struggling on. Rest, work, solitude, and the frankness of intercourse with his kind were alike forbidden to him. Everything was gone. His existence was a great cold blank, something like the enormous plain of the whole of Russia levelled with snow and fading gradually on all sides into shadows and mists.

He sat down, with swimming head, closed his eyes, and remained like that, sitting bolt upright on the sofa and perfectly awake for the rest of the night ; till the girl bustling into the outer room with the samovar thumped with her fist on the door, calling out, " Kirylo Sidorovitch, please ! It is time for you to get up ! "

Then, pale like a corpse obeying the dread summons of judgment, Razumov opened his eyes and got up.

.   .   .   .   .   .

Nobody will be surprised to hear, I suppose, that when the summons came he went to see Coun-cillor Mikulin. It came that very morning, while, looking white and shaky, like an invalid just out of bed, he was trying to shave himself. The envelope was addressed in the little attorney's handwriting. That envelope contained another, superscribed to Razumov, in Prince K——'s hand, with the request " Please forward under cover at once " in a corner. The note inside was an autograph of Councillor Mikulin. The writer stated candidly that nothing had arisen which needed clearing up, but never-theless appointed a meeting with Mr. Razumov at a certain address in town which seemed to be that of an oculist.

Razumov read it, finished shaving, dressed, looked at the note again, and muttered gloomily,

" Oculist." He pondered over it for a time, lit a match, and burned the two envelopes and the enclosure carefully. Afterwards he waited, sitting perfectly idle and not even looking at anything in particular till the appointed hour drew near—and then went out.

Whether, looking at the unofficial character of the summons, he might have refrained from attending to it is hard to say. Probably not. At any rate, he went ; but, what's more, he went with a certain eagerness, which may appear incredible till it is remembered that Councillor Mikulin was the only person on earth with whom Razumov could talk, taking the Haldin adventure for granted. And Haldin, when once taken for granted, was no longer a haunting, falsehood-breeding spectre. Whatever troubling power he exercised in all the other places of the earth, Razumov knew very well that at this oculist's address he would be merely the hanged murderer of Mr. de P—— and nothing more. For the dead can live only with the exact intensity and quality of the life imparted to them by the living. So Mr. Razumov, certain of relief, went to meet Councillor Mikulin with the eagerness of a pursued person welcoming any sort of shelter.

This much said, there is no need to tell anything more of that first interview and of the several others. To the morality of a Western reader an account of these meetings would wear perhaps the sinister character of old legendary tales where the Enemy of

Mankind is represented holding subtly mendacious dialogues with some tempted soul. It is not my part to protest. Let me but remark that the Evil One, with his single passion of satanic pride for the only motive, is yet, on a larger, modern view, allowed to be not quite so black as he used to be painted. With what greater latitude, then, should we appraise the exact shade of mere mortal man, with his many passions and his miserable ingenuity in error, always dazzled by the base glitter of mixed motives, everlastingly betrayed by a shortsighted wisdom.

Councillor Mikulin was one of those powerful officials who, in a position not obscure, not occult, but simply inconspicuous, exercise a great influence over the methods rather than over the conduct of affairs. A devotion to Church and Throne is not in itself a criminal sentiment ; to prefer the will of one to the will of many does not argue the possession of a black heart or prove congenital idiocy. Councillor Mikulin was not only a clever but also a faithful official. Privately he was a bachelor with a love of comfort, living alone in an apartment of five rooms luxuriously furnished ; and was known by his intimates to be an enlightened patron of the art of female dancing. Later on the larger world first heard of him in the very hour of his downfall, during one of those State trials which astonish and puzzle the average plain man who reads the newspapers, by a glimpse of unsuspected intrigues. And in the stir of vaguely seen monstrosities, in that momentary, mysterious disturbance of muddy waters, Councillor Mikulin went under, dignified, with only a calm, emphatic protest of his innocence —nothing more. No disclosures damaging to a harassed autocracy, complete fidelity to the secrets of the miserable *arcana imperii* deposited in his patriotic breast, a display of bureaucratic stoicism in a Russian official's ineradicable, almost sublime contempt for truth ; stoicism of silence understood only by the very few of the initiated, and not without a certain cynical grandeur of self-sacrifice on the part of a sybarite. For the terribly heavy sentence turned Councillor Mikulin civilly into a corpse, and actually into something very much like a common convict.

It seems that the savage autocracy, no more than the divine democracy, does not limit its diet exclusively to the bodies of its enemies. It devours its friends and servants as well. The downfall of His Excellency Gregory Gregorievitch Mikulin (which did not occur till some years later) completes all that is known of the man. But at the time of Mr. de P——'s murder (or execution) Councillor Mikulin, under the modest style of Head of Department at the General Secretariat, exercised a wide influence as the confidant and right-hand man of his former schoolfellow and lifelong friend, General T——. One can imagine them talking over the case of Mr. Razumov, with the full sense of their unbounded power over all the lives in Russia, with

cursory disdain, like two Olympians glancing at a
worm. The relationship with Prince K—— was
enough to save Razumov from some carelessly
arbitrary proceeding, and it is also very probable
that after the interview at the Secretariat he would
have been left alone. Councillor Mikulin would
not have forgotten him (he forgot no one who ever
fell under his observation), but would have simply
dropped him for ever. Councillor Mikulin was a
good-natured man and wished no harm to any one.
Besides (with his own reforming tendencies) he
was favourably impressed by that young student,
the son of Prince K——, and apparently no fool.

But as fate would have it, while Mr. Razumov
was finding that no way of life was possible to him,
Councillor Mikulin's discreet abilities were rewarded
by a very responsible post—nothing less than the
direction of the general police supervision over
Europe. And it was then, and then only, when
taking in hand the perfecting of the service which
watches the revolutionist activities abroad, that he
thought again of Mr. Razumov. He saw great
possibilities of special usefulness in that uncommon
young man on whom he had a hold already, with
his peculiar temperament, his unsettled mind and
shaken conscience, struggling in the toils of a false
position. . . . It was as if the revolutionists themselves had put into his hand that tool so much finer
than the common base instruments, so perfectly
fitted, if only vested with sufficient credit, to

penetrate into places inaccessible to common informers. Providential! Providential! And Prince K——, taken into the secret, was ready enough to adopt that mystical view too. "It will be necessary, though, to make a career for him afterwards," he had stipulated anxiously. "Oh! absolutely. We shall make that our affair," Mikulin had agreed. Prince K——'s mysticism was of an artless kind; but Councillor Mikulin was astute enough for two.

Things and men have always a certain sense, a certain side by which they must be got hold of if one wants to obtain a solid grasp and a perfect command. The power of Councillor Mikulin consisted in the ability to seize upon that sense, that side in the men he used. It did not matter to him what it was—vanity, despair, love, hate, greed, intelligent pride or stupid conceit, it was all one to him as long as the man could be made to serve. The obscure, unrelated young student Razumov, in the moment of great moral loneliness, was allowed to feel that he was an object of interest to a small group of people of high position. Prince K—— was persuaded to intervene personally, and on a certain occasion gave way to a manly emotion which, all unexpected as it was, quite upset Mr. Razumov. The sudden embrace of that man, agitated by his loyalty to a throne and by suppressed paternal affection, was a revelation to Mr. Razumov of something within his own breast.

" So that was it ! " he exclaimed to himself.   A sort of contemptuous tenderness softened the young man's grim view of his position as he reflected upon that agitated interview with Prince K——.   This simple-minded, worldly ex-Guardsman and senator whose soft grey official whiskers had brushed against his cheek, his aristocratic and convinced father, was he a whit less estimable or more absurd than that famine-stricken, fanatical revolutionist, the red-nosed student ?

And there was some pressure, too, besides the persuasiveness. Mr. Razumov was always being made to feel that he had committed himself.   There was no getting away from that feeling, from that soft, unanswerable " Where to ? " of Councillor Mikulin. But no susceptibilities were ever hurt. It was to be a dangerous mission to Geneva for obtaining, at a critical moment, absolutely reliable information from a very inaccessible quarter of the inner revolutionary circle.   There were indications that a very serious plot was being matured. . . . The repose indispensable to a great country was at stake. . . . A great scheme of orderly reforms would be endangered. . . . The highest personages in the land were patriotically uneasy, and so on. In short, Councillor Mikulin knew what to say. This skill is to be inferred clearly from the mental and psychological self-confession, self-analysis of Mr. Razumov's written journal—the pitiful resource of a young man who had near

25

him no trusted intimacy, no natural affection to turn to.

How all this preliminary work was concealed from observation need not be recorded. The expedient of the oculist gives a sufficient instance. Councillor Mikulin was resourceful, and the task not very difficult. Any fellow-student, even the red-nosed one, was perfectly welcome to see Mr. Razumov entering a private house to consult an oculist. Ultimate success depended solely on the revolutionary self-delusion which credited Razumov with a mysterious complicity in the Haldin affair. To be compromised in it was credit enough—and it was their own doing. It was precisely *that* which stamped Mr. Razumov as a providential man, wide as poles apart from the usual type of agent for " European supervision."

And it was *that* which the Secretariat set itself the task to foster by a course of calculated and false indiscretions.

It came at last to this, that one evening Mr. Razumov was unexpectedly called upon by one of the " thinking " students whom formerly, before the Haldin affair, he used to meet at various private gatherings ; a big fellow with a quiet, unassuming manner and a pleasant voice.

Recognising his voice raised in the anteroom, " May one come in ? " Razumov, lounging diiy on his couch, jumped up. " Suppose he were coming to stab me ? " he thought sardonically, and, assuming a green shade over his left eye, said in a severe tone, " Come in."

The other was embarrassed ; hoped he was not intruding.

" You haven't been seen for several days, and I've wondered." He coughed a little. " Eye better ? "

" Nearly well now."

" Good. I won't stop a minute ; but you see I, that is, we—anyway, I have undertaken the duty to warn you, Kirylo Sidorovitch, that you are living in false security maybe."

Razumov sat still with his head leaning on his hand, which nearly concealed the unshaded eye.

" I have that idea too."

" That's all right, then. Everything seems quiet now, but those people are preparing some move of general repression. That's of course. But it isn't that I came to tell you." He hitched his chair closer, dropped his voice. " You will be arrested before long—we fear."

An obscure scribe in the Secretariat had overheard a few words of a certain conversation, and had caught a glimpse of a certain report. This intelligence was not to be neglected.

Razumov laughed a little, and his visitor became very anxious.

" Ah, Kirylo Sidorovitch, this is no laughing matter. They have left you alone for a while, but . . .! Indeed, you had better try to leave the country, Kirylo Sidorovitch, while there's yet time."

Razumov jumped up and began to thank him for the advice with mocking effusiveness, so that the other, colouring up, took himself off with the notion that this mysterious Razumov was not a person to be warned or advised by inferior mortals.

Councillor Mikulin, informed the next day of the incident, expressed his satisfaction. " H'm. Ha ! Exactly what was wanted to . . ." and glanced down his beard.

" I conclude," said Razumov, " that the moment has come for me to start on my mission."

" The psychological moment," Councillor Mikulin insisted softly—very gravely—as if awed.

All the arrangements to give verisimilitude to the appearance of a difficult escape were made. Councillor Mikulin did not expect to see Mr. Razumov again before his departure. These meetings were a risk, and there was nothing more to settle.

" We have said everything to each other by now, Kirylo Sidorovitch," said the high official feelingly, pressing Razumov's hand with that unreserved heartiness a Russian can convey in his manner. " There is nothing obscure between us. And I will tell you what ! I consider myself fortunate in having—h'm—your . . ."

He glanced down his beard, and, after a moment of thoughtful silence, handed to Razumov a half-sheet of notepaper—an abbreviated note of matters already discussed, certain points of inquiry, the line of conduct agreed on, a few hints as to personalities, and so on. It was the only compromising document in the case, but, as Councillor Mikulin observed, " it could be easily destroyed. Mr. Razumov had better not see any one now—till on the other side of the frontier, when, of course, it will be just that . . . See and hear and . . ."

He glanced down his beard ; but when Razumov declared his intention to see one person at least before leaving St. Petersburg, Councillor Mikulin failed to conceal a sudden uneasiness. The young man's studious, solitary, and austere existence was well known to him. It was the greatest guarantee of fitness. He became deprecatory. Had his dear Kirylo Sidorovitch considered whether, in view of such a momentous enterprise, it wasn't really advisable to sacrifice every sentiment ? . . .

Razumov interrupted the remonstrance scornfully. It was not a young woman, it was a young fool he wished to see for a certain purpose. Councillor Mikulin was relieved, but surprised.

" Ah ! And what for—precisely ? "

" For the sake of improving the aspect of verisimilitude," said Razumov curtly, in a desire to affirm his independence. " I must be trusted in what I do."

Councillor Mikulin gave way tactfully, murmuring, " Oh, certainly, certainly. Your judgment . . ."

And with another handshake they parted.

The fool of whom Mr. Razumov had thought was the rich and festive student known as Madcap

Kostia. Feather-headed, loquacious, excitable, one could make certain of his utter and complete indiscretion. But that riotous youth, when reminded by Razumov of his offers of service some time ago, passed from his usual elation into boundless dismay.

" Oh, Kirylo Sidorovitch, my dearest friend—my saviour—what shall I do ? I've blown last night every rouble I had from my dad the other day. Can't you give me till Thursday ? I shall rush round to all the usurers I know. . . . No, of course you can't ! Don't look at me like that. What shall I do ? No use asking the old man. I tell you he's given me a fistful of big notes three days ago. Miserable wretch that I am."

He wrung his hands in despair. Impossible to confide in the old man. " They " had given him a decoration, a cross on the neck only last year, and he had been cursing the modern tendencies ever since. Just then he would see all the intellectuals in Russia hanged in a row rather than part with a single rouble.

" Kirylo Sidorovitch, wait a moment. Don't despise me. I have it. I'll, yes—I'll do it—I'll break into his desk. There's no help for it. I know the drawer where he keeps his plunder, and I can buy a chisel on my way home. He will be terribly upset, but, you know, the dear old duffer really loves me. He'll have to get over it—and I, too. Kirylo, my dear soul, if you can only wait for a few hours—till this evening—I shall steal all the blessed lot I can lay my hands on ! You doubt me ! Why ? You've only to say the word."

" Steal, by all means," said Razumov, fixing him stonily.

" To the devil with the Ten Commandments ! " cried the other, with the greatest animation. " It's the new future now."

But when he entered Razumov's room late in the evening it was with an unaccustomed soberness of manner, almost solemnly.

" It's done," he said.

Razumov, sitting bowed, his clasped hands hanging between his knees, shuddered at the familiar sound of these words. Kostia deposited slowly in the circle of lamplight a small brown-paper parcel tied with a piece of string.

" As I've said—all I could lay my hands on. The old boy'll think the end of the world has come."

Razumov nodded from the couch, and contemplated the hare-brained fellow's gravity with a feeling of malicious pleasure.

" I've made my little sacrifice," sighed mad Kostia. " And I've to thank you, Kirylo Sidorovitch, for the opportunity."

" It has cost you something ? "

" Yes, it has. You see, the dear old duffer really loves me. He'll be hurt."

" And you believe all they tell you of the new future and the sacred will of the people ? "

" Implicitly. I would give my life . . . Only, you see, I am like a pig at a trough. I am no good. It's my nature."

Razumov, lost in thought, had forgotten his existence till the youth's voice, entreating him to fly without loss of time, roused him unpleasantly.

" All right. Well—good-bye."

" I am not going to leave you till I've seen you out of St. Petersburg," declared Kostia unexpectedly, with calm determination. " You can't refuse me that now. For God's sake, Kirylo, my soul, the police may be here any moment, and when they get you they'll immure you somewhere for ages—till your hair turns grey. I have down there the best trotter of dad's stables and a light sledge. We shall do thirty miles before the moon sets, and find some roadside station . . ."

Razumov looked up amazed. The journey was decided—unavoidable. He had fixed the next day for his departure on the mission. And now he discovered suddenly that he had not believed in it. He had gone about listening, speaking, thinking, planning his simulated flight, with the growing conviction that all this was preposterous. As if anybody ever did such things ! It was like a game of make-believe. And now he was amazed ! Here was somebody who believed in it with desperate earnestness. " If I don't go now, at once," thought Razumov, with a start of fear, " I shall never go." He rose without a word, and the anxious Kostia thrust his cap on him, helped him into his cloak, or else he would have left the room bareheaded as he stood. He was walking out silently when a sharp cry arrested him.

" Kirylo ! "

" What ? " He turned reluctantly in the doorway. Upright, with a stiffly extended arm, Kostia, his face set and white, was pointing an eloquent forefinger at the brown little packet lying forgotten in the circle of bright light on the table. Razumov hesitated, came back for it under the severe eyes of his companion, at whom he tried to smile. But the boyish, mad youth was frowning. " It's a dream," thought Razumov, putting the little parcel into his pocket and descending the stairs ; " nobody does such things." The other held him under the arm, whispering of dangers ahead, and of what he meant to do in certain contingencies. " Preposterous," murmured Razumov, as he was being tucked up in the sledge. He gave himself up to watching the development of the dream with extreme attention. It continued on foreseen lines, inexorably logical— the long drive, the wait at the small station sitting by a stove. They did not exchange half a dozen words altogether. Kostia, gloomy himself, did not care to break the silence. At parting they embraced twice—it had to be done ; and then Kostia vanished out of the dream.

When dawn broke, Razumov, very still in a hot, stuffy railway-car full of bedding and of sleeping people in all its dimly lighted length, rose quietly, lowered the glass a few inches, and flung out on the great plain of snow a small brown-paper parcel. Then he sat down again muffled up and motionless. " For the people," he thought, staring out of the window. The great white desert of frozen, hard earth glided past his eyes without a sign of human habitation.

That had been a waking act ; and then the dream had him again : Prussia, Saxony, Würtemberg, faces, sights, words—all a dream, observed with an angry, compelled attention. Zurich, Geneva—still a dream, minutely followed, wearing one into harsh laughter, to fury, to death—with the fear of awakening at the end. . . .

II

" Perhaps life is just that," reflected Razumov, pacing to and fro under the trees of the little island, all alone with the bronze statue of Rousseau. " A dream and a fear." The dusk deepened. The pages written over and torn out of his notebook were the first-fruit of his " mission." No dream that. They contained the assurance that he was on the eve of real discoveries. " I think there is no longer anything in the way of my being completely accepted."

He had resumed his impressions in those pages, some of the conversations. He even went so far

as to write : " By-the-bye, I have discovered the
personality of that terrible N.N. A horrible,
paunchy brute. If I hear anything of his future
movements I shall send a warning."

The futility of all this overcame him like a curse.
Even then he could not believe in the reality of his
mission. He looked round despairingly, as if for
some way to redeem his existence from that uncon-
querable feeling. He crushed angrily in his hand
the pages of the notebook. " This must be posted,"
he thought.

He gained the bridge and returned to the north
shore, where he remembered having seen in one of
the narrower streets a little obscure shop stocked
with cheap wood carvings, its walls lined with
extremely dirty cardboard-bound volumes of a
small circulating library. They sold stationery
there too. A morose, shabby old man dozed
behind the counter. A thin woman in black,
with a sickly face, produced the envelope he had
asked for without even looking at him. Razumov
thought that these people were safe to deal with
because they no longer cared for anything in the
world. He addressed the envelope on the counter
with the German name of a certain person living
in Vienna. But Razumov knew that this, his first
communication for Councillor Mikulin, would find
its way to the Embassy there, be copied in cypher
by somebody trustworthy, and sent on to its desti-
nation, all safe, along with the diplomatic corre-

spondence. That was the arrangement contrived to cover up the track of the information from all unfaithful eyes, from all indiscretions, from all mishaps and treacheries. It was to make him safe—absolutely safe.

He wandered out of the wretched shop and made for the post office. It was then that I saw him for the second time that day. He was crossing the Rue Mont Blanc with every appearance of an aimless stroller. He did not recognise me, but I made him out at some distance. He was very good-looking, I thought, this remarkable friend of Miss Haldin's brother. I watched him go up to the letter-box and then retrace his steps. Again he passed me very close, but I am certain he did not see me that time, either. He carried his head well up, but he had the expression of a somnambulist struggling with the very dream which drives him forth to wander in dangerous places. My thoughts reverted to Natalia Haldin, to her mother. He was all that was left to them of their son and brother.

The Westerner in me was discomposed. There was something shocking in the expression of that face. Had I been myself a conspirator, a Russian political refugee, I could have perhaps been able to draw some practical conclusion from this chance glimpse. As it was, it only discomposed me strongly, even to the extent of awakening an indefinite apprehension in regard to Natalia Haldin. All this is rather inexplicable, but such was the origin of the purpose I formed there and then to call on these ladies in the evening, after my solitary dinner. It was true that I had met Miss Haldin only a few hours before, but Mrs. Haldin herself I had not seen for some considerable time. The truth is, I had shirked calling of late.

Poor Mrs. Haldin! I confess she frightened me a little. She was one of those natures, rare enough, luckily, in which one cannot help being interested, because they provoke both terror and pity. One dreads their contact for oneself, and still more for those one cares for, so clear it is that they are born to suffer and to make others suffer too. It is strange to think that, I won't say liberty, but the mere liberalism of outlook which for us is a matter of words, of ambitions, of votes (and if of feeling at all, then of the sort of feeling which leaves our deepest affections untouched), may be for other beings very much like ourselves and living under the same sky, a heavy trial of fortitude, a matter of tears and anguish and blood. Mrs. Haldin had felt the pangs of her own generation. There was that enthusiast brother of hers—the officer they shot under Nicholas. A faintly ironic resignation is no armour for a vulnerable heart. Mrs. Haldin, struck at through her children, was bound to suffer afresh from the past, and to feel the anguish of the future. She was of those who do not know how to heal themselves, of those who are too much aware of their heart, who, neither cowardly nor selfish, look passionately at its wounds—and count the cost.

Such thoughts as these seasoned my modest, lonely bachelor's meal. If anybody wishes to remark that this was a roundabout way of thinking of Natalia Haldin, I can only retort that she was well worth some concern. She had all her life before her. Let it be admitted, then, that I was thinking of Natalia Haldin's life in terms of her mother's character, a manner of thinking about a girl permissible for an old man, not too old yet to have become a stranger to pity. There was almost all her youth before her—youth robbed arbitrarily of its natural lightness and joy, overshadowed by an un-European despotism ; a terribly sombre youth given over to the hazards of a furious strife between equally ferocious antagonisms.

I lingered over my thoughts more than I should have done. One felt so helpless, and even worse —so unrelated in a way. At the last moment I hesitated as to going there at all. What was the good ?

The evening was already advanced when, turning into the Boulevard des Philosophes, I saw the light in the window at the corner. The blind was down, but I could imagine behind it Mrs. Haldin seated in the chair, in her usual attitude, looking out for some one, which had lately acquired the poignant quality of mad expectation.

I thought that I was sufficiently authorised by

the light to knock at the door. The ladies had not retired as yet. I only hoped they would not have any visitors of their own nationality. A broken-down, retired Russian official was to be found there sometimes in the evening. He was infinitely forlorn and wearisome by his mere dismal presence. I think these ladies tolerated his frequent visits because of an ancient friendship with Mr. Haldin, the father, or something of that sort. I made up my mind that if I found him prosing away there in his feeble voice I should remain but a very few minutes.

The door surprised me by swinging open before I could ring the bell. I was confronted by Miss Haldin, in hat and jacket, obviously on the point of going out. At that hour! For the doctor, perhaps?

Her exclamation of welcome reassured me. It sounded as if I had been the very man she wanted to see. My curiosity was awakened. She drew me in, and the faithful Anna, the elderly German maid, closed the door, but did not go away afterwards. She remained near it as if in readiness to let me out presently. It appeared that Miss Haldin had been on the point of going out to find me.

She spoke in a hurried manner very unusual with her. She would have gone straight and rung at Mrs. Ziegler's door, late as it was, for Mrs. Ziegler's habits . . .

Mrs. Ziegler, the widow of a distinguished professor who was an intimate friend of mine, lets me have three rooms out of her very large and fine

apartment, which she didn't give up after her husband's death ; but I have my own entrance opening
on the same landing. It was an arrangement of at
least ten years' standing. I said that I was very
glad that I had the idea to . . .

Miss Haldin made no motion to take off her
outdoor things. I observed her heightened colour,
something pronouncedly resolute in her tone. Did
I know where Mr. Razumov lived ?

Where Mr. Razumov lived ? Mr. Razumov ? At
this hour—so urgently ? I threw my arms up in
sign of utter ignorance. I had not the slightest idea
where he lived. If I could have foreseen her question only three hours ago, I might have ventured
to ask him on the pavement before the new post-
office building, and possibly he would have told me,
but very possibly, too, he would have dismissed me
rudely to mind my own business. And possibly, I
thought, remembering that extraordinary hallucined,
anguished, and absent expression, he might have
fallen down in a fit from the shock of being spoken
to. I said nothing of all this to Miss Haldin, not
even mentioning that I had a glimpse of the young
man so recently. The impression had been so
extremely unpleasant that I would have been glad
to forget it myself.

" I don't see where I could make inquiries," I
murmured helplessly. I would have been glad to
be of use in any way, and would have set off to
fetch any man, young or old, for I had the greatest

confidence in her common sense. " What made you think of coming to me for that information ? " I asked.

" It wasn't exactly for that," she said, in a low voice. She had the air of some one confronted by an unpleasant task.

" Am I to understand that you must communicate with Mr. Razumov this evening ? "

Natalia Haldin moved her head affirmatively ; then, after a glance at the door of the drawing-room, said in French :

" *C'est maman*," and remained perplexed for a moment. Always serious, not a girl to be put out by any imaginary difficulties, my curiosity was suspended on her lips, which remained closed for a moment. What was Mr. Razumov's connection with this mention of her mother ? Mrs. Haldin had not been informed of her son's friend's arrival in Geneva.

" May I hope to see your mother this evening ? " I inquired.

Miss Haldin extended her hand as if to bar the way.

" She is in a terrible state of agitation. Oh, you would not be able to detect . . . It's inward, but I who know mother, I am appalled. I haven't the courage to face it any longer. It's all my fault ; I suppose I cannot play a part ; I've never before hidden anything from mother. There has never been an occasion for anything of that sort between

26

us. But you know yourself the reason why I
refrained from telling her at once of Mr. Razumov's
arrival here. You understand, don't you ? Owing
to her unhappy state. And—there——— I am no
actress. My own feelings being strongly engaged, I
somehow . . . I don't know. She noticed something in my manner. She thought I was concealing
something from her. She noticed my longer ab-
sences, and, in fact, as I have been meeting Mr.
Razumov daily, I used to stay away longer than
usual when I went out. Goodness knows what
suspicions arose in her mind. You know that she
has not been herself ever since. . . . So this evening
she—who has been so awfully silent for weeks—
began to talk all at once. She said that she did not
want to reproach me ; that I had my character as
she had her own ; that she did not want to pry into
my affairs or even into my thoughts ; for her part,
she had never had anything to conceal from her
children. . . . Cruel things to listen to. And all
this in her quiet voice, with that poor, wasted face
as calm as a stone. It was unbearable."

Miss Haldin talked in an undertone and more
rapidly than I had ever heard her speak before.
That in itself was disturbing. The anteroom being
strongly lighted, I could see under the veil the
heightened colour of her face. She stood erect,
her left hand was resting lightly on a small table.
The other hung by her side without stirring. Now
and then she caught her breath slightly.

" It was too startling. Just fancy! She thought
that I was making preparations to leave her without
saying anything. I knelt by the side of her chair
and entreated her to think of what she was saying!
She put her hand on my head, but she persists in her
delusion all the same. She had always thought
that she was worthy of her children's confidence,
but apparently it was not so. Her son could not
trust her love nor yet her understanding—and now
I was planning to abandon her in the same cruel
and unjust manner, and so on, and so on. Nothing
I could say . . . It is morbid obstinacy. . . .
She said that she felt there was something, some
change in me. . . . If my convictions were calling
me away, why this secrecy, as though she had been
a coward or a weakling not safe to trust? ' As if
my heart could play traitor to my children,' she
said. . . . It was hardly to be borne. And she
was smoothing my head all the time. . . . It was
perfectly useless to protest. She is ill. Her very
soul is . . ."

I did not venture to break the silence which fell
between us. I looked into her eyes, glistening
through the veil.

" I ! Changed ! " she exclaimed in the same
low tone. " My convictions calling me away ! It
was cruel to hear this, because my trouble is that I
am weak and cannot see what I ought to do. You
know that. And to end it all I did a selfish thing.
To remove her suspicions of myself I told her of

Mr. Razumov. It was selfish of me. You know we were completely right in agreeing to keep the knowledge away from her. Perfectly right. Directly I told her of our poor Victor's friend being here I saw how right we have been. She ought to have been prepared ; but in my distress I just blurted it out. Mother got terribly excited at once. How long has he been here ? What did he know, and why did he not come to see us at once, this friend of her Victor ? What did that mean ? Was she not to be trusted even with such memories as there were left of her son ? . . . Just think how I felt seeing her, white as a sheet, perfectly motionless, with her thin hands gripping the arms of the chair. I told her it was all my fault."

I could imagine the motionless dumb figure of the mother in her chair, there, behind the door, near which the daughter was talking to me. The silence in there seemed to call aloud for vengeance against an historical fact and the modern instances of its working. That view flashed through my mind, but I could not doubt that Miss Haldin had had an atrocious time of it. I quite understood when she said that she could not face the night upon the impression of that scene. Mrs. Haldin had given way to most awful imaginings, to most fantastic and cruel suspicions. All this had to be lulled at all costs and without loss of time. It was no shock to me to learn that Miss Haldin had said to her, " I will go and bring him here at once." There was

nothing absurd in that cry, no exaggeration of sentiment. I was not even doubtful in my " Very well,
but how ? "

It was perfectly right that she should think of
me, but what could I do in my ignorance of Mr.
Razumov's quarters ?

" And to think he may be living near by, within
a stone's-throw, perhaps ! " she exclaimed.

I doubted it ; but I would have gone off cheerfully to fetch him from the other end of Geneva. I
suppose she was certain of my readiness, since her
first thought was to come to me. But the service
she meant to ask of me really was to accompany
her to the Château Borel.

I had an unpleasant mental vision of the dark
road, of the sombre grounds, and the desolately
suspicious aspect of that home of necromancy and
intrigue and feminist adoration. I objected that
Madame de S—— most likely would know nothing
of what we wanted to find out. Neither did I
think it likely that the young man would be found
there. I remembered my glimpse of his face, and
somehow gained the conviction that a man who
looked worse than if he had seen the dead would
want to shut himself up somewhere where he could
be alone. I felt a strange certitude that Mr. Razumov was going home when I saw him.

" It is really of Peter Ivanovitch that I was
thinking," said Miss Haldın quietly.

Ah ! He, of course, would know. I looked at

my watch. It was twenty minutes past nine only.
. . . Still.

"I would try his hotel, then," I advised. "He
has rooms at the Cosmopolitan, somewhere on the
top floor."

I did not offer to go by myself, simply from
mistrust of the reception I should meet with. But
I suggested the faithful Anna, with a note asking for
the information.

Anna was still waiting by the door at the other
end of the room, and we two discussed the matter in
whispers. Miss Haldin thought she must go herself.
Anna was timid and slow. Time would be lost in
bringing back the answer, and from that point of
view it was getting late, for it was by no means
certain that Mr. Razumov lived near by.

"If I go myself," Miss Haldin argued, "I can
go straight to him from the hotel. And in any case
I should have to go out, because I must explain to
Mr. Razumov personally—prepare him in a way.
You have no idea of mother's state of mind."

Her colour came and went. She even thought
that both for her mother's sake and for her own it
was better that they should not be together for a
little time. Anna, whom her mother liked, would
be at hand.

"She could take her sewing into the room,"
Miss Haldin continued, leading the way to the door.
Then, addressing in German the maid who opened
it before us, "You may tell my mother that this

gentleman called and is gone with me to find Mr. Razumov. She must not be uneasy if I am away for some length of time."

We passed out quickly into the street, and she took deep breaths of the cool night air. " I did not even ask you," she murmured.

" I should think not," I said, with a laugh. The manner of my reception by the great feminist could not be considered now. That he would be annoyed to see me, and probably treat me to some solemn insolence, I had no doubt, but I supposed that he would not absolutely dare to throw me out. And that was all I cared for. " Won't you take my arm ? " I asked.

She did so in silence, and neither of us said anything worth recording till I let her go first into the great hall of the hotel. It was brilliantly lighted, and with a good many people lounging about.

" I could very well go up there without you," I suggested.

" I don't like to be left waiting in this place," she said in a low voice. " I will come too."

I led her straight to the lift then. At the top floor the attendant directed us to the right : " End of the corridor."

The walls were white, the carpet red, electric lights blazed in confusion, and the emptiness, the silence, the closed doors all alike and numbered, made me think of the perfect order of some severely luxurious model penitentiary on the solitary confinement principle. Up there under the roof of that enormous pile for housing travellers no sound of any kind reached us, the thick crimson felt muffled our footsteps completely. We hastened on, not looking at each other till we found ourselves before the very last door of that long passage. Then our eyes met, and we stood thus for a moment lending ear to a faint murmur of voices inside.

" I suppose this is it," I whispered unnecessarily. I saw Miss Haldin's lips move without a sound, and after my sharp knock the murmur of voices inside ceased. A profound stillness lasted for a few seconds, and then the door was brusquely opened by a short black-eyed woman in a red blouse, with a lot of nearly white hair, done up negligently in an untidy and unpicturesque manner. Her thin, jetty eyebrows were drawn together. I learned afterwards with interest that she was the famous—or the notorious—Sophia Antonovna, but I was struck then by the quaint Mephistophelian character of her inquiring glance, because it was so curiously evil-less, so—I may say—un-devilish. It got softened still more as she looked up at Miss Haldin, who stated, in her rich, even voice, her wish to see Peter Ivanovitch for a moment.

" I am Miss Haldin," she added.

At this, with her brow completely smoothed out now, but without a word in answer, the woman in the red blouse walked away to a sofa and sat down, leaving the door wide open.

And from the sofa, her hands lying on her lap, she watched us enter, with her black, glittering eyes.

Miss Haldin advanced into the middle of the room ; I, faithful to my part of mere attendant, remained by the door after closing it behind me. The room, quite a large one, but with a low ceiling, was scantily furnished, and an electric bulb with a porcelain shade pulled low down over a big table (with a very large map spread on it) left its distant parts in a dim, artificial twilight. Peter Ivanovitch was not to be seen, neither was Mr. Razumov present. But, on the sofa, near Sophia Antonovna, a bony-faced man with a goatee beard leaned forward with his hands on his knees, staring hard with a kindly expression. In a remote corner a broad, pale face and a bulky shape could be made out, uncouth, and as if insecure on the low seat on which it rested. The only person known to me was little Julius Laspara, who seemed to have been poring over the map, his feet twined tightly round the chair-legs. He got down briskly and bowed to Miss Haldin, looking absurdly like a hook-nosed boy with a beautiful false pepper-and-salt beard. He advanced, offering his seat, which Miss Haldin declined. She had only come in for a moment to say a few words to Peter Ivanovitch.

His high-pitched voice became painfully audible in the room.

" Strangely enough, I was thinking of you this

very afternoon, Natalia Victorovna. I met Mr. Razumov. I asked him to write me an article on anything he liked. You could translate it into English—with such a teacher."

He nodded complimentarily in my direction. At the name of Razumov an indescribable sound, a sort of feeble squeak, as of some angry small animal, was heard in the corner occupied by the man who seemed much too large for the chair on which he sat. I did not hear what Miss Haldin said. Laspara spoke again.

" It's time to do something, Natalia Victorovna. But I suppose you have your own ideas. Why not write something yourself? Suppose you came to see us soon? We could talk it over. Any advice . . ."

Again I did not catch Miss Haldin's words. It was Laspara's voice once more.

" Peter Ivanovitch? He's retired for a moment into the other room. We are all waiting for him."

The great man, entering at that moment, looked bigger, taller, quite imposing in a long dressing-gown of some dark stuff. It descended in straight lines down to his feet. He suggested a monk or a prophet, a robust figure of some desert-dweller— something Asiatic ; and the dark glasses in conjunction with this costume made him more mysterious than ever in the subdued light.

Little Laspara went back to his chair to look at the map, the only brilliantly lit object in the room.

Even from my distant position by the door I could make out, by the shape of the blue part representing the water, that it was a map of the Baltic provinces. Peter Ivanovitch exclaimed slightly, advancing towards Miss Haldin, checked himself on perceiving me, very vaguely no doubt, and peered with his dark, bespectacled stare. He must have recognised me by my grey hair, because, with a marked shrug of his broad shoulders, he turned to Miss Haldin in benevolent indulgence. He seized her hand in his thick cushioned palm, and put his other big paw over it like a lid.

While those two standing in the middle of the floor were exchanging a few inaudible phrases no one else moved in the room; Laspara, with his back to us, kneeling on the chair, his elbows propped on the big-scale map, the shadowy enormity in the corner, the frankly staring man with the goatee on the sofa, the woman in the red blouse by his side— not one of them stirred. I suppose that really they had no time, for Miss Haldin withdrew her hand immediately from Peter Ivanovitch and before I was ready for her was moving to the door. A disregarded Westerner, I threw it open hurriedly and followed her out, my last glance leaving them all motionless in their varied poses : Peter Ivanovitch alone standing up, with his dark glasses like an enormous blind teacher, and behind him the vivid patch of light on the coloured map, pored over by the diminutive Laspara.

Later on, much later on, at the time of the newspaper rumours (they were vague and soon died out) of an abortive military conspiracy in Russia, I remembered the glimpse I had of that motionless group with its central figure. No details ever came out, but it was known that the revolutionary parties abroad had given their assistance, had sent emissaries in advance, that even money was found to dispatch a steamer with a cargo of arms and conspirators to invade the Baltic provinces. And while my eyes scanned the imperfect disclosures (in which the world was not much interested), I thought that the old, settled Europe had been given in my person attending that Russian girl something like a glimpse behind the scenes. A short, strange glimpse on the top floor of a great hotel of all places in the world : the great man himself ; the motionless great bulk in the corner of the slayer of spies and gendarmes ; Yakovlitch, the veteran of ancient terrorist campaigns ; the woman, with her hair as white as mine and the lively black eyes, all in a mysterious half-light, with the strongly lighted map of Russia on the table. The woman I had the opportunity to see again. As we were waiting for the lift she came hurrying along the corridor, with her eyes fastened on Miss Haldin's face, and drew her aside as if for a confidential communication. It was not long. A few words only.

Going down in the lift, Natalia Haldin did not break the silence. It was only when out of the hotel and as we moved along the quay in the fresh darkness spangled by the quay lights, reflected in the black water of the little port on our left hand, and with lofty piles of hotels on our right, that she spoke.

" That was Sophia Antonovna—you know the woman ? "

" Yes, I know—the famous . . ."

" The same. It appears that after we went out Peter Ivanovitch told them why I had come. That was the reason she ran out after us. She named herself to me, and then she said, ' You are the sister of a brave man who shall be remembered. You may see better times.' I told her I hoped to see the time when all this would be forgotten, even if the name of my brother were to be forgotten too. Something moved me to say that, but you understand ? "

" Yes," I said. " You think of the era of concord and justice."

" Yes. There is too much hate and revenge in that work. It must be done. It is a sacrifice—and so let it be all the greater. Destruction is the work of anger. Let the tyrants and the slayers be forgotten together, and only the reconstructors be remembered."

" And did Sophia Antonovna agree with you ? " I asked sceptically.

" She did not say anything except, ' It is good for you to believe in love.' I should think she

understood me. Then she asked me if I hoped to
see Mr. Razumov presently. I said I trusted I
could manage to bring him to see my mother this
evening, as my mother had learned of his being
here and was morbidly impatient to learn if he
could tell us something of Victor. He was the only
friend of my brother we knew of, and a great
intimate. She said, 'Oh! Your brother—yes.
Please tell Mr. Razumov that I have made public
the story which came to me from St. Petersburg.
It concerns your brother's arrest,' she added. 'He
was betrayed by a man of the people who has since
hanged himself. Mr. Razumov will explain it all
to you. I gave him the full information this
afternoon. And please tell Mr. Razumov that
Sophia Antonovna sends him her greetings. I am
going away early in the morning—far away.'"

And Miss Haldin added, after a moment of
silence :

"I was so moved by what I heard so unexpectedly that I simply could not speak to you
before. . . . A man of the people ! Oh, our poor
people ! "

She walked slowly, as if tired out suddenly. Her
head drooped ; from the windows of a building with
terraces and balconies came the banal sound of
hotel music ; before the low mean portals of the
Casino two red posters blazed under the electric
lamps, with a cheap provincial effect—and the
emptiness of the quays, the desert aspect of the

streets, had an air of hypocritical respectability
and of inexpressible dreariness.

I had taken for granted she had obtained the
address, and let myself be guided by her. On the
Mont Blanc bridge, where a few dark figures seemed
lost in the wide and long perspective defined by
the lights, she said :

" It isn't very far from our house. I somehow
thought it couldn't be. The address is Rue de
Carouge. I think it must be one of those big new
houses for artisans."

She took my arm confidingly, familiarly, and
accelerated her pace. There was something primi-
tive in our proceedings. We did not think of the
resources of civilisation. A late tramcar overtook
us ; a row of fiacres stood by the railing of the
gardens. It never entered our heads to make use of
these conveyances. She was too hurried, perhaps,
and as to myself—well, she had taken my arm
confidingly. As we were ascending the easy incline
of the Corraterie, all the shops shuttered and no
light in any of the windows (as if all the mercenary
population had fled at the end of the day), she said
tentatively :

" I could run in for a moment to have a look at
mother. It would not be much out of the way."

I dissuaded her. If Mrs. Haldin really expected
to see Razumov that night it would have been
unwise to show herself without him. The sooner
we got hold of the young man and brought him

along to calm her mother's agitation the better. She assented to my reasoning, and we crossed diagonally the Place de Théâtre, bluish grey with its floor of slabs of stone, under the electric light, and the lonely equestrian statue all black in the middle. In the Rue de Carouge we were in the poorer quarters and approaching the outskirts of the town. Vacant building plots alternated with high, new houses. At the corner of a side street the crude light of a whitewashed shop fell into the night, fanlike, through a wide doorway. One could see from a distance the inner wall with its scantily furnished shelves, and the deal counter painted brown. That was the house. Approaching it along the dark stretch of a fence of tarred planks, we saw the narrow pallid face of the cut angle, five single windows high, without a gleam in them, and crowned by the heavy shadow of a jutting roof slope.

"We must inquire in the shop," Miss Haldin directed me.

A sallow, thinly whiskered man, wearing a dingy white collar and a frayed tie, laid down a newspaper, and, leaning familiarly on both elbows far over the bare counter, answered that the person I was inquiring for was indeed his *locataire* on the third floor, but that for the moment he was out.

"For the moment," I repeated, after a glance at Miss Haldin. "Does this mean that you expect him back at once ? "

He was very gentle, with ingratiating eyes and soft lips. He smiled faintly as though he knew all about everything. Mr. Razumov, after being absent all day, had returned early in the evening. He was very surprised about half an hour or a little more ago to see him come down again. Mr. Razumov left his key, and in the course of some words which passed between them had remarked that he was going out because he needed air.

From behind the bare counter he went on smiling at us, his head held between his hands. Air. Air. But whether that meant a long or a short absence it was difficult to say. The night was very close certainly.

After a pause, his ingratiating eyes turned to the door, he added :

" The storm will drive him in."

" There's going to be a storm ? " I asked.

" Why, yes ! "

As if to confirm his words we heard a very distant, deep rumbling noise.

Consulting Miss Haldin by a glance, I saw her so reluctant to give up her quest that I asked the shopkeeper, in case Mr. Razumov came home within half an hour, to beg him to remain downstairs in the shop. We would look in again presently.

For all answer he moved his head imperceptibly. The approval of Miss Haldin was expressed by her silence. We walked slowly down the street, away from the town ; the low garden walls of the modest

27

villas doomed to demolition were overhung by the boughs of trees and masses of foliage, lighted from below by gas lamps. The violent and monotonous noise of the icy waters of the Arve falling over a low dam swept towards us with a chilly draught of air across a great open space, where a double line of lamplights outlined a street as yet without houses. But on the other shore, overhung by the awful blackness of the thunder-cloud, a solitary dim light seemed to watch us with a weary stare. When we had strolled as far as the bridge, I said :

" We had better get back. . . ."

In the shop the sickly man was studying his smudgy newspaper, now spread out largely on the counter. He just raised his head when I looked in and shook it negatively, pursing up his lips. I rejoined Miss Haldin outside at once, and we moved off at a brisk pace. She remarked that she would send Anna with a note the first thing in the morning. I respected her taciturnity, silence being perhaps the best way to show my concern.

The semi-rural street we followed on our return changed gradually to the usual town thoroughfare, broad and deserted. We did not meet four people altogether, and the way seemed interminable, because my companion's natural anxiety had communicated itself sympathetically to me. At last we turned into the Boulevard des Philosophes, more wide, more empty, more dead—the very desolation of slumbering respectability. At the sight of the two lighted windows, very conspicuous from afar, I had the mental vision of Mrs. Haldin in her armchair keeping a dreadful, tormenting vigil under the evil spell of an arbitrary rule : a victim of tyranny and revolution, a sight at once cruel and absurd.

III

" You will come in for a moment ? " said Natalia Haldin.

I demurred on account of the late hour. " You know mother likes you so much," she insisted.

" I will just come in to hear how your mother is."

She said, as if to herself, " I don't even know whether she will believe that I could not find Mr. Razumov, since she has taken it into her head that I am concealing something from her. You may be able to persuade her. . . ."

" Your mother may mistrust me too," I observed.

" You ! Why ? What could you have to conceal from her ? You are not a Russian nor a conspirator."

I felt profoundly my European remoteness, and said nothing, but I made up my mind to play my part of helpless spectator to the end. The distant rolling of thunder in the valley of the Rhône was coming nearer to the sleeping town of prosaic virtues and universal hospitality. We crossed the street opposite the great dark gateway, and Miss Haldin rang at the door of the apartment. It was opened almost instantly, as if the elderly maid had been waiting in the anteroom for our return. Her flat physiognomy had an air of satisfaction. The gentleman was there, she declared, while closing the door.

Neither of us understood. Miss Haldin turned round brusquely to her. " Who ? "

" Herr Razumov," she explained.

She had heard enough of our conversation before we left to know why her young mistress was going out. Therefore, when the gentleman gave his name at the door, she admitted him at once.

" No one could have foreseen that," Miss Haldin murmured, with her serious grey eyes fixed upon mine. And, remembering the expression of the young man's face seen not much more than four hours ago, the look of a haunted somnambulist, I wondered with a sort of awe.

" You asked my mother first ? " Miss Haldin inquired of the maid.

" No. I announced the gentleman," she answered, surprised at our troubled faces.

" Still," I said in an undertone, " your mother was prepared."

" Yes. But he has no idea . . ."

It seemed to me she doubted his tact. To her question how long the gentleman had been with her mother, the maid told us that *der Herr* had

been in the drawing-room no more than a short
quarter of an hour.

She waited a moment, then withdrew, looking a
little scared.   Miss Haldin gazed at me in silence.

" As things have turned out," I said, " you
happen to know exactly what your brother's friend
has to tell your mother.   And surely after that . . ."

" Yes," said Natalia Haldin slowly. " I only
wonder, as I was not here when he came, if it
wouldn't be better not to interrupt now."

We remained silent, and I suppose we both
strained our ears, but no sound reached us through
the closed door. The features of Miss Haldin
expressed a painful irresolution ; she made a
movement as if to go in, but checked herself. She
had heard footsteps on the other side of the door.
It came open, and Razumov, without pausing,
stepped out into the anteroom.   The fatigue of
that day and the struggle with himself had changed
him so much that I would have hesitated to recognise that face, which, only a few hours before, when
he brushed against me in front of the post office, had
been startling enough but quite different. It had
been not so livid then, and its eyes not so sombre.
They certainly looked more sane now, but there was
upon them the shadow of something consciously
evil.

I speak of that, because, at first, their glance fell
on me, though without any sort of recognition or
even comprehension. I was simply in the line of

his stare. I don't know if he had heard the bell or expected to see anybody. He was going out, I believe, and I do not think that he saw Miss Haldin till she advanced towards him a step or two. He disregarded the hand she put out.

" It's you, Natalia Victorovna. . . . Perhaps you are surprised . . . at this late hour. But, you see, I remembered our conversations in that garden. I thought really it was your wish that I should—without loss of time . . . so I came. No other reason. Simply to tell . . ."

He spoke with difficulty. I noticed that, and remembered his declaration to the man in the shop that he was going out because he " needed air." If that was his object, then it was clear that he had miserably failed. With downcast eyes and lowered head he made an effort to pick up the strangled phrase.

" To tell what I have heard myself only to-day —to-day . . ."

Through the door he had not closed I had a view of the drawing-room. It was lighted only by a shaded lamp—Mrs. Haldin's eyes could not support either gas or electricity. It was a comparatively big room, and in contrast with the strongly lighted anteroom its length was lost in semi-transparent gloom backed by heavy shadows ; and on that ground I saw the motionless figure of Mrs. Haldin, inclined slightly forward, with a pale hand resting on the arm of the chair.

She did not move. With the window before her she had no longer that attitude suggesting expectation. The blind was down ; and outside there was only the night-sky harbouring a thunder-cloud, and the town indifferent and hospitable in its cold, almost scornful, toleration—a respectable town of refuge to which all these sorrows and hopes were nothing. Her white head was bowed.

The thought that the real drama of autocracy is not played on the great stage of politics came to me as, fated to be a spectator, I had this other glimpse behind the scenes, something more profound than the words and gestures of the public play. I had the certitude that this mother refused in her heart to give her son up after all. It was more than Rachel's inconsolable mourning, it was something deeper, more inaccessible in its frightful tranquillity. Lost in the ill-defined mass of the high-backed chair, her white, inclined profile suggested the contemplation of something in her lap, as though a beloved head were resting there.

I had this glimpse behind the scenes, and then Miss Haldin, passing by the young man, shut the door. It was not done without hesitation. For a moment I thought that she would go to her mother, but she sent in only an anxious glance. Perhaps if Mrs. Haldin had moved . . . but no. There was in the immobility of that bloodless face the dreadful aloofness of suffering without remedy.

Meantime the young man kept his eyes fixed on

the floor. The thought that he would have to repeat the story he had told already was intolerable to him. He had expected to find the two women together. And then, he had said to himself, it would be over for all time—for all time. " It's lucky I don't believe in another world," he had thought cynically.

Alone in his room after having posted his secret letter, he had regained a certain measure of composure by writing in his secret diary. He was aware of the danger of that strange self-indulgence. He alludes to it himself, but he could not refrain. It calmed him—it reconciled him to his existence. He sat there scribbling by the light of a solitary candle, till it occurred to him that having heard the explanation of Haldin's arrest, as put forward by Sophia Antonovna, it behoved him to tell these ladies himself. They were certain to hear the tale through some other channel, and then his abstention would look strange, not only to the mother and sister of Haldin, but to other people also. Having come to this conclusion, he did not discover in himself any marked reluctance to face the necessity, and very soon an anxiety to be done with it began to torment him. He looked at his watch. No ; it was not absolutely too late.

The fifteen minutes with Mrs. Haldin were like the revenge of the unknown : that white face, that weak, distinct voice ; that head, at first turned to him eagerly, then, after a while, bowed again

and motionless—in the dim, still light of the room
in which his words which he tried to subdue re-
sounded so loudly—had troubled him like some
strange discovery. And there seemed to be a secret
obstinacy in that sorrow, something he could not
understand ; at any rate, something he had not
expected. Was it hostile ? But it did not matter.
Nothing could touch him now ; in the eyes of the
revolutionists there was now no shadow on his
past. The phantom of Haldin had been indeed
walked over, was left behind lying powerless and
passive on the pavement covered with snow. And
this was the phantom's mother consumed with grief
and white as a ghost. He had felt a pitying surprise.
But that, of course, was of no importance. Mothers
did not matter. He could not shake off the poignant
impression of that silent, quiet, white-haired woman,
but a sort of sternness crept into his thoughts.
These were the consequences. Well, what of it ?
" Am I then on a bed of roses ? " he had exclaimed
to himself, sitting at some distance with his eyes
fixed upon that figure of sorrow. He had said all
he had to say to her, and when he had finished she
had not uttered a word. She had turned away her
head while he was speaking. The silence which had
fallen on his last words had lasted for five minutes
or more. What did it mean ? Before its incomprehensible character he became conscious of anger
in his stern mood, the old anger against Haldin reawakened by the contemplation of Haldin's mother.

And was it not something like enviousness which gripped his heart, as if of a privilege denied to him alone of all the men that had ever passed through this world ? It was the other who had attained to repose and yet continued to exist in the affection of that mourning old woman, in the thoughts of all these people posing for lovers of humanity. It was impossible to get rid of him. " It's myself whom I have given up to destruction," thought Razumov. " He has induced me to do it. I can't shake him off."

Alarmed by that discovery, he got up and strode out of the silent, dim room with its silent old woman in the chair, that mother ! He never looked back. It was frankly a flight. But on opening the door he saw his retreat cut off. There was the sister. He had never forgotten the sister, only he had not expected to see her then—or ever any more, perhaps. Her presence in the anteroom was as unforeseen as the apparition of her brother had been. Razumov gave a start as though he had discovered himself cleverly trapped. He tried to smile, but could not manage it, and lowered his eyes. " Must I repeat that silly story now ? " he asked himself, and felt a sinking sensation. Nothing solid had passed his lips since the day before, but he was not in a state to analyse the origins of his weakness. He meant to take up his hat and depart with as few words as possible, but Miss Haldin's swift movement to shut the door took him by surprise. He half turned after her, but without raising his eyes, passively, just as a feather might stir in the disturbed air. The next moment she was back in the place she had started from, with another half-turn on his part, so that they came again into the same relative positions.

"Yes, yes," she said hurriedly. "I am very grateful to you, Kirylo Sidorovitch, for coming at once—like this. . . . Only, I wish I had . . . Did mother tell you?"

"I wonder what she could have told me that I did not know before," he said, obviously to himself, but perfectly audible. "Because I always *did* know it," he added louder, as if in despair.

He hung his head. He had such a strong sense of Natalia Haldin's presence that to look at her he felt would be a relief. It was she who had been haunting him now. He had suffered that persecution ever since she had suddenly appeared before him in the garden of the Villa Borel with an extended hand and the name of her brother on her lips. . . . The anteroom had a row of hooks on the wall nearest to the outer door, while against the wall opposite there stood a small dark table and one chair. The paper, bearing a very faint design, was all but white. The light of an electric bulb high up under the ceiling searched that clear square box into its four bare corners, crudely, without shadows—a strange stage for an obscure drama.

"What do you mean?" asked Miss Haldin. "What is it that you knew always?"

He raised his face, pale, full of unexpressed suffering. But that look in his eyes of dull, absent obstinacy, which struck and surprised everybody he was talking to, began to pass away. It was as though he were coming to himself in the awakened consciousness of that marvellous harmony of feature, of lines, of glances, of voice, which made of the girl before him a being so rare, outside, and, as it were, above the common notion of beauty. He looked at her so long that she coloured slightly.

"What is it that you knew?" she repeated vaguely.

That time he managed to smile.

"Indeed, if it had not been for a word of greeting or two, I would doubt whether your mother was aware at all of my existence. You understand?"

Natalia Haldin nodded; her hands moved slightly by her side.

"Yes. Is it not heart-breaking? She has not shed a tear yet—not a single tear."

"Not a tear! And you, Natalia Victorovna? You have been able to cry?"

"I have. And then I am young enough, Kirylo Sidorovitch, to believe in the future. But when I see my mother so terribly distracted, I almost forget everything. I ask myself whether one should feel proud—or only resigned. We had

such a lot of people coming to see us. There were
utter strangers who wrote asking for permission to
call to present their respects. It was impossible
to keep our door shut for ever. You know that
Peter Ivanovitch himself . . . Oh yes, there was
much sympathy, but there were persons who
exulted openly at that death. Then, when I was
left alone with poor mother, all this seemed so
wrong in spirit, something not worth the price she
is paying for it. But directly I heard you were
here in Geneva, Kirylo Sidorovitch, I felt that
you were the only person who could assist me . . ."

" In comforting a bereaved mother ? Yes ! "
he broke in, in a manner which made her open her
clear, unsuspecting eyes. " But there is a question
of fitness. Has this occurred to you ? "

There was a breathlessness in his utterance
which contrasted with the monstrous hint of mockery
in his intention.

" Why ! " whispered Natalia Haldin with feeling.
" Who more fit than you ? "

He had a convulsive movement of exasperation,
but controlled himself.

" Indeed ! Directly you heard that I was in
Geneva, before even seeing me ? It is another
proof of that confidence which . . ."

All at once his tone changed, became more
incisive and more detached.

" Men are poor creatures, Natalia Victorovna.
They have no intuition of sentiment. In order to

speak fittingly to a mother of her lost son one must have had some experience of the filial relation. It is not the case with me—if you must know the whole truth. Your hopes have to deal here with ' a breast unwarmed by any affection,' as the poet says. . . . That does not mean it is insensible," he added in a lower tone.

"I am certain your heart is not unfeeling," said Miss Haldin softly.

"No. It is not as hard as a stone," he went on in the same introspective voice, and looking as if his heart were lying as heavy as a stone in that unwarmed breast of which he spoke. "No, not so hard. But how to prove what you give me credit for—ah! that's another question. No one has ever expected such a thing from me before. No one whom my tenderness would have been of any use to. And now you come. You! Now! No, Natalia Victorovna. It's too late. You come too late. You must expect nothing from me."

She recoiled from him a little, though he had made no movement, as if she had seen some change in his face, charging his words with the significance of some hidden sentiment they shared together. To me, the silent spectator, they looked like two people becoming conscious of a spell which had been lying on them ever since they first set eyes on each other. Had either of them cast a glance then in my direction, I would have opened the door quietly and gone out. But neither did; and I remained, every fear of indiscretion lost in the sense of my enormous remoteness from their captivity within the sombre horizon of Russian problems, the boundary of their eyes, of their feelings—the prison of their souls.

Frank, courageous, Miss Haldin controlled her voice in the midst of her trouble.

" What can this mean ? " she asked, as if speaking to herself.

" It may mean that you have given yourself up to vain imaginings while I have managed to remain amongst the truth of things and the realities of life —our Russian life—such as they are."

" They are cruel," she murmured.

" And ugly. Don't forget that — and ugly. Look where you like. Look near you, here abroad where you are, and then look back at home, whence you came."

" One must look beyond the present." Her tone had an ardent conviction.

" The blind can do that best. I have had the misfortune to be born clear-eyed. And if you only knew what strange things I have seen ! What amazing and unexpected apparitions ! . . . But why talk of all this ? "

" On the contrary, I want to talk of all this with you," she protested with earnest serenity. The sombre humours of her brother's friend left her unaffected, as though that bitterness, that suppressed anger, were the signs of an indignant rectitude.

She saw that he was not an ordinary person, and perhaps she did not want him to be other than he appeared to her trustful eyes. " Yes, with you especially," she insisted. " With you of all the Russian people in the world. . . ." A faint smile dwelt for a moment on her lips. " I am like poor mother in a way. I too seem unable to give up our beloved dead, who, don't forget, was all in all to us. I don't want to abuse your sympathy, but you must understand that it is in you that we can find all that is left of his generous soul."

I was looking at him ; not a muscle of his face moved in the least. And yet, even at the time, I did not suspect him of insensibility. It was a sort of rapt thoughtfulness. Then he stirred slightly.

" You are going, Kirylo Sidorovitch ? " she asked.

" I ! Going ? Where ? Oh yes, but I must tell you first . . ." His voice was muffled and he forced himself to produce it with visible repugnance, as if speech were something disgusting or deadly. " That story, you know — the story I heard this afternoon . . ."

" I know the story already," she said sadly.

" You know it ! Have you correspondents in St. Petersburg too ? "

" No. It's Sophia Antonovna. I have seen her just now. She sends you her greetings. She is going away to-morrow."

He had lowered at last his fascinated glance ;

she too was looking down, and standing thus before each other in the glaring light, between the four bare walls, they seemed brought out from the confused immensity of the Eastern borders to be exposed cruelly to the observation of my Western eyes. And I observed them. There was nothing else to do. My existence seemed so utterly forgotten by these two that I dared not now make a movement. And I thought to myself that, of course, they had to come together, the sister and the friend of that dead man. The ideas, the hopes, the aspirations, the cause of Freedom, expressed in their common affection for Victor Haldin, the moral victim of autocracy,—all this must draw them to each other fatally. Her very ignorance and his loneliness to which he had alluded so strangely must work to that end. And, indeed, I saw that the work was done already. Of course. It was manifest that they must have been thinking of each other for a long time before they met. She had the letter from that beloved brother kindling her imagination by the severe praise attached to that one name ; and for him to see that exceptional girl was enough. The only cause for surprise was his gloomy aloofness before her clearly expressed welcome. But he was young, and however austere and devoted to his revolutionary ideals, he was not blind. The period of reserve was over ; he was coming forward in his own way. I could not mistake the significance of this late visit, for in

28

what he had to say there was nothing urgent. The true cause dawned upon me : he had discovered that he needed her—and she was moved by the same feeling. It was the second time that I saw them together, and I knew that next time they met I would not be there, either remembered or forgotten. I would have virtually ceased to exist for both these young people.

I made this discovery in a very few moments. Meantime, Natalia Haldin was telling Razumov briefly of our peregrinations from one end of Geneva to the other. While speaking she raised her hands above her head to untie her veil, and that movement displayed for an instant the seductive grace of her youthful figure, clad in the simplest of mourning. In the transparent shadow the hat rim threw on her face her grey eyes had an enticing lustre. Her voice, with its unfeminine yet exquisite timbre, was steady, and she spoke quickly, frank, unembarrassed. As she justified her action by the mental state of her mother, a spasm of pain marred the generously confiding harmony of her features. I perceived that with his downcast eyes he had the air of a man who is listening to a strain of music rather than to articulated speech. And in the same way, after she had ceased, he seemed to listen yet, motionless, as if under the spell of suggestive sound. He came to himself, muttering :

" Yes, yes. She has not shed a tear. She did not seem to hear what I was saying. I might have told her anything. She looked as if no longer belonging to this world."

Miss Haldin gave signs of profound distress. Her voice faltered. "You don't know how bad it has come to be. She expects now to *see him*!" The veil dropped from her fingers and she clasped her hands in anguish. "It will end by her seeing him," she cried.

Razumov raised his head sharply and attached on her a prolonged, thoughtful glance.

"H'm. That's very possible," he muttered in a peculiar tone, as if giving his opinion on a matter of fact. "I wonder what . . ." He checked himself.

"That would be the end. Her mind will be gone then, and her spirit will follow."

Miss Haldin unclasped her hands and let them fall by her side.

"You think so?" he queried profoundly. Miss Haldin's lips were slightly parted. Something unexpected and unfathomable in that young man's character had fascinated her from the first. "No! There's neither truth nor consolation to be got from the phantoms of the dead," he added after a weighty pause. "I might have told her something true; for instance, that your brother meant to save his life—to escape. There can be no doubt of that. But I did not."

"You did not! But why?"

"I don't know. Other thoughts came into my

head," he answered. He seemed to me to be watching himself inwardly, as though he were trying to count his own heart-beats, while his eyes never for a moment left the face of the girl. "You were not there," he continued. "I had made up my mind never to see you again."

This seemed to take her breath away for a moment.

"You . . . How is it possible?"

"You may well ask. . . . However, I think that I refrained from telling your mother from prudence. I might have assured her that in the last conversation he held as a free man he mentioned you both . . ."

"That last conversation was with you," she struck in, in her deep, moving voice. "Some day you must . . ."

"It was with me. Of you he said that you had trustful eyes. And why I have not been able to forget that phrase I don't know. It meant that there is in you no guile, no deception, no falsehood, no suspicion—nothing in your heart that could give you a conception of a living, acting, speaking lie, if ever it came in your way. That you are a pre-destined victim . . . Ha! what a devilish suggestion!"

The convulsive, uncontrolled tone of the last words disclosed the precarious hold he had over himself. He was like a man defying his own dizziness in high places and tottering suddenly on the very edge of the precipice. Miss Haldin

pressed her hand to her breast. The dropped black
veil lay on the floor between them. Her movement
steadied him. He looked intently on that hand till
it descended slowly, and then raised again his eyes
to her face. But he did not give her time to speak.

"No? You don't understand? Very well."
He had recovered his calm by a miracle of will.
"So you talked with Sophia Antonovna?"

"Yes. Sophia Antonovna told me . . ." Miss
Haldin stopped, wonder growing in her wide eyes.

"H'm. That's the respectable enemy," he
muttered, as though he were alone.

"The tone of her references to you was extremely friendly," remarked Miss Haldin, after
waiting for a while.

"Is that your impression? And she the most
intelligent of the lot, too. Things then are going as
well as possible. Everything conspires to . . . Ah!
those conspirators," he said slowly, with an accent
of scorn ; " they would get hold of you in no time !
You know, Natalia Victorovna, I have the greatest
difficulty in saving myself from the superstition of
an active Providence. It's irresistible. . . . The
alternative, of course, would be the personal Devil
of our simple ancestors. But, if so, he has overdone
it altogether—the old Father of Lies—our national
patron—our domestic god, whom we take with us
when we go abroad. He has overdone it. It seems
that I am not simple enough . . . That's it ! I
ought to have known . . . And I did know it," he

added in a tone of poignant distress which overcame my astonishment.

" This man is deranged," I said to myself, very much frightened.

The next moment he gave me a very special impression beyond the range of commonplace definitions. It was as though he had stabbed himself outside and had come in there to show it ; and more than that—as though he were turning the knife in the wound and watching the effect. That was the impression, rendered in physical terms. One could not defend oneself from a certain amount of pity. But it was for Miss Haldin, already so tried in her deepest affections, that I felt a serious concern. Her attitude, her face, expressed compassion struggling with doubt on the verge of terror.

" What is it, Kirylo Sidorovitch ? " There was a hint of tenderness in that cry. He only stared at her in that complete surrender of all his faculties which in a happy lover would have had the name of ecstasy.

" Why are you looking at me like this, Kirylo Sidorovitch ? I have approached you frankly. I need at this time to see clearly in myself . . ." She ceased for a moment as if to give him an opportunity to utter at last some word worthy of her exalted trust in her brother's friend. His silence became impressive, like a sign of a momentous resolution.

In the end Miss Haldin went on appealingly :

" I have waited for you anxiously. But now

that you have been moved to come to us in your kindness, you alarm me. You speak obscurely. It seems as if you were keeping back something from me."

" Tell me, Natalia Victorovna," he was heard at last in a strange, unringing voice, " whom did you see in that place ? "

She was startled, and as if deceived in her expectations.

" Where ? In Peter Ivanovitch's rooms ? There was Mr. Laspara and three other people."

" Ha ! The vanguard—the forlorn hope of the great plot," he commented to himself. " Bearers of the spark to start an explosion which is meant to change fundamentally the lives of so many millions in order that Peter Ivanovitch should be the head of a State."

" You are teasing me," she said. " Our dear one told me once to remember that men serve always something greater than themselves—the idea."

" Our dear one," he repeated slowly. The effort he made to appear unmoved absorbed all the force of his soul. He stood before her like a being with hardly a breath of life. His eyes, even as under great physical suffering, had lost all their fire. "Ah ! your brother . . . But on your lips, in your voice, it sounds . . . and indeed in you everything is divine. . . . I wish I could know the innermost depths of your thoughts, of your feelings."

" But why, Kirylo Sidorovitch ? " she cried,

alarmed by these words coming out of strangely lifeless lips.

" Have no fear. It is not to betray you. So you went there ? . . . And Sophia Antonovna, what did she tell you, then ? "

" She said very little, really. She knew that I should hear everything from you. She had no time for more than a few words." Miss Haldin's voice dropped and she became silent for a moment. " The man, it appears, has taken his life," she said sadly.

" Tell me, Natalia Victorovna," he asked after a pause, " do you believe in remorse ? "

" What a question ! "

" What can *you* know of it ? " he muttered thickly. " It is not for such as you . . . What I meant to ask was whether you believed in the efficacy of remorse."

She hesitated as though she had not understood, then her face lighted up.

" Yes," she said firmly.

" So he is absolved. Moreover, that Ziemianitch was a brute, a drunken brute."

A shudder passed through Natalia Haldin.

" But a man of the people," Razumov went on, " to whom they, the revolutionists, tell a tale of sublime hopes. Well, the people must be forgiven. . . . And you must not believe all you've heard from that source, either," he added, with a sort of sinister reluctance.

"You are concealing something from me," she exclaimed.

"Do you, Natalia Victorovna, believe in the duty of revenge?"

"Listen, Kirylo Sidorovitch. I believe that the future will be merciful to us all. Revolutionist and reactionary, victim and executioner, betrayer and betrayed, they shall all be pitied together when the light breaks on our black sky at last. Pitied and forgotten; for without that there can be no union and no love."

"I hear. No revenge for you, then? Never? Not the least bit?" He smiled bitterly with his colourless lips. "You yourself are like the very spirit of that merciful future. Strange that it does not make it easier. . . . No! But suppose that the real betrayer of your brother—Ziemianitch had a part in it too, but insignificant and quite involuntary —suppose that he was a young man, educated, an intellectual worker, thoughtful, a man your brother might have trusted lightly, perhaps, but still— suppose . . . But there's a whole story there."

"And you know the story! But why, then——"

"I have heard it. There is a staircase in it, and even phantoms, but that does not matter if a man always serves something greater than himself—the idea. I wonder who is the greatest victim in that tale?"

"In that tale!" Miss Haldin repeated. She seemed turned into stone.

"Do you know why I came to you? It is simply because there is no one anywhere in the whole great world I could go to. Do you understand what I say? Not one to go to. Do you conceive the desolation of the thought—no one—to—go—to?"

Utterly misled by her own enthusiastic interpretation of two lines in the letter of a visionary, under the spell of her own dread of lonely days, in their overshadowed world of angry strife, she was unable to see the truth struggling on his lips. What she was conscious of was the obscure form of his suffering. She was on the point of extending her hand to him impulsively when he spoke again.

"An hour after I saw you first I knew how it would be. The terrors of remorse, revenge, confession, anger, hate, fear, are like nothing to the atrocious temptation which you put in my way the day you appeared before me with your voice, with your face, in the garden of that accursed villa."

She looked utterly bewildered for a moment; then, with a sort of despairing insight went straight to the point.

"The story, Kirylo Sidorovitch, the story!"

"There is no more to tell!" He made a movement forward, and she actually put her hand on his shoulder to push him away; but her strength failed her, and he kept his ground, though trembling in every limb. "It ends here—on this very spot."

He pressed a denunciatory finger to his breast with force, and became perfectly still.

I ran forward, snatching up the chair, and was in time to catch hold of Miss Haldin and lower her down. As she sank into it she swung half round on my arm, and remained averted from us both, drooping over the back. He looked at her with an appalling expressionless tranquillity. Incredulity, struggling with astonishment, anger, and disgust, deprived me for a time of the power of speech. Then I turned on him, whispering from very rage :

" This is monstrous. What are you staying for ? Don't let her catch sight of you again. Go away ! . . ." He did not budge. " Don't you understand that your presence is intolerable—even to me ? If there's any sense of shame in you . . ."

Slowly his sullen eyes moved in my direction. " How did this old man come here ? " he muttered, astounded.

Suddenly Miss Haldin sprang up from the chair, made a few steps, and tottered. Forgetting my indignation, and even the man himself, I hurried to her assistance. I took her by the arm, and she let me lead her into the drawing-room. Away from the lamp, in the deeper dusk of the distant end, the profile of Mrs. Haldin, her hands, her whole figure had the stillness of a sombre painting. Miss Haldin stopped, and pointed mournfully at the tragic immobility of her mother, who seemed to watch a beloved head lying in her lap.

That gesture had an unequalled force of expression, so far-reaching in its human distress that one could not believe that it pointed out merely the ruthless working of political institutions. After assisting Miss Haldin to the sofa, I turned round to go back and shut the door. Framed in the opening, in the searching glare of the white anteroom, my eyes fell on Razumov, still there, standing before the empty chair, as if rooted for ever to the spot of his atrocious confession. A wonder came over me that the mysterious force which had torn it out of him had failed to destroy his life, to shatter his body. It was there unscathed. I stared at the broad line of his shoulders, his dark head, the amazing immobility of his limbs. At his feet the veil dropped by Miss Haldin looked intensely black in the white crudity of the light. He was gazing at it spellbound. Next moment, stooping with an incredible, savage swiftness, he snatched it up and pressed it to his face with both hands. Something, extreme astonishment perhaps, dimmed my eyes, so that he seemed to vanish before he moved.

The slamming of the outer door restored my sight, and I went on contemplating the empty chair in the empty anteroom. The meaning of what I had seen reached my mind with a staggering shock. I seized Natalia Haldin by the shoulder.

" That miserable wretch has carried off your veil ! " I cried, in the scared, deadened voice of an awful discovery. " He . . ."

The rest remained unspoken. I stepped back and looked down at her in silent horror. Her hands were lying lifelessly, palms upwards, on her lap. She raised her grey eyes slowly. Shadows seemed to come and go in them as if the steady flame of her soul had been made to vacillate at last in the cross-currents of poisoned air from the corrupted dark immensity claiming her for its own, where virtues themselves fester into crimes in the cynicism of oppression and revolt.

" It is impossible to be more unhappy. . . ." The languid whisper of her voice struck me with dismay. " It is impossible. . . . I feel my heart becoming like ice."

IV

Razumov walked straight home on the wet glistening pavement. A heavy shower passed over him ; distant lightning played faintly against the fronts of the dumb houses with the shuttered shops all along the Rue de Carouge ; and now and then, after the faint flash, there was a faint, sleepy rumble ; but the main forces of the thunderstorm remained massed down the Rhône valley as if loath to attack the respectable and passionless abode of democratic liberty, the serious-minded town of dreary hotels, tendering the same indifferent hospitality to tourists of all nations and to international conspirators of every shade.

The owner of the shop was making ready to close when Razumov entered and without a word extended his hand for the key of his room. On reaching it for him, from a shelf, the man was about to pass a small joke as to taking the air in a thunderstorm, but, after looking at the face of his lodger, he only observed, just to say something :

" You've got very wet."

" Yes, I am washed clean," muttered Razumov, who was dripping from head to foot, and passed through the inner door towards the staircase leading to his room.

He did not change his clothes, but, after lighting the candle, took off his watch and chain, laid them on the table, and sat down at once to write. The book of his compromising record was kept in a locked drawer, which he pulled out violently, and did not even trouble to push back afterwards.

In this queer pedantism of a man who had read, thought, lived, pen in hand, there is the sincerity of the attempt to grapple by the same means with another profounder knowledge. After some passages which have been already made use of in the building up of this narrative, or add nothing new to the psychological side of this disclosure (there is even one more allusion to the silver medal in this last entry), comes a page and a half of incoherent writing where his expression is baffled by the novelty and the mysteriousness of that side of our emotional life to which his solitary existence had been a stranger. Then only he begins to address directly the reader he had in his mind, trying to express in broken sentences, full of wonder and awe, the sovereign (he uses that very word) power of her person over his imagination, in which lay the dormant seed of her brother's words.

" . . . The most trustful eyes in the world—your brother said of you when he was as well as a dead man already. And when you stood before me with your hand extended, I remembered the very sound of his voice, and I looked into your eyes —and that was enough. I knew that something had happened, but I did not know then what. . . . But don't be deceived, Natalia Victorovna. I believed that I had in my breast nothing but an inexhaustible fund of anger and hate for you both. I remembered that he had looked to you for the perpetuation of his visionary soul. He, this man who had robbed me of my hard-working, purposeful existence. I, too, had my guiding idea ; and remember that, amongst us, it is more difficult to lead a life of toil and self-denial than to go out in the street and kill from conviction. But enough of that. Hate or no hate, I felt at once that, while shunning the sight of you, I could never succeed in driving away your image. I would say, addressing that dead man, ' Is this the way you are going to haunt me ? ' It is only later on that I understood—only to-day, only a few hours ago. What could I have known of what was tearing me to pieces and dragging the secret for ever to my lips ? You were appointed to undo the evil by making me betray myself back into truth and peace. You ! And you have done it in the same way, too, in which he ruined me : by forcing upon me your confidence. Only what I detested him for, in you ended by appearing noble and exalted. But, I repeat, be not deceived. I was given up to evil. I exulted in having induced that silly innocent fool to steal his father's money. He was a fool, but not a thief. I made him one. It was necessary. I had to confirm myself in my contempt and hate for what I betrayed. I have suffered from as many vipers in my heart as any social democrat of them all—vanity, ambitions, jealousies, shameful desires, evil passions of envy and revenge. I had my security stolen from me, years of good work, my best hopes. Listen—now comes the true confession. The other was nothing. To save me, your trustful eyes had to entice my thought to the very edge of the blackest treachery. I could see them constantly looking at me with the confidence of your pure heart which had not been touched by evil things. Victor Haldin had stolen the truth of my life from me, who had nothing else in the world, and he boasted of living on through you on this earth where I had no place to lay my head. She will marry some day, he had said—and your eyes were trustful. And do you know what I said to myself ? I shall steal his sister's soul from her.

When we met that first morning in the gardens, and
you spoke to me confidingly in the generosity of
your spirit, I was thinking, ' Yes, he himself by
talking of her trustful eyes has delivered her into
my hands ! ' If you could have looked then into
my heart, you would have cried out aloud with
terror and disgust.

" Perhaps no one will believe the baseness of
such an intention to be possible. It's certain that,
when we parted that morning, I gloated over it. I
brooded upon the best way. The old man you
introduced me to insisted on walking with me. I
don't know who he is. He talked of you, of your
lonely, helpless state, and every word of that friend
of yours was egging me on to the unpardonable sin
of stealing a soul. Could he have been the devil
himself in the shape of an old Englishman ? Natalia
Victorovna, I was possessed ! I returned to look at
you every day, and drink in your presence the poison
of my infamous intention. But I foresaw difficulties.
Then Sophia Antonovna, of whom I was not thinking—I had forgotten her existence—appears suddenly
with that tale from St. Petersburg. . . . The only
thing needed to make me safe—a trusted revolutionist for ever.

" It was as if Ziemianitch had hanged himself
to help me on to further crime. The strength of
falsehood seemed irresistible. These people stood
doomed by the folly and illusion that was in them
—they being themselves the slaves of lies. Natalia

29

Victorovna, I embraced the might of falsehood, I exulted in it—I gave myself up to it for a time. Who could have resisted! You yourself were the prize of it. I sat alone in my room, planning a life, the very thought of which makes me shudder now, like a believer who had been tempted to an atrocious sacrilege. But I brooded ardently over its images. The only thing was that there seemed to be no air in it. And also I was afraid of your mother. I never knew mine. I've never known any kind of love. There is something in the mere word . . . Of you I was not afraid—forgive me for telling you this. No, not of you. You were truth itself. You could not suspect me. As to your mother, you yourself feared already that her mind had given way from grief. Who could believe anything against me? Had not Ziemianitch hanged himself from remorse? I said to myself, ' Let's put it to the test, and be done with it once for all.' I trembled when I went in ; but your mother hardly listened to what I was saying to her, and, in a little while, seemed to have forgotten my very existence. I sat looking at her. There was no longer anything between you and me. You were defenceless—and soon, very soon, you would be alone. . . . I thought of you. Defenceless. For days you have talked with me—opening your heart. I remembered the shadow of your eyelashes over your grey, trustful eyes. And your pure forehead! It is low like the forehead of statues —calm, unstained. It was as if your pure brow bore a light which fell on me, searched my heart and saved me from ignominy, from ultimate undoing. And it saved you too. Pardon my presumption. But there was that in your glances which seemed to tell me that you . . . Your light! your truth! I felt that I must tell you that I had ended by loving you. And to tell you that I must first confess. Confess, go out—and perish.

"Suddenly you stood before me! You alone in all the world to whom I must confess. You fascinated me—you have freed me from the blindness of anger and hate—the truth shining in you drew the truth out of me. Now I have done it; and as I write here, I am in the depths of anguish, but there is air to breathe at last—air! And, by-the-bye, that old man sprang up from somewhere as I was speaking to you, and raged at me like a disappointed devil. I suffer horribly, but I am not in despair. There is only one more thing to do for me. After that—if they let me—I shall go away and bury myself in obscure misery. In giving Victor Haldin up, it was myself, after all, whom I have betrayed most basely. You must believe what I say now, you can't refuse to believe this. Most basely. It is through you that I came to feel this so deeply. After all, it is they and not I who have the right on their side!—theirs is the strength of invisible powers. So be it. Only don't be deceived, Natalia Victorovna, I am not converted. Have I then the soul of a slave? No! I am independent—and therefore perdition is my lot."

On these words, he stopped writing, shut the book, and wrapped it in the black veil he had carried off. He then ransacked the drawers for paper and string, made up a parcel which he addressed to Miss Haldin, Boulevard des Philosophes, and then flung the pen away from him into a distant corner.

This done, he sat down with the watch before him. He could have gone out at once, but the hour had not struck yet. The hour would be midnight. There was no reason for that choice except that the facts and the words of a certain evening in his past were timing his conduct in the present. The sudden power Natalia Haldin had gained over him he ascribed to the same cause. " You don't walk with impunity over a phantom's breast," he heard himself mutter. " Thus he saves me," he thought suddenly. " He himself, the betrayed man." The vivid image of Miss Haldin seemed to stand by him, watching him relentlessly. She was not disturbing. He had done with life, and his thought even in her presence tried to take an impartial survey. Now his scorn extended to himself. " I had neither the simplicity nor the courage nor the self-possession to be a scoundrel, or an exceptionally able man. For who, with us in Russia, is to tell a scoundrel from an exceptionally able man ? . . ."

He was the puppet of his past, because at the very stroke of midnight he jumped up and ran swiftly downstairs as if confident that, by the power of destiny, the house door would fly open before the absolute necessity of his errand. And as a matter of fact, just as he got to the bottom of the stairs, it was opened for him by some people of the house coming home late—two men and a woman. He slipped out through them into the street, swept then by a fitful gust of wind. They were, of course, very much startled. A flash of lightning enabled them to observe him walking away quickly. One of the men shouted, and was starting in pursuit, but the woman had recognised him. " It's all right. It's only that young Russian from the third floor." The darkness returned with a single clap of thunder, like a gun fired for a warning of his escape from the prison of lies.

He must have heard at some time or other and now remembered unconsciously that there was to be a gathering of revolutionists at the house of Julius Laspara that evening. At any rate, he made straight for the Laspara house, and found himself without surprise ringing at its street door, which, of course, was closed. By that time the thunderstorm had attacked in earnest. The steep incline of the street ran with water, the thick fall of rain enveloped him like a luminous veil in the play of lightning. He was perfectly calm, and between the crashes listened attentively to the delicate tinkling of the doorbell somewhere within the house.

There was some difficulty before he was admitted. His person was not known to that one of the guests who had volunteered to go downstairs and see what was the matter. Razumov argued with him patiently. There could be no harm in admitting a caller. He had something of importance to communicate to the company upstairs.

" Something of importance ? "

" That'll be for the hearers to judge."

" Urgent ? "

" Without a moment's delay."

Meantime, one of the Laspara daughters descended the stairs, small lamp in hand, in a grimy and crumpled gown, which seemed to hang on her by a miracle, and looking more than ever like an old doll with a dusty brown wig, dragged from under a sofa. She recognised Razumov at once.

" How do you do ? Of course you may come in."

Following her light, Razumov climbed two flights of stairs from the lower darkness. Leaving the lamp on a bracket on the landing, she opened a door and went in, accompanied by the sceptical guest. Razumov entered last. He closed the door behind him, and stepping on one side, put his back against the wall.

The three little rooms *en suite*, with low, smoky ceilings and lit by paraffin lamps, were crammed with people. Loud talking was going on in all three, and tea-glasses, full, half-full, and empty, stood everywhere, even on the floor. The other Laspara girl sat, dishevelled and languid, behind an enormous samovar. In the inner doorway Razumov had a glimpse of the protuberance of a large stomach,

which he recognised. Only a few feet from him
Julius Laspara was getting down hurriedly from his
high stool.

The appearance of the midnight visitor caused
no small sensation. Laspara is very summary in
his version of that night's happenings. After some
words of greeting, disregarded by Razumov, Laspara
(ignoring purposely his guest's soaked condition and
his extraordinary manner of presenting himself)
mentioned something about writing an article. He
was growing uneasy, and Razumov appeared absent-
minded. " I have written already all I shall ever
write," he said at last, with a little laugh.

The whole company's attention was riveted on
the newcomer, dripping with water, deadly pale,
and keeping his position against the wall. Razumov
put Laspara gently aside, as though he wished to be
seen from head to foot by everybody. By then the
buzz of conversation had died down completely,
even in the most distant of the three rooms. The
doorway facing Razumov became blocked by men
and women, who craned their necks and certainly
seemed to expect something startling to happen.

A squeaky, insolent declaration was heard from
that group.

" I know this ridiculously conceited individual."

" What individual ? " asked Razumov, raising
his bowed head, and searching with his eyes all the
eyes fixed upon him. An intense surprised silence
lasted for a time. " If it's me . . ."

He stopped, thinking over the form of his confession, and found it suddenly, unavoidably suggested by the fateful evening of his life.

" I am come here," he began, in a clear voice, " to talk of an individual called Ziemianitch. Sophia Antonovna has informed me that she would make public a certain letter from St. Petersburg . . ."

" Sophia Antonovna has left us early in the evening," said Laspara. " It's quite correct. Everybody here has heard . . ."

" Very well," Razumov interrupted, with a shade of impatience, for his heart was beating strongly. Then, mastering his voice so far that there was even a touch of irony in his clear, forcible enunciation :

" In justice to that individual, the much ill-used peasant, Ziemianitch, I now declare solemnly that the conclusions of that letter calumniate a man of the people—a bright Russian soul. Ziemianitch had nothing to do with the actual arrest of Victor Haldin."

Razumov dwelt on the name heavily, and then waited till the faint, mournful murmur which greeted it had died out.

" Victor Victorovitch Haldin," he began again, " acting with, no doubt, noble-minded imprudence, took refuge with a certain student of whose opinions he knew nothing but what his own illusions suggested to his generous heart. It was an unwise display of confidence. But I am not here to appreciate the actions of Victor Haldin. Am I to tell you of the feelings of that student, sought out in his obscure solitude, and menaced by the complicity forced upon him ? Am I to tell you what he did ? It's a rather complicated story. In the end the student went to General T—— himself, and said, ' I have the man who killed de P—— locked up in my room, Victor Haldin, a student like myself.' "

A great buzz arose, in which Razumov raised his voice.

" Observe—that man had certain honest ideals in view. But I didn't come here to explain him."

" No. But you must explain how you know all this," came in grave tones from somebody.

" A vile coward ! " This simple cry vibrated with indignation. " Name him ! " shouted other voices.

" What are you clamouring for ? " said Razumov disdainfully, in the profound silence which fell on the raising of his hand. " Haven't you all understood that I am that man ? "

Laspara went away brusquely from his side and climbed upon his stool. In the first forward surge of people towards him, Razumov expected to be torn to pieces, but they fell back without touching him, and nothing came of it but noise. It was bewildering. His head ached terribly. In the confused uproar he made out several times the name of Peter Ivanovitch, the word "judgment," and the phrase, "But this is a confession," uttered by somebody in a desperate shriek. In the midst of the tumult, a young man, younger than himself, approached him with blazing eyes.

"I must beg you," he said, with venomous politeness, "to be good enough not to move from this spot till you are told what you are to do."

Razumov shrugged his shoulders.

"I came in voluntarily."

"Maybe. But you won't go out till you are permitted," retorted the other.

He beckoned with his hand, calling out, "Louisa! Louisa! come here, please"; and, presently, one of the Laspara girls (they had been staring at Razumov from behind the samovar) came along, trailing a bedraggled tail of dirty flounces, and dragging with her a chair, which she set against the door, and, sitting down on it, crossed her legs. The young man thanked her effusively, and rejoined a group carrying on an animated discussion in low tones. Razumov lost himself for a moment.

A squeaky voice screamed, "Confession or no confession, you are a police spy!"

The revolutionist Nikita had pushed his way in front of Razumov, and faced him with his big, livid cheeks, his heavy paunch, bull neck, and enormous hands. Razumov looked at the famous slayer of gendarmes in silent disgust.

"And what are you?" he said, very low, then shut his eyes, and rested the back of his head against the wall.

"It would be better for you to depart now." Razumov heard a mild, sad voice, and opened his eyes. The gentle speaker was an elderly man, with a great brush of fine hair making a silvery halo all round his keen, intelligent face. "Peter Ivanovitch shall be informed of your confession—and you shall be directed . . ."

Then, turning to Nikita, nicknamed Necator, standing by, he appealed to him in a murmur:

"What else can we do? After this piece of sincerity he cannot be dangerous any longer."

The other muttered, "Better make sure of that before we let him go. Leave that to me. I know how to deal with such gentlemen."

He exchanged meaning glances with two or three men, who nodded slightly, then turning roughly to Razumov, "You have heard? You are not wanted here. Why don't you get out?"

The Laspara girl on guard rose and pulled the chair out of the way unemotionally. She gave a sleepy stare to Razumov, who started, looked round the room and passed slowly by her as if struck by some sudden thought.

"I beg you to observe," he said, already on the landing, "that I had only to hold my tongue. To-day, of all days since I came amongst you, I was made safe, and to-day I made myself free from falsehood, from remorse—independent of every single human being on this earth."

He turned his back on the room, and walked towards the stairs, but, at the violent crash of the door behind him, he looked over his shoulder and saw that Nikita, with three others, had followed him out. "They are going to kill me, after all," he thought.

Before he had time to turn round and confront them fairly, they set on him with a rush. He was driven headlong against the wall. "I wonder how," he completed his thought.

Nikita cried, with a shrill laugh right in his face, "We shall make you harmless. You wait a bit."

Razumov did not struggle. The three men held him pinned against the wall, while Nikita, taking up a position a little on one side, deliberately swung off his enormous arm. Razumov, looking for a knife in his hand, saw it come at him open, unarmed, and received a tremendous blow on the side of his head over his ear. At the same time he heard a faint, dull, detonating sound, as if some one had fired a pistol on the other side of the wall. A raging fury awoke in him at this outrage. The people in Laspara's rooms, holding their breath, listened to the desperate scuffling of four men all over the landing; thuds against the walls, a terrible crash against the very door, then all of them went down together with a violence which seemed to shake the whole house. Razumov, overpowered, breathless, crushed under the weight of his assailants, saw the monstrous Nikita squatting on his heels near his head, while the others held him down, kneeling on his chest, gripping his throat, lying across his legs.

" Turn his face the other way," the paunchy terrorist directed, in an excited, gleeful squeak.

Razumov could struggle no longer. He was exhausted ; he had to watch passively the heavy open hand of the brute descend again in a degrading blow over his other ear. It seemed to split his head in two, and all at once the men holding him became perfectly silent—soundless as shadows. In silence they pulled him brutally to his feet, rushed with him noiselessly down the staircase, and, opening the door, flung him out into the street.

He fell forward, and at once rolled over and over helplessly, going down the short slope together with the rush of running rain water. He came to rest in the roadway of the street at the bottom, lying on his back, with a great flash of lightning over his face—a vivid, silent flash of lightning which blinded him utterly. He picked himself up and put his arm over his eyes to recover his sight. Not a sound reached him from anywhere, and he began to walk, staggering, down a long, empty street. The lightning waved and darted round him its silent flames, the water of the deluge fell, ran, leaped, drove—noiseless like the drift of mist. In this unearthly stillness his footsteps fell silent on the pavement, while a dumb wind drove him on and on, like a lost mortal in a phantom world ravaged by a soundless thunderstorm. God only knows where his noiseless feet took him to that night, here and there, and back again without pause or rest. Of one place, at least, where they did lead him, we heard afterwards ; and, in the morning, the driver of the first south-shore tramcar, clanging his bell desperately, saw a bedraggled, soaked man without a hat, and walking in the roadway unsteadily with his head down, step right in front of his car, and go under.

When they picked him up, with two broken limbs and a crushed side, Razumov had not lost consciousness. It was as though he had tumbled, smashing himself, into a world of mutes. Silent men, moving unheard, lifted him up, laid him on the sidewalk, gesticulating and grimacing round him their alarm, horror, and compassion. A red face with moustaches stooped close over him, lips moving, eyes rolling. Razumov tried hard to understand the reason of this dumb show. To those who stood around him, the features of that stranger, so grievously hurt, seemed composed in meditation. Afterwards his eyes sent out at them a look of fear and closed slowly. They stared at him. Razumov made an effort to remember some French words.

" *Je suis sourd*," he had time to utter feebly, before he fainted.

" He is deaf," they exclaimed to each other.
" That's why he did not hear the car."

They carried him off in that same car. Before
it started on its journey, a woman in a shabby black
dress, who had run out of the iron gate of some
private grounds up the road, clambered on to the
rear platform and would not be put off.

" I am a relation," she insisted, in bad French.
"This young man is a Russian, and I am his
relation."

On this plea they let her have her way. She sat
down calmly, and took his head on her lap ; her
scared faded eyes avoided looking at his deathlike
face. At the corner of a street, on the other side
of the town, a stretcher met the car. She followed
it to the door of the hospital, where they let her come
in and see him laid on a bed. Razumov's new-found
relation never shed a tear, but the officials had some
difficulty in inducing her to go away. The porter
observed her lingering on the opposite pavement
for a long time. Suddenly, as though she had
remembered something, she ran off.

The ardent hater of all Finance Ministers, the
slave of Madame de S——, had made up her mind
to offer her resignation as lady companion to the
Egeria of Peter Ivanovitch. She had found work
to do after her own heart.

But hours before, while the thunderstorm still
raged in the night, there had been in the rooms of
Julius Laspara a great sensation. The terrible

Nikita, coming in from the landing, uplifted his squeaky voice in horrible glee before all the company :

" Razumov ! Mr. Razumov ! The wonderful Razumov ! He shall never be any use as a spy on any one. He won't talk, because he will never hear anything in his life—not a thing ! I have burst the drums of his ears for him. Oh, you may trust me. I know the trick. Ha, ha, ha ! I know the trick."

V

It was nearly a fortnight after her mother's funeral that I saw Natalia Haldin for the last time.

In those silent, sombre days the doors of the *appartement* on the Boulevard des Philosophes were closed to every one but myself. I believe I was of some use, if only in this, that I alone was aware of the incredible part of the situation. Miss Haldin nursed her mother alone to the last moment. If Razumov's visit had anything to do with Mrs. Haldin's end (and I cannot help thinking that it hastened it considerably), it is because the man, trusted impulsively by the ill-fated Victor Haldin, had failed to gain the confidence of Victor Haldin's mother. What tale, precisely, he told her cannot be known—at any rate, I do not know it—but to me she seemed to die from the shock of an ultimate disappointment borne in silence. She had not believed him. Perhaps she could not longer believe any one, and consequently had nothing to say to any one—not even to her daughter. I suspect that Miss Haldin lived the heaviest hours of her life by that silent death-bed. I confess I was angry with the broken-hearted old woman passing away in the obstinacy of her mute distrust of her daughter.

When it was all over I stood aside. Miss Haldin had her compatriots round her then. A great number of them attended the funeral. I was there too, but afterwards managed to keep away from Miss Haldin, till I received a short note rewarding my self-denial. " It is as you would have it. I am going back to Russia at once. My mind is made up. Come and see me."

Verily, it was a reward of discretion. I went without delay to receive it. The *appartement* of the Boulevard des Philosophes presented the dreary signs of impending abandonment. It looked desolate and as if already empty to my eyes.

Standing, we exchanged a few words about her health, mine, remarks as to some people of the Russian colony, and then Natalia Haldin, establishing me on the sofa, began to talk openly of her future work, of her plans. It was all to be as I had wished it. And it was to be for life. We should never see each other again. Never !

I gathered this success to my breast. Natalia Haldin looked matured by her open and secret experiences. With her arms folded she walked up and down the whole length of the room, talking slowly,

30

smooth-browed, with a resolute profile. She gave me a new view of herself, and I marvelled at that something grave and measured in her voice, in her movements, in her manner. It was the perfection of collected independence. The strength of her nature had come to surface because the obscure depths had been stirred.

" We two can talk of it now," she observed, after a silence and stopping short before me. " Have you been to inquire at the hospital lately ? "

" Yes, I have." And as she looked at me fixedly, " He will live, the doctors say. But I thought that Tekla . . ."

" Tekla has not been near me for several days," explained Miss Haldin quickly. " As I never offered to go to the hospital with her, she thinks that I have no heart. She is disillusioned about me."

And Miss Haldin smiled faintly.

" Yes. She sits with him as long and as often as they will let her," I said. " She says she must never abandon him—never as long as she lives. He'll need somebody—a hopeless cripple, and stone deaf with that."

" Stone deaf ? I didn't know," murmured Natalia Haldin.

" He is. It seems strange. I am told there were no apparent injuries to the head. They say, too, that it is not very likely that he will live so very long for Tekla to take care of him."

Miss Haldin shook her head.

"While there are travellers ready to fall by the way our Tekla will never be idle. She is a good Samaritan by an irresistible vocation. The revolutionists didn't understand her. Fancy a devoted creature like that being employed to carry about documents sewn in her dress, or made to write from dictation."

"There is not much perspicacity in the world."

No sooner uttered, I regretted that observation. Natalia Haldin, looking me straight in the face, assented by a slight movement of her head. She was not offended, but turning away began to pace the room again. To my Western eyes she seemed to be getting farther and farther from me, quite beyond my reach now, but undiminished in the increasing distance. I remained silent as though it were hopeless to raise my voice. The sound of hers, ɔ close to me, made me start a little.

"Tekla saw him picked up after the accident. The good soul never explained to me really how it came about. She affirms that there was some understanding between them—some sort of compact— that in any sore need, in misfortune, or difficulty, or pain, he was to come to her."

"Was there?" I said. "It is lucky for him that there was, then. He'll need all the devotion of the good Samaritan."

It was a fact that Tekla, looking out of her window at five in the morning, for some reason

or other, had beheld Razumov in the grounds of
the Château Borel, standing stock-still, bareheaded
in the rain, at the foot of the terrace. She had
screamed out to him, by name, to know what was
the matter. He never even raised his head. By the
time she had dressed herself sufficiently to run
downstairs he was gone. She started in pursuit,
and rushing out into the road, came almost directly
upon the arrested tramcar and the small knot of
people picking up Razumov. That much Tekla
had told me herself one afternoon we happened to
meet at the door of the hospital, and without any
kind of comment. But I did not want to meditate
very long on the inwardness of this peculiar episode.

" Yes, Natalia Victorovna, he will need somebody when they dismiss him, on crutches and stone
deaf, from the hospital. But I do not think that
when he rushed like an escaped madman into the
grounds of the Château Borel it was to seek the
help of that good Tekla."

" No," said Natalia, stopping short before me,
" perhaps not." She sat down and leaned her head
on her hand thoughtfully. The silence lasted for
several minutes. During that time I remembered
the evening of his atrocious confession—the plaint
she seemed to have hardly enough life left in her to
utter, " It is impossible to be more unhappy. . . ."
The recollection would have given me a shudder if
I had not been lost in wonder at her force and her
tranquillity. There was no longer any Natalia

Haldin, because she had completely ceased to think of herself. It was a great victory, a characteristically Russian exploit in self-suppression.

She recalled me to myself by getting up suddenly like a person who has come to a decision. She walked to the writing-table, now stripped of all the small objects associated with her by daily use—a mere piece of dead furniture ; but it contained something living still, since she took from a recess a flat parcel which she brought to me.

" It's a book," she said rather abruptly. " It was sent to me wrapped up in my veil. I told you nothing at the time, but now I've decided to leave it with you. I have the right to do that. It was sent to me. It is mine. You may preserve it, or destroy it after you have read it. And while you read it, please remember that I *was* defenceless. And that he . . ."

" Defenceless ! " I repeated, surprised, looking hard at her.

" You'll find the very word written there," she whispered. " Well, it's true ! I *was* defenceless— but perhaps you were able to see that for yourself." Her face coloured, then went deadly pale. " In justice to the man, I want you to remember that I was. Oh, I was, I was ! "

I rose, a little shakily.

" I am not likely to forget anything you say at this our last parting."

Her hand fell into mine.

" It's difficult to believe that it must be good-bye with us."

She returned my pressure and our hands separated.

" Yes. I am leaving here to-morrow. My eyes are open at last and my hands are free now. As for the rest—which of us can fail to hear the stifled cry of our great distress ? It may be nothing to the world."

" The world is more conscious of your discordant voices," I said. " It is the way of the world."

" Yes." She bowed her head in assent, and hesitated for a moment. " I must own to you that I shall never give up looking forward to the day when all discord shall be silenced. Try to imagine its dawn ! The tempest of blows and of execrations is over ; all is still ; the new sun is rising, and the weary men united at last, taking count in their conscience of the ended contest, feel saddened by their victory, because so many ideas have perished for the triumph of one, so many beliefs have abandoned them without support. They feel alone on the earth and gather close together. Yes, there must be many bitter hours ! But at last the anguish of hearts shall be extinguished in love."

And on this last word of her wisdom, a word so sweet, so bitter, so cruel sometimes, I said good-bye to Natalia Haldin. It is hard to think I shall never look any more into the trustful eyes of that girl—wedded to an invincible belief in the advent of

loving concord springing like a heavenly flower from
the soil of men's earth, soaked in blood, torn by
struggles, watered with tears.

. . . .

It must be understood that at that time I didn't
know anything of Mr. Razumov's confession to
the assembled revolutionists. Natalia Haldin might
have guessed what was the " one thing more "
which remained for him to do ; but this my Western
eyes had failed to see.

Tekla, the ex-lady companion of Madame de
S——, haunted his bedside at the hospital. We
met once or twice at the door of that establishment,
but on these occasions she was not communicative.
She gave me news of Mr. Razumov as concisely
as possible. He was making a slow recovery, but
would remain a hopeless cripple all his life. Personally, I never went near him : I never saw him
again, after the awful evening when I stood by, a
watchful but ignored spectator of his scene with
Miss Haldin. He was in due course discharged
from the hospital, and his " relative "—so I was
told—had carried him off somewhere.

My information was completed nearly two years
later. The opportunity, certainly, was not of my
seeking ; it was quite accidentally that I met a
much-trusted woman revolutionist at the house of a
distinguished Russian gentleman of liberal convictions, who came to live in Geneva for a time.

He was a quite different sort of celebrity from

Peter Ivanovitch—a dark-haired man with kind eyes, high-shouldered, courteous, and with something hushed and circumspect in his manner. He approached me, choosing the moment when there was no one near, followed by a grey-haired, alert lady in a crimson blouse.

"Our Sophia Antonovna wishes to be made known to you," he addressed me, in his guarded voice. "And so I leave you two to have a talk together."

"I would never have intruded myself upon your notice," the grey-haired lady began at once, "if I had not been charged with a message for you."

It was a message of a few friendly words from Natalia Haldin. Sophia Antonovna had just returned from a secret excursion into Russia, and had seen Miss Haldin. She lived in a town "in the centre," sharing her compassionate labours between the horrors of overcrowded jails and the heart-rending misery of bereaved homes. She did not spare herself in good service, Sophia Antonovna assured me.

"She has a faithful soul, an undaunted spirit, and an indefatigable body," the woman revolutionist summed it all up, with a touch of enthusiasm.

A conversation thus engaged was not likely to drop from want of interest on my side. We went to sit apart in a corner where no one interrupted us. In the course of our talk about Miss Haldin, Sophia Antonovna remarked suddenly :

" I suppose you remember seeing me before ? That evening when Natalia came to ask Peter Ivanovitch for the address of a certain Razumov, that young man who . . ."

" I remember perfectly," I said. When Sophia Antonovna learned that I had in my possession that young man's journal given me by Miss Haldin she became intensely interested. She did not conceal her curiosity to see the document.

I offered to show it to her, and she at once volunteered to call on me next day for that purpose.

She turned over the pages greedily for an hour or more, and then handed me the book with a faint sigh. While moving about Russia, she had seen Razumov too. He lived, not " in the centre," but " in the south." She described to me a little two-roomed wooden house, in the suburb of some very small town, hiding within the high plank-fence of a yard overgrown with nettles. He was crippled, ill, getting weaker every day, and Tekla the Samaritan tended him unweariedly with the pure joy of unselfish devotion. There was nothing in that task to become disillusioned about.

I did not hide from Sophia Antonovna my surprise that she should have visited Mr. Razumov. I did not even understand the motive. But she informed me that she was not the only one.

" Some of *us* always go to see him when passing through. He is intelligent. He has ideas. . . . He talks well, too."

Presently I heard for the first time of Razumov's public confession in Laspara's house. Sophia Antonovna gave me a detailed relation of what had occurred there. Razumov himself had told her all about it, most minutely.

Then, looking hard at me with her brilliant black eyes :

" There are evil moments in every life. A false suggestion enters one's brain, and then fear is born—fear of oneself, fear for oneself. Or else a false courage—who knows ? Well, call it what you like ; but tell me, how many of them would deliver themselves up deliberately to perdition (as he himself says in that book) rather than go on living, secretly debased in their own eyes ? How many ? . . . And please mark this—he was safe when he did it. It was just when he believed himself safe and more—infinitely more—when the possibility of being loved by that admirable girl first dawned upon him, that he discovered that his bitterest railings, the worst wickedness, the devil work of his hate and pride, could never cover up the ignominy of the existence before him. There's character in such a discovery."

I accepted her conclusion in silence. Who would care to question the grounds of forgiveness or compassion ? However, it appeared later on that there was some compunction, too, in the charity extended by the revolutionary world to Razumov the betrayer. Sophia Antonovna continued uneasily :

" And then, you know, he was the victim of an outrage. It was not authorised. Nothing was decided as to what was to be done with him. He had confessed voluntarily. And that Nikita who burst the drums of his ears purposely, out on the landing, you know, as if carried away by indignation —well, he has turned out to be a scoundrel of the worst kind—a traitor himself, a betrayer—a spy ! Razumov told me he had charged him with it by a sort of inspiration . . ."

" I had a glimpse of that brute," I said. " How any of you could have been deceived for half a day passes my comprehension ! "

She interrupted me.

" There ! There ! Don't talk of it. The first time I saw him, I, too, was appalled. They cried me down. We were always telling each other, ' Oh ! you mustn't mind his appearance.' And then he was always ready to kill. There was no doubt of it. He killed—yes ! in both camps. The fiend . . ."

Then Sophia Antonovna, after mastering the angry trembling of her lips, told me a very queer tale. It went that Councillor Mikulin, travelling in Germany (shortly after Razumov's disappearance from Geneva), happened to meet Peter Ivanovitch in a railway carriage. Being alone in the compartment, these two talked together half the night, and it was then that Mikulin the Police Chief gave a hint to the arch-revolutionist as to the true character of the arch-slayer of gendarmes. It looks as though Mikulin had wanted to get rid of that particular agent of his own ! He might have grown tired of him, or frightened of him. It must also be said that Mikulin had inherited the sinister Nikita from his predecessor in office.

And this story, too, I received without comment in my character of a mute witness of things Russian, unrolling their Eastern logic under my Western eyes. But I permitted myself a question :

" Tell me, please, Sophia Antonovna, did Madame de S—— leave all her fortune to Peter Ivanovitch ? "

" Not a bit of it." The woman revolutionist shrugged her shoulders in disgust. " She died without making a will. A lot of nephews and nieces came down from St. Petersburg, like a flock of vultures, and fought for her money amongst themselves. All beastly Kammerherrs and Maids of Honour—abominable court flunkeys. Tfui ! "

" One does not hear much of Peter Ivanovitch now," I remarked, after a pause.

" Peter Ivanovitch," said Sophia Antonovna gravely, " has united himself to a peasant girl."

I was truly astonished.

" What ! On the Riviera ? "

" What nonsense ! Of course not."

Sophia Antonovna's tone was slightly tart.

" Is he, then, living actually in Russia ? It's a tremendous risk—isn't it ? " I cried. " And all for the sake of a peasant girl.   Don't you think it's very wrong of him ? "

Sophia Antonovna preserved a mysterious silence for a while, then made a statement :

" He just simply adores her."

" Does he ?   Well, then, I hope that she won't hesitate to beat him."

Sophia Antonovna got up and wished me good-bye, as though she had not heard a word of my impious hope ; but, in the very doorway, where I attended her, she turned round for an instant, and declared in a firm voice :

" Peter Ivanovitch is an inspired man."

THE END

CHINUA ACHEBE
Things Fall Apart

THE ARABIAN NIGHTS
(tr. Husain Haddawy)

MARCUS AURELIUS
Meditations

JANE AUSTEN
Emma
Mansfield Park
Northanger Abbey
Persuasion
Pride and Prejudice
Sanditon and Other Stories
Sense and Sensibility

HONORÉ DE BALZAC
Cousin Bette
Eugénie Grandet
Old Goriot

SIMONE DE BEAUVOIR
The Second Sex

SAUL BELLOW
The Adventures of Augie March

WILLIAM BLAKE
Poems and Prophecies

JORGE LUIS BORGES
Ficciones

JAMES BOSWELL
The Life of Samuel Johnson

CHARLOTTE BRONTË
Jane Eyre
Villette

EMILY BRONTË
Wuthering Heights

MIKHAIL BULGAKOV
The Master and Margarita

SAMUEL BUTLER
The Way of all Flesh

ITALO CALVINO
If on a winter's night a traveler

ALBERT CAMUS
The Stranger

WILLA CATHER
Death Comes for the Archbishop
My Ántonia

MIGUEL DE CERVANTES
Don Quixote

GEOFFREY CHAUCER
Canterbury Tales

ANTON CHEKHOV
The Steppe and Other Stories
My Life and Other Stories

KATE CHOPIN
The Awakening

CARL VON CLAUSEWITZ
On War

SAMUEL TAYLOR COLERIDGE
Poems

WILKIE COLLINS
The Moonstone
The Woman in White

JOSEPH CONRAD
Heart of Darkness
Lord Jim
Nostromo
The Secret Agent
Typhoon and Other Stories
Under Western Eyes

DANTE ALIGHIERI
The Divine Comedy

DANIEL DEFOE
Moll Flanders
Robinson Crusoe

CHARLES DICKENS
Bleak House
David Copperfield
Dombey and Son
Great Expectations
Hard Times
Little Dorrit
Martin Chuzzlewit
Nicholas Nickleby
The Old Curiosity Shop
Oliver Twist
Our Mutual Friend
A Tale of Two Cities

Everyman's Library, founded in 1906 and relaunched in 1991, aims to offer the most complete library in the English language of the world's classics. Each volume is printed in a classic typeface on acid-free, cream-wove paper with a sewn full cloth binding.